VILLAIN

Shuichi Yoshida was born in Nagasaki, Japan, in 1968. He is the author of nine books. The winner of numerous literary awards in Japan, he has also had several of his short stories adapted for television. *Villain* won the Osaragi Jiro Prize and the Mainichi Publishing Culture Award, two prestigious Japanese prizes.

SHUICHI YOSHIDA

Villain

TRANSLATED FROM THE JAPANESE BY
Philip Gabriel

VINTAGE BOOKS
London

Published by Vintage 2011

2 4 6 8 10 9 7 5 3 1

First published as *Akunin* in Japan by Asah: Shimbun
Publications Inc., Tokyo, in 2007

First published in Great Britain by Harvill Secker in 2010

Vintage
Random House, 20 Vauxhall Bridge Road,
London SW1V 2SA

www.vintage-books.co.uk

Addresses for companies within The Random House Group Limited
can be found at: www.randomhouse.co.uk/offices.htm

The Random House Group Limited Reg. No. 954009

A CIP catalogue record for this book
is available from the British Library

ISBN 9780099526650

The Random House Group Limited supports The Forest
Stewardship Council (FSC), the leading international forest
certification organisation. All our titles that are printed on
Greenpeace approved FSC certified paper carry the FSC logo.
Our paper procurement policy can be found at:
www.randomhouse.co.uk/environment

Printed and bound in Great Britain by
CPI Cox & Wyman, Reading, RG1 8EX

VILLAIN

CHAPTER 1

WHO DID SHE WANT TO SEE?

Route 263 runs north and south some forty-eight kilometers, connecting Fukuoka and Saga Prefectures and straddling Mitsuse Pass in the Sefuri mountain range. The highway begins at the Arae intersection in Sawara Ward in Fukuoka City, an ordinary intersection in an area that, since the mid-1960s, has become a bedroom suburb of Fukuoka with a mushrooming of large and medium-size condos, including, on the east side, the massive Arae housing complex. Sawara Ward is also an educational hub, with three well-known universities—Fukuoka University, Seinan Gakuin, and Nakamura Gakuen—within a three-kilometer radius of the intersection. Perhaps because of all the students living in the vicinity, everyone you see walking at the intersection, or waiting for buses—even the elderly—seems young and full of life.

Known at this point as Sawara Avenue, Route 263 runs straight south. Down the avenue there's a Daiei department store, a Mos Burger fast-food restaurant, a 7-Eleven convenience store, and one of those big-box suburban chain bookstores with a massive sign that proclaims, in no-nonsense fashion, *Books*. The first convenience store has an entrance directly facing the street, but after the Noke intersection the next one has a small parking space for one or two cars, the store after that enough space for five or six, then one with a larger parking lot to accommodate up to ten cars. Past the Muromi River, the convenience stores are surrounded by parking lots that can accommodate several huge eighteen-wheelers, the stores themselves like small boxes almost lost in the midst of massive parking lots.

Here the road begins to gently rise, and just before Suga Shrine curves sharply to the right. There are fewer houses along the roadside; just the brand-new asphalt road and white guardrails leading up toward Mitsuse Pass.

Mitsuse Pass has always had ghostly, otherworldly stories connected to it. In the beginning of the Edo period it was rumored to be a hideout for robbers. In the mid-1920s rumor had it that someone murdered seven women in Kitagata township in Saga Prefecture and escaped to the pass. More recently the pass has become infamous as the place where, so the story goes, someone staying at a nearby inn went crazy and killed another guest. Aware of this tale, young people liked to dare each other to drive over the pass. There have been supposed sightings of ghosts as well, usually near the exit to the Mitsuse Tunnel on the border between Fukuoka and Saga.

The road through the tunnel, a toll road known as Echo Road, was built to bypass the sharp curves and slopes that slow down traffic in the winter. Construction was begun in 1979 and completed in 1986. The toll road costs ¥250 for passenger cars and ¥870 for larger vehicles, and truck drivers on the route between Nagasaki and Fukuoka, weighing the trade-off between time and cost, often choose to drive over the pass.

Taking the regular expressway from Nagasaki to Hakata, a part of Fukuoka City, costs ¥3,650 in tolls for a passenger car, one way, so including the toll for the tunnel, taking the pass road saves nearly ¥1,000. The downside, however, is the drive over an eerie road that, even in daytime, is covered with thick, overhanging trees. At night no matter how fast you drive it feels as if you are tottering over a mountain path with only a flashlight to guide you.

Even so, cars setting out from Nagasaki that take the pass road to save money take the Nagasaki Expressway from Nagasaki to Omura, then to Higashi-Sonogi and Takeo, and get off at the Saga Yamato interchange. Intersecting this east-west Nagasaki Expressway at the interchange is Route 263.

Despite its reputation, until January 6, 2002, Mitsuse Pass was merely a road over a mountain pass, one long overlooked once the expressway was built. For those who lived in the area it was nothing more than a mountain road on the border of the two prefectures with a mammoth tunnel that had cost upwards of five billion yen to complete. But in the beginning of January 2002, an uncommon snowfall lay on the land. There, among the countless networks of artery-like roads spread out over the country, Route 263 and the Nagasaki Expressway linking Nagasaki and Fukuoka suddenly stood out, like a blood vessel bulging near the skin.

On this day, a young construction worker living outside Nagasaki was arrested by the Nagasaki police. The crime? He was suspected of strangling Yoshino Ishibashi, an insurance saleswoman who lived in Fukuoka, and abandoning her body.

On December 9, 2001, Yoshio Ishibashi was standing outside his barbershop near the JR Kurume station. Though he usually had a few customers on a Sunday, no one had visited his shop all morning, so he went out in front, hoping to lure some in. Dressed in his white barber's smock, he gazed down the road, the cold north wind rushing past. An hour had passed since he had finished the lunch his wife, Satoko, had prepared, and the scent of curry lingered even outside.

From the front of the barbershop he could see the JR Kurume station in the distance. Two taxis were parked in the deserted square in front of the station, waiting for over an hour for customers. Whenever Yoshio saw this deserted square, he thought he would have more business if only his shop were located near the other railroad station in town, the private Nishitetsu Kurume station. These two railroad lines—one state owned, the other private—basically ran parallel from Kurume to Fukuoka City, but while the JR special express train cost ¥1,320 one way and took twenty-six minutes, the Nishitetsu express took forty-two minutes but cost only ¥600.

You either spend sixteen more minutes or ¥720, one or the other.

Every time Yoshio gazed out from his shop at the JR station, it struck him how people would so easily sell sixteen minutes of their time for ¥720. Not that this applied to everybody, of course. It was highly unlikely that another Ishibashi who lived in this town, the world-renowned founder of Bridgestone Tires, and his descendants, would sell their precious time for such small change. But there was only a handful of people like that in this town, and on a late Sunday afternoon at the end of the year, most people were like him. The Nishitetsu station might be a bit farther away, but when they wanted to go to Fukuoka, that's where they headed.

Once Yoshio calculated his own value based on the difference between the two stations. If you live to age seventy and your time is worth ¥720 per sixteen minutes, how much is a person's life worth? When he first saw the result on the calculator he was sure he had made a mistake. The bottom line was ¥1.6 billion. He hurriedly punched in the numbers again but came up with the same result. A person's life is worth ¥1.6 billion. My life, he thought, is worth ¥1.6 billion.

This might have been a meaningless figure, something he'd calculated to kill time, but to Yoshio, the owner of a little barbershop whose customers were deserting him, the number gave a brief moment of happiness.

Yoshio had one child, a daughter named Yoshino, who had graduated the previous spring from junior college and had started working as a door-to-door salesperson for an insurance company in Fukuoka City. When she took the job, Yoshio had argued for a solid two weeks that she should continue to live at home, as she'd done in college, and commute via the Nishitetsu line. Her job and their house were in the same prefecture, after all, and she shouldn't count on her salary, which was based mostly on commissions. Yoshino countered that her company gave its employees a housing allowance, and that if she lived at home it would interfere with work. So in the end she moved into an apartment building rented by her company, not far from her firm.

Perhaps there were other reasons, but after Yoshino moved to Fukuoka she rarely came home. Once, when Yoshio told her to come back on a Saturday, she'd flatly refused, saying she had to entertain customers. Yoshio was sure she'd at least come back for New Year's, but just the other day his wife had informed him that Yoshino planned to take a trip to Osaka with friends from her company at the end of the year.

"*Osaka?* What's she going there for?" Yoshio growled.

His wife half expected this reaction. "Don't yell at me. She said she and her girlfriends are going to some place called Universal Studio or something." She strode off to the kitchen to begin making dinner for the two of them.

"Why in the world didn't you let me know about this earlier?" Yoshio yelled at her as she shuffled away.

Pouring soy sauce into a pan, Satoko said quietly, "Yoshino's an adult. She hardly ever gets a vacation, so when she does we should let her do what she wants."

When Yoshio had first met his wife she'd been so pretty she could have been selected Miss Kurume, but after she'd had Yoshino she put on weight and now looked nothing like her former self.

"When did you find out about this?"

As he yelled this, the door chime at their shop rang. Clicking his tongue, Yoshio plodded out to the front. His wife hadn't replied, but he could well imagine his daughter telling her to keep it a secret from Dad that she'd already bought a plane ticket, and Satoko replying, as if it was all too much trouble, "Okay, okay, I get it. . . ."

In the shop stood an elementary school boy from the neighborhood, who until recently always came with his mother. The boy was as cute as one of those chubby little helmeted samurai dolls, but the back of his head was as flat as a cliff, the result, no doubt, of his mother letting him lie too long on his back as a baby.

Still, Yoshio was happy that there were still a few neighborhood children like this who came to get their hair cut. Once they got into junior or senior high, boys started to care too much about their appearance and either let their hair grow long or stopped coming to his shop, claiming that the haircuts he gave were out of style. Before he realized what was happening, local boys were making appointments in salons in Fukuoka and traveling there on weekends to get their hair styled.

The other day there'd been a meeting of the local barber and hair-salon union and when Yoshio mentioned this trend, the female owner of the Lillie Salon, who was drinking *shochu*, butted in. "You're lucky you work with boys," she said. "With girls, the ones in elementary school are already going to get their hair cut in salons in Fukuoka."

"I remember you were pretty precocious, too, back when you were a kid," Yoshio joked. "So you can't just say it's kids these days." Yoshio and the woman were the same age, so he felt comfortable kidding her.

"Back in my day, we didn't go to salons in Fukuoka," the woman replied. "We stood in front of the mirror, curling iron in hand, for two or three hours, doing it ourselves."

"The Seiko cut, I'll bet."

Yoshio laughed and several people sitting nearby, glasses in hand, joined the conversation. "You're talking twenty years ago, aren't you," one of them said.

Yoshio was of a slightly older generation, but still he knew that Kurume had produced a phenomenally popular female singer, Seiko Matsuda. In the early 1980s, Yoshio mused, this young girl's clear singing voice really had transformed drab Kurume into something bright and glittering again.

Yoshio had been to Tokyo himself only once, when he was young, as part of a third-rate rockabilly band, his hair slicked back with pomade. He and his bandmates took the night train to Tokyo and checked out the wide pedestrian-only streets of Harajuku.

On the first day there he was bowled over by the crowds. By the second day he was used to the masses of people, but felt a growing sense of inferiority and irritation at being from a country town, and he started picking fights with some of the kids dancing in the Harajuku streets. His rough, dialect-laden challenge didn't faze the young

Tokyoites, though, who calmly asked him to get out of the way. He remembered, too, how when they were searching for a bar written up in a guidebook, Masakatsu, their drummer, muttered a heartfelt comment: "You know, Seiko Matsuda is really something. To come from Kurume and make it here in Tokyo." Yoshio always remembered these words. And how right after they got back home, Satoko announced that she was pregnant with Yoshino. They weren't married yet.

Now he stood in front of his shop, which at least seemed like it was paying off; all of a sudden in the evening people came in for haircuts, one after another. The first was a man from the neighborhood who'd retired from the prefectural office the year before. With his retirement pay and pension he seemed to be well off, for he'd recently purchased three miniature dachshunds, each one of which went for ¥100,000. Whenever he went out for a walk, he'd carry the three little dogs in his arms.

Just as the man tied up his three yappy dogs outside and sat down to have his thinning hair trimmed, a junior high student, also from the neighborhood, came in. Without a word of greeting, he plopped down on the bench in the back of the shop and was soon lost in the manga magazine he'd brought with him. For a moment Yoshio considered calling in his wife to have her help out, but he would soon be finished with the dachshund owner so he told the sullen boy, "I'll be finished soon—please be patient." When he and his wife married, she commuted to a barber school in Fukuoka and got a license. Their dream was to open a second shop, but the economy in the '80s was already starting to sputter, and besides, after Satoko's mother died three years ago of a stroke, she claimed that touching other people's hair reminded her of touching a corpse, and she stopped working in the shop altogether. Still, when it rains it pours. As Yoshio was in the middle of shaving the retiree, a third customer came in, and he had no choice but to ask Satoko for help.

"I'm kind of busy," she replied sullenly.

"What do you mean you're busy? I've got customers waiting here."

"I'm in the middle of gutting these shrimp."

"Can't it wait?"

"It's better if I do it now. . . ."

Yoshio had given up on her even before she finished replying. In the mirror the man he was shaving gave him a sympathetic smile. This wasn't the first time he'd heard an exchange like this between them.

"I'm sorry. You'll have to wait just a little bit longer," Yoshio said to the junior high student. Still absorbed in his manga, the boy barely noticed.

"She's a barber's daughter, not that that makes any difference." Shifting the scissors in his hand, Yoshio clicked his tongue. His eyes met those of the customer in the mirror.

"My wife's exactly the same," the man said. "If I ask her to take the dogs for a walk, she gets all hot and bothered and says, 'You have no idea how much work it takes to run this house! You think I'm a maid or something?' "

Yoshio gave a forced smile at the customer's words, but couldn't help but think that taking this retired civil servant's dogs for a walk, and a barber asking his wife to help cut customers' hair, were entirely different things.

The rest of the day they had a steady stream of customers, eight in all, including a man who wanted his white hair dyed, until they closed up at seven p.m. It was as if all the regulars who came once a month decided to come on the same day, and Yoshio was kept running from one to the next. Satoko had finished with the shrimp, but had gone out shopping, so he couldn't ask again for help.

After the final customer left, and Yoshio was sweeping up the hair from the floor, he thought how nice it would be if—not every day, but at least once a week—they had this many customers. His legs and back were about to give out from standing for so long, but the leather bag he used instead of a cash register was full of thousand-yen bills, more stuffed than he'd seen it in a decade.

When he closed up shop and stepped up into their living room, his wife was on the phone with their daughter. Yoshino always managed, barely, to keep her promise to phone them on Sunday evenings. As he watched his wife talking, Yoshio was less concerned with what they were saying than with how much the call was costing. A few months ago Yoshino had canceled her contract for her PHS phone and had bought a cell phone. Yoshio had told her over and over to use the landline in her apartment, but Yoshino preferred the convenience of the cell phone and always used it when she called.

Yoshino was sitting in her studio apartment in Fairyland Hakata, the building that her company, Heisei Insurance, rented in Chiyo, Hakata Ward, in Fukuoka City. She was redoing her nails and only half listening to her mother drone about how adorable some customer's miniature dachshunds were.

Fairyland Hakata consisted of thirty studio apartments, all occupied by saleswomen for Heisei Insurance. It was a different setup from a company dorm, for there was no cafeteria and no dorm rules. The women worked in different areas throughout town. They often talked to their neighbors across their verandas, and every evening you could hear some of them in the small arbor in the courtyard, cans of juice in their hands, as they laughed and chatted. Rent for the apartments cost sixty thousand yen per month, half of which the company subsidized. Their studio apartments each had a small bathroom and a kitchen, but many of the women cooked together to save money.

After a while Yoshino grew bored by her mother's story of the cute dogs. "Mom," she said, cutting her off, "I gotta go. I'm having dinner with some friends."

Satoko had already asked her, as soon as she called, whether she'd eaten, but now acted as if she didn't realize her daughter had yet to have dinner. "Oh, is that right? I'd better let you go. Hold on a second," she added, "I'll put Dad on." She went to get him without waiting for Yoshino's reply.

Yoshino was bored. She stepped out onto the veranda. Her apartment was on the second floor, and from there she could hear Suzuka

Nakamachi talking in the courtyard. Suzuka, perhaps proud that she didn't have a Kyushu accent like most of the girls, was talking louder than anyone else about some TV drama.

As Yoshino came back in from the veranda, her father said hello.

"I'm on my way out to eat with friends," she said, trying to keep their conversation short, but her father didn't seem to have much to say. Instead of his usual complaints about how bad business was, he seemed in a rare good mood. "Is that right?" he said. "Well, stay safe, okay? . . . By the way, how's work?"

"Work?" she replied quickly. "Cold calls are hard. Hard to get people to sign up. Anyway, gotta go. See ya." And she hung up.

She had no idea that this was the last time she'd ever talk with her parents.

Yoshino was waiting by the entrance of the building when her friends Sari and Mako came down the stairs together. All three of them worked in different parts of town, but they were her two best friends in the apartment building.

As tall, thin Sari and short, chubby Mako descended, the distance between each step, which was obviously the same, appeared different.

Earlier that day the three of them had wandered around department stores in Tenjin, but since it was still too early for dinner, they had come back home before going out again.

Sari had purchased a pair of Tiffany Open Heart earrings earlier in the day at Mitsukoshi and was already wearing them. The earrings cost twenty thousand yen, and Sari had paced the store for nearly an hour, agonizing over whether to buy them. When Sari was checking out the prices and trying on different earrings, Yoshino, who was getting tired of waiting, told her, "When you can't make up your mind, it's best to just go for their signature item."

Now she casually told Sari how nice the earrings looked, and stooped down to adjust her boots, which didn't feel right. The heels were worn out already, the buckles starting to come apart. The two girls beside her had on similar boots.

Yoshino stood up. "So where should we go?" Mako rarely gave her own opinion, but spoke up this time. "How 'bout some *gyoza* at Tetsunabe?"

"I could go for some *gyoza*," Sari agreed readily, and looked at Yoshino to gauge her reaction.

Yoshino slipped her cell phone into the Louis Vuitton Cabas Piano bag her father had bought her as a graduation present when she finished junior college, then pulled out her wallet, also a Vuitton. There was less than ten thousand yen inside, and she sighed.

"Kind of a pain to go all the way to Nakasu, yeah?" Yoshino said.

Sensing something in her reply, Sari asked, "What, you got a date or something?" Yoshino just inclined her a head a bit.

"With Keigo?" Sari, half disbelieving, half suspicious, gazed at Yoshino. "Why do you say that?" Yoshino asked, dodging the question. "I'm just gonna see him for a short time," she quickly added.

"Better not to have any *gyoza*, then," Mako butted in. "You know what it'll do to your breath." Her tone was so earnest that Yoshino had to laugh.

It took less than three minutes to walk from their building to the Chiyo-Kenchoguchi subway station, but along the way the road ran past the densely thick Higashi Park. Walking there in the daytime was no problem, but as the neighborhood-watch group's bulletin board cautioned, it was better to avoid the place at night.

Higashi Park, established by the Fukuoka prefectural office, was home to two bronze statues. One was dedicated to the cloistered emperor Kameyama, who at the time of the thirteenth-century Mongol invasion made a famous prayer at Ise Shrine asking that his life be taken in order to spare the nation. The second statue was that of Nichiren, the founder of the Nichiren sect of Buddhism. The grounds of the park also housed the Toka Ebisu Shrine—dedicated to Ebisu, one of the seven gods of good fortune—as well as the Mongol Invasion Museum. But once the sun set, these buildings seemed to disappear, and the park turned back into dense, thick woods.

As they headed to the subway, Yoshino showed Sari and Mako the e-mail she'd received a few days before from Keigo Masuo.

I'd love to go to Universal Studios too! But it's pretty crowded at the end of the year. Well, time to get some sleep. Good night.

Sari and Mako each read the message, and in turn each gave a huge, exaggerated sigh.

"Sounds to me like he's asking you to go with him to Universal Studios." Mako, who generally took things at face value, was openly envious.

"I don't know." Yoshino smiled vaguely.

"I bet he'd go if you asked him," Sari said.

Keigo Masuo was a senior, a business major at Seinan Gakuin University. His parents owned a Japanese-style inn in the upscale resort town of Yufuin, which would account for Keigo's expensive condo in front of Hakata station and his Audi A6. Yoshino and her two friends had first met Keigo at the end of October, at a bar in Tenjin. The three girls were out for the evening and, at the bar, they were invited to join Keigo and his lively group of friends to play darts, which they did until nearly midnight.

Keigo asked her for her e-mail address that night—that much was true. But Yoshino's stories about the dates they'd had since then were all a lie.

"You're going to see Keigo after this, right? Why don't you invite him?"

Yoshino had tried to dodge the question of who she was going to meet later that evening, but her two friends were convinced it had to be Keigo.

Yoshino avoided Sari's eyes and repeated, "We're just getting together for a little while."

The footsteps of the three girls were absorbed into the darkness of the empty park. They continued to talk about Keigo until they arrived at the station, their cheerful voices making the eerie path by the park brighter, as if the number of streetlights had increased.

At the station, and in the subway on the way to Tenjin, Keigo continued to be the subject of conversation. They speculated on which actor he most resembled, one of them mentioning that she looked up his family's inn on the Internet and saw that it had a separate cottage with an outdoor natural hot spring.

Yoshino was proud that she was the only one Keigo had asked for her e-mail address when they'd met in the bar. And that pride had led her, when Sari had first asked if he'd sent her a message, to suddenly lie: "Yeah, he did. I'm going to see him this weekend." When the weekend came, she had her two friends check her hair and makeup, and they gave her a cheery send-off as she left the apartment. The white lie she'd told had ballooned into something out of her control, and she wound up taking the Nishitetsu line back to her parents' home to kill the day there.

It was true that Keigo had contacted her. But she was the one who had to take the initiative. Still, if she sent him a message he'd always reply. *I really want to go to Universal Studios,* she'd e-mailed once, and he said that he did, too, adding, she noted, an exclamation mark. But this didn't lead to an invitation to go together. Despite the exchanged e-mails, since that first chance meeting at the bar, Yoshino had never laid eyes on Keigo Masuo.

They were still talking about Keigo even after they entered the *gyoza* restaurant in Nakasu and sat down to a meal of chicken wings, potato salad, and the main dish, grilled *gyoza,* washed down by draft beer. Mako was envious of Yoshino for having a steady boyfriend, while Sari, half jealous, cautioned Yoshino to make sure he didn't play around with anyone else.

"Yoshino, you still okay on time?" Mako said, and Yoshino glanced at the wall clock. The hands behind the greasy glass face showed nine p.m.

"No problem," she replied. "He's going to see some friends afterward, so we can only see each other for a few minutes."

Mako sighed predictably. "Of course you want to see him, even if it's just for a short time."

Yoshino didn't correct her misunderstanding but added with a shrug, "And besides, I've got work tomorrow."

The man Yoshino had plans to meet that night, though, wasn't

Keigo Masuo. Irritated that Keigo wasn't replying to her recent messages, out of boredom she'd registered with a dating site and she was instead going to meet someone she'd met online.

※

As Yoshino, Sari, and Mako discussed Keigo, about fifteen kilometers away, on a curve over Mitsuse Pass, the man Yoshino was going to meet had pulled his car over onto the gravel shoulder of the road. It was the kind of forsaken stretch of highway that hardly merited being called an interstate.

As he had driven over the white center line on the narrow road, it rose up in the halogen headlights and looked for an instant like a writhing white snake. The snake stretched out in the distance as if to bind up the pass. Trussed up as tight as it could get, the pass twisted from side to side, making the leaves on the trees appear to shake and tremble.

Far in the distance, in the pitch-black background of this road over the pass, lay the gaping mouth of the Mitsuse Tunnel. Farther down that road, the lights of Hakata would come into view.

The headlights of the stopped car illuminated the dust and, beyond that, palely lit up the surrounding woods. A single moth flitted across the light.

From the Saga Yamato interchange to here was one sharp curve after another, and every time the man turned his wheel over, a ten-yen coin on the dashboard slid back and forth.

The coin was change he got when he stopped for gas at a station just before the pass. Usually he'd just prepay a certain amount, ¥3,000 or ¥3,500, but the attendant was cute so he couldn't help showing off, and told her to fill it up with premium. That cost ¥5,990, and after he paid with thousand-yen notes, he was left with just a single ¥5,000 bill in his wallet.

The gas attendant shoved the nozzle into his tank. The man watched her the whole time in his side mirror. As the tank filled, the girl walked around to the front and cleaned the windshield, her generous breasts smashed against the glass. The girl's cheeks were red in the cold night wind. The gas station, alone in the middle of nowhere, was as bright as day.

The man recalled Yoshino's voice on the phone a few days earlier. "I have a date with some friends for dinner on Sunday, but if we can meet kind of late it'd be okay. . . ."

"That works for me."

He picked up the ten-yen coin on the dashboard and stuck it in his pocket. As he did, his fingertips brushed against his stiff penis. Thoughts of Yoshino hadn't given him an erection, but all the swaying back and forth on the sharp curves had.

The man's name was Yuichi Shimizu. He was twenty-seven, lived in Nagasaki City, and worked in construction. He and Yoshino had gone on two dates the month before, but since then, he'd had trouble getting in touch with her. Now, though, he was on his way to see her. He was supposed to meet her at ten, but even with the time it took to get over the pass he figured he had plenty of time. He was going to meet her at the place he'd dropped her off last time, the main gate of Higashi Park in Fukuoka. He remembered seeing a huge bronze statue when he'd pulled over.

Yuichi opened his door and swung his legs out the driver's side. He'd customized the car so it rode low and his legs had no trouble reaching the ground.

It was a perfect time to take a break and have a cigarette, but Yuichi didn't smoke. At the construction site, when the other workers took a break and all of them started puffing away, he'd sometimes join them for lack of something else to do, but he much preferred just closing his eyes and letting time drift by.

The warm air from inside the car rushed out, brushing against his neck. In the distance he could see the tunnel exit, but nothing else with any color. Still, he could see how the darkness that enveloped the pass came in many shades: the nearly purplish darkness of the mountain ridge, the whitish darkness surrounding the cloud-hidden moon, the blackish darkness covering the woods nearby.

Yuichi closed his eyes for a bit, then opened them to compare the difference between that sort of darkness and the darkness that surrounded him; as he opened his eyes he spotted the small headlights of a car climbing the pass. The lights disappeared when it rounded a curve, only to reappear again. The lights were dim, but still enough to illuminate the white guardrail and the orange mirror set up on each curve.

Just then a small truck appeared from the direction of the tunnel and flew right by him, leaving behind the stink of farm animals. The sudden bestial smell hit him like a jellyfish stinging his nose.

Yuichi closed his door to shut out the smell, pushed back his seat, and lay down. He took his cell phone out of his pocket and checked to see if there were any messages from Yoshino, but there weren't. When he opened the screen, though, he saw her photo, clad only in her underwear. Her face was off the picture, but the rest of her body appeared clearly, even down to a small telltale pimple on her shoulder.

This one photo had cost him three thousand yen.

"Hey, stop it!"

They were in a love hotel built on reclaimed land in Hakata Bay, and when Yuichi pointed his cell-phone camera at Yoshino, she quickly reached for her white shirt and hid her chest. She was just about to put the shirt on; grabbing it so abruptly got it all wrinkled. "Now look what you've made me do," she moaned.

Their room in the love hotel was a cheap, claustrophobic place that rented for ¥4,320 for three hours. Its concrete walls were wall-papered, the rug was shoddy, and although the pipe-frame bed did have a mattress cover, the quilt on top was, for some unknown reason, one size too small for the double bed. The window didn't open. It overlooked a highway overpass, not the harbor.

"Come on, let me take your picture."

Yuichi tried again, vaguely, to persuade her, but Yoshino just laughed at him. "Don't be an idiot," she said. She seemed more concerned about the wrinkles on her shirt.

"Just one photo. I won't take your face."

Yuichi sat up formally on the bed and made his request. Yoshino glanced up at him for a second and said wearily, "How much are you willing to pay?"

Yuichi only had on underwear. His jeans lay discarded on the floor, the wallet in his back pocket bulging out.

When he didn't reply Yoshino said, "I'll do it for three thousand yen." She no longer hid her chest with the shirt, and her shiny bra was visible, her breasts straining against the fabric.

Yuichi pushed the button with his thumb, the shutter snapped, and he was left with a photo of a half-naked Yoshino.

Yoshino leaped onto the bed and pestered him to show her the photo. After making sure her face wasn't in it, she said, "I really have to get going. I have curfew." She got up off the bed and buttoned up her shirt.

From the parking lot of the love hotel they could see Fukuoka Tower off in the distance. Yuichi was craning his neck for a better look, but Yoshino said, "I'm kind of in a hurry here," urging him to get going.

"You ever been up to the observation platform on the tower?" Yuichi asked.

"When I was a kid, yeah," Yoshino replied, as if she couldn't be bothered. She motioned with her chin for him to get into the car. "It looks just like a lighthouse," Yuichi was about to say, but Yoshino was already in the passenger seat.

"If Keigo and I do go to Universal Studios during New Year's break, we probably should stay two days, don't you think?" Yoshino said, picking up an already cold *gyoza* from the pan.

Her date with Yuichi was scheduled for ten p.m. and the clock on the wall showed it was already past that.

"You ever been to Osaka, Yoshino?" Mako asked, her face flushed from two draft beers.

"Nope, never have," Yoshino replied.

"Me neither. But I have a cousin who lives there."

Mako was usually the quiet one, but she became talkative when she was drunk. Generally she lisped a bit, but when drunk she talked in a syrupy sort of voice. At parties with guys, she was always kind of a pain.

"I've never been abroad, either. . . ." Mako said, seated casually on her cushion, elbows splayed on the table.

"Me neither," Yoshino said.

"Sari's been to Hawaii," Mako said, eyeing the cushion where Sari had been sitting before she got up to use the restroom. Mako didn't seem particularly envious.

Yoshino sometimes found Mako's indifferent attitude frustrating. Mako never said things overtly, but she always spoke about herself in a self-deprecating way.

Yoshino, Mako, and Sari were a tight threesome at the apartment building. Sometimes they'd gather for dinner at one of their rooms, or take over the arbor in the courtyard and sit there laughing until dark. Their poor sales records also bound them together. In the beginning Yoshino and Sari competed to see who could close more deals, but once they started turning to relatives to improve their sales figures, they quickly lost interest. Now, after attending the morning meeting at their head office, they more often than not joined Mako in skipping out on pointless cold calls and going to see a movie instead.

Mako, the easygoing one, was like a buffer between Yoshino and Sari.

"Hey, if Keigo and I do end up going to Universal Studios, you want to go with us?"

Sari hadn't come back from the restroom yet.

"Me?" Mako was resting her head in her hands on the table, and raised her chin in surprise.

"I'll get Keigo to invite one of his friends and the four of us can go together. At a place like that, the more the merrier, don't you think?"

Keigo of course hadn't promised he'd take Yoshino to Universal Studios at this point, but including others in her fantasy plans made the whole picture seem more real and gave her a small thrill. Even if she was deceiving Mako, when the actual time came to go, she could always claim that something came up and Keigo couldn't make it, and then she and Mako could use the tickets instead of letting them go to waste. Going with Keigo, just the two of them, would be amazing, but if it didn't work out and she had to settle for Mako, Yoshino still wanted to go over New Year's.

"But shouldn't you invite Sari, too?" Mako looked forlornly into Yoshino's eyes.

"The thing is, Keigo doesn't get along with her," Yoshino said, deliberately keeping her voice down.

"You're kidding. But they seemed to get along so well at the bar."

"Don't tell Sari, okay? It'd hurt her feelings."

Mako nodded solemnly at Yoshino's mock-serious warning.

Of course it was an outright lie that Keigo disliked Sari. Mako was so gullible that sometimes Yoshino liked making something up and seeing how she'd react.

Mako was from Hitoyoshi City in Kumamoto Prefecture. Her father owned a used-car lot, where her mother had worked part-time, and Mako was their only daughter. As might be expected of a daughter from a good family where the parents got along well, Mako Adachi saw work as a stopgap and wanted, soon after she graduated from junior college, to get married. She was generally pretty passive: since childhood, she had waited to be chosen by others rather than choosing her own friends. After she graduated from high school she decided to go to the junior college in Fukuoka affiliated with her high school, a move that eliminated any worries about entrance exams. She didn't care if she knew anybody there or not, and as it turned out, she didn't. After college she was hoping to return home to Hitoyoshi, but couldn't find a job there. So with no other alternative, she took the job at Heisei Insurance, moved into the company apartment building, and eventually made two friends, Yoshino and Sari. They were flashier than her friends in high school, but she was relieved to have someone to keep her company until she found a man to marry.

"You know, the other day Suzuka Nakamachi called out to me in the courtyard," Mako said, as if suddenly remembering it. With her chopsticks she skillfully peeled a slice of cucumber stuck in the potato salad from the side of the bowl.

"When was this?" Yoshino made a face, remembering how Suzuka liked to hang out in the arbor in the courtyard, letting every-one hear her Tokyo accent.

"Like—three days ago? She goes, 'So I hear from Sari that Yoshino and Keigo are going out. Is that true?' You remember how one of her friends goes to the same college as Keigo?" Mako didn't seem all that interested in the topic as she chewed the crunchy slice of cucumber.

"So what did you say to her?" Yoshino asked, pretending to be calm.

"I told her I thought so."

Startled perhaps by Yoshino's severe tone, Mako stopped chewing for a moment. Just then Sari came back from the downstairs restroom.

"So, what're you talking about?" Sari said, taking off her boots. Restaurants like this with tatami rooms provided clogs and slippers for customers to use when they went to the restroom, but Sari, a stickler for cleanliness, claimed she felt uncomfortable using communal slippers and always wore her own shoes. Yoshino had her doubts about this explanation.

Yoshino watched Mako reach into the potato salad again with her chopsticks. "I think Suzuka likes Keigo," she said. "So she sees me as a rival."

This was another lie, something that just popped into her head, but it might help keep a lid on things. If indeed Suzuka found out more from her friend who went to the same college, Yoshino's lie could turn anything Suzuka said into a simple case of jealousy.

"No kidding?" Sari said, leaping at this bit of gossip as she stepped up into the tatami room. Yoshino again thought about Sari and her boots and couldn't believe that fastidiousness had anything to do with her wearing them to the restroom. Yoshino recalled a time when she was eating bread in her apartment; Sari had said, "Give me some," and then grabbed a bite. She used the same handkerchief every day. Sari also insisted that she had a serious boyfriend when she was in high school, but Yoshino had once told Mako that she thought this was a lie, and that Sari was still a virgin.

And in fact Sari, all of twenty-one, had yet to spend the night with a man. She'd made up a story about dating the same boy from the basketball team in high school for three years. But the truth was that it was another girl who'd gone out with the boy, not Sari, who spent those years pining away for him on her own. Nobody knew her in Fukuoka, so she used the opportunity to reinvent her past. She liked to show Yoshino and Mako a photo of her with the boy taken at Sports Day in high school.

"Wow, he's really cute," Mako said when she saw the photo, and this was all it took for Sari to blur the boundary between fact and fiction.

Every time Mako exclaimed over how cute the boy was, how tall he was, how he had such nice eyes and white teeth, Sari was under the illusion that she was the one being praised. It was exactly these qualities that she herself had liked, and she had started to convince herself that she and the boy really had been a couple. In Fukuoka Sari had discovered the joy of inventing an ideal self.

Naïve Mako might be fooled by this, but Sari had to consider Yoshino, too, as she sat there looking suspicious. When Sari had first showed them the Sports Day photo, Mako had been blithely ecstatic about it, but Yoshino had asked, "Hey, why don't you call him now?"

Sari of course demurred. "But I'm sure he still likes you, right?" Yoshino badgered her. "He must have cried his eyes out when you moved to Fukuoka. Don't you think he'd be happy to hear from you?" Seeing how flustered this made Sari, Yoshino gloated to herself.

For Sari, then, being alone with Yoshino felt claustrophobic. When she was just with Mako, she could be the center of attention, but Yoshino made her feel guilty, as though she were wearing a cheap knockoff brand. Still, if she was with shy Mako in town and some guys tried to pick them up, it was never any fun; but with Yoshino guys would treat them to dinner or to sing karaoke. She'd enjoy it and then feel bold enough to use curfew as an excuse to say a quick goodbye.

The last single order of *gyoza* came and the three of them made short work of it. They'd already had four orders, which meant they'd gobbled down some thirteen *gyoza* each.

Yoshino, stretching her legs out under the low table, rubbed her stomach exaggeratedly and said, "I shouldn't have eaten so much. And after I'd just lost a couple of pounds." Sari and Mako, their legs also splayed out, both sighed deeply, completely stuffed.

As Yoshino looked at the bill and calculated her third of it, Mako said, "You sure you're okay? It's already ten-thirty."

For a second Yoshino didn't know what she was getting at. "What do you mean?" she asked.

"You know . . . with Keigo and all . . ." Mako said, inclining her head.

Yoshino had momentarily forgotten she'd told her friends that she had a date with him.

"That's right . . . I better get going," Yoshino said, pretending to be flustered.

When it was ten p.m. Yoshino had actually considered e-mailing Yuichi that she'd be a little late, but then she'd gotten so involved in bad-mouthing Suzuka Nakamachi that she hadn't sent a message.

Yuichi had been so insistent on meeting her that she'd reluctantly agreed. "I still have to pay you for the photo," he said. If that was all it was, five minutes should be enough.

Yoshino divided the bill into thirds. The *gyoza* cost ¥470 per order, the potato salad ¥520, and adding on the chicken wings, sardines stuffed with snap eggs, and draft beers, the total came to ¥2,366 each. Sari and Mako took the money from their purses and laid out the exact amount they owed on the table. Meanwhile, Yoshino pulled out her cell phone and checked to see if she had any messages. She had a few, but nothing from Yuichi, let alone from Keigo.

At five after ten, Yuichi was wondering whether he should send Yoshino a message.

He was already in the parking lot in front of Higashi Park with his engine turned off, looking like all the other cars parked in the tree-lined two-hundred-yen-per-hour lot—as if he'd been here for days.

The JR Yoshizuka station was nearby, but at this time of night there weren't many cars driving on the road along the park. Occasionally a taxi rounding the curve would light up the parked cars. None of the others had drivers in them. Only Yuichi, his face sunburned from construction work, was lit up by the headlights.

Yoshino had definitely said to meet her at the entrance to the park. She said she was having dinner with friends but would be able to make it.

Yuichi considered driving once around the park, but with the narrow paths, that would take at least three minutes. He worried that Yoshino might arrive from the station and figure that he hadn't shown up.

Yuichi took his hand off the ignition key. He'd turned the engine off over five minutes ago, but the car was still warm from the drive. He could feel the road as he drove over the pass, lit up only by the pale light from his halogen headlights; he felt himself stepping on the gas as if to plunge into that light, the back end of his car sliding as he rounded the curves. No matter how much he pursued this ball of light ahead of him, he never could reach it.

Still, every time he drove over the pass, he had the fantasy that his car would be able to catch that ball of light. In this dream, a moment after his car caught up with it he'd pass through the light to the other side, to a world he'd never seen before. But Yuichi couldn't imagine what he'd see there. He tried conjuring scenes from movies he'd seen—the green Mediterranean, the Milky Way—but nothing seemed right. Sometimes he tried to imagine his own scene, not one based on TV or movies, but when he did everything went blank before him and he knew he'd never find it.

Yuichi closed his eyes and pictured in his mind the mountain pass he'd just crossed, and the bright lights of Tenjin.

It was now fifteen minutes past the time they were supposed to meet. Even if Yoshino did show up, they wouldn't have much time to talk; and try as he might, Yuichi couldn't think of anything he wanted to talk to her about.

The footpath was deserted, just like the road along the park. If they had a half hour alone, he thought, maybe he could get Yoshino to suck him off. She'd resist at first, but if he grabbed her and kissed her, and stroked her breasts, then who knows what she might be willing to do.

After coming down off the pass he'd stopped at the first vending machine he spotted and bought a bottle of oolong tea, which he'd gulped down. Now he suddenly had to pee.

The roads were still deserted. The public restroom in the park was nearby, but once before when he'd parked there and used the restroom, a young man had appeared out of nowhere and stood behind him, unmoving, until he finished peeing, even though the urinal next to the man was unoccupied. Yuichi was afraid the guy would say something to him, so he hurriedly finished, zipped his pants, and leaped out of the restroom as if he were being chased. All the way back to his car he'd glanced around nervously, but there was no sign of the man. It felt creepy.

He flipped open his cell phone and saw that another five minutes had passed. He didn't think Yoshino would stand him up, but he was getting worried, so he climbed out of his car.

Outside, he realized that the cold air from the pass had swept down to the city. He stretched and took a deep breath, and the chilled air caught in his throat. In the distance the sky over Tenjin was dyed purple. Suddenly the thought hit him that Yoshino was planning to spend the night with him. Since he came all the way from Nagasaki to see her, maybe she was going to go with him to that love hotel they went to before? If that was the case, he didn't mind her being twenty minutes late. But he couldn't stay at a love hotel in Hakata tonight. He had to be back at work at seven a.m.

He climbed over the fence, checked to see that no one was coming, and urinated on a hedge in the park. The foamy spray of his urine covered the hedge like a wet cloth and dribbled down at his feet.

❈

"Hey, remember how some guys tried to pick us up at the Meeting Bridge? Yoshino, you remember?" Sari called out to her from behind, and Yoshino turned around.

"When was this?" Yoshino asked.

The three girls had left Tetsunabe, the *gyoza* restaurant, and were hurrying toward the subway, along the Naka River, its surface lit up by all the neon signs.

"Last summer," Sari said. She was walking next to Yoshino and she glanced over at the bright surface of the Fukuhaka Meeting Bridge, a semi-covered footbridge.

"Really?" Yoshino asked.

"You remember—those two guys on a business trip from Osaka."

Yoshino finally nodded. "Um," she said. Last summer, one time after they'd eaten in Tenjin and were on their way home, two men had called out to them on the bridge, asking if they'd like to go sing karaoke. The men, slim in their suits, were nice looking enough, but Mako had had too much to drink, so the women turned them down.

"I got them to give me their business cards and I found the cards yesterday. They work for a TV station in Osaka."

"Are you kidding me?" Yoshino replied, not showing much interest.

"I was thinking if I change jobs I'd like to go into mass media, so maybe I'll get in touch with them."

"With guys who tried to pick you up?" Yoshino chuckled. Considering the kind of junior college Sari had graduated from, no one in the media was going to hire her, particularly a TV station.

"Hey," Sari said, changing the subject, "whatever happened to that guy who tried to pick you up in the park next to Solaria?"

"Solaria?"

"You know, the guy who came from Nagasaki, driving some kind of cool-looking car?"

This was the man Yoshino was on the way to see now. "Hmm," Yoshino said, trying to cut off the topic. She glanced at Mako.

Yoshino had told her friends he'd tried to pick her up at the park in Tenjin. But they had indeed met for the first time in person in front of Solaria. Since he was from Nagasaki, Yuichi didn't know Solaria, a popular Hakata fashion mall.

"You've never been to Tenjin?" Yoshino had asked him, and he said, "I've driven here a few times but never walked around." Yoshino had been hesitant about meeting him, but when he sent her his photo the day before, and she saw how good-looking he was, she e-mailed him, agreeing to meet.

On the day of their date, she arrived at Solaria and saw a tall man who looked like he must be Yuichi, leaning against a show window at the entrance. He was even more handsome than his photo. Yoshino suddenly regretted not having been more honest with him in their phone conversations and messages.

She hesitantly approached him and when he saw her approaching, he got flustered and mumbled something she couldn't catch.

"Excuse me?" Yoshino asked and he mumbled again.

He must be nervous, Yoshino figured. She deliberately brushed his arm, repeated herself, and looked up at him.

"I—I don't know any restaurants around here," he said in a small voice.

"That doesn't matter. Anywhere's fine."

When he saw Yoshino's smile, the man's face relaxed.

Yoshino figured his mumbling was just first-date nerves, but as time passed he kept it up. She couldn't understand a thing he said. It wasn't nervousness that made him mumble, she realized, it was just the way he normally talked.

"It kind of irritates me being with him," Yoshino said curtly. She was walking between Sari and Mako, down the stairs to the subway.

"But isn't he really handsome?" Mako said enviously.

"Yeah, he's good-looking, all right," Yoshino replied. "But he's boring. And besides, I have Keigo."

"That's right. . . . But how come you're the one that always gets to meet guys like that?" Mako asked.

After a pause, Sari said, snidely, "She's only been going out with Keigo for a short time, so of course she wants to see other guys."

As she held on tightly to the strap in the crowded subway car, Yoshino looked at the reflection of her two friends in the window. "His car is a tricked-out Skyline GT-R, plus he's taller than Keigo, I think. The problem is, he's a total bore. I think he might be slightly retarded."

"How many times have you guys dated?"

"Two or three times, I guess," Yoshino said, her eyes on the window.

"But the guy comes all the way from Nagasaki to see you."

"It only takes an hour and a half."

"He can get here that fast?"

"He drives crazy fast."

"You've gone driving with him?"

"Just as far as Momochi."

Sari, who'd been listening to their conversation as both of them stared straight ahead at the window, lowered her voice and poked Yoshino playfully in the side. "If you went to Momochi you must have stayed over, like at the Hyatt?"

"The Hyatt? No way." Yoshino deliberately left her reply open to interpretation.

That first day when she met Yuichi at Solaria, they went to eat at a nearby pizza restaurant. Yuichi seemed totally unsure of himself. He couldn't get the busy waitress's attention, and when she brought the wrong order to them, he didn't know what to do, and didn't complain. Mentally, Yoshino was already comparing him to Keigo, when they'd played darts at the bar in Tenjin.

When Yoshino first moved into the Fairyland Hakata apartments, there was a time when she was totally wrapped up in online dating sites. This was before she became friends with Sari and Mako, and she'd spend every night, bored, alone in her room punching out replies to ten or more so-called online friends. All of them wanted to meet her. At night, typing out replies to turn them down, she felt like a girl with a busy, full social schedule, when in fact, not yet used to Hakata, all she was doing was sitting alone in a corner of her little apartment, busily moving her thumbs along a keypad.

After she and Sari and Mako became friends, she didn't have the time to deal with her online friends. Then she'd met Keigo in October, and given him her e-mail address; but when she became irritated that he hadn't contacted her much, she registered again with the same online dating site. In three days she got over a hundred e-mails, some of them from older men looking to have a relationship. She separated the replies by age. Next she decided, based on their language, which ones were lying about their age, and replied just to the handful who seemed like real possibilities.

Yuichi was one of these. In his first reply he said he was *into cars*. When Yoshino read this, she had a mental image of herself sitting next to Keigo in his Audi. He hadn't invited her for a drive, of course, but she daydreamed about his car: where they would go and what CDs they'd play. Out of the hundred or so replies she received, Yuichi's e-mail probably stuck with her for this reason.

The moment she first saw Yuichi she regretted having told him, via phone and e-mail, that she had a boyfriend but that they weren't getting along well, and that she didn't feel like going out with anyone right now. Yuichi's skittishness became more pronounced over time. Once he did start to talk, he told long, pointless stories about his car. Yoshino mentally classified him as a Loser. Unlike Yuichi, she didn't just want to go for a drive. She wanted to look cool whizzing down the streets of Hakata as she rode with a man everyone would envy.

The rough hands of this construction worker from Nagasaki should have been sexy to her, but instead they struck her as just those of an overworked manual laborer.

Yoshino and the other girls got off the subway at the Chiyo prefectural office stop, two stops away from Nakasu-Kawabata station, and climbed the cramped stairs, emerging behind the City Sports Center. During the day this part of town was usually lively, but at night and on weekends it was so quiet it felt like stepping into a dream.

"Where are you meeting him?" Mako asked, from a few steps ahead of Yoshino.

"Um . . . In front of Yoshizuka station," she lied. She couldn't believe the two of them planned to follow her and check things out, but since she'd already lied about meeting Keigo, she had to be cautious.

"You okay getting to the station by yourself?" Mako was worried that Yoshino would have to walk alone past the dark park.

"Yeah, I'll be fine," Yoshino said. She nodded with a smile.

"Well, then we'll see you," Sari said, and she quickly turned the corner.

Yoshino would have to walk down this gloomy path until she reached the entrance of the park.

After saying goodbye at the corner, Yoshino sped up. She could hear her friends' footsteps gradually fade into the distance. Finally she was left with just the sound of her own footsteps echoing on the narrow path.

It was already ten-forty. Yoshino was sure the whole business would take at most three minutes. She felt bad that he'd come all the way from Nagasaki, but he'd insisted on meeting her tonight to pay her the ¥18,000 he'd promised for an evening with her. Even after she'd told him she was busy and that he could just transfer it to her account.

Sari and Mako both listened to the sound of Yoshino's footsteps disappearing. At the end of the road they could see the brightly lit entrance to their apartment building.

"I wonder if Yoshino's really gonna come back soon," Mako said, glancing behind her. Sari looked back, too. The only color on the monochrome street was a solitary red mailbox at the corner where they'd said goodbye.

"Do you really think Yoshino's going to see Keigo?" The words suddenly spilled out of Sari.

"What do you mean? If she isn't, then where'd she go?"

"Somehow I just can't believe that Yoshino and Keigo are going out."

"But Yoshino's always going out on dates with him these days, isn't she?"

"Yeah, but think about it—have we ever seen them together? Like right now, maybe she's just going to hang out at a convenience store or something."

Mako laughed it off. "No way," she said.

Yuichi turned on the overhead light in his car and angled the rearview mirror toward him. In the darkness the reflection of his face was indistinct. He moved his head from side to side, combing his fingers through his hair. His hair was soft and feline; the fine strands flowed through his rough fingers.

In the spring of last year, Yuichi had dyed his hair for the first time in his life. He dyed it a brown that almost appeared black, and when none of the guys on his construction site noticed, he dyed it a lighter brown, then even lighter the next time, until finally now, a year and a half later, his hair was nearly blond.

Since the change in hair color was so gradual, no one kidded him about it. Only once did another worker, Nosaka, laugh and say, "Hey, since when are you a blond?" His blond hair went well with his skin, tanned from outdoor work, so perhaps that explained the lack of teasing.

Yuichi was not a flashy guy, though when he went to Uniqlo and other inexpensive clothing stores to buy sweatshirts and sweatpants, he always wound up going for bright colors, reds and pinks. He would tell himself he'd get something subdued, black or beige, something that didn't show dirt easily, but when he got to the store and stood in front of the racks of clothes, for some reason he'd reach for the brighter colors. It's only going to get dirty anyway, he told himself.

His old chest of drawers at home was stuffed full of similar sweatshirts and T-shirts, all of them with threadbare collars, frayed sleeves, the cloth all worn out. All of this made the colors stand out even more, like colors in a deserted theme park. He liked these old sweatshirts and T-shirts, though, because they absorbed the sweat and grease well, and the more he wore them the more they felt like part of his skin, a feeling he found liberating.

Yuichi leaned forward and looked again in the rearview mirror. His hair was in place. His eyes were slightly bloodshot, but at least the pimple between his eyebrows was gone.

Until he graduated from high school, Yuichi was the type of boy who never combed his hair. He wasn't on any sports team, but every couple of months he'd go to the neighborhood barbershop and get a buzz cut.

Around the time he started attending an industrial high school, the barber had sighed and said, "Yuichi, pretty soon I bet you're going to get all particular about your hair, telling me how to cut it." The huge mirror in the barbershop reflected a young boy, tall and skinny, who was far from being very masculine.

"If you have anything special you want me to do, let me know, okay?" said the barber. The barber liked to sing *enka*, and he made his own recordings, posters for which were plastered on the wall.

But Yuichi had no idea what *anything special* meant when it came to hair. He had no idea where to begin. Until he graduated from high school, Yuichi always got his hair cut at this shop. Afterward, he worked for a short time at a small health food store, and then, after he quit, just hung out at home. A former classmate invited him to work at a karaoke box place, but within half a year the place closed down and he took a series of short-term jobs, at a gas station for a few months, then at a convenience store. And before he knew it he was twenty-three.

It was around that time that he started working in construction. He was considered more of a day laborer than a regular employee, but since the owner of the company was a relative, he earned more than he would have otherwise. He'd been working with this company now for four years. Yuichi liked the irregularity of the work, how they worked in good weather and didn't wh⸱⸱ i⸱ ⸱ained.

Fewer and fewer cars passed in front of the park. It had become so quiet that the presence of the young couple two cars ahead of him, who had driven away quite some time ago, still lingered.

And right then he spotted Yoshino walking, not so quickly, down the path that ran parallel to the park. Yuichi had been cleaning his nails under the interior light in his car.

He gave his horn a light tap. Surprised by the sound, Yoshino stopped for a moment.

On Monday morning, December 10, 2001, Sari woke up five minutes ahead of her alarm, a rare occurrence. Sari was not a morning person, and when she was living with her parents in Kagoshima City, almost every morning her mother got upset when she wouldn't get up on time. Even after Sari moved out and started living in Fukuoka, her mother would occasionally call her to remind her to get up.

Part of the reason she had trouble getting up was that she couldn't fall asleep easily. Back when she was still in school she'd go to bed early, but as soon as she closed her eyes, her mind started replaying conversations she had had with her friends. *If only I'd said this to her,* she'd think. *If only I'd come back to the classroom earlier.* She couldn't help worrying about all the little things that happened. A lot of people do this, of course, but in Sari's case her regret over trivial events of the day would, before she realized it, balloon into the same imaginary scenario.

It was hard to explain what this scene was, exactly. She had just entered junior high and was in bed one night when it popped into her mind, and ever since, no matter how much she'd try not to think of it, it came to her as she struggled to sleep.

The time period wasn't clear, perhaps the late 1920s or early '30s. In this mental scene Sari was locked up in a cramped room, a photograph of an actress clutched in her hands. Sometimes in the photograph the actress wore Western clothes like a pinup film star; at other times it was a newspaper clipping, an ad for what appeared to be the actress's new movie. Sari had no idea who the actress was, but she did know that in her fantasy she was ragingly, overwhelmingly jealous of this woman. Through the latticed window, she sometimes saw gallant young soldiers marching down a cherry-tree-lined street; sometimes she heard the shouts of children throwing snowballs at each other.

In this fantasy, Sari always felt irritated. *If only I could get out of this room*, she thought, then she would be able to take the actress's place in the movie. Her fantasy had no plot, no other characters. Just this one protagonist, Sari's alter ego, whose feelings became her own when Sari couldn't sleep.

Just before her alarm buzzed, Sari reached out and turned it off. It hadn't rung, but she felt as if she could hear it. She flipped open her cell phone to see if there were any messages from Yoshino, but there were none.

She got out of bed and opened the curtains. From her third-floor window she had a nice view of Higashi Park bathed in the early morning sunshine.

Last night, just before twelve, she'd phoned Yoshino, certain she'd be back by then, but there was no answer.

Yoshino's phone had rung but eventually gone to voice mail, so Sari had hung up and gone out on the veranda to peer down at Yoshino's apartment, which was directly beneath hers. The lights weren't on. If she really had met up with Keigo and come home afterward, twelve was too early for her to have gone to sleep.

Flustered, Sari had then decided to phone Mako, who sounded as if she was brushing her teeth when she answered the phone.

"So Yoshino isn't back yet?" Sari asked her.

"Huh?"

"Didn't she say something about coming back right away? But I just called her cell and she didn't pick up."

"Maybe she's taking a shower?"

"But her light's off."

"So maybe she's still with Keigo."

Mako sounded like she couldn't be bothered, so Sari just let it be.

"She'll be back soon. Did you want something?" Mako asked her.

"No, not really . . ." Sari replied and hung up.

No, she didn't have anything else she wanted to ask Mako. Instead, the sound of Yoshino's footsteps, fading as she walked toward the darkened park, came back to her.

Normally Sari wouldn't have given it another thought, but after she took a shower and went back to bed, she was still concerned. She knew she was being a pest, but she called Yoshino's cell phone one more time. This time, though, the call went immediately to voice messaging, as if the phone had been turned off. Right as it did, Sari pictured Keigo's condo in front of Hakata station. Feeling foolish, she tossed the cell phone aside.

That morning Sari arrived at her company's Hakata branch, also in front of Hakata station, just in time for the eight-thirty morning meeting. Normally she rode her bicycle for the one-kilometer commute to the office, but today, just as she was straddling the bike, Mako—who usually commuted by subway to the company's Seinan branch—called out to her. "I've got to stop by the Hakata office," Mako told her, so Sari decided to take the subway, too.

As they were walking to the station Sari asked, "So, have you heard from Yoshino?"

"Yoshino? She hasn't come back?" Mako asked, mellow as usual.

"She never answered her cell."

"Then I suppose she must have stayed overnight at Keigo's. She'll go to work from there."

Mako's laid-back attitude convinced Sari that she must be right. They stopped discussing it and rushed into the subway.

When their morning meeting at work was over, the branch manager switched on the TV set on top of a shelf in the small reception area. He'd never turned it on before, so all the employees collectively turned toward the screen.

"Something has happened at Mitsuse Pass," the branch manager said, turning toward the others. Several employees had already heard something and, from the corner of the room, they began to talk loudly. Several others moved closer to the TV.

The morning light shone through a large window, over which hung a decoration left over from the Tanabata midsummer festival. It was the only spot in the office where the summer heat still seemed to linger.

Sari turned to Mako, who was busy counting promotional gifts packed into a cardboard box. "Mako," she asked, "don't tell me you're planning to buy those? Aren't they kind of expensive?"

"New ones are coming out, they said. Plus we can buy these at seventy percent off."

The box was crammed with not very appealing stuffed bunnies.

"Who's going to sign a contract with us just because we hand out this kind of junk?" Sari asked.

"Yeah, but there are some people who ask specifically for the stuffed toy animals," Mako said seriously.

Then several staff members in front of the TV exclaimed loudly: "No way." "How awful." Their voices weren't so much tense as indifferent, so Sari merely glanced around at the TV.

Normally this local morning show reported on bargain sales in town, but today on the TV a young reporter, frowning very seriously, was standing in front of the road that ran through the mountains.

"They found a dead body up at Mitsuse Pass," one of the staff members said, turning around.

Everyone began to move toward the TV.

"The young woman's body was discovered this morning at the base of the cliff that's visible over there. The police have roped off the area, but even from here it's clear that the cliff is quite steep."

The reporter, out of breath, was almost shouting, as if he'd just arrived at the site.

Sari was struck by an awful premonition and glanced over at Mako, who was obliviously pawing through the stuffed animals.

"Mako," Sari said, and Mako—thinking Sari wanted some of the stuffed animals—held out the one in her hand, the smallest of the bunnies in the box.

"Not that. *Look*," Sari said, irritated, motioning with her chin. Mako slowly turned to the screen.

". . . The victim has not yet been indentified. According to authorities the body was abandoned there today, before dawn. Most likely the victim has been dead for eight to ten hours. . . ."

Mako returned to her box. Sari, half afraid, waited for what Mako might say. Mako's face stiffened and she said, "Mitsuse Pass is where there're all those ghosts, right?"

"That's not the point!" Sari shouted. If she explained it, she was sure Mako could catch her drift, but she was reluctant to put her thoughts into words.

"What?" Mako said, reaching again for the box.

"Yoshino did go to work today, didn't she?"

Sari finally got this much out, but Mako still didn't follow. "Yeah, I guess so," she said.

"Should we call her?"

Sari looked helplessly at the TV again and Mako finally got it. "No way!" she said in disbelief. "I'm sure she went to work from Keigo's place.

"If you're so worried, why don't you call her?" she added.

"I don't know. . . ."

"Want me to call her?" Mako wearily pulled her cell phone out of her bag. "I'm only getting voice mail," she said. "Hi, Yoshino? When you get this give me a call."

"Why don't you call the other branch directly?" Sari suggested.

"She's gotta be there," Mako said, but at Sari's urging she dialed the number in Tenjin.

"Hello? This is Miss Adachi from the Seinan branch. I was wondering if Yoshino Ishibashi is there?"

Cell phone pressed against her ear, Mako knelt down and stuck her hand among the plush toy animals.

After a moment she stood up. "Yes? Is that right?" she said. "I see. Yes, I understand." Her voice was cheery enough, but after she hung up she turned to Sari with a dazed look.

"She didn't come to work?" Sari asked.

"On the schedule board it said she was going directly to meet a client. It's probably the owner of that coffee shop. You know, the guy Yoshino did a cold call to the other day."

People were starting to drift back to work, but Sari wasn't finished.

"Mitsuse Pass is a creepy place. I drove through there once," Suzuka Nakamachi said, her eyes still glued to the TV. She shuddered dramatically.

Later Sari realized that if Suzuka hadn't spoken to her right then, it might have been the end of it. They worked in the same sales district but weren't close. Still, Suzuka always spoke to Sari in an overly familiar way. Mako didn't mind her, but Yoshino disliked Suzuka intensely. Once she'd said, trembling with emotion, "I hate the way she acts."

"Suzuka," Sari said, shooting a quick glance at the TV. "You know Keigo Masuo, right, who goes to Seinan University? Do you know how to get in touch with him?"

"Keigo?" Suzuka said, guardedly. "Why do you ask?"

"Yoshino went to stay over at his place, but isn't answering her cell. Do you know his number?"

Suzuka listened, expressionless. "I don't really know him, but my friend sort of does."

"Would he know how to get in touch with Keigo?"

"Gee, I don't know. . . ."

Sari was pretty sure she wasn't going to get any help from her.

Mako was listening to their conversation. "Well, it's time for me to get going," she said and closed the lid of the cardboard box. Just then the TV showed an interview with the old man who had first discovered the body. Several people in the office were watching and burst out laughing. The old man had exceedingly long nose hairs. The laughter broke the tension in the room and the office's normal, peaceful atmosphere returned.

"I noticed that the rope tying down the load on the back of my truck had broken," the old man was explaining, "so I stopped right at that curve over there. I got out and happened to glance over the edge of the cliff and saw something stuck in a tree. When I looked more closely . . . I couldn't believe my eyes."

That same morning, Suzuka Nakamachi arrived at the coffee shop in the Mitsukoshi department store just after ten a.m. She had an appointment with a client, the first contract she'd managed to land in some time. Though the premiums for the new account were neglible, the client had promised he'd introduce her to his cousin and his wife, which could mean more business for her.

They were scheduled to meet at ten-thirty, so she had a little time. Suzuka decided to phone a friend, a guy named Yosuke Tsuchiura, who attended Seinan Gakuin University. She was hoping to use this opportunity to get closer to Keigo. She'd liked him for some time.

Yosuke and Suzuka were both from Saitama Prefecture and had been classmates in high school. After Yosuke graduated he decided to attend a private university in Fukuoka, where he had no relatives or any connections, and his friends were surprised. Why Fukuoka of all places? they asked him. "If I'm going to go to college," Yosuke explained, "I'd like to go someplace where I don't know anybody." Suzuka alone found the idea appealing.

After she graduated from a junior college outside Tokyo, she felt exhausted trying to find a job there and she suddenly recalled his words. She wasn't chasing after him, but two years after Yosuke moved to Fukuoka, so did she. They saw each other fairly often, and though their relationship wasn't totally platonic, they didn't consider themselves a couple.

Yosuke must have still been asleep when she called. "Ah—hello?" he answered sleepily, a bit annoyed.

"You're still sleeping?"

"Suzuka? What time is it?"

"It's after ten. Don't you have classes today?"

Yosuke gradually woke up. She quickly apologized for waking him, and turned to the real reason for her call. "There's a guy named Keigo Masuo a year ahead of you in school, right?"

"Keigo?"

"You know—when we were drinking in that bar in Tenjin, you pointed him out."

"Oh, Keigo. Right."

"Do you know his phone number?"

"His phone number?"

Suzuka could detect a hint of jealousy, and it gave her a tiny thrill.

"One of my co-workers is supposedly going out with him, and she's been out of touch since yesterday. So I was wondering if you could tell me how to contact him." Suzuka tried to make it sound straightforward.

"No, I don't know his number. He's a year above me and he's not really the kind of guy who hangs out with someone like me," Yosuke said, self-deprecatingly.

"So you don't know his number?'

"No, I don't. . . . Oh—wait a sec. You know, I think I heard some rumor about him a couple of days ago. They said he's disappeared."

"Disappeared?"

"Yeah. The word's going around that he hasn't been in his apartment the last few days, and apparently didn't go back home to see his parents, either."

"So what happened? He just vanished?"

"I think he's off on a trip by himself. His folks run an inn in Yufuin so he's got to be loaded, right?"

Yosuke was so casual about it that Suzuka started to find his explanation plausible. Keigo had gone off on a trip.

"The thing is, though, one of the girls at work was supposed to meet him yesterday in our neighborhood."

"Yesterday? Then maybe it's just a rumor after all, about him disappearing," Yosuke said. "He must still be there, at his place."

Suzuka could picture them—Yoshino and Keigo—making out on his bed.

The truth was, Suzuka had fallen in love with Keigo the moment she first saw him in the bar in Tenjin, but the more she'd heard about him from Yosuke and his friends, the more she felt he was out of her league. When Suzuka had heard Sari and Mako, in the courtyard at their apartment building, talking about how Yoshino and Keigo were going out, she frankly didn't buy it. Everything she'd heard about Keigo indicated that he led a flamboyant life—he was the best-known guy in his college and he was dating a local newscaster. Could a man like this really be going out with someone like Yoshino who was—among the girls at their building—at best only slightly above average?

❦

After finishing her morning rounds collecting premiums from her main clients, Sari anxiously hurried back to the Hakata branch office. She'd e-mailed Yoshino several times while making her rounds, with no response, and on her breaks she'd called Yoshino's cell, which immediately went to voice mail. She knew this could mean anything but still, ever since Sari had seen the morning TV report on the murder at Mitsuse Pass, she'd felt uneasy.

As soon as she got back to the Hakata branch, she phoned

Yoshino's office. *Please, let her be there,* she prayed, at the same time feeling she wouldn't be. Her finger shook as she dialed.

The middle-aged woman who answered the phone gave her the same message as in the morning: Yoshino wasn't at work.

"She was going to go directly to see clients this morning and be here by eleven. It, uh, doesn't look like she's back yet, though."

Sari hung up and glanced around the office, empty during lunch hour. The section chief was gone, the tag on his desk turned over to indicate that he was out. The instant Sari saw this she thought, *That's it. I'll call the Tenjin branch one more time and get Yoshino's parents' phone number.*

Just then, from the TV in the next room, she heard the beginning of another report on the discovery at Mitsuse Pass. Drawn by the sound, Sari drifted into the reception area. No one else was there to turn around at the click of her high heels on the floor.

The reporter, a helicopter above him droning over the valley where the body had been discovered, was listing the characteristics of the dead woman.

"Sari . . ."

Sari turned. She'd been so engrossed in the scene on TV she hadn't noticed Mako.

"Have you heard from Yoshino?" Mako asked. She looked more plaintive than worried.

Sari shook her head. "Take a look," she said, and pointed to the screen.

The scene changed from the deep valley to an illustration of the characteristics of the dead woman. The physical description matched Yoshino, as did the hairstyle and clothes she'd been wearing when they'd said goodbye to her last night.

Sari took Mako's hand and tugged her away from the TV. Mako had been too scared to watch the TV at her own office after the morning meeting, and before she knew it, she'd come over to Sari's branch.

"Shouldn't we let somebody know?" Sari said.

"But who would we tell?" Mako asked forlornly.

"How about the section chief? Oh, Mako, d'you know Yoshino's parents' phone number?"

"That's right! Maybe she went back home." Mako nodded, relieved, and pulled her cell phone out of her bag.

As Mako made the call, Sari looked back and forth between her and the broadcast from Mitsuse Pass.

"Hello, my name is Mako Adachi. I was wondering if Yoshino is there?" The phone had apparently rung for some time before anyone answered. Mako spoke hurriedly, glancing in Sari's direction.

"Ah, no—thank *you*. It's so nice to talk with you. . . . Uh, no. . . . No. . . . I see. . . . No. . . ."

Mako held the phone away from her, cupped her hand over it, and said to Sari, "What do you think? Is it okay to tell them that Yoshino didn't come back last night?"

"Tell them we're calling 'cause Yoshino said something about going back to her parents' home this afternoon. Tell them she may very well be coming back here soon."

Sari listened as Mako repeated her lie. Sari began to feel that all their fears were groundless.

Mako hung up and said, quite casually, "They just said to tell her to call them when she gets back."

Sari and Mako sat for a while, watching the continuing TV coverage, going round and round about whether they should tell their general manager or even the police, or just wait a while longer to see if Yoshino came back.

Then Suzuka returned to the office.

"Any luck getting Keigo's phone number?" Sari called out to her.

With one eye on the TV, Suzuka ran over.

"He seems to have disappeared."

Sari and Mako exchanged a look. "*Disappeared?*" they chorused.

"Yeah. I didn't hear this from him directly, naturally, but from a friend of his friend. The last couple of days nobody can get in touch with him. Maybe *disappeared* isn't the right word. Seems like he might have just gone on a trip by himself somewhere."

"Wait a sec!" Mako said loudly.

"He was supposed to meet up with Yoshino at the park last night!" Sari continued.

"You still haven't got in touch with her?" Suzuka said, turning to the TV.

"No, not yet," Sari and Mako said, both shaking their heads.

"Don't you think you should tell somebody? The whole thing about Keigo disappearing might just be a rumor, and maybe he actually did hook up with Yoshino."

Suzuka was suddenly acting very friendly, and Sari felt that she was being forced into doing something she'd rather not.

"The police?" Sari said, tilting her head.

Suzuka replied, "Telling her general manager's enough right now, don't you think? Not by phone, but just go there and tell him directly. I'll go with you."

Sari and Mako felt as if Suzuka was leading them by the hand as, together, they exited the building.

It was only a few minutes by taxi to the Tenjin branch where Yoshino worked. The TV was on there, too, and several staff members were watching events unfold as they ate their lunches.

Nervously, all three of them made their way to see Goro Terauchi, the general manager of the Tenjin branch.

Mr. Terauchi had been napping at his desk. Sari briefly explained their concerns. She emphasized that it might all prove groundless. But when she mentioned how much the police sketch of the victim resembled Yoshino, Terauchi turned pale.

Terauchi was finishing his fourth year as general manager. He'd been hired by the company twenty years ago, and finally, after working furiously for years, had achieved his present position, supervising a fifty-six-person branch, the second largest in Fukuoka.

He had a bad leg, which he dragged a little, but it didn't interfere with his ability to do his job. His pace when he walked around the office was slow, but he was sharp at sniffing out potential new customers. In his younger days it was rumored that he flirted with older female employees near retirement, in order to get them to pass along their clients to him, which is what led to his eventually getting promoted.

After he was promoted to general manager, Terauchi decided to start fresh. He no longer had to struggle anymore, calculating how much commission he'd earn for each client. Instead, he decided he would be a good father figure to the young female employees who were working their hardest to earn money, women younger than his own daughter.

And in fact he always was willing to lend an ear to whatever the girls had to say. The more they talked with him, he thought, the stronger their bonds would be. He wanted to hear personal details but the girls didn't usually seek advice about life and love. Instead they wanted to talk about the kind of professional topics he had, over the past twenty years, experienced and grown sick of: "One of the other girls is coming on to her clients," one would say. "My relatives are starting to hate me for trying to sign them up," another would complain.

Still, Terauchi was proud of the fact that in his years as head of the Tenjin branch their sales had grown dramatically. The previous manager had been somewhat hysterical and many new employees had quit in protest before they'd even finished their probationary period. In the world of insurance, where the best way to get new clients is to take good care of the employees, the job of the manager is less to soothe the clients than to keep up the morale of the sales force.

So when Sari and Mako told him they were worried about Yoshino, his first reaction was mild anger. He was worried that it might negatively affect the Tenjin branch's reputation, that it would all lead to a fight over who would take over Yoshino's clients. He thought Sari and the others lacked a sense of urgency over what could be something very serious.

First, Terauchi phoned the Heisei Insurance Fukuoka branch. The receptionist didn't seem to grasp the situation and told him roughly that she'd transfer him to the chief of general affairs.

When the chief heard what Terauchi had to say, he replied timidly, "I . . . I think you'd . . . better call the police." It was clear that he was hoping Terauchi would handle the whole thing.

As Terauchi hung up, he looked up at the three girls standing in front of him.

"I'm going to call the police now," he said.

"Huh? Oh—I see," they said, nodding.

"You said—you haven't been able to contact her since last night, correct? And the description of her clothes on TV matches?" Terauchi asked, his tone sharp. The three girls, huddled closer together, nodded fearfully.

Terauchi dialed 911. After speaking with several detectives, he called a taxi. Sari and the others wanted to come with him, but thinking there was an outside chance he might have to identify the body, Terauchi told them he'd go alone.

When he arrived at the precinct and identified himself at the front desk, he was immediately escorted to the fifth-floor investigation headquarters. The main detective he'd spoken to on the phone appeared, and Terauchi proffered his company ID and business card. He was immediately hustled down to the morgue. As they walked, the detective asked him details about the location of the Tenjin branch and the Fairyland Hakata apartment building.

The experience was just as he'd seen on TV and in the movies. Incense was burning in the room, and the detective ostentatiously drew back the thin green sheet covering the body.

There was no doubt about it. The body lying there was Yoshino Ishibashi.

"It's definitely her," Terauchi gulped. He was surprised at how naturally this line came out.

"She was strangled," the detective said, and Terauchi's gaze fell on Yoshino's white neck. It was ringed with a purplish bruise.

Terauchi remembered how Yoshino looked when she smiled, how she used to rush into the office barely in time for the mandatory morning meeting. It surprised him that he could remember so clearly the face of one employee out of the fifty-odd people who worked for him.

✻

As Terauchi was identifying the body, thirty kilometers away in Kurume, Yoshino's father, Yoshio, was in his house after a late lunch, lying down, using his zabuton seat cushion as a pillow.

From where he lay he could see into the darkened barbershop, closed as always on Mondays. With the lights out inside, the sunlight shone through the window at the front of the shop, projecting the name *Ishibashi Barbershop*, painted in white on the window, as a shadow on the floor.

Yoshio had taken over the business from his father around the time that Yoshino was born. Up until then, he'd mainly hung out with his delinquent friends from the band, living off the money he'd pestered his parents to give him, but at his wife's urging he started training at the barbershop. The year Yoshino started elementary school, his father died of a cerebral hemorrhage. His mother had passed away ten years before, so Yoshio, his wife, and their daughter moved from their apartment into the vacant family house. Yoshio sometimes wondered how his life would have worked out if Satoko hadn't become pregnant so early, but it was just a random thought. He couldn't picture any other life. But truthfully Yoshio had always hated his father's profession. He'd taken over the family business reluctantly. It was a profession he took on for his daughter, but Yoshio had started to sense the instinctive dislike Yoshino had for her father's work.

As Yoshio gazed vacantly around the dark shop, Satoko called out to him from the kitchen. "You think she's coming back?" Apparently one of Yoshino's colleagues had called in the afternoon saying she was.

"I bet she'll ask us to introduce her to somebody she can sell insurance to. . . ."

Yoshio had nothing else to do today, so he thought he'd ride his bike over to the station to meet her, though he knew she wouldn't be happy about it.

Yoshio was half dozing when the call came from the police. As if in a dream he heard Satoko say, "Yes. Yes. That's right. Yes, that's correct." She called out, "Honey!" and he snapped awake. Her voice sounded far away, but echoed nearby in the tiny house.

He rolled over and saw Satoko looming over him as if she were going to trample him, her hand cupped over the phone.

"Honey . . . I, I don't know what it's all about. . . . It's the police. . . ."

Yoshio sat up. Satoko's hand was shaking as she held the cordless phone.

"What do they want?" Yoshio asked, leaning away from the phone.

"*You* ask them. . . . I don't know what they're talking about. . . ."

Satoko's eyes were out of focus, her face drained of blood.

Yoshio grabbed the phone from her and shouted an angry hello.

It was a woman's voice on the phone—slightly unprofessional, small and hard to hear. The cordless phone was always full of static and Yoshio couldn't get used to it. "That's normal. It's just the signal," Yoshino had explained, and Yoshio had been putting up with it for nearly a year. Today the static was a loud buzzing in his ears.

Yoshino had been involved in an accident, the woman explained, so they would need to please come to the station as soon as possible for identification. "Eh? What'd you say?" Yoshio said, feeling as if he were talking more to the static than to a person.

When he hung up, Satoko was sitting beside him. She looked less astonished than resigned.

"Come on, let's go!" Yoshio said, tugging at her hand. "No way a company director's going to remember the face of every employee!"

Satoko seemed paralyzed and Yoshio yanked her to her feet. After she'd given birth to Yoshino, Satoko had put on weight, and her rear end slid heavily across the worn-out tatami.

"But Yoshino's coming back today! She's coming home!"

❀

The call from Terauchi to the Tenjin branch came in after three p.m. Sari, Mako, and other employees were gathered around the TV in the reception area, quickly switching from one channel to the next to find coverage of the incident. Sari answered the phone.

Mako had a premonition: "It's true. Yoshino's been murdered. . . ."

Sari was listening intently. Suddenly she screamed out, "*What?*" Several others turned to look at Mako.

"See? I knew it. . . ." Mako said weakly.

As soon as Sari put down the phone, she began to talk as if she'd been jolted by electricity. There was too much she needed to say and the words tumbled out all at once.

"It was Yoshino, she was strangled, Mr. Terauchi wants us to wait here until he gets back." Sari's body began trembling uncontrollably.

"Are you okay?" someone next to Mako asked, holding her, but Mako couldn't bring herself to look up to see who it was. The office, usually nearly empty at this time of day, seemed claustrophobic. She tried to breathe, but it seemed as if someone had sucked away all the air, and no matter how she tried to take in a breath, the air wouldn't go inside. Sari was standing there, still blabbing away, but Mako couldn't hear her. People's mouths were moving but it was as if they were all drowning, their mouths just moving. *Please, someone cry*, she prayed. If somebody cried she knew she could, too. And then she could breathe again.

"Someone's coming here from the police! They want to find out exactly when and where we left her last night!" Sari shouted.

Finally, Mako could react. She nodded, and stood up from her chair without really knowing what she was doing. Her body was still shaking and the floor looked miles away.

From the outset Mako had always sensed a rivalry between Yoshino and Sari. They'd never quarreled openly or anything, but they had used Mako as a sounding board to bad-mouth each other. Yoshino bragged to Mako about dating men she'd met at online dating sites, but always cautioned her to keep it a secret from Sari. Mako didn't see why meeting guys and having dinner with them was something she had to hide, but Yoshino seemed to find it embarrassing as well as fun, and Mako didn't want Sari to use this against Yoshino.

When she first moved into the Fairyland Hakata apartments, Sari had said to Yoshino, half joking, "You're from Kurume, right? And your last name is Ishibashi? Hey, maybe you're related to the president of Bridgestone?" By then Mako already knew that Yoshino's family ran a barbershop, so she was sure Yoshino would deny this, but instead she nonchalantly replied, "Hm? Me? We're sort of distant relatives."

Sari of course nearly shrieked when she heard this. Surprised at her reaction, Yoshino hurriedly added, "But, we're just . . . very, very distant relatives."

When Sari had left, Yoshino told Mako, "Don't tell anybody my family runs a barbershop." Mako had been thinking of calling her on this lie, but Yoshino looked so fierce and Mako was afraid of losing a new friend, so she nodded weakly.

Mako couldn't figure out why Yoshino would lie like that, especially when the three of them had just become friends.

Mako wasn't sure of the exact number, but Yoshino always seemed to be corresponding with four or five guys she'd met online. Sometimes, when Sari wasn't with them, she'd let Mako see the messages from the men.

"Isn't this sick?" she'd say, showing Mako a message that said, *Thanks for the photo! You're so cute! I spent a whole hour just looking at your picture!* Most of the messages were, indeed, fairly repulsive.

Of the men Yoshino met online she'd actually met three—no, four—of them.

Whenever Yoshino met one of these men, she always told Mako all about it. Not what they did for a living or what they looked like, but things like how one man took her to a famous *teppanyaki* place and bought her a fifteen-thousand-yen tenderloin steak. Or comments on the guy's possessions, how one drove a BMW.

Mako listened without comment whenever Yoshino reported

back on these dates. She never once felt envious. She knew that having dinner with a man she'd just met would make her too nervous, and she much preferred spending an evening alone in her room reading. But she never had a problem listening to Yoshino talk about her exploits. There was a vicarious pleasure in hearing about Yoshino and the kind of life Mako would never know.

"Sari said the person Yoshino went to see last night wasn't Keigo Masuo, but I think it had to have been." Mako was in the lobby of the Fairyland Hakata, answering questions from a police officer. "I heard from Suzuka Nakamachi that for the last couple of days no one knew where Keigo was. But if they wanted to get in touch with each other, they could have. So if she really wanted to see him last night they could have hooked up. . . ."

Mako felt regretful. The young detective had urged her to tell him anything she might know about Yoshino, so she'd told him how Yoshino and Sari didn't get along, and how Yoshino had met men online. Mako felt she'd given the detective a bad impression of Yoshino.

Mako and the young detective weren't alone in the apartment-building lobby. Every so often a uniformed policeman would come over and report to the detective. Still, it was just the two of them facing each other across the lace-covered table, and talking with a police detective was, of course, a first for her. The young detective had a small scar from stitches next to his right eyebrow. His muscular upper arms strained the fabric of his suit.

"I'd like you to tell me more about these online friends of Ms. Ishibashi's."

At the beginning of last month, a Sunday, a cold rain had fallen since morning. It was just a light drizzle, but to Mako, looking out from the third-floor veranda of her apartment, it seemed as if the rain had erased all the sounds of the city.

Yoshino had stopped by to see her and stood looking out at the same scene. She turned to Mako and asked her to come with her to the convenience store. Whenever she did this, Mako always thought,

The convenience store? Can't you manage that on your own? But she never said anything, figuring it would cause a rift between them, and she never lied about having something else to do. After all, it wasn't that big a deal.

They were walking, holding umbrellas, to the convenience store in front of Yoshizuka station, avoiding the rain puddles, when Yoshino said, "Take a look at this," and held out her cell phone.

On the screen was a picture of a young man. "We started e-mailing each other recently," Yoshino explained.

Mako looked at the phone, which had a few raindrops on the LCD. The photo wasn't that good, but she could see the sort of rough look of the man, his dark skin, his nicely shaped nose, the lonely look in his eyes as he gazed at the camera. He was good-looking enough that she couldn't take her eyes off him.

"So what d'you think?" Yoshino asked.

"He's sexy," Mako replied honestly. *If this is the kind of guy Yoshino hooks up with,* Mako thought, *maybe online dating isn't so bad after all.*

Apparently satisfied, Yoshino said, "But I don't feel like seeing him anymore. I mean, I've got Keigo now and everything." She intentionally banged her cell phone shut.

"What do you mean you don't feel like meeting him anymore? . . . You mean you've already *met* him?"

"Yeah, last Sunday."

"You're kidding."

"Remember the guy I was talking about who tried to pick me up at the park in front of Solaria?"

"What?" Mako said loudly.

"Don't tell Sari, okay? That wasn't just some pickup. We had a date."

"No way. . . ."

If you're so embarrassed about meeting guys online, thought Mako, *then why don't you quit?* She couldn't figure Yoshino out sometimes. She acted embarrassed about online dating, yet here she was showing off the photo of one of the guys she met.

"He's good-looking, all right, but a complete bore. It's no fun being with him. Plus he's a construction worker, which doesn't turn me on."

Yoshino continued talking about the guy as she folded up her umbrella and went into the convenience store.

Mako hadn't gone to the store thinking to buy anything, but as soon as she went in she found she wanted something sweet.

"The only thing is, he's good in bed," Yoshino suddenly whispered in Mako's ear, just as she was reaching for a strawberry pudding cup.

"Huh?"

Mako reflexively glanced around them. Luckily there were no other customers by the dessert counter, and the two clerks were back at the register, helping a woman mail a package.

"The sex is great," Yoshino whispered again, a knowing smile on her lips, and reached for an éclair.

"Are you telling me . . . you did it with him already? The first time you met him?" Mako asked, eyes wide.

Examining the éclairs one by one, Yoshino laughed strangely. "Well, isn't that the whole point?

"He's like, so good at it," she went on. "It's like I completely lose it, and can't help screaming. The way he moves his fingers is so smooth. I was on my back, but before I knew what was going on I was on my stomach, and his fingers were all over my back and butt. It was like all the strength had left me. I tried to move, but all he has to do is touch my knees and I'm a complete wreck. Usually I'm too shy to make much noise, but when I'm with him, I don't care anymore. I shout as loud as I can. And the more I cry out, the more I lose control, and it's like I know we're in a small hotel room but it feels like we're in some vast open place. I've never sucked a guy's fingers as crazily as I did with him."

Yoshino didn't mind talking about such shameless things even in public like this, but Mako did, and glanced around anxiously. A part of her rejected lewd talk like this, but as she listened she pictured herself on the white sheets with the man, writhing under his touch.

She could see the man in the photo, his fingers moving over her body, his voice telling her to *just let go*.

Outside the rain was gloomy and heavy. Yoshino changed gears and began instead to recount how squeamish she felt when she recently watched the movie *Battle Royale* with all its cruel, violent scenes.

"So you're not going to see that guy anymore?" Mako asked.

A mean look flashed across Yoshino's eyes. "If I dump him, you want me to introduce you?"

Mako was flustered. "No, no way," she demurred. It felt as if Yoshino had seen into her mind and all her silly fantasies.

Mako could sense how Yoshino looked down on her as a woman. Maybe that was inevitable, for Mako was twenty and had never gone out with a man, which, unlike Sari, she didn't hide. And of the three of them, Yoshino was by far the most experienced.

Strangely enough, though, Mako never felt inferior to Yoshino, no matter how much she bragged about her sex life. All her stories about hooking up with men from dating sites, and Keigo Masuo, were like something far away, like a TV drama, and Mako never felt contempt for her, or envy. But this time was different. For the first time, one of Yoshino's stories took hold of her. She knew she should just let it go, but her rainy-day convenience-store fantasies about the man and his caresses made her overwhelmed by a mixture of jealousy for Yoshino, who really had been touched by this man, and contempt for her for leaping into bed with a guy she'd just met online, despite already having a boyfriend, Keigo. The more contempt Mako felt, though, the more uneasy she became, concerned that deep down she wanted to be just as shameless as Yoshino.

Mako knew she wasn't the type to try to date men she met online. But she also knew she wasn't like Sari, who was distressed that she couldn't act like Yoshino, secretly trashing her because Yoshino could. If possible, Mako wanted to marry someone also from Kumamoto, settle down there, and raise a happy family. That's all she really wanted—but the instant she pictured herself in the arms of Yoshino's man, her dream evaporated.

. . .

"Um . . ."

The detective with the scar beside his right eyebrow looked at Mako.

Bright sunshine lit up the apartment-building lobby. The automatic front door must have had a slight gap in it, for the wind was blowing in, making a strange whistling sound. In addition to Mako and the detective interviewing her, five or six other policemen had entered and were making their way between the lobby and Yoshino's apartment, on the second floor.

Every time they brought down another box of Yoshino's possessions, Mako thought, *Ah, Yoshino really* was *murdered.* Sari, who'd been questioned before her, had broken down, wailing loudly, but Mako couldn't do that. Not that she wasn't sad. But the tears just wouldn't flow.

"So those were the only three men you heard about from Miss Ishibashi?"

Mako tried to focus. "Uh, yes, that's—that's right." She nodded.

"Two last summer and then one more this autumn. The two men from last summer were both from Fukuoka? And they took her out to dinner, bought her clothes and so on, and though you don't know their ages, they seemed much older?"

"Yes, that's right."

"And the man she met this autumn is a college student, and they went for drives together sometimes?"

"Yes, that's what I heard."

"There weren't any others?"

"No, these are the only three I remember. She might have mentioned others. . . . Of course there were a lot more she e-mailed with." Mako got this out in a rush, telling herself that she was helping the investigation, not putting down her friend.

"Is there anybody else besides yourself that Miss Ishibashi might have told these things to?"

The young detective's long fingers had very healthy-looking nails. Perhaps it was his bad habit, but the backs of his fingers were marked where he had pressed his nails into them.

"I think I'm the only one she told," Mako replied.

"All right. Let's go over it one more time. You believe that last night Miss Ishibashi went to meet Keigo Masuo, correct?" The detective sighed deeply.

"Sari has her doubts," Mako replied, "but I think that's what happened."

"I see. . . ."

"Maybe somebody took her away after that. . . ."

"We're checking into that possibility," the detective said, cutting her off, and Mako looked down meekly, knowing she'd been too pushy.

The detective looked down at his notebook and his scrawled notes.

"I understand. I'm really sorry I had to ask you all these questions."

Mako was taken aback. "You—you mean we're finished?"

Brusquely, the detective yelled out to a policeman standing at the entrance.

"Excuse me . . ." Mako said.

"Yes?"

"Is that all?"

"Yes, we're finished here. I'm sorry to have taken up so much of your time. Especially now, with what happened to your friend."

Mako went out in the hallway and saw Suzuka standing there, eyes puffy from crying. She was next to be questioned, it seemed. Mako silently slipped past her.

As soon as she was in the elevator, Mako wondered why she hadn't told the detective one more thing. About one more man Yoshino met online. But she just couldn't bring herself to tell the young detective about him. If she did, he'd think she was the same sort of girl as Yoshino, a girl who hunted for men online. She would hate for him to think that.

Mako didn't realize it at the time, but this decision of hers threw off the subsequent investigation.

CHAPTER 2

WHO DID HE WANT TO SEE?

Early Monday morning, December 10, 2001, Norio Yajima—who ran a wrecking business on the outskirts of Nagasaki City—was driving his old van to work. He'd had the van, which now had more than two hundred thousand kilometers on it, for so long it felt like a part of him, and he drove it lovingly, gingerly.

His throat had been bothering him since the previous night, and he kept clearing it. It felt full of phlegm, but no matter how hard he coughed he couldn't bring any up. When he forced himself to cough, this only brought up the sour taste of bile in his mouth. Last night in bed he'd vomited, and his wife, Michiyo, told him he should gargle. He'd done that long before and he muttered, to no one in particular, "Damn it! I *hate* this!"

Norio turned left at the usual intersection, and as he did, the traffic protector amulet Michiyo had hung on his rearview mirror swung back and forth.

The way the intersection came together looked grotesque, as if a wide road constructed by a giant and a narrow little path made by dwarves had been forced to merge. Going down the broad highway, the intersection appeared to be an L-shaped road that curved right at a 90-degree angle. But farther down, the curve became a narrow alley and then opened into a small bridge that spanned the waterway paralleling the highway. In 1971 they'd finished filling in the shore between the mainland and an island, and the road now connected the two.

The island was home to a mammoth shipbuilding dock. This was where the giant lived. And the narrow alley still ran through the fishing village, whose shoreline had been stolen from it.

Norio steered smoothly off the highway into the alley. On his left was a church, its stained glass sparkling in the morning sun. Here there was always the presence of the sea. As Norio reached the end of the alley, there stood Yuichi Shimizu as always, outfitted in his tacky sweatshirt, a sleepy look on his face.

Norio pulled up in front of him, and Yuichi yanked open the door, said a desultory good morning, and climbed into the middle row of seats. Norio grunted out a hello and stepped on the gas.

Every morning on their way to the construction site in Nagasaki City, Norio picked up three workers in this order: first Yuichi, then another man in Kogakura, and a third in Tomachi.

After his abbreviated greeting, Yuichi was invariably silent. As Norio accelerated he asked, "Not enough sleep again? Bet you were out driving around again till late."

Yuichi glanced for a second at the rearview mirror. "Not really," he said.

Norio knew it was hard for a young guy like Yuichi to be picked up at six every morning, but between his disheveled hair and his eyes still encrusted with sleep, he looked as if he'd been in bed until three minutes ago. Norio couldn't help scolding him.

If Yuichi had been a total stranger Norio wouldn't have found his appearance and attitude so irksome, but they were relatives. Norio's mother and Yuichi's grandmother were sisters, which made Yuichi and Norio's only daughter, Hiromi, second cousins.

At the end of the alley was a communal parking lot used by local residents. Among the old cars and vans was Yuichi's precious white Skyline, bathed in the morning sunlight as if it were just out of the showroom. Yuichi bought the car used, but he had still paid more than two million yen for it, taking out a seven-year loan.

"Can't you buy something cheaper?" Yuichi's grandmother Fusae said when he bought it. "I asked him this, but he insisted he had to have this one. Well, I suppose a big car is convenient, when we have to take Grandpa to the hospital." It had been hard to tell if she was happy or worried about his purchase.

Fusae and her husband, Katsuji, who was bedridden most of the time, had two daughters, Shigeko and Yoriko. The older, Shigeko, was living in Nagasaki City with her husband, who ran a high-end confectionary shop. She'd put her two sons through college and now they were out on their own. According to Fusae she was "the daughter I never have to worry about." In contrast, her second daughter, Yuichi's mother, never seemed able to settle down. When she was young, she married a man she worked with at a bar and they had Yuichi. This was fine as far as it went, but around the time that Yuichi entered elementary school, his father ran off with another woman. Not knowing what else to do, Yoriko brought Yuichi back to her parents' home and stayed for a time but then took off, leaving her parents with no choice but to raise him. Rumor had it that she was working as a maid in an inn in the resort town of Unzen. Norio thought that it had worked out better for the boy this way, better for him to be raised by his grandfather, who worked for years in the shipyard, and his grandmother, rather than be dragged all over the place by irresponsible parents. Because of this, when Yuichi entered junior high and his grandparents proposed to adopt him, Norio didn't hesitate to support the idea.

When Yuichi was adopted by his grandparents his last name, naturally enough, changed, from Honda to Shimizu. At New Year's the next year, when Norio stopped by to give Yuichi the traditional gift of money, he asked, half joking, "What do you think? Doesn't Yuichi Shimizu sound better than Yuichi Honda?"

But Yuichi, who was getting interested in motorcycles and cars, replied, "No, Honda is way more cool," as he traced the English letters on the tatami.

. . .

Now, driving, Norio returned to the intersection—the spot where the giant's land and the dwarves' had been forcibly stitched together—and as they were waiting for the light to change, Yuichi spoke up from the backseat. "Uncle, this morning we're gonna remove the blue sheet on the concrete, right?"

"We could wait till the afternoon," Norio replied. "How long you think it'll take to get rid of all of it?"

"If we leave just the front, about an hour should do it."

At this time of morning the lane going in the other direction was packed with cars all headed toward the shipyard, full of men trying their best to suppress yawns.

The light changed and Norio stepped on the gas. The tools stacked in the back of the van clanked together. Yuichi must have opened the window, for the scent of the sea wafted into the van.

"What'd you do last night?" Norio glanced back at him in the rearview mirror. He saw Yuichi grow suddenly tense.

"Why are you asking?"

Norio actually wanted to ask about Yuichi's grandfather Katsuji, who would probably have to go back in the hospital before long, but Yuichi's response made him keep asking questions. "I just figured you must have been out driving around last night."

"I didn't go anywhere yesterday," Yuichi replied.

"What kind of mileage do you get with that car, anyway?" Norio tried to change the subject but he saw a slightly disgusted look on Yuichi's face. "Bet you get ten kilometers to the liter."

"No way. It depends on the road, but if I get seven I'm doing okay." Yuichi's tone was curt, but he perked up at a conversation about cars.

Already the line of cars headed for the city was starting to show signs of turning into a traffic jam. If they had come thirty minutes later they would have been caught in a massive tie-up.

The road they were on was the only interstate that ran north and south along the Nagasaki peninsula. In the opposite direction, past the city, the highway ran past an abandoned offshore industrial island called Battleship Island, so named because of its shape; past

Takahama Beach, crowded with people in the summer; then past the swimming beaches at Wakamisaki; and finally, at the end of the highway, the beautiful lighthouse at Kabashima.

"Hey, how's your grandpa? Still not feeling so good?" Norio asked as they continued down the highway toward the city.

There was no response, so Norio asked, "Is he going to go back in the hospital?"

"I'm taking him there today after work."

Yuichi was looking out the window, and his reply was half blown away by the breeze.

"You should have told me. You could have taken him first and then come to work." Most likely Fusae had told him to go to work first, but Norio thought this was a little cold of her.

"It's the same hospital as always, so it can wait till evening," Yuichi said, protective of his grandmother.

For the last seven years Yuichi's grandfather had suffered from a severe case of diabetes. He was getting on in years, and no matter how often he went to the hospital he never seemed to improve. When Norio called on him once a month to check on how he was doing, he was struck by the older man's increasingly ashen complexion.

"I know it's my own daughter's fault, but I'm really happy Yuichi's with us. Without him I'd have a heck of a time getting Grandpa back 'n' forth to the hospital."

Recently every time Norio and Fusae saw each other she'd say the same thing. Yuichi might be helpful to have around, but the more Fusae said this, the sorrier Norio felt for his quiet cousin—whom he treated like a nephew—as he was practically bound hand and foot to this elderly couple. Besides this, Yuichi was almost the only young person in his village. The rest of the residents were old couples, or old people living alone, and Yuichi was kept busy shuttling not just his grandparents but other elderly neighbors to the hospital. But he always brought his car around without a word of complaint.

For Norio, Yuichi was like the son he'd never had, which is why he'd been so upset when Yuichi had taken out a loan to buy his flashy car. Once Norio had calmed down, though, he started to feel sorry for him—since the whole point of having the car seemed to be to ferry old people back and forth to the hospital.

Unlike the other young guys on the construction site, Yuichi never overslept and he always worked hard. But Norio had no idea what made this young man happy.

On this particular day Norio made his usual rounds to pick up the other workers. Yuichi was the only one of all of them who wasn't in his late fifties—the others, including Norio, filled the van with cigarette smoke and groans about married life, about how much their knees ached, or how much their wife snored.

They all knew Yuichi wasn't talkative, so they barely spoke to him. When Yuichi had first joined their construction gang, they tried to take good care of him, inviting him to boat races, or out to bars in Doza in Nagasaki. But at the races he wouldn't even make a single bet, and wouldn't sing even one karaoke song when they went drinking. *Young guys these days are no fun at all*, they concluded, and washed their hands of him.

"Hey, Yuichi! What's the matter? You look pale."

Norio glanced in the rearview mirror. He'd almost forgotten that Yuichi was there, but now he saw that his face was white as a sheet. They were just about to enter the city, at a spot where they could see the harbor between the row of warehouses along the coast.

"What's wrong? You don't feel good?" Norio asked.

Yoshioka, seated behind Yuichi, said, "You gonna throw up? Open the window! Right now!" and hurriedly leaned forward to roll it down.

Yuichi weakly brushed his hand aside and whispered, "No, I'm okay."

Yuichi looked so bad that Norio decided to pull over. As he did, the truck behind them roared past, blaring its horn, the wind rocking their van.

As soon as the van stopped Yuichi tumbled out, holding his stomach, and vomited on the ground. Nothing seemed to come up from his stomach, though, and he just stayed there, his breathing ragged and labored.

"You got a hangover?" Yoshioka called out from the van. Yuichi, hands on the paving stones of the sidewalk, shuddered as he nodded.

❀

Koki Tsuruta held the curtain, dyed in the evening sun, open a crack and peered down at the street below. From the twelfth-floor window he could see all of Ohori Park. Two white vans were parked on the street and the young detective who had just questioned him was climbing into one of them. His parents had bought this condo for him near the university, but Koki had never liked the view. The broad vista outside it made him feel small, like a worthless, spoiled rich kid.

The digital clock beside his bed showed five past five. The detective had banged on his door at four-thirty, and Koki, who'd just dragged himself out of bed, answered his questions for a half hour.

Koki sat down on his bed and took a sip of lukewarm water from a plastic bottle.

Until it dawned on him that the detective was after Keigo Masuo, Koki had answered him sullenly. He'd been watching videos until morning and couldn't hide how upset he felt at having someone pounding on his door. When the detective, not too much older than himself, showed him his badge and said he'd like to ask him some questions, Koki figured that the guy who molested women in the park must have been at it again.

"I hear that you and Keigo Masuo are close."

When he heard this, Koki put the two together, concluding that Keigo must have molested somebody—or maybe picked up some girl at a bar and raped her. Somehow the word *raped* seemed a better fit for Keigo than *molested*.

Koki was fully awake at last as the young detective summarized the facts as they knew them. *Mitsuse Pass. Yoshino Ishibashi. Dead body. Strangled. Keigo Masuo. Disappeared.* As he listened, Koki's knees gave out. Keigo had done something far worse than rape, and had fled. Koki started to sink to the floor, and the detective said, "We don't know exactly what happened, but thought that maybe you could tell us where Mr. Masuo might be. Has he gotten in touch with you recently?"

Koki lightly tapped his sleepy face and tried to remember. The detective stood there patiently, pen and notebook in hand.

"Well . . ." Koki began, gazing at the detective. "How should I put it. . . . I haven't been able to get in touch with him the last three or four days. Everybody's saying he just dropped off the grid for a laugh, but I figure he went off on a trip somewhere by himself." Koki got this out in a rush of words, then stopped and glanced at the detective again.

"Yes, that seems to be the case. When was the last time you talked with him?" The detective's expression remained unchanged, and he tapped the notebook with the tip of his pen.

"The last time? Umm . . . it must have been over the weekend."

Koki searched his memory. He remembered talking to Keigo on the phone, but what day of the week that was, he couldn't say. The signal had been bad and it was hard to hear him. "Where are you?" Koki had asked him, to which Keigo replied, laughing, "I'm up in the hills."

He hadn't called for any special reason. He'd just wanted to double-check the time for their seminar exam the following week. Koki was sure he'd been watching the movie *Whacked* on video that night. He remembered wanting to tell Keigo about it when the phone went dead.

Koki hurried to his bedroom and checked the receipt from the video store. "It was last Wednesday," he told the detective standing in the entrance.

Whenever Keigo came over, Koki always made him watch videos that he liked. Keigo wasn't interested in movies so he'd either fall asleep or go home; but Koki, who dreamed of making a film some-day, had talked with Keigo about producing something together.

Sometimes Keigo would invite him out drinking at night, saying they could talk more about movies, but as soon as they arrived at a bar, Keigo would forget about movies and start trolling for girls. Keigo was a flashy guy—even other guys could see that—and it wouldn't be long before he'd snag a girl. He'd bring her back to where Koki was sitting and introduce him, saying, "My friend here's gonna make a film next year. You want to be in it?"

The girls Keigo picked up were themselves far from flashy. Koki had asked him about this and he'd replied, laughing, "It's the down-and-out-looking ones that make me hard."

Koki remembered hearing the name the young detective had mentioned, Yoshino Ishibashi. When the detective had told him that they'd discovered the body of a woman with that name at Mitsuse Pass, the first image that flashed in front of Koki's eyes was from a film he'd seen sometime, of a white woman's frozen corpse. But after the detective had repeated the name, it finally dawned on him that this was the name of a girl that Keigo had tried to pick up in a bar in Tenjin a few months ago.

Koki had been with him that night. They were playing darts, and Koki remembered sitting at the end of the bar and discussing the films of Eric Rohmer with the bartender. Keigo had just invited Yoshino and her two friends to go sing karaoke, but they'd demurred, saying they had a curfew and were about to leave. Koki and the bartender were deep into their debate over Rohmer's films, the bartender arguing that Conte d'été was his best, while Koki insisted that Le genou de Claire was his masterpiece.

Keigo followed him to the counter and was standing just behind Koki when he said, "Tell me your e-mail address. I'll take you out to dinner next time." Koki turned around, and sure enough the girl wasn't much to speak of. She quickly gave him her address.

As the girls walked up the stairs, Keigo gave them a casual, "Bye now! See you!" and then came back to the bar, ordered a beer, and showed Koki the coaster with the girl's e-mail address on it. The name scrawled on the coaster was Yoshino Ishibashi.

Koki remembered the name since it was the same name, with just one character different, as that of a girl in the film club he belonged to who was below him in college.

As Keigo took the beer from the bartender, Koki had said, "The Ishibashi I know's much cuter than this girl."

Keigo continued to toy with the coaster. "Yeah," he said, "but I like that kind of girl. The kind that you know isn't quite grown up. She runs around, looking all cross, with her Louis Vuitton handbag, but still deep down is a farmer's daughter. Give me a girl with a Louis Vuitton bag and cheap shoes walking on a path between rice fields and I'm all over her."

When Koki first met Keigo in college he found it strange how, even though their likes and personalities were so different, they got along so well. It must have been because they were both from wealthy families and could afford to be laid-back. If Keigo were a prima donna movie star, then Koki was the director, the only one who could coax a good performance out of him.

Koki remembered a time when he and Keigo were eating ramen at an outdoor stand in Nagahama. Keigo had just bought a new car and spent all his free time tooling around town in it.

As they were slurping down their noodles Keigo asked him, "Koki, is your dad the type who cheats on his wife?"

"What?"

"Nothing. I was just wondering."

Koki's father owned a number of rental buildings in central Fukuoka. He'd inherited all of them from his own father, and even to his son he was a man with too much time and money on his hands. Koki found it hard to respect him.

"Well, I can't say for sure he hasn't played around. . . . But I imagine the most he's done is just fool around with some bar hostesses or something."

Keigo didn't seem too interested. A pile of ramen still remained in his bowl, but he snapped his disposable chopsticks in half and dropped them into the bowl.

"How 'bout your dad?" Koki said, trying to be casual. Keigo took a sip of water from the worn-out plastic cup and said, "My dad? Well, remember he runs an inn." He practically spat out the words.

"What does that have to do with anything?"

"Inns have maids," Keigo said with a knowing grin. "Since I was a kid I saw my dad taking maids into one of the back rooms. I wonder about that. . . . Those women probably hated it, right? . . . No, of course they hated it, though it didn't look that way to me."

As they exited the ramen stand, Keigo turned to the owner and said, "Thanks for the meal. It was awful."

For an instant the other customers froze. It was an awkward moment, but Koki liked this about Keigo. And in fact the stand they'd eaten at was aimed at tourists and charged way too much.

As Yuichi scrubbed away the dirt from his hands in the water-filled drum, Norio stood behind him, smoking and watching him. The drum was used for mixing cement and no matter how much clean water was poured in it, a snakelike pattern remained on your skin after your hands dried.

It was six p.m. and the various work crews on the site were getting ready to go home. Several pieces of heavy machinery now sat quietly in a row; only a few minutes ago, they were in use, tearing down a wall.

It was their fourth day tearing down a former maternity hospital, and two-thirds of it had now been mercilessly ripped apart. In a large-scale site like this, Norio had to subcontract out some of the work. His company owned a 15m heavy-duty power backhoe, but one machine wasn't nearly enough to pull down a three-story steel-and-concrete structure.

Yuichi dried his hands on the towel around his neck. "You know," Norio said, crushing out his cigarette in an ashtray, "it's about time you got a heavy-equipment license."

Yuichi turned toward him. "Yeah," he replied listlessly, and began scrubbing his face with the towel. The more he scrubbed, the dirtier his face seemed to get.

"I'll give you a week off next month. Why don't you go get your license then?"

Yuichi pouted and nodded, but it was hard to tell if this meant he'd like to do it.

Norio had been waiting for a long time, hoping Yuichi himself would suggest that he take the licensing exam, but he never took the initiative.

As Yuichi was stowing away his rubber gloves in his bag Norio asked, "So, how are you feeling now?" Despite vomiting on the way to work, after they got to the site Yuichi worked quietly, as always. Norio had noticed, though, that he'd hardly touched the lunch he'd brought with him.

"You've got to take your grandpa to the hospital, right? As soon as you get home?" Norio asked.

"Probably after dinner," Yuichi said absently as he shouldered his bag and stood up in the dusty wind.

Kurami, Yoshioka, and Yuichi climbed back into the van with Norio, just as they did every day.

The setting sun was bathing Nagasaki Harbor in red as they drove back down the highway, and Kurami popped open his usual can of *shochu.*

"You'll be home in thirty minutes. Can't you hold out till then?" Norio asked, frowning as the sharp smell of liquor hit him.

"I've been holding out for the last hour we were working, so how do you expect me to last another half hour?" Kurami gave a half-disgusted laugh, and lifted the single-serving can to his lips. Some of the liquid dribbled down and wet his thick whiskers. The window was open but still the van was filled with the odor of *shochu* and dried dirt.

"Hey, I heard a girl was murdered yesterday at the Mitsuse Pass in Fukuoka," said Yoshioka, gazing out the window.

"They said she sold insurance. Her parents must be out of their minds," said Kurami, who had a daughter about the same age, as he licked his *shochu*-smeared fingers.

Yoshioka, who lived with his common-law wife, didn't have kids and probably couldn't feel what the parents were going through. Yoshioka had never given them the details, but he lived with this woman in public housing, and though they'd been together ten years, she was still officially married to her husband. He changed the subject. "Mitsuse Pass," he said. "When I drove trucks I used to use that road all the time.

"Yuichi, you go driving over Mitsuse Pass often, don't you?" Yoshioka asked.

Yuichi was staring out the window. He shifted his gaze to the interior of the van. His face was reflected in the rearview mirror.

Traffic in the opposite direction heading back to town was starting to back up. The cars of the shipyard workers formed a long chain that stretched down the road. The faces of the men in the cars, lit by the setting sun, looked somehow demonic, like *hannya* masks.

"You drive there pretty often, right? Mitsuse Pass?" Yuichi hadn't replied, so Yoshioka repeated his question.

"I don't much like . . . Mitsuse Pass. It's creepy at night."

Somehow this reply of Yuichi's stayed with Norio as he continued to drive.

After letting out Kurami, and then Yoshioka, Norio headed for Yuichi's house.

They left the highway and drove into a narrow alley, so narrow their side mirrors nearly scraped the nameplates on the front of the houses. The alley wound its way toward the fishing village. The coastline had nearly disappeared when the sea around the village had been filled in, but a tiny harbor still remained, with a handful of fishing boats anchored there. The part of the harbor surrounded by piers was calm, the only sound the occasional creak of the boats tugging at their lines.

There were several warehouses around the harbor, all with their shutters down. At first glance it seemed as though they were connected to the fishing industry, but in fact they contained boats for the annual Chinese-style Peron dragon-boat racing festival.

Dragon-boat racing was popular in this region, with districts competing against each other every summer. It was an inspiring sight to see a dozen or so men paddling in tandem, and every year the events attracted crowds of tourists.

"You're going to be in the Peron next year, too, right?" Norio asked as he glanced at one of the warehouses, whose shutter was only half down. Yuichi had his bag in his lap and was getting ready to exit the van.

"When is it they start practicing?" Norio asked, glancing in the rearview mirror.

"Same time as always," Yuichi replied.

When Yuichi first participated in the Peron races, when he was in high school, Norio had been the district leader. Unlike the other young men, who were always moaning and groaning about practice, Yuichi silently paddled on. That was all well and good, but he overdid it, the skin on his hands scraped so raw that when it came time for the actual competition he couldn't compete.

Ten years had passed since then and Yuichi had participated in the races every year. He always claimed he didn't especially enjoy it—but when practice began, he was always the first one to show up at the warehouses.

"I think I'll stop by and say hello." Norio stopped his van in front of Yuichi's house, and switched off the engine.

Yuichi, already halfway out, turned toward him.

"What time was it that you're taking Uncle to the hospital?" Norio asked.

"After dinner," Yuichi answered vacantly, and stepped down from the van.

Norio followed him in and as soon as he entered he was hit by the distinctive odor of a sick person's house. Despite Yuichi's presence, the house was that of an old couple, and as soon as you set foot in it, it was as if all color had drained away. The dirty red sneakers Yuichi kicked off at the entrance were the only bright spot.

"Fusae-san!" Norio followed Yuichi, who briskly strode inside, and called out toward the interior of the house. It bothered Norio how the young man just kicked off his shoes and didn't neatly line them up at the entrance.

As Norio was removing his own shoes he heard Fusae's voice: "Oh, is Norio with you? We haven't seen him in quite a while."

"You're taking Uncle to the hospital?" Norio stepped up into the house as Fusae came out of the kitchen to greet him, wiping her wet hands on a dish towel.

"He just got released, but now he has to go in again."

"Yeah, that's what Yuichi was saying. . . ."

Norio strode down the hall and slid open the door into Katsuji's bedroom.

"Uncle, I hear you're going back in the hospital? Bet you'd rather stay at home, huh?"

As soon as he pulled back the sliding door, Norio caught a faint whiff of urine. The streetlight outside shone into the room, mixing with the blinking fluorescent light hanging over the faded tatami.

"As soon as he goes to the hospital, he says he wants to come home. But once we're home, he says he prefers the hospital. I don't know what I'm going to do with him."

Fusae switched the fluorescent light off, and back on again. In the futon Katsuji gave a muffled cough.

Norio sat down next to the old man's bed and roughly pulled back the futon. Katsuji's wrinkled face was revealed, resting on the hard pillow.

"Uncle," Norio said, and rested his hand on the old man's forehead. Maybe his own hand was hot, he thought with a start, for the old man's skin was chilly.

"Where's Yuichi?" Katsuji asked in a phlegmy voice, brushing Norio's hand off his forehead.

Just then Yuichi could be heard clomping around upstairs, making the whole house shake.

"You can't rely on Yuichi to do everything," Norio said, his words aimed not just at Katsuji, but at Fusae standing behind him.

"We don't," Fusae pouted.

"I know you don't, but he's still a young guy. If he spends all his time taking care of an old man and woman, he's never going to get married," Norio said, deliberately playful.

Fusae's stern look softened. "I know, but if Yuichi wasn't here I wouldn't even be able to give Uncle a bath."

"That's why you should hire a caregiver."

"Do you have any idea how much they cost?"

"That expensive?"

"Well, look at what the Okazakis are paying for—"

"Be quiet!" shouted an angry voice from the futon, followed by a painful cough.

"Sorry, sorry." Norio lightly patted the futon, stood up, and guided Fusae out of the room.

A fresh-looking yellowtail lay on the cutting board in the kitchen, darkish blood spreading out on the board. The eyes looking at the ceiling and the half-opened mouth seemed to be complaining about something.

"By the way, was Yuichi out late last night?" Norio said casually, standing behind Fusae, who was back at the cutting board, cleaver in hand. He was remembering how that morning Yuichi had looked so pale and had jumped out of the van and vomited.

"I don't know. He must have gone out."

"I was surprised he had a hangover."

"A hangover? Yuichi?"

"He was white as a sheet."

"He went drinking? But he was driving."

Fusae was slicing up the yellowtail with a practiced hand, the bones of the fish snapping as she cut through them.

"How about you take one of these yellowtail back to Michiyo? Mr. Morishita from the fishing co-op gave them to me this morning, and Yuichi's the only other one here who'll eat them." Fusae turned around and pointed to beneath the table. A single drop of water dripped down from the tip of the cleaver onto the dark, shiny floor.

Norio looked under the table and found a single yellowtail in a Styrofoam container. He carried the yellowtail, case and all, over to the front hall, then went upstairs. The door to Yuichi's room was right at the top of the stairs.

Norio felt a bit hesitant about knocking, and instead called out "Hey!" and opened the door.

Yuichi was in his underwear, probably about to take a bath, and he nearly collided with the door as Norio opened it.

"You going to take a bath?" Norio said, gazing at Yuichi's upper body, the muscles visible under a thin layer of skin.

"A bath, then eat, and then the hospital." Yuichi nodded and started out of the room. Norio twisted to one side to let him pass.

Norio was going to follow him downstairs, but he saw a pamphlet entitled *Getting Your Crane License* that had fallen on the floor.

"Ah, so you *are* thinking of getting your license."

There was no reply, just the sound of Yuichi stomping down the stairs.

Norio drifted into the room and picked up the pamphlet. Yuichi's footsteps faded off down the hallway downstairs.

Norio sat down on a flattened cushion and let his eyes wander about the room. On the tan walls there were several car posters, fixed to the wall with yellowed Scotch tape, and a pile of car magazines on the floor. But other than that the room was empty. No pinups, not even a TV or a radio/cassette player.

Fusae had once said, "Yuichi's real room isn't here, but his car," and Norio could see that this was no exaggeration.

Norio tossed aside the pamphlet and picked up the pay envelope on the low table. He'd given the envelope to Yuichi last week, but the moment he felt it he knew it was empty. Next to the envelope was a receipt from a gasoline station. Norio hadn't planned to look at it, but found it in his hand anyway. It was from a station in Saga Yamato, for ¥5,990.

"Yesterday," Norio said, looking at the date.

Yuichi had insisted that he hadn't driven anywhere far yesterday. Norio tilted his head, puzzled.

❈

Fusae slipped the head of the yellowtail off the cutting board. It hit the sink with a loud thunk and slid toward the drain, its half-open mouth facing her.

She turned at the sound of footsteps in the corridor and saw Yuichi, in only his underwear, chewing on a piece of *kamaboko* he'd grabbed from the table as he headed toward the bath.

"Did Norio go home already?" she asked his retreating figure.

Still chewing on the *kamaboko*, Yuichi turned and silently pointed upstairs to his room.

"What's he doing in your room?"

"No idea," Yuichi said, sliding open the door to the bath. The door, glass set in a wooden frame, creaked loudly like a thin sheet of corrugated iron as it bowed inward.

There was no changing room attached to the bath, so Yuichi just dropped his underwear where he was and, shivering, rushed into the bath, his white rear end like a blurred afterimage. There was another loud bang as he slammed the door to the bath shut.

Fusae shifted the cleaver in her hand and began slicing up the flesh of the yellowtail.

Footsteps rang out coming down the stairs, and when Norio called out "Auntie, I'll be going," Fusae was dissolving miso into a pot and couldn't see him off.

"Thanks for stopping by," she called out.

The old front door creaked and then slammed shut, shaking the whole house. After the sound of Norio's footsteps faded, the only sound was the pot, bubbling away.

It's so quiet, Fusae thought. *Only Katsuji, nearly bedridden, and me, an old woman in the house*. And young Yuichi, of course, there in the bath. But the house was so still it was scary.

As she leaned over to sniff the miso, Fusae called out to Yuichi. "I hear you had a hangover this morning?" Instead of a reply there was a loud splash of water.

"Where did you go drinking?"

No reply, just the sound of Yuichi pouring water over himself.

"You shouldn't drink and drive, you know."

By this point Fusae no longer expected any response.

She turned off the nearly boiling pot of soup and put the cutting board, bloody from slicing up the fish, into the sink to soak.

So Yuichi could eat as soon as he came out of the bath, she sliced up a healthy portion of sashimi and put it out with the fried ground fish meat she'd cooked the night before. She opened the rice cooker and the fluffy hot rice sent a cloud of steam into the chilly kitchen.

Before Katsuji became bedridden she'd always cooked three cups of rice in the morning and five in the evening. Sometimes she felt like all she'd done for the last fifteen years was rinse rice to make sure these two men had enough to fill their stomachs. Yuichi had loved rice, ever since he was a child. Give him a couple of daikon pickles and he could easily down a large bowl.

And everything he ate made him grow. From the time he entered junior high Fusae could swear she actually saw him growing taller by the day. Sometimes she couldn't believe it, found it incredible how the food she provided him helped him blossom into a grown man. She'd had only daughters herself, and could sense how raising a boy, her grandson, struck a chord deep within her, some female instinct she'd never felt with her daughters.

In the beginning she deferred to Yuichi's mother, Yoriko. After Yoriko ran off with a man, leaving behind Yuichi, who was in elementary school, and Fusae knew it was up to her to raise the child, she naturally enough was upset by her daughter's unfaithfulness. But more than that, she felt a new energy rising up within her. Fusae was just about to turn fifty at the time.

When Yuichi had first come to live in this house, after his mother had been abandoned by her husband, he'd already lost all trust in her. He'd call out "Mom!" to her and act spoiled, but he really wasn't focused on her at all.

Once Fusae had taken out an old photo album to show Yuichi,

taking care that Yoriko didn't see them. "Don't you think Grandma was prettier than your mother?" she asked. She'd meant it as a joke, but as she pulled the dusty old album out of the closet she felt a certain tension within her. Yuichi gazed at the photo she pointed out and was silent. Looking down on his small head from behind, Fusae suddenly realized what a terrible thing she had done. She quickly snapped shut the album. "I'm so sorry," she said. "I was never, ever beautiful." Despite her age, she found herself blushing.

At Katsuji's bedside, Fusae packed some underwear and toiletries in his leather bag. She'd bought the bag the first time he'd gone into the hospital. Figuring they'd use it only one time she'd chosen a cheap one, but with him in and out of the hospital all the time the bag, even the stitching, had started to fall apart.

"Tomorrow I'll bring you some tea and *furikake*," Fusae said. Katsuji's mouth must have been dry, for he swallowed audibly.

"Has Yuichi eaten already?" Katsuji slowly rolled over and half crawled out of bed toward the dinner Fusae had brought on a tray.

"He had yellowtail sashimi. If you'd like, I'll bring you some," Fusae hurriedly added. Katsuji had let out a sigh when he saw the bland boiled vegetables and rice porridge.

"I don't need any sashimi. But I want you to make sure to give something to the nurses at the hospital." Katsuji picked up his chopsticks, his hands trembling slightly.

"What do you mean, *give something*?"

"Money, of course."

"Money? Again with the money. Nurses these days don't accept money from patients." As she always did, Fusae turned this notion down flat. She hated this aspect of Katsuji's personality, something she saw in all men and disliked intensely. It was fine to think about giving tips to the nurses, but where did he imagine the money was going to come from?

"Even if you give them something extra, they're not going to do anything special for you. They're respected professionals nowadays, and if you give them money they'll think you're looking down on them," Fusae said, and slowly rose to her feet with a grunt. These days if she got up too quickly, her knees hurt.

Fusae watched as Katsuji, hunched over, slurped down his porridge. As she watched him, she remembered what her neighbor, old Mrs. Okazaki, had told her: "Every other month when I get a pension check I think, 'Ah, he's really dead, isn't he.'"

The first time she heard this, Fusae thought about how this elderly woman had loved her husband. But as Katsuji's condition deteriorated and he grew steadily weaker, the words took on a completely different meaning: when either a husband or wife died, your daily expenses were cut in half.

After his bath Yuichi sat cross-legged on a chair, wolfing down his meal. He must have been starving, for he followed each slice of sashimi with two or three huge mouthfuls of rice.

"I made some daikon miso soup," Fusae called out to him, and ladled some into the soup bowl she'd turned over. Yuichi didn't wait for it to cool but slurped it down as soon as she passed it to him.

"I should go along with you, don't you think?" Fusae said, and sat down. She noticed a grain of rice stuck to Yuichi's chin.

"No, you don't need to come. All I have to do is take him to the nurse station on the fifth floor, right?" Yuichi mixed some wasabi in a plate of soy sauce, the sweeter variety found in Kyushu.

"We have a meeting again at seven in the community center. They're talking about health foods. Don't worry, I'm not planning to buy any. But hearing about it doesn't cost anything," Fusae said, pouring hot water out of the thermos into a teapot. The thermos made a gurgling sound as she pushed the button a couple of times to get out the last drops of water.

She stood up to add more water to the teapot, and that's when it happened. Yuichi had been enjoying the sashimi and deep-fried fish paste, but he suddenly groaned and put a hand to his mouth.

"What's wrong?" Fusae hurried around behind him and pounded him sharply on the back. She was sure that something was stuck in his throat, but he stood up, pushed her aside, and with his hand to his mouth he rushed to the toilet. Fusae stood there, flabbergasted.

She heard him retching. Flustered, Fusae sniffed the sashimi and the fish paste but neither one smelled off.

After throwing up for a while, Yuichi finally emerged, his face deathly pale.

"What's wrong?" Fusae asked, gazing intently at him. Yuichi shoved past her, saying, "Nothing . . . Just got something stuck in my throat." It was clear to both of them that this wasn't the real problem.

"You sure? . . ." Fusae bent over and retrieved his chopsticks from the floor. Yuichi's legs were right in front of her. She noticed that he was trembling—even though he'd just taken a bath and shouldn't be cold.

Grumbling the entire time, Katsuji managed to get out of bed and get dressed, and Yuichi drove him to the hospital. It was only fifty meters to the parking lot where Yuichi had his car, and Katsuji should have been able to walk there, but he ordered Yuichi to bring the car around to the front door, which he did, reluctantly.

Yuichi tossed the bag into the backseat, raised the passenger seat up, and Katsuji, looking unhappy, struggled to sit down. Yuichi walked around to the driver's side and Fusae said, "If the head nurse isn't there, then Ms. Imamura will be in charge."

Yuichi's white car looked out of place in the dark alley alongside the row of old houses. Inside, the subdued glow of the car stereo and radio lights looked like out-of-season fireflies.

As soon as Fusae shut the passenger-side door the car roared off. For a brief moment the far-off sound of waves was drowned out by the engine.

After seeing them off, Fusae hustled back into the kitchen to straighten up after dinner. Once she was finished, she went around switching off the lights, then slipped on some sandals and headed to the community center.

The wind was cold, but the sea was calm. Moonlight bathed the boats anchored in the harbor, and an occasional burst of wind teased the electric lines overhead and made them hum.

When Fusae spotted Mrs. Okazaki on the wharf, with its sprinkling of streetlights, heading to the community center, she picked up her pace. In the moonlight of the tiny wharf, the older woman shuffling along looked eerie yet somehow comical.

"So, Grannie, you're headed there, too?" As Fusae caught up with her, Mrs. Okazaki, who was using a shopping cart as a walker, halted and looked up.

"Oh, Fusae, it's you."

"Did you try the Chinese herbal medicine from last time?" Fusae asked.

The old woman started walking again, slowly, and replied, "Yes, and I feel a bit better."

"Me, too. I had my doubts it would work at first, but the morning after I drank some, I did feel better."

Starting a month before, a pharmaceutical company, headquartered in Tokyo, apparently, had been holding health seminars at the community center. Fusae hadn't been interested, but the head of the local women's association had invited her, and after that she hadn't missed a session.

As she walked along the wharf, the cold sea wind made her joints ache. The distinctive fishing-harbor tidal smell mixed in with the cold wind and tickled her nose, which had started to lose all feeling. Fusae deliberately walked on the seaward side to block the cold wind from hitting the elderly Mrs. Okazaki.

"I was wondering if I could bother Yuichi to buy some more rice for me," Mrs. Okazaki said just as the community center came into view. "Whenever you go out shopping is fine."

"You should have asked me sooner. I just had him do some shopping." Fusae put her hand on the old woman's back and guided her into the center.

"The Daimaru store will deliver, but they charge four thousand yen for ten kilograms of rice, and on top of that a three-hundred-yen delivery fee."

"Don't ever shop at Daimaru. Four thousand yen for ten

kilograms? If you drive to the bargain store, you can get it at half price."

Mrs. Okazaki had stepped up onto a stone step and Fusae took her arm. The older woman grabbed tightly on to her wrist.

"I knew that, but I don't have anyone like you do, Fusae, with a car who can go shopping for me."

"We're friends, so don't hesitate to ask us. We'll be happy to. I'm always asking Yuichi to go shopping for us. It's no trouble for him to pick up a few things for you, too."

Directly ahead of the short flight of steps was the community center, which with its imposing gate resembled a shrine. Fluorescent lights lit up the interior, reflecting a shadow of someone looking down at them.

"But you do still have some rice left, right?" Fusae asked.

As she stepped up the last stone step Mrs. Okazaki said, in a forlorn voice, "I should be okay for another four or five days."

"I'll have Yuichi pick up some tomorrow."

Just as she spoke, a voice came from the community center. "Is that Mrs. Okazaki?" it called. It came from the shadow, who was, in fact, the instructor of the seminar, a plump medical doctor named Tsutsumishita. As he spoke, he hurried down to them.

"Did you try the herbal medicine from last time?" he asked.

Mrs. Okazaki strained to stand up straight and smiled happily.

Dr. Tsutsumishita guided them into the community center and they found many of their neighbors already there, seated on cushions spread out at random on the floor and chatting with each other.

Fusae went to get cushions for herself and Mrs. Okazaki, then sat down next to the head of the women's association, Mrs. Sanae, and eavesdropped as she chatted with Mrs. Okazaki about how well the herbal medicine had worked, how their legs weren't so cold when they went to bed.

Dr. Tsutsumishita brought over a paper cup with hot tea. "That's so kind of you," Fusae said gratefully. "I shouldn't be having a man wait on me." She took the cup from the tray.

"Grannie, I wasn't lying about that herbal medicine, now was I? Didn't you still feel hot even after you came out of the bath?" Dr. Tsutsumishita patted Mrs. Okazaki's shoulder and sat down beside her.

"It's true, I did feel warm. Though when I first got it I thought it had to be a joke." Mrs. Okazaki spoke in a loud voice, and around the hall other people laughed, agreeing with her.

"Well, I'm not about to come all this way on my short little legs just to pull a fast one on you." Still seated, Dr. Tsutsumishita wiggled his short legs, evoking a burst of laughter.

For the last month Dr. Tsutsumishita had been lecturing on how to maintain good health after age sixty. Fusae at first had gone unwillingly, but she gradually found this doctor—who used his own shortcomings as grist for his talks—an enjoyable speaker, and since the afternoon had been counting the minutes to this evening's seminar.

"Well, let's get started." Dr. Tsutsumishita stood up and addressed the group of old people scattered around the hall. One old man in the group had a red face, and must have been imbibing some *shochu* before he came.

"Today's topic is blood circulation." Dr. Tsutsumishita's voice carried well throughout the hall. As he stepped up to the podium, the audience smiled in anticipation, as if they were about to hear a performance of comic *rakugo*.

Right beside the podium was a colorful *Big Catch* flag that nowadays was used only during the dragon-boat races.

❄

At night the atmosphere in the hospital changed. There was a heaviness, a sadness in the air, a total absence of anything cheerful or happy.

That evening, Miho Kaneko sat down on a bench in the waiting room and started flipping through a magazine she'd brought from the hospital recreation area.

It was not yet eight p.m., but the light in the outpatient reception desk was off and the worn-out benches in the waiting area were illuminated only by the remaining fluorescent lights overhead. The waiting area was so small it was hard to believe that during the day over a hundred people crowded in, waiting their turn.

With everyone gone now the only things left in the waiting area were the benches and the color-coded arrows painted on the walls indicating the different wings of the hospital. The pink arrow for the ob-gyn wing, yellow for pediatrics, light blue for neurology. Under the fluorescent lights, the arrows looked colorful and out of place.

A patient would occasionally hurry down the hall to go outside to smoke. At nine the front door was locked and they couldn't go outside to the designated smoking area. So out they went for the final smoke of the day—patients pushing IV poles, some holding colostomy bags in one hand, some leaning on canes, others in wheelchairs. One man past middle age, and a young man, probably from the same ward, were discussing baseball as they made their way outside. A woman in a wheelchair was talking to her husband on a cell phone. Each of them, each with his own illness or injury, headed out into the cold for the final smoke of the day.

When she turned to look farther down the hall, Miho saw, as she had on other nights, an old woman with dyed red hair, seated in front of the large TV that was left on during the day. A baby carriage was in front of her. She was just sitting there, doing nothing, though occasionally she'd rouse herself to rock the baby carriage and speak gently to the baby boy inside. "Hmm? What is it?" she asked him. Inside the baby carriage was a boy with polio. He was a little too big for the frilly carriage, and his twisted hand stuck out of it.

The old woman came here every night at this time. She sat here, speaking to this boy who couldn't respond, stroking his painful, twisted body.

Miho figured the ward that housed the boy must be filled with young mothers. She didn't know the story, but she decided that the red-haired old woman must feel uncomfortable among them, so she brought the boy out here to the hall every night.

Miho sat there, turning the pages of the magazine and half listening to the voices of the patients going out for a smoke, and the voice of the old woman soothing the boy.

It was a glossy women's magazine, and she was slowly reading through each page of a report on the marriage of an actress and a Kabuki actor. She'd read about a third of the article when the nurse in charge of her case rushed out from the elevator and approached her. "Ah, Miss Kaneko," she said, and Miho nodded a greeting.

As she approached, the nurse noted her magazine and said, grimacing, "It's hard to read a magazine on the ward, isn't it."

"No, not really. It's just that spending the whole day on the ward gets a little depressing. . . ."

"Did Dr. Moroi talk to you this morning?"

"He did. He said that if the test results are good, I can be released on Thursday."

"That's wonderful. You look so much better than when you were first admitted."

Two weeks ago Miho had a fever that lasted three days. She'd just opened her own little diner and couldn't very well take time off, even though she knew she was pushing herself too hard. Soon afterward she'd suddenly collapsed, and fortunately a regular customer was at her place and called for an ambulance.

The diagnosis was overwork. She was also on the verge of getting pneumonia, the doctor told her. Her diner was small, but still she'd overdone it. She'd finally been able to open her own place, something she'd always wanted to do, and now had to close it just two months later. Miho couldn't believe her luck.

The nurse stood up and went over to the red-haired old woman.

"You're lucky, Mamoru, that your grandmother's always with you." The nurse's gentle voice as she spoke to the boy in the baby carriage echoed in the still waiting area. As if replying to her, the motor of the vending machine kicked in with a groan.

Miho closed her magazine and stood up to return to her ward. Just then the automatic front door slid open, the cold air rushing in, and she casually glanced over, expecting it to be some patients coming in after their final cigarette. Instead, it was a tall young man with dyed blond hair supporting an old man who was walking gingerly inside. The faded pink warm-up clothes the young man wore went well, oddly enough, with his blond hair. He was staring at his feet as he walked. He had his arm under the old man's armpit, supporting him, and it was clear the old man was leaning on him heavily.

As she casually watched the two of them, Miho went over and stood in front of the elevator. She pushed the Up button and the door opened right away. She was planning to wait for the two men coming in the entrance. She went inside the elevator and pushed the Open button and the two of them appeared again from the shadows of a pillar. And that's when she realized who it was.

Miho hurriedly lifted her finger from Open and stabbed the Close button. The door slid shut. Just before it did, the young man had started to look up and she'd seen his face. There was no doubt about it. The young man supporting the older man was Yuichi Shimizu. As the elevator started Miho instinctively edged backward, her back bumping against the wall.

Two years ago, when Miho had worked at a massage parlor, Yuichi had come there almost every night, always asking for her.

The parlor, which was in the busiest shopping district in Nagasaki City, had just opened. There was a game center on the first floor and a river just across the street. On the street along the river, girls who worked at the cabaret clubs stood outside, dressed up as sexy nurses and high school students, trying to induce men passing by to come in. It was that sort of neighborhood.

Yuichi never asked her to do anything weird, but in the end it was because of him that she quit working there, feeling as if she were fleeing. The only way she could explain it was to say that she was frightened by him. If pressed to explain how he frightened her, she could only say that it was how very ordinary Yuichi was, despite the kind of establishment he was patronizing.

When the elevator reached the fifth floor, Miho walked back to her ward, casting nervous glances behind her. All of the visitors had left and of the six beds, three lined up on each side of the room, only Miho's had its curtain open.

Miho headed to her bed and quickly pulled the curtain shut. From the bed next to her she heard the elderly Mrs. Yoshii, asleep already and snoring. Miho sat down on her bed and told herself, *There's nothing to be afraid of. Nothing to be afraid of.*

The first time Yuichi Shimizu had come to the massage parlor was, as she recalled, a Sunday. The parlor opened at nine a.m. on weekends, and at this time of day they could mostly expect married men who had slipped out of the house on some excuse. That morning Miho was running the parlor with just one other woman, an Osaka native who was already in her midthirties.

As always, after the client had chosen the girl he wanted from the photo list, the manager called Miho. She'd just gotten to work and hurriedly slipped into an orange negligee and headed for one of the rooms.

Five identical rooms were on one corridor, and when Miho opened the door to the tiny, two-mat room furthest back, she found a tall man standing there. Miho smiled and introduced herself, then guided the awkward young man to the bed, where she had him sit down.

Clients who came at this time of day usually started by sheepishly explaining why they were there. The most common explanation was that they had worked the whole night through and hadn't caught a wink of sleep. Miho didn't care one way or the other, but men who came this early in the morning were invariably apologetic.

Yuichi sat on the bed, looking nervously around the cramped room as if to confess that he'd never been in a place like this before. Following the training manual, Miho invited him to take a shower, but he said, in a forlorn vice, "But I've already taken a bath. . . ."

Yuichi didn't appear to be one of those clients who wanted a girl to touch him when he was dirty, and indeed he smelled as if he'd just stepped out of the shower.

"I'm sorry, but those are the rules," Miho told him.

The shower was in a tiny bathroom, so cramped that if two people were in it their bodies couldn't help but touch.

Miho asked him to take off his clothes, while she touched the water to make sure the shower was the right temperature. When she turned around, Yuichi was still wearing his underwear, his thighs pushed tightly together. He looked around the tiny room as if he didn't know where to rest his eyes.

"You're going to take a shower with your underwear on?"

Miho smiled at him, and after a second's hesitation, he quickly pulled his briefs off. His penis caught in the elastic and slapped against his belly.

Miho had had a lot of older clients recently. Although she knew that this wasn't the type of business where you could choose your customers, and that she would just have to get used to it, she was starting to get fed up with this life, with all these men who could only get it up after a tremendous effort on her part.

Miho took Yuichi's hand and had him stand under the lukewarm shower. The water slid down his shoulders to his chest, wetting his almost painfully erect penis.

"Are you off work today?" Miho asked as she scrubbed his back with a soapy sponge. He was tense and she was hoping this would help him relax.

"Or maybe you're still in college?" she asked, rinsing the bubbles from his back.

"No, I've got a job," Yuichi finally replied.

"You must be into sports. You're so muscular." Miho didn't really care, but had to keep the conversation going.

With barely a word, Yuichi just stood there, staring at her hand, looking terribly serious.

When Miho was about to touch his soapy penis, Yuichi quickly twisted away from her. His penis was pulsing, as if a single touch was all it would take for him to come.

"Don't be shy. That's the kind of place this is." As Miho smiled, half fed up, Yuichi suddenly grabbed the showerhead from her and rinsed the rest of his body himself.

She wiped him dry with a bath towel and sent him on ahead into the room. One of the rules was to make sure to wipe clean the entire bathroom after using it. After cleaning up the bathroom she returned to their room and found Yuichi, towel still wrapped around his waist, standing there, his clothes in his hands.

"Are you from Nagasaki?" Miho asked. She'd never asked a client anything private before, but the words just slipped out.

Yuichi hesitated a moment, then told her the name of a town outside the city that she'd never heard of.

"I only moved here a half a year ago, so I'm afraid I don't know much about the area." At her words, Yuichi's face clouded over slightly.

Miho guided Yuichi to the bed and had him lie down. She removed the bath towel and there was his penis, looking like a coyote off in the distance, head raised and about to howl.

Truth be told, she was sure he would be a one-time-only client. After they came out of the shower, it took only three minutes for him to finish up, and though Miho had suggested that there was enough time left to do it again, Yuichi hurriedly slipped on his clothes and left.

Even for a first visit to such a place, he didn't seem to enjoy himself much. He hadn't even waited for her to wipe him off, and appeared eager to get away. Still, two days later he was back again, asking for Miho without even glancing at the folder of other girls' photos. The manager called her, and when she entered the room she found him seated on the bed this time, as if used to the place. This was a weekday evening and the massage parlor was crowded.

"Oh, you came back!" She smiled pleasantly, and Yuichi gave a slight nod and held out a plastic bag to her.

"What is that?" Afraid that it might be some weird sex toy, Miho cautiously accepted the bag. As soon as she did she let out a shriek, for the bag was warm.

She was about to toss it aside when Yuichi muttered, "It's *butaman*, pork buns. The place where I bought them has the best ones."

"*Butaman?*" Miho made an effort not to throw it aside. "For me?" she asked, and Yuichi gave a slight nod.

On occasion she'd received presents from other clients, but when they were food it was the usual cookies and chocolates. Getting hot food was a first.

Miho looked a bit stunned, and Yuichi asked, "What, you don't like *butaman?*"

"No, I do," Miho replied.

Yuichi took the bag from her and opened it on his lap. For a second he seemed to be looking around for small plates to use, though it was highly unlikely a tiny room in a massage parlor would have any.

As soon as he ripped open the plastic bag the hot, meaty, yeasty odor filled the windowless room. Through the thin walls they heard a man's vulgar laugh.

After this he came back three days in a row.

According to the manager, when Miho was off duty Yuichi didn't choose another girl, but instead walked away, shoulders slumped in disappointment.

Miho had no idea what it was about her that kept Yuichi returning. The first time she'd just done the usual things to him and hadn't made him particularly satisfied. But then two days later, here he was back again, looking totally unconcerned, with a bag of hot *butaman* as a present.

In the cramped room the two of them ate the *butaman*. Their conversation never went anywhere. To Miho's questions, Yuichi gave only short, evasive answers, and never asked her anything himself.

"Are you on your way home from work?" she asked.

"Yeah."

"Your job's nearby?"

"We work in all kinds of places. Construction sites."

Before he came to see her Yuichi always stopped home and took a bath first.

"We have a shower, so you should just come straight here from work."

Yuichi didn't reply.

That day, after they'd finished the *butaman*, Miho took him to the shower. He wasn't as hesitant as before, though he still turned away when she tried to touch his soapy penis.

Yuichi invariably chose the most popular forty-minutes-for-¥5,800 menu. Subtracting the time they were in the shower, that left them a scant thirty minutes alone, but that was usually more than enough for the client to get what he came for.

Whenever there was any time left over, most clients, greedy to get their money's worth, wanted to do it a second time. But Yuichi came soon after they took a shower, and when she tried to touch him afterward, he rebuffed her. He was content for them to just rest their heads on their arms and gaze up at the ceiling.

He was an easy client. The more he visited her, the more relaxed she became with him, even nodding off occasionally as she lay there staring at the ceiling. And before long, Yuichi began to open up more about himself.

The next time he brought her cakes. He always brought something to eat and they would share the food in the cramped little room. She grew more used to him, and rather than insist on a shower, she started making cold tea or coffee for him at the start of each session.

It was probably the fifth, or maybe the sixth, time he paid her a visit that he brought a homemade box lunch for them. It was the afternoon of a holiday.

Ah, so he's brought something again, she thought, taking the paper bag from him, but when she opened it she found a two-tier lunch box with a picture of Snoopy on it.

"A box lunch?" Miho couldn't keep from asking in surprise, and Yuichi shyly lifted the lid.

The top tier contained fried omelets, sausages, chicken nuggets, and potato salad. The layer below was packed with rice, and different colored *furikake* flakes, each carefully separated from the other.

As she took the lunch box from him, for an instant the idea

flashed before her that Yuichi had a girlfriend, that this girlfriend had made him the lunch but he was giving it to her. But when she asked, "Why did you bring me this?" Yuichi, shyly looking down, muttered, "I'm afraid it might not be so good. . . ."

"You mean *you* made it?" Miho couldn't help asking in surprise as Yuichi pulled apart a pair of disposable chopsticks and passed them over.

"The chicken nuggets are leftover ones my grandmother made last night. . . ."

Miho looked at Yuichi, astonished. Yuichi sat there, like a child awaiting the results of a test, waiting for Miho to taste it.

Miho had already heard that he lived with his grandparents. She never wanted to know about her clients' background, so she hadn't asked any more.

"No kidding? You really made this yourself?"

Miho picked up a piece of the fluffy omelets with her chopsticks. They tasted slightly sweet.

"I like omelets with a bit of sugar in them," Yuichi explained, and Miho replied, "I like sweet omelets, too."

"The potato salad's really good."

It wasn't as if they were on some spring picnic in a park. They were in a tiny, windowless room in a massage parlor, a stack of tissue boxes to one side.

After this day Yuichi always brought homemade box lunches with him when he came to see her.

When he asked her about her shift, she'd tell him her schedule, and say things like "I'm usually hungriest around nine." Before she knew it she was looking forward to his box lunches.

"Nobody really taught me how to cook, but I picked it up. I kind of like to watch my grandma prepare fish, though I hate all the cleaning up afterward. . . ."

Yuichi said all this as he watched Miho, in her gaudy negligee, eating the box lunch.

His lunches really were tasty, and Miho started to put in requests. "Can you include the *hikiji* like last time?" she'd ask.

After they finished eating Yuichi liked to lie beside her, hands behind his head.

As she reviewed the lunch they'd just eaten, Miho would play with his penis. She was paid for her services, of course, but she also felt she needed to thank him for the tasty food.

"You never ask to see me outside of here, do you?" she asked once, just after the alarm went off signaling that they had five minutes left. Miho's hand was inside his underpants, and Yuichi was busily kneading her breasts.

"Most regular customers always invite us out. It's like, Hey, let's go on a date next time."

Yuichi didn't reply, so Miho asked him again. At that instant, Yuichi's fingers suddenly stopped moving over her breasts.

"What do you mean, invite you? You mean like we meet outside of here!?"

Yuichi was seething. To Miho it felt as though his fingers were speaking, for they squeezed her breasts hard, not so hard they hurt, but hard enough.

She twisted away. "I'm not going to date you. No way," she announced, and got out of bed. Yuichi roughly grabbed her arm.

"Just seeing you here is enough for me," Yuichi said. "We can be by ourselves here. Just the two of us, with nobody bothering us."

"Well, for forty minutes, at least," Miho said, laughing.

"Then next time I'll do the hour menu," Yuichi said, looking serious.

At first she thought he was joking, but he didn't smile.

It was time for lights out on the ward, and the nurse came by to switch off the overhead light. Miho lay in bed, staring at the ceiling and thinking about Yuichi, but as soon as the lights were off, she slipped out of bed.

In the bed nearest the entrance there was still a small light on; it seemed as if that was the only place where time still flowed. Through the curtain she could see the shadow of somebody reading. Behind the curtain was a girl attending a local junior college, who'd had liver problems since she was young. She had darkish skin but a cute face. It was clear she'd been raised in a loving family.

Miho went out of the ward, trying not to make a sound in her slippers, and headed toward the bank of elevators. In the hallway was a line of orange vinyl tape indicating the toilets and bathroom.

She got into one of the oversize elevators, big enough to accommodate gurneys. As she descended she was hit by the sensation that the whole building was ascending and she alone was standing still.

On the first floor the old lady was still soothing the little boy, but the place was otherwise quiet, the only sound the hum of the vending machine.

Even if she saw Yuichi, it wasn't as if there was anything she wanted to talk with him about. She'd been the one who trampled on his feelings, and she couldn't very well face him now. Maybe two weeks in the hospital with hardly anyone coming to see her had weakened her will.

Still, she wanted to say something to him, especially after seeing him helping an old man into the hospital. If he could only tell her he was all right, that he was going out with an ordinary girl now. She'd been cruel when she broke up with him, and if he told her that, she felt that she could be forgiven for the way she'd acted.

Even though she worked for a massage parlor, Yuichi had rented an apartment on his own and had wanted them to live together.

As Miho watched her soothing the boy in the baby carriage, the old woman suddenly turned and said, "It's nice and quiet here so I can relax." She'd seen the old woman a number of times, but this was the first time she'd spoken to her.

Still wondering if she was going to see Yuichi again, Miho stiffened and approached the old woman, as if drawn to her. It was the first time she'd looked at the little boy up close. She'd imagined how twisted his body was, but the reality was far worse, and his weak, unfocused eyes wandered.

"Hey there, Mamoru." Miho rubbed the boy's frail arm.

The old woman gave her a suspicious look, apparently wondering how she knew the boy's name.

"The nurse called him that," Miho explained quickly, and the old woman, looking satisfied, said, "Mamoru's a popular little boy, now, aren't you? Everybody knows you." She stroked the boy's sweaty forehead as she spoke.

"If you rub him like this it takes away some of the pain," the old woman said, stroking the limp little boy's shoulder. The vending machine started humming a bit more loudly.

Lots of things to say sprang to Miho's mind, but for some reason she couldn't say them. She sat down next to the old woman and, following her lead, rubbed the arms and legs sticking out of the baby carriage.

Just then the elevator door slid open and Yuichi came out. The old man wasn't with him now, and he had a sullen look on his face, hands stuck in his jeans pockets. Yuichi glanced in Miho's direction but apparently didn't notice her. He looked away and strode off.

"Yuichi!" Miho called out to him, as his retreating figure headed toward the entrance that was soon to be locked up for the night. Yuichi halted, startled for a second, and turned around guardedly. Miho stood up from the bench and looked directly at him.

The little boy's leg, which she'd just been rubbing, brushed against her thigh. It moved, as if he was asking her to rub him some more.

The moment Yuichi's eyes met hers the strength drained out of him. Without thinking, though she was still standing far away, Miho reached out her hand to him.

She hurriedly went over to him. She could see his face grow paler with each step.

"Are you—okay?" she asked, taking his arm. She'd just been holding the little boy's arm, and for an instant the feeling gave her goose bumps. "I saw you a little while ago bringing in an old man and so I waited here for you."

For a second the thought struck Miho that he wasn't bringing the old man to the hospital, but that it was Yuichi himself who was sick.

"Anyway, why don't we just sit down for a while?"

Miho tugged at his arm but he shrugged loose as if trying to get away.

"It's not like I'm trying to apologize or anything," she said. "It's been two years, after all. . . . It's just that I haven't seen you in so long, and it brings back lots of memories."

She'd gotten closer than she'd realized and took a step back. The color slowly returned to Yuichi's pale face.

"Excuse me, I didn't mean to keep you," Miho apologized.

She wanted him to tell her that he was okay now. That's all she wanted to hear, why she'd called out to him. But the instant Yuichi had spotted her, he'd blanched.

She could only conclude that Yuichi still hadn't forgiven her. She'd called out to him, thinking that the passage of time had softened things, only to be struck by the realization that that was the self-centered thinking of someone who'd betrayed another person.

"I, uh . . . have to get going," Yuichi managed to say, glancing at the entrance.

"Oh, I'm so sorry, I shouldn't have . . ." Miho apologized.

It was obvious he had no feelings for her anymore, but still Miho found his attitude cold.

Yuichi hurriedly exited the hospital. His figure as he headed toward the parking lot was lit up in the moonlight. The parking lot was nearby, Miho knew, but to her it looked as if he were heading somewhere far, far away. As if he were making his way toward another night altogether, one that lay beyond the present.

Yuichi disappeared into the lot. As if they hadn't just seen each other for the first time in two years, he didn't turn around, not once.

Three days had passed since the murder at Mitsuse Pass and all the TV talk shows were filled with reports on the incident. No matter what channel you turned to, there was the cold winter pass, the usual reporters standing in front of it as they professed their hatred for the murderer and his crime.

The talk show reports all basically boiled down to the same story line: A twenty-one-year-old woman working for an insurance company in Fukuoka City was murdered and her body was dumped at Mitsuse Pass. At approximately ten-thirty that night the woman said goodbye to her colleagues near the apartment building their company leased and went to see her boyfriend at a place a three-minute walk away. The boyfriend had not been heard from since. The police were looking for him as a material witness, but according to his friends, he'd been missing the past three or four days.

Along with the summary of the murder details scrolling along the screen, the TV showed scenes of the freezing pass to dramatize the cruelty of the deed. In contrast, when they discussed the missing boyfriend, relating how he was the *most popular student on campus*, how he drove an expensive foreign car and lived alone in a condo in a *high-end section of Fukuoka*, the screen was filled with lively scenes from the upscale Tenjin and Nakasu neighborhoods. To viewers it was obvious from the newscasters' tones that it was 99 percent certain that this boyfriend was the criminal.

Kanji Hayashi, an instructor at a local *juku*, a prep school, was one of these viewers. As he stared fixedly at the TV screen in his apartment, he didn't seem to notice that the piece of toast with marmalade in his hand was growing cold. It was three p.m., about time he had to get going or else he'd be late to class, but he remained glued to his chair.

Hayashi had first learned of the murder two days before, after he got up in the afternoon and had switched on the TV, just as now. At first he'd just thought, *Hmm . . . over at Mitsuse Pass, huh?* but when the photo of the victim came on the screen he'd nearly choked on his orange juice.

To him she wasn't Yoshino Ishibashi, but Mia, a girl he'd met three months ago online.

Hayashi hurriedly checked his call records, and though it was unlikely he'd saved any since it was a while ago, he did find one e-mail from her:

Thank you very much for everything the other day. It was lots of fun. But as I was telling you, I'm being transferred next month to Tokyo and it doesn't look like I'll be able to see you anymore. I'm really sorry about the bad timing. Thank you so much. Bye bye. Mia.

So the only message from her left on his phone was this last one, basically telling him not to get in touch anymore. All the enormous numbers of messages they'd exchanged before that had vanished, but not the memory of the day he'd met Yoshino Ishibashi/Mia. That was still crystal clear in his mind.

They'd arranged to meet in the lobby of a hotel next to the Fukuoka Dome. A long bench encircled the spacious lobby, and it was nearly filled with families staying at the hotel.

Mia showed up ten minutes late. She didn't quite live up to the photo she'd e-mailed him, but to a forty-two-year-old bachelor like Hayashi, this young girl was still as cute as a ladybug. There was nothing hesitant about her. She pulled out a taxi receipt for the ride over to the hotel and asked him to reimburse her. He'd told her to take a taxi when she'd said that the hotel was far away for her, but still, when she pulled out the receipt and demanded payment before she'd even said hello, it struck Hayashi that their meeting was definitely a business transaction.

"I don't have a lot of time," Mia told him. Hayashi decided to skip going to a coffee shop first, as he'd been planning to do, and they drove directly to a love hotel.

This wasn't the first time Hayashi had done this. He handed over the thirty thousand yen he'd promised and they wasted no time going up to their cramped little guest room.

It was obvious that this wasn't the first time for Mia, either. As soon as she got the cash, she stripped off her clothes and, just in her underwear, asked, "Okay with you if I order some drinks?" and called the front desk. Her ribs showed just below her full breasts, but her belly had a slight roll of fat.

Hayashi had never been with a prostitute, but watching her seated on the bed phoning the front desk, to him that's what she looked like. She seemed to enjoy their time in bed. Her skin and vagina got so wet he couldn't see it as just an act done for money.

An amateur pretending to be a prostitute, or an amateur prostitute— Hayashi couldn't decide which was more erotic. Maybe it didn't matter, they were women all the same, but Hayashi couldn't help thinking that there was something very different about the two.

The talk-show report on the murder at Mitsuse Pass finished, and Hayashi finally put down his piece of toast, a neat half-moon of tooth marks from the single bite he'd taken carved out of it.

Over the past couple of days he'd mulled over this notion that a girl he'd met just once had been killed by someone, and though he could understand it on a conceptual level, emotionally he couldn't absorb the reality.

If he were to compare it to anything, it was maybe like the mixed feelings he'd had when he saw a girl from his junior high school days appear on local TV as a newscaster, the mixture of ridicule and envy he'd felt when he couldn't believe she was actually on TV reporting the news. Mia was no newscaster, however. The only reason she was on TV was because somebody had strangled her and dumped her body out in the cold.

The criminal must be somebody just like me, Hayashi thought. *She met another guy like me online, the only difference being that this other guy turned out to be a murderer.*

Hayashi didn't know if he was trying to justify, or ridicule, himself. *Of course I didn't kill her,* he thought, *but the murdered girl is some-one I knew, and was killed by someone very much like me.* The mur-derer must have viewed her as an amateur playing at being a prostitute. If he'd seen her as an amateur prostitute he might never have felt like killing her.

He was going to be late for class, so he switched off the TV and adjusted his tie before heading out. That's when a knock came at the front door. Thinking it must be a poorly timed delivery, Hayashi gruffly yanked open the door. Two men in suits stood there, like a wall blocking his way.

"Kanji Hayashi?"

At first he couldn't figure out which one had spoken. Both men were around thirty, with identical crew cuts.

"Uh . . . yeah. Yes."

He knew immediately that it was about the murder. He'd known this day would come. Once they examined her cell phone, his number would surely come out.

"We have a few things we'd like to ask you. . . ."

The two detectives spoke almost simultaneously. "I understand," Hayashi said, nodding quietly, and hurriedly added, "No, that isn't what I mean. You're here about the murder at Mitsuse Pass, right?"

The two glanced at each other, then shot him a sharp look.

"I know her, but I don't have anything to do with what happened."

Hayashi let them come in and shut the door. The cramped entrance was littered with shoes and the three hulking men stood there awkwardly, trying not to step on them.

"I knew you'd be coming. You found out about me on her cell phone, right? About her and me having a, what should I say? A friendship."

Hayashi spoke without any hesitation. Ever since he heard about the murder he'd been thinking about what he should say. The two crew-cut detectives listened silently, exchanging an occasional glance. Their faces were expressionless and it was hard to tell whether they believed him.

"I met her online about three months ago," Hayashi went on. "We went out on one date, but that was it."

"A date?" the detective with the polka-dot tie asked, smiling wryly.

"There's nothing illegal about it. She was an adult and it was consensual. . . . And the money was . . . something I earned on the stock market and I just gave it to her so she could have some spending money, that's all. . . ."

Spittle flew out as Hayashi spoke. One of the detectives stepped way back, crushing a discarded sneaker. "Take it easy," he said, trying to calm him down while looking around for a better spot to stand.

As he looked up at the two tall detectives, Hayashi began to suspect that he wasn't the first man they'd questioned who knew her.

"Let's not get into the question of this spending money right now. But I do want to make one thing clear: we don't know the contents of e-mails and conversations from cell-phone numbers we've retrieved."

The polka-dot-tie detective finally pulled out his notebook, flicking it open in front of Hayashi. "Where were you this past Sunday? At about ten p.m.?" The detective, for some reason, rubbed his eyebrows as he asked this.

Here we go, Hayashi thought, and let out a deep breath.

"I was at work then. I teach at a *juku*, and finished my last class at ten-thirty. For an hour after that I worked with some colleagues writing a supplementary curriculum for the winter break. Then I went out to a bar and left there at three-thirty. On the way home I stopped by a video-rental place. I still have the video here."

They finished in under ten minutes. The detectives smiled and left, and without realizing it, Hayashi sank to the floor where he stood.

He'd been bold enough when he told them about his alibi for Sunday, but when the detective told him because of the nature of the crime they'd have to investigate his workplace, Hayashi pleaded with them not to. "Look, I've worked there twenty years," he said. "It will put me in a real spot if you do that. Can't you look into it in secret? Like, ask the owner of the bar, or use some other excuse to question my colleagues?" He nearly broke down in tears.

The detectives gave a noncommittal reply and left. It didn't look as though they really suspected him, but neither did they seem to care about how this might affect his future.

Everything he'd told the detectives was the truth. But he'd never realized how hard it was to tell the truth. *Telling a lie would have been so much easier on me,* Hayashi thought. But he was late for work. He'd just focus on doing his job, and if any of this happened to leak out, he'd apologize and promise never to do it again. And there was one other thing he could most definitely swear to. That he never, *ever*, had any sexual interest in the elementary school girls who studied at his *juku*.

He found he could talk again, though he was still frozen, slumped to the floor.

The detectives hadn't given him an exact number, but had indicated that they'd questioned other men who'd had a relationship with the girl. These men had signed on to an online site for fun and had got to know her, and now they were at their wits' end. It was the same with him—he couldn't believe any of them had hooked up with her in order to kill her. But the fact remained: she'd been murdered.

A hooker having an evil customer and getting killed sounded like a stereotypical story line. But the girl in this case wasn't a hooker. This was a young girl who hid her secret life, who worked hard every day as a salesperson for an insurance company. A girl who wasn't a prostitute, but liked to pretend she was.

When they were in the love hotel Hayashi had complimented her. "Your body is so supple," he'd said. Dressed only in her underwear, Yoshino had bent forward proudly to show him.

"I was in the rhythmic gymnastics club. I used to be much more flexible than this."

Her spine showed through her white skin as she turned and smiled at him. He could never have imagined that just three months later that smiling face would be lying beside a road, dead.

On the morning of the same day, outside Nagasaki City and about a hundred kilometers from Fukuoka, Yuichi's grandmother Fusae had bought some produce from the truck that came to peddle vegetables once a week, and was stuffing it into her refrigerator, all the while rubbing her throbbing knee. She'd bought some eggplants, thinking she'd pickle them, but then regretted it, remembering that Yuichi wasn't fond of the dish.

She thought a thousand yen would be enough, but the total had come to ¥1,630. The peddler had knocked off thirty yen, but Fusae had been left with so little in her purse that she knew she couldn't wait until next week, as she'd been planning, to withdraw some cash from her postal account.

She planned to take the bus that day to visit her husband in the hospital. If she went to see him, he was sure to say something mean to her, but if she didn't go he'd complain about that, so she knew she had to. The insurance covered all the costs of the hospital, but she had to pay for the daily bus fare herself. From the nearby bus stop to the stop in front of Nagasaki station cost ¥310. Then she'd transfer to another bus that would let her out in front of the hospital and that would cost another ¥180. A round trip every day set her back ¥980.

For Fusae, who was trying to keep their expenses for vegetables every week to ¥1,000, spending ¥980 every day on bus fare made her feel terribly guilty, as guilty as if she had been staying in a hot-springs inn, being waited on hand and foot.

After she'd put the vegetables away in the fridge, she took a pick-led plum out of a plastic container and popped it in her mouth.

"Fusae-san, are in you in?" a man's voice at the front door said, a voice she recognized.

Chewing on the pickled plum, she went out to the entrance, where she found the local patrolman and another man she didn't know.

"Oh, having a late breakfast, are we?" the plump policeman asked with a friendly smile.

As Fusae removed the plum pit from her mouth, the policeman went on, "I just heard that Katsuji is back in the hospital?"

Fusae hid the pit in her hand and glanced at the man in the suit. His suntanned skin looked leathery and she noticed that the hands dangling at his sides had very short fingers.

"This is Mr. Hayata from the prefectural police. He has a few questions for Yuichi."

"For Yuichi?" As she said this, her mouth suddenly filled with a sour burst of flavor from the pickled plum.

Whenever she stopped by the police box to chat and have a cup of tea, the pistol at the patrolman's hip never bothered her, but now she couldn't take her eyes off it.

"Did Yuichi go out this past Sunday night?"

They were in the entrance to the house. The patrolman, seated on the step up to the house, had to twist around to ask her this. The detective, standing beside him, put his hand on his shoulder. "I'll ask the questions," he said with a stern look.

As if nestling closer to the patrolman, Fusae sat down formally next to him.

"It seems that the girl killed at Mitsuse Pass was a friend of Yuichi's," the patrolman said, ignoring the warning.

"What! Yuichi's friend was killed?"

Still seated formally, legs tucked under her, Fusae leaned back. Pain shot through her knees and she groaned.

The patrolman hurriedly took her arm and helped her to her feet. "Having trouble standing again?" he said.

"If it's one of Yuichi's friends, you must mean someone from his junior high school?" Fusae asked.

Yuichi had attended an all-male technical high school, so it must be someone from his junior high, she thought. Which would mean that a girl from this neighborhood had been murdered.

"No, not from his junior high. A friend he made recently."

"Recently?" she asked. She'd always been worried that there *weren't* any girls in her grandson's life. When it came to friends, not only did she know of zero girls, but she also knew that he had, at most, only one or two close male friends.

The detective seemed upset with the talkative patrolman, and said, frowning, "I told you I'd ask the questions here. . . . I'd like to ask you about last Sunday, whether . . ."

Before the detective's overbearing voice had even finished, Fusae replied. "On Sunday I'm pretty sure he was at home."

"Ah, so he was at home," the patrolman interrupted, obviously relieved. "Just before we came here," he went on, "we stopped by old Mrs. Okazaki's. When Yuichi goes out he always takes his car. She lives right next to the parking lot and she told me she can hear whenever a car goes in or out. But according to her, on Sunday Yuichi's car never left the lot."

Neither Fusae nor the detective said anything as the patrolman rattled on. But Fusae noticed a slight softening in the detective's harsh eyes.

"I told you to be quiet, but you never listen, do you," the detective said, warning the talkative patrolman again. This time, though, there was a hint of warmth in his voice.

"My husband and I go to bed early," Fusae said, "so I'm not sure, but I think Yuichi was in his room Sunday evening."

The patrolman turned to the detective. "With what Mrs. Okazaki told us, and what his grandmother here says, I think it's certain he was."

"Yes, but actually I . . ." the detective began where the patrolman left off, finally taking control of the conversation. Fusae suddenly noticed the pickled-plum pit in her hand.

"On the call list of the cell phone of the woman found at Mitsuse Pass, we found your grandson's number."

"Yuichi's?"

"Not just his. She apparently knew a lot of people."

"Is she from around here?"

"No, from Hakata."

"Hakata? Yuichi has friends from Hakata? I had no idea."

The detective figured if he explained things one by one he'd have to deal with endless questions, so he quickly outlined what they knew about the murder. Since it now seemed certain that Yuichi had been home all that night, his explanation came off sounding more like an apology for the sudden intrusion.

The dead girl was a twenty-one-year-old named Yoshino Ishibashi, a salesperson for an insurance company in Hakata. She apparently had a wide circle of friends—people from her hometown, colleagues, and other casual friends—for, according to her phone records, in the week before the incident she'd been in contact with nearly fifty different people. And Yuichi was one of them.

"The last time your grandson e-mailed her was four days before the murder, and the last message she sent to him was the day after that. She got in touch with nearly ten other people as well after that."

As the detective went on, Fusae pictured the girl who'd been killed. If she had so many friends, Yuichi couldn't have anything to do with it. It was a horrible crime, of course, but there was no way she could believe that Yuichi was connected to it.

Once the detective finished his summary, Fusae suddenly recalled what Norio had told her, how the day after the murder Yuichi had had a hangover and vomited on the way to work. These had to be related, Fusae concluded. Yuichi must have heard about the girl's death on TV or somewhere and felt sad about losing a friend, and that's why he got sick. The instinct she'd developed over twenty years of raising him told her that this had to be true.

The detective seemed in a hurry, and after he finished he added, gently, "Anyway, I don't think you need to worry."

Fusae wasn't worried, but her face was still grim. "You think so?" she asked.

"What time does Yuichi come home from work?" the detective asked.

"Usually around six-thirty," she replied.

"Well, if I have any more questions, I'll get in touch. Thanks for your time."

Fusae stood up to see him out. "Thank you," she said, and bowed. The detective's words about getting in touch again seemed more like a formality.

After they'd seen the detective out, the patrolman sat back down in the entrance and said, a comical look on his face, "Boy, I bet you were surprised by all this, huh? When I heard they wanted to see Yuichi as a material witness, I was shocked. But Mrs. Okazaki just happened to be in the police box when the call came in, and she said that Yuichi's car never left the parking lot on Sunday. I was so relieved. Just between you and me, it looks like they already know who the criminal was. They just have to check out everybody else."

"So they know who did it?" Fusae gave an exaggerated look of relief. "I just couldn't picture him having a girlfriend in Hakata," she added.

"Well, he's a young guy, so what're you going to do? Seems like that girl had lots of boyfriends she made on dating sites."

"Dating sites? What're those?"

"Well . . . it's kind of like being pen pals."

"I had no idea Yuichi was exchanging letters with a girl in Hakata."

Fusae remembered the pickled-plum pit in her hand again, and tossed it outside.

The Wonderland pachinko parlor was set down in an unexpected spot on the highway. Just as the highway along the sea curved sharply to the left, there first was a huge, garish sign and then the place itself, a cheap imitation of Buckingham Palace. The gate into the mammoth parking lot that surrounded the parlor was supposed to look like the Arc de Triomphe, while next to the building entrance sat a miniature Statue of Liberty.

It was a gaudy eyesore of a building by any standard. Compared to the pachinko places in the city, however, the machines paid off better, so the parking lot was packed with cars, like bees swarming over sugar, not just on the weekends but during the week.

On the second floor by the slot machines, Hifumi Shibata shoved in the last dozen or so coins he had. The slot machine he'd had his eye on was occupied, so he had to choose another and decided he'd just play it until the coins he had in his pocket were gone.

Thirty minutes before, Hifumi had e-mailed Yuichi.

I'm at Wonder. Can you stop by on the way back from work? To which he soon received a short reply: *Sounds good.*

Hifumi and Yuichi had been friends since they were children.

Hifumi and his parents once lived in the same school district as Yuichi, but half a year before he graduated from junior high, Hifumi's parents sold their small house and their land to rent a condo in the city. Naturally Hifumi's parents hadn't expected to sell their land for very much — it was near the little harbor whose seacoast had all been filled in — and on top of that his father had gambling debts that took up most of what they earned. So when they moved to the tiny apartment in the city it almost felt as if they were skipping out in shame over their past.

After they moved, Yuichi was the only friend who contacted him and they'd kept in touch ever since.

When they were together, Yuichi never lightened up. He wasn't much fun to be with, but still, for whatever reason, Hifumi kept on seeing him.

Some three years before, Hifumi had taken his then girlfriend for a drive to Hirado, and on their way back his engine died. He didn't have the money to pay for a tow truck, so he called a couple of his friends, but they all turned him down, either too busy or simply unwilling to come to his aid. The only one ready to drive out to give him a tow was Yuichi.

"Sorry about this," Hifumi had apologized.

As Yuichi, a blank look on his face, attached the tow cable, he replied, "I was just lying around at home anyway."

Hifumi didn't want his girlfriend to be in the towed car so he had her ride with Yuichi in his car instead.

They towed the car to a garage that Hifumi often used, and then Yuichi left with barely a word. As the girlfriend waved goodbye, Hifumi asked her a leading question: "Nice-looking guy, huh?" But she replied, laughing, "He didn't talk at all in the car. When I thanked him he just nodded and curtly said, 'Um.' I felt like I couldn't breathe." That, indeed, was the kind of guy he was.

The slot machine finally began to pay off. Hifumi looked around the pachinko place for one of the miniskirted young attendants who brought complimentary cups of coffee.

As he turned toward the entrance, he saw Yuichi climbing the spiral staircase. Hifumi raised a hand and Yuichi spotted him and made his way over, down the narrow aisle.

Yuichi was on his way home from the construction site and his navy blue trousers were dirty. His jacket was the same navy blue color, but from the open zipper you could see a swath of the pink sweatshirt underneath.

Yuichi sat down next to Hifumi and popped open a can of coffee he'd no doubt purchased on the first floor. Yuichi pulled a thousand-yen note from his pocket and without a word started to play the slot machine in front of him.

As Yuichi had come close, Hifumi could smell him. It wasn't the sweaty smell he had in summer, but more the dusty cement smell of a deserted house.

"Did you hear about the murder at Mitsuse Pass?" Yuichi suddenly asked, after quickly running through the thousand yen.

"I heard that a girl got killed there," Hifumi said, still facing his machine. His luck had turned as soon as Yuichi sat down next to him.

Yuichi had brought up the topic but sat there silently, as usual.

"They said she was involved with a bunch of guys she'd met on a dating site. I saw that on TV today." Hifumi kept the conversation going as he went on pushing the slot-machine button.

"Think they'll find him soon?" Yuichi asked.

"Find who?"

No response.

"You mean the criminal?"

No response again.

"Yeah, they'll find him pretty soon. All they have to do is check the phone records." Hifumi didn't glance at Yuichi at all as he spoke.

After thirty minutes with the slots, the two of them exited the pachinko parlor. Hifumi wound up losing fifteen thousand yen, Yuichi two thousand. The sun had already set but the parking lot was brightly lit. Their dark shadows bisected the white parking lines as they walked.

Hifumi, unlike Yuichi, had absolutely no interest in cars and drove a cheap economy car. He unlocked it, and Yuichi quickly sat down beside him. Hifumi glanced up at the sky. The waves nearby sounded as if they were coming down from above. The sky was usually filled with stars, but tonight he could see only Venus. *Maybe it'll rain tomorrow*, Hifumi thought.

As they drove along the coast toward Yuichi's home, Hifumi complained about the trouble he was having finding work. He'd spent the morning at an employment agency, and as he checked through the classified ads, had invited one of the young girls working there out for a drink. He struck out on both counts—no job and no date. But after spending the morning there, he was optimistic about finding a job. "There are a lot of jobs out there if you're looking for one," he concluded.

After the music ended on the radio, a short news broadcast came on. The lead story was the murder at Mitsuse Pass.

Hifumi turned to Yuichi, who hadn't said a word since he'd climbed aboard. "Speaking of Mitsuse Pass . . ." Hifumi began. Yuichi had been gazing out the window but he leaned back and turned toward Hifumi in the cramped car.

"You remember how I saw a ghost there?" Hifumi went on, turning into a sharp curve. The sudden curve threw Yuichi against the door.

"Remember? I went for a job interview in Hakata, and took the road over the pass on the way home? And my headlights suddenly went out. I was scared, and pulled over and started the engine again, and suddenly there was this guy sitting next to me, covered in blood. You remember when I told you that?"

As he pulled up close to a Honda Cub motorcycle lazily tooling down the middle of the road, Hifumi shot a glance at Yuichi.

"I was terrified. The engine wouldn't start, and this bloody man was sitting in the passenger seat. I must have screamed as I was turning the key."

Hifumi laughed at this memory, but Yuichi just said, "Hurry up and pass him," motioning to the motorcycle with his chin.

On the night in question it was just after eight p.m. when Hifumi had driven over the pass. After finishing the interview at the company—he couldn't recall now which one it was—he was disappointed, knowing he wouldn't get the job, so to make up for it he went to a massage parlor in Tenjin. Choosing a good massage parlor probably meant more to him at the time than the job interview. After being satisfied at the massage parlor, he went out for some ramen and then headed back home, over the pass.

It was still early, but he saw no other cars headed in the opposite direction, let alone ones headed in the same direction. The woods lit up in his headlights looked eerie, and he began to regret having taken this back road instead of the main highway to save on tolls.

To drown out this lonely feeling he started singing loudly, but his voice only seemed to be sucked out into the forest surrounding him. His headlights—his only lifeline in this pitch-black mountain pass— started to act strangely just as he was reaching the highest point of the road. At first Hifumi had thought something was wrong with his eyes.

The next instant something black flashed in front of his flickering lights. Hifumi slammed on the brakes, clutching the steering wheel to keep it straight. Now his headlights went out completely. Straight ahead was a darkness so deep it was as if his eyes were closed, and though the engine was still running, the incessant chirping of insects from the woods was so loud he wanted to clap his hands over his ears to drown it out. The AC was freezing cold, but he was starting to sweat. He felt as if lukewarm water had been poured all over him.

Just then the whole car vibrated and the engine cut out. And he sensed something—or someone—in the passenger seat beside him. Fear gives us tunnel vision. He couldn't look to the side, or turn to see what was there. All he could manage was to stare straight ahead.

The engine wouldn't start. Hifumi let out a scream. He knew something was sitting beside him. But what it was, he had no idea.

. . . *It hurts so much.* . . .

A man's voice said it from beside him. Hifumi tried to drown it out with another scream. The engine still wouldn't start.

... This is it. ... I can't stand it anymore. ...

Again the man's voice. Hifumi put his hand on the door, ready to flee.

At that very instant a man's bloody face was reflected in the windshield. The man was gazing steadily in his direction.

❧

Fusae heard something at the front door. She glanced at the clock, then hurriedly stuffed the manila envelope she'd been vaguely looking at into her apron pocket. On the envelope was written *Receipt enclosed*. Still seated, Fusae reached toward the gas range and reheated the small *arakabu* fish cooked in soy sauce.

"Evening!"

Fusae heard Hifumi's cheerful voice and stood up. "Oh, Hifumi's with you?" she said, and went out to the hallway.

Hifumi quickly removed his shoes and went in, almost elbowing Yuichi out of the way. "Hi, Grandma. Something smells really good," he said, peering into the kitchen.

"You haven't eaten yet? It'll be ready in a minute, so would you like to eat with Yuichi?"

"I'd love to!" Hifumi happily replied, nodding several times.

"Did you play pachinko?" Fusae placed the lid on the pan.

"No, the slots. But we had no luck. Lost again."

"How much?"

Hifumi held up his fingers to indicate fifteen thousand yen.

Fusae felt relieved that Yuichi had come home with Hifumi. She knew he had absolutely nothing to do with the murder at Mitsuse Pass, but still the detective's visit—his questions about Yuichi's whereabouts on Sunday and the lie she'd told him—left her with an unpleasant aftertaste.

Yuichi had most definitely gone out that evening in his car. But since Mrs. Okazaki had insisted that he hadn't, even if he had, it couldn't have been for very long. The same thing had happened before, when Yuichi had taken Katsuji to the hospital. Even when he went out for a couple of hours, Mrs. Okazaki would always insist his car had never left the lot.

"Hifumi, were you with Yuichi on Sunday?" Fusae asked after making sure that Yuichi had gone upstairs.

As she checked the fish in the pan, Hifumi said, tilting his head, "Sunday? No, I wasn't. . . . Uh—I think he must have gone to the repair place. He was talking about getting a part for his car." As he spoke, he reached out to snare a piece of fish from the pan.

"Hey, I told you it would be ready soon," Fusae said, lightly slapping his hand away. Hifumi obediently pulled back.

"Do you have any sashimi?" he asked, opening the refrigerator.

Fusae prepared a plate of food for Hifumi first, then took the clean laundry she'd folded in the evening upstairs to Yuichi's room. She opened the door and found him sprawled out on his bed. "I'll be down in a minute," he muttered curtly.

Fusae placed the clean clothes into the drawers of the worn-out dresser, the one with little bear faces as handles that he'd used since he moved here with his mother.

"The police came here today," Fusae said as she pushed the clothes into the drawers, deliberately looking away from him. "So there's a girl in Fukuoka you were writing to? I'm sure you already heard this, but that girl died."

Fusae turned toward Yuichi for the first time. He was still on the bed, and had only lifted his head. He was expressionless, as if his mind was elsewhere.

"You heard about it, right? What happened to that girl," Fusae started to ask again.

"Yeah, I heard," Yuichi said slowly.

"Did you ever meet her, or did you just write to her?"

"Why do you want to know?"

"If you met her, maybe you should at least go to her funeral?"

"Her funeral?"

"That's right. If you only wrote to her, you don't need to. But it's different if you actually met her. . . ."

"No, I never met her."

Fusae could see that the bottoms of Yuichi's socks were soiled, the dirt tracing the shape of his toes. Yuichi was staring so fixedly at her that Fusae had the feeling someone else was standing behind her.

"I don't know this girl," Fusae continued, "but my gosh, people do some awful things in this world, don't they. . . . The police said they already know who did it, and that that person is trying to get away and they're searching for him."

"They know who did it?"

"That's what the patrolman told me. He said the man ran off, and they haven't located him yet."

"Are you talking about that college student?" Yuichi asked.

"What college student?"

"Isn't that what they said on TV?"

The certainty with which he said this finally convinced Fusae of one awful fact:

He is mixed up in all this, after all.

"The police really said that?" Yuichi asked. "That that college student is the murderer?" Fusae nodded. She had no idea how far his relationship with the girl had gone, but it was understandable that he'd feel hatred toward the criminal.

"They'll find him soon. He can't run forever," Fusae said, consoling him.

When Yuichi got up from the bed, his face was flushed. Fusae was sure he must be angry, but at the same time he looked relieved that they had identified the murderer.

"I wanted to ask you, where did you go last Sunday? You went out for a while at night, right?"

"Last Sunday?"

"Did you go to the service garage?"

Yuichi nodded at Fusae's tone.

"The police asked me. They're going around questioning all the girl's friends. Mrs. Okazaki told them you didn't go anywhere, and I didn't mean to lie, but I went along with it. Even if you take your car out for an hour or two, she never counts that as your having actually gone out. Oh, would you like to take a bath before supper?"

As soon as she finished her monologue Fusae left the room, without waiting for a reply. Halfway down the stairs she turned around. With Katsuji in and out of the hospital, she thought, Yuichi was the only one she could rely on. Her eldest daughter wouldn't come to see how her father was, let alone her second daughter.

After coming back down to the first floor Fusae reached into her apron pocket and took out the manila envelope. Inside was a single receipt that said:

For purchases: One set of Chinese herbal medicine. ¥263,500.

Dr. Tsutsumishita, the man who led the health seminars at the community center, had told her, "Come over to my office in town and we can give you a good price on some herbal medicine." Yesterday, half out of curiosity, Fusae decided to stop by on the way home from the hospital. She hadn't planned to buy anything. Traveling back and forth to the hospital had worn her out, and she just thought it might be amusing to hear some more of Dr. Tsutsumishita's funny stories. But when she went there, a rough-looking bunch of young men suddenly surrounded her, intimidating her into signing a contract.

I don't have this kind of money on me, she'd tearfully told them, and the men forced her to go with them to the post office, where she had a savings account. She was so frightened she couldn't ask anyone for help. As they stood watch over her, she withdrew what little savings she had.

CHAPTER 3

WHO DID SHE HAPPEN TO MEET?

Mitsuyo Magome was staring out the window of the men's clothing store Wakaba as the rain-swept cars went rushing by. The shop was on the outskirts of Saga City, next to Highway 34, a kind of bypass route around the city. There was usually a lot of traffic on the highway, but all the drivers saw was a monotonous repetition of the same scenery they'd seen a few minutes before.

Mitsuyo was in charge of the men's suit corner on the second floor of Wakaba.

Until about a year before she'd run the casual-wear corner on the first floor, but her manager had decided to move her upstairs. "With casual wear it's better to have the employees be around the same age as the customers," he explained amiably. "That way they have the same sort of tastes." And wasting no time, the next week he reassigned her to the suits corner.

If it had merely been a question of her age, Mitsuyo would have protested, but when it came to "tastes" there wasn't much she could say. She was actually relieved to hear that her fashion sense didn't match what was found in the casual-wear corner of the shop.

The shop sold what might be termed *trendyish* jeans and shirts, *ish* being the operative element. And there was a great difference between what was trendy and what was *almost*. For instance, she remembered coming across a shirt in a high-end store in Hakata that had the same design as one they sold at Wakaba, with prints of horses on it. Somehow the horses on the Wakaba knockoff shirt were ever so slightly larger, and that almost undetectable difference of a few millimeters was all it took to make the Wakaba shirts look kitschy.

But she also remembered a junior high school student who bought one of these horse-print shirts, and how happy he was as he carefully put on his yellow helmet and pedaled off on his low-seat bicycle, the precious shirt under one arm. She knew it contradicted the earlier feelings she had when her manager transferred her out of casual wear, but when she saw this junior high school boy pedaling away down along the highway she felt like shouting out to him: *That's right—who cares if the horses are a little bigger. Be proud of your shirt!* At that moment, Mitsuyo realized she was almost fond of her hometown.

"Miss Magome! How 'bout taking a break?"

Mitsuyo turned and saw the plump face of Kazuko Mizutani, the floor manager, peeking up above the rack of suits. From where Mitsuyo stood by the window, the rows of suits looked like waves rushing in to the shore. On a weekday morning like this they couldn't expect many customers. Occasionally someone would rush in to buy a dark suit for a funeral, but there didn't seem to be any tragedies in the neighborhood today.

"Did you bring your lunch?" Kazuko asked as she weaved her way through the maze of suit racks.

"These days making my lunch is the only thing I enjoy doing," Mitsuyo replied.

When the shop wasn't busy, they took turns going for lunch during the morning. The shop was spacious, but there were only three employees. Quite often they outnumbered the customers.

"I hate this winter rain. I wonder when it's going to let up." Kazuko came up beside her and went over to the window. Her breath clouded a tiny portion as she breathed on the pane. The heat was on in the shop but with no customers the place felt empty and cold.

"Did you ride your bike to work again?"

As Kazuko asked this, Mitsuyo gazed down at the large parking lot below, wet in the rain. They shared the lot with a fast-food place next door, and there were a few cars, but they were all parked close to the other store. Just her one little bike sat next to a fence near Wakaba, as if it were standing up alone to the cold winter downpour.

"If it's still raining when you get off, we'll give you a ride," Kazuko said, patting Mitsuyo's shoulders and then heading off toward the checkout counter.

Kazuko was forty-two this year. Her husband, one year older, was manager of an electric appliance store in the city and always came by to pick her up after work. He was a quiet man, and Mitsuyo found it cute how even after twenty years of marriage, he still called her Kazu-chan. The two of them had one child, a twenty-year-old son who was a junior in college. Kazuko was worried about him, calling him a *hikikomori*, a self-imposed shut-in. From what she said, though, he didn't seem to be a hard-core shut-in. She was just worried that he preferred staying in his room and fooling around with his computer to going out, and that he still didn't have a girlfriend. Using the buzzword *hikikomori* was, Mitsuyo felt, Kazuko's way of convincing herself and those around her that her worries were justified.

She wasn't trying to explain away Kazuko's son and his shut-in qualities, but really, there was so little to do in this town. Go out three days in a row and you were sure to run across someone you met the day before. It was like living in a continuous tape loop; it was much more fun to connect with the world through your computer than to live in the real world.

After she took an early lunch, and before her evening break, three different customers came in. One was an elderly couple. The husband had no interest in buying a new shirt, but his wife kept holding up one shirt after another in front of him, apparently less interested in the color or design than in the price.

Just before Mitsuyo's evening break a man in his early thirties came in. The staff had been told to wait until the customers asked a question before approaching them, so Mitsuyo stood across the room, eyeing the man as he pawed through the racks of suits. Even from that distance, she spied the man's wedding ring.

"There're just no good eligible men our age in this town," her twin sister, Tamayo, once said. "I mean there *are* some good men, but they're all married."

Mitsuyo's friends who worked in town said the same thing. These friends, though, were all married, so their tone was different from that of her unmarried sister. "There's a guy I'd love to introduce you to," they'd tell her. "But unfortunately he's already married. It's a real shame. . . ."

Not that she'd even asked them to introduce her to someone, but the truth remained that it took some courage, in a town like Saga, to be turning thirty next year and to still be single. Her three best friends from high school were all married, with children. One of them had a son who had already started elementary school this year.

"Excuse me," the customer looking through the suits suddenly asked. He was holding up a mocha-colored suit.

"Would you like to try it on?" Mitsuyo smiled as she approached.

"So is this suit one of the ones that are thirty-eight thousand nine hundred yen for two?" he asked, pointing to the poster hanging from the ceiling.

"Yes. All of them are." Mitsuyo smiled again and led him to the fitting room.

The man was tall, and must work out, she figured. After he put on the suit and opened the curtain Mitsuyo could see his muscular thighs bulging through the tight slacks.

"Don't you think they're a little tight?" the man asked as he looked at her in the mirror.

"Most slacks are styled that way these days."

She crouched down in front of him to measure the length of the legs. The man smelled slightly milky, as if he might have a baby at home.

A man's large legs were right in front of her. He was wearing socks, but still she could see the outlines of his toenails. Mitsuyo wondered how many men she'd knelt down in front of. When she first started doing this, measuring trouser legs, she'd hated it, feeling as if she were kneeling in submission.

All those men's legs. Legs with dirty socks, with clean socks. Thick ankles, thin ankles, long calves, short calves. Sometimes men's legs looked brutal to her, at other times strong and reliable.

Back when she was twenty-two or twenty-three and was called on to help measure trousers, she had the illusion that among all these men whose trouser legs she was taking up would be her future husband. She laughed at this memory now, but back then she held on to the hope that as she knelt before a man, pinning up a trouser leg, she'd look up and there would be the face of her future husband, gazing gently down at her. For a while she had this fantasy about each customer she served.

This was her first period of expectation about marriage, she realized now. But no matter how many trouser legs she shortened, she never saw the face of the man she was to marry.

The winter rain kept on falling, even after dark.

Mitsuyo closed out the register, turned off the lights in the spacious shop, and went to the locker room to change out of her uniform. Kazuko, already in her street clothes, said, "You can't go home on a bike in this rain. We'll give you a ride."

Mitsuyo glanced at her tired face in the locker-room mirror. "That would be nice," she said. But then she worried that the next morning she'd have to take the bus to work.

They left through the employee entrance, the rain continuing to pound down on the large parking lot. Behind the store, a fallow field beyond a fence smelled wet and earthy.

Cars hissed by on the wet highway, spraying water. The mammoth, brightly lit sign for the store with the name *Wakaba* was reflected on the rainy pavement and flickered in a dreamy way.

Mitsuyo heard a car horn and turned toward the sound. Kazuko was already in the passenger seat of her husband's minicar, which was edging toward Mitsuyo.

Mitsuyo ran out from under the eaves, leaving her umbrella

closed. "Thank you so much," she said as she clambered into the backseat. It took only a few seconds, but her neck was wet and the rain was so cold it hurt.

"Another day, huh?" Kazuko's husband, who wore thick glasses, said.

"Thank you for always helping me out," Mitsuyo replied.

Mitsuyo's apartment was in a corner of a rice field that had a watercourse running through it. It was fairly new, but had that tacky, instantly obsolete look of a place that was built only to be torn down in a few years. Drenched in the rain this evening, the building looked even more dreary than usual.

As they always did, Kazuko and her husband dropped her off right in front of her building. As Mitsuyo climbed out of the backseat, her sneakers sank with a squish into the mud.

Mitsuyo waved goodbye and splashed through the mud up the stairs. She was only on the second floor, but when she got upstairs the view made her feel as if she were at some scenic overlook. The scent of drenched soil, blown toward her by the wind, tickled her nose.

She opened the door to No. 201 and light filtered out from inside.

"Hey, I thought you were going to that party with the Chamber of Commerce," Mitsuyo called out as she tugged off her wet, muddy skirt. The smell of the kerosene stove hit her, along with the voice of her sister: "It wasn't mandatory, so I didn't go."

In the six-mat living room, her sister, Tamayo, was toweling off her wet hair. She must have just lit the stove, for the room was still cold and had the acrid stink of kerosene.

"I used to hate having to pour drinks for the men, but now the younger girls are pouring *me* drinks. Kind of makes me uncomfortable," Tamayo said, standing in front of the stove.

"Did you buy anything?" Mitsuyo asked her, speaking to her back.

"No, nothing. It was raining and everything."

Tamayo tossed her the damp towel.

"Anything in the fridge?" As she wiped her wet neck Mitsuyo opened the refrigerator.

"Did Mrs. Mizutani give you a ride again?"

"Yeah, I left my bike, so tomorrow I'll have to take the bus."

There was half a cabbage in the fridge, and a bit of pork, so she decided to sauté these and make some *udon* as well. She shut the fridge.

"Your skirt's going to get wrinkled," Mitsuyo cautioned Tamayo, who was sitting on the tatami in her damp clothes.

"So you think it's really okay for a couple of twin sisters turning thirty next year to sit here enjoying *udon*?" Tamayo said, twirling some *tororo konbu* around her noodles.

Mitsuyo sprinkled some pepper flakes in her bowl. "These noodles are a bit overcooked," she said.

"Twenty years ago the neighbors would have definitely looked at us like we're weird."

"Why?"

"Two women, twins, living alone in an apartment? Think they wouldn't gossip about that?"

Tamayo, her long hair pulled back and fastened with a rubber band, noisily slurped down the noodles.

"Plus we have names that make us sound like a comedy team— Mitsuyo and Tamayo. The kids in the neighborhood would definitely have called us the Witch Twins."

"The Witch Twins . . ." Half laughing, Mitsuyo felt a shudder of dread at the thought. This didn't hurt her appetite, though, as she continued to down the noodles.

They lived in a 2DK apartment, two bedrooms plus a dining room–kitchen that rented for ¥42,000 a month. On paper it sounded like a nice place, but the two bedrooms actually consisted of two identical six-mat tatami rooms separated by a sliding door. The other residents of this cheap apartment building were all young couples with small children.

After graduating from a local high school, the twins had worked at a food-processing plant in Tosu City. They hadn't planned to work in the same factory, but after they'd applied at several places only one had hired them. They both worked on the production line. They were assigned to various stations on the line over the three years they worked there, and over this time had watched tens of thousands of instant-noodle cups flow past.

Tamayo was the first to grow sick of it and she quit to work as a caddie at a nearby golf course. But she soon hurt her back and took an office job at the Chamber of Commerce. Around the time she quit the caddie job, Mitsuyo was let go by the food factory. The company was downsizing, and the first to be fired were the girls like Mitsuyo who'd only graduated from high school.

The employment office at the factory introduced her to the menswear shop. She wasn't good at dealing with customers, but wasn't in a position to wait for something that suited her better.

They rented this apartment around the time that Mitsuyo first started working at Wakaba. Tamayo claimed that if they kept living at home, they'd never get married, and so she half forced Mitsuyo into the idea of moving in with her.

The twins always got along well and continued to do so after living together. Their parents were glad to get the two nagging older sisters out of the house, for it gave them the chance to seriously start preparing for the girls' younger brother, their eldest son, to get married. And sure enough, three years later he married a former high school classmate. The girl was twenty-two at the time, three years younger than the twins. In attendance at the wedding were several of their brother's friends, themselves already married with babies—not an uncommon scene at this suburban wedding hall.

"Hey, what d'you think one of the girls at the Chamber of Commerce asked me?"

After they finished their *udon*, Mitsuyo was washing the dishes in the kitchen, Tamayo sprawled out in front of the TV.

" '*What're you doing for Christmas?*' she asked. How am I supposed to answer a nineteen-year-old who asks me that?" Tamayo was watching a show on dieting and doing leg lifts as she watched.

"But weren't you going to take some vacation time and go on a trip?"

"Yeah, but taking a bus trip around the Shimanami Kaido Expressway with a bunch of women seems kind of sad, don't you think? Hey, do you want to go with me?"

"No way. We're together every day. Just the thought of taking a trip with you on my vacation makes me tired."

Mitsuyo added a little dishwashing liquid to her sponge. In the kitchen hung a calendar from the local supermarket. Other than notations of garbage days and her days off, the calendar was blank.

Christmas, Mitsuyo murmured as she squeezed the sponge. The last few years Mitsuyo had spent Christmas with her parents. Her brother's little boy, born not too long after the wedding, had his birthday on Christmas Eve, so he'd always go home with an armful of presents.

She'd been squeezing the sponge too hard and the suds had dripped down on her rubber glove. She stood there, watching as the suds slid down the glove to her elbow and then, once enough suds accumulated, into the sink with all the dirty dishes. The soapy suds made her elbow itch. Her whole body felt itchy.

Yuichi rolled over several times in bed, as if to test how creaky the springs were.

It was 8:50 p.m. Too early to sleep, but these past few days he'd tried to fall asleep as soon as he could, so right after taking a bath and having dinner he went to bed, even though his eyes remained wide open.

He'd toss and turn, and start to notice the smell of his pillow, and the feel of his blanket and how it rubbed against his neck the wrong way.

And most nights, before he knew it, he had an erection. His hard penis under the blanket was nearly as hot as the infrared space heater next to his bed.

Nine days had passed since the murder. The TV talk shows had all reported how the Fukuoka college student sought as a material witness was still missing, but the last couple of days, the shows had been silent about the murder at Mitsuse Pass.

As the local patrolman had told Fusae, the only lead the police were pursuing was to find the missing college student. Since then, the police hadn't contacted Yuichi's home, or tried to question him. Nothing at all happened, as if he'd disappeared from their radar.

When he closed his eyes, he felt as if he were driving over the pass again, holding on to the steering wheel so tightly he nearly spun out on some of the curves. The headlights of his car lit up the forest as the white guardrails drew closer.

Yuichi rolled over again. *Go to sleep!* he commanded himself, burying his face in the pillow, smelling its mixture of sweat, body odor, and shampoo.

Right then his phone beeped, signaling an e-mail. Suddenly freed from being forced to go to sleep, he reached out for the cell phone, which lay inside the pocket of the pants he'd tossed on the floor.

It has to be Hifumi, he thought, but he didn't recognize the number.

He got up and sat cross-legged. Though it was winter, he still slept just in his underwear, and his back facing the heater soon got hot.

Hello. Remember me? We exchanged a few messages a couple of months ago. I'm the elder of twin sisters who live in Saga, and you were going on and on about some lighthouse. Have you forgotten? Sorry for the sudden e-mail.

After he read the message Yuichi scratched his back, which was still facing the heater. In just a short time, it felt as if he'd been burned.

He got out of bed and sat on the tatami. As he slid forward his trousers and sweatshirt got twisted in his knees.

Yuichi remembered the girl. Two months ago he had registered his address on a dating site and gotten five or six replies. Hers was one of them, and they'd e-mailed for a while, but when he invited her to go for a drive she suddenly stopped replying.

Hey, it's been a while. So what's up all of a sudden?

His fingers worked smoothly over the keys. Usually when he spoke, something in his mind interfered before he could get the words out, but when he sent e-mails, the words flowed easily.

You remember me? I'm happy. No, nothing's really going on. I just felt like e-mailing you.

He couldn't remember her name, but even if he did, he was sure it was an alias.

How have you been? Yuichi replied. *You were talking about buying a car, so did you get one?*

No, I didn't. I'm still commuting by bike. How about you? Anything nice happen lately?

Nice?

A new girlfriend, maybe?

Nope. How about you?

No such luck. Hey, have you gone to any new lighthouses since then?

No, I haven't gone at all. On the weekends I just hang out at home.

No kidding? Hey, where was that lighthouse you recommended, the one you said was so pretty?

Where did I say it was? In Nagasaki? Or Saga?

Nagasaki. You said there's a little island next to it you can walk to with a lookout platform. You said the sunset from there is so gorgeous it makes you almost cry.

Oh, that's Kabashima Lighthouse. It's near where I live.

How far is it?

Fifteen, twenty minutes by car.

Really? You live in such a nice place.

I wouldn't say that.

But it's near the sea, right?

Yeah, the sea's right nearby.

Just then, as he e-mailed about the sea, Yuichi heard the sound of the waves against the breakwaters outside. The waves sounded louder at night. He could hear the waves the whole night long, washing over his body as he lay in his narrow bed.

At those times Yuichi felt as though he were a piece of driftwood bobbing in the waves. The waves were about to wash over him, but never quite reached him; he was about to be washed up on the beach but never quite reached it, either. A piece of driftwood tumbling about at the shoreline.

Is there one in Saga, too? A pretty lighthouse?

Yuichi replied right away: *Yeah, there's one in Saga.*

But it must be around Karatsu, right? I live in Saga City.

Yuichi had never heard this girl speak, but with each word he felt he could hear her voice.

Yuichi had driven through Saga many times and tried to picture the scenery. Compared to Nagasaki, Saga was boringly flat, with the same monotonous roads wherever you went. No mountains anywhere. No steep slopes or little cobblestone alleys like in Nagasaki. Just newly paved, arrow-straight roads lined with big-box bookstores, pachinko parlors, and fast-food places. Each store's massive parking lot was filled with cars, but somehow the only thing missing was people.

It came to him all of a sudden, as he was exchanging messages with the girl, that she was a part of this scene, walking down the very streets he was picturing. It made perfect sense, but Yuichi, who only knew these streets from the window of his car, had no idea how this plodding scenery appeared to someone who actually lived there and walked down those streets. You walk and walk and nothing around you ever changes. A slow-motion kind of scenery.

These days I haven't talked to anybody.

He looked down and saw these words on the screen. They weren't words someone had e-mailed him. Without realizing it, he'd typed the message.

He was about to erase the message, but added *All I do is go back and forth between home and work*—and after a moment's hesitation, he sent it.

He'd never felt lonely before. He hadn't even known what it meant. But ever since that night he'd felt terribly lonely. Loneliness, he thought, must mean being anxious for somebody to listen to you.

He'd never had anything he really wanted to tell someone else, before this. But now he did. And he wanted someone to tell it to.

"Tamayo! I might be late tonight."

Mitsuyo was still on her futon as she heard Tamayo behind the sliding door getting ready to go to work. She listened to these sounds, and tried to decide whether to voice this thought. Finally, when Tamayo was at the front door pulling on her shoes, she did.

"Inventory?" she heard Tamayo say from the front door.

"Uh . . . yeah. No, that's not it. I'm taking the day off. . . . I just have something I need to do, so I'll be back late."

Mitsuyo crawled out of bed, slid open the sliding door, and peeked out toward the front door. Tamayo had her shoes on and was standing there, hand on the doorknob.

"Something to do?" Tamayo asked. "What do you mean? And what time will you be back? You won't need dinner?"

Her flurry of questions was more perfunctory, and didn't mean she was actually interested. She'd already turned the knob and had one foot out the door.

"If you're getting up, then I don't have to lock the door, right? Jeez, why do I have to go to work on a Saturday?"

Without waiting for a reply, Tamayo shut the door.

"See you later," Mitsuyo called out to the door.

Tamayo had left the electric rug on, so as Mitsuyo crawled out of her futon her palms and knees felt the warmth. She held the calendar and traced the green 22 with her fingertips.

The weekend was usually the busiest time at her store, and she hadn't taken Saturday and Sunday off in a row like this since that time a year and a half ago.

It had been Golden Week, the string of holidays at the end of April and beginning of May, and she'd taken off a few vacation days she'd accumulated so she could stay over at a former high school friend's place in Hakata. Her friend's husband was back in his hometown for a Buddhist memorial service for a relative, and the two young women were looking forward to a night of chatting. Mitsuyo also wanted to hold her friend's two-year-old son.

The bus for Tenjin left from in front of the Saga railway station. She'd bicycled to the station, arriving a little past twelve-thirty, ten minutes before the express bus to Hakata was scheduled to leave. She was in line to buy her ticket when her friend phoned. "My son has a fever," she explained. It was kind of last minute, but if your child's sick there's nothing you can do about it. Without any fuss, Mitsuyo got out of the line and, sulking a bit, went home.

She was back in her apartment, trying to figure out how she would spend these vacation days she'd wasted. The TV was on but Mitsuyo wasn't paying much attention to it when a news flash came on the screen. At first she expected it to be about a girl who'd been kidnapped years ago, and was in the news lately, that they'd found her. The story had always frightened her, and a shiver ran through her.

But the news flash was about a bus hijacking. For a second she was relieved, but then she couldn't believe her eyes. On the screen flashed the name of the highway bus she'd been about to board.

"What the—?" Mitsuyo yelled in the empty apartment. She hurriedly switched to another channel and there was a live report on the hijacking. "My God. I can't believe this. . . ." She hadn't planned to say this aloud, but the words just came out.

The scene on TV was taken from a helicopter shadowing the bus, which was tearing down the Chugoku Highway. Above the clamor of the helicopter a reporter was excitedly shouting out, "Ah, that was a close one! It just passed a truck."

Mitsuyo's cell phone, on her table, rang at that moment, the call from her friend in Hakata.

"Where are you?" the friend suddenly asked.

"I'm fine," Mitsuyo replied. "I'm at home."

Her friend had just heard about the hijacking. She was sure Mitsuyo must have given up and gone home, but just in case she decided to call and check. Phone in hand, Mitsuyo couldn't take her eyes off the screen. The bus sped up and barely slipped by several unsuspecting cars.

"I . . . I was supposed to be on that bus. On that same bus," Mitsuyo muttered as she stared at the screen.

Her friend was relieved, and after hanging up Mitsuyo continued to stare at the TV. The announcer gave the bus's time of departure and route. There was no doubt about it—this was the bus she had almost boarded. The bus she saw outside as she was waiting in line to buy a ticket. The bus the old lady in front of her took, the one the giddy high school girls behind were riding.

She sat transfixed by the images. "We know nothing about the situation inside the bus," the announcer kept repeating, and Mitsuyo felt like shouting, "But the old lady in front of me is in there! And the girls in line behind me!"

The TV kept showing the roof of the bus barreling down the highway. Mitsuyo started to feel as if she herself were in the bus. She could see the scenery rushing by the window. The old woman from the ticket line was seated across the aisle from her, her face ashen. A few seats in front were the two high school girls, pressed close to each other, sobbing.

The bus didn't look as if it was going to slow down. It blasted past one car after another filled with families out enjoying the Golden Week holidays.

In her mind, Mitsuyo desperately wanted to move from her aisle seat to the window seat. She'd been ordered not to look toward the front, but her eyes drifted there. A young man holding a knife was standing next to the driver. Every once in a while he'd stab the foam rubber of a nearby seat, and shout out something unintelligible.

"The bus . . . the bus is pulling into a rest area!" The reporter's yell brought Mitsuyo back to reality.

The bus had overshot its original destination, Tenjin, and had taken the Kyushu Expressway and now the Chugoku Highway. A patrol car had led the bus into the rest area, where it pulled to a stop.

Mitsuyo was watching this scene on TV, but somehow she saw the scene from the interior of the bus, the police outside surrounding them.

"Someone . . . someone appears to be injured inside! Stabbed and seriously wounded!" The reporter's voice said over the scene of the spacious parking lot.

If she looked to her side, Mitsuyo would see the old woman there, stabbed. Mitsuyo knew she was in her apartment watching all this on TV, but she was too frightened to look.

Ever since she was a child, she'd felt unlucky. The world was filled with lots of different people, but if you divided them into two groups—the lucky and the unlucky—she was definitely one of the latter. And she was surely in the unluckiest cohort of all. It was a conviction she'd had her entire life.

As if to shake off these memories of the hijacking Mitsuyo opened the window. The warm air inside the apartment rushed out, the cold winter wind flowing in and brushing against her body. Mitsuyo shivered once, stretched, and took a deep breath.

When things got divided up into good and bad, she always ended up with the bad. She'd always been certain she was that kind of person. *But I didn't take that bus back then*, she thought. *I was just about to, but I didn't, so for the first time in my life I got lucky.*

Mitsuyo looked up and saw the still rice fields in front of her. She glanced at her cell phone in the sunlight coming in the open window. When she checked for new e-mails, she found the dozens of messages she'd exchanged recently.

Three days before, she'd gathered her courage and e-mailed this man named Yuichi Shimizu, and his response had been encouraging. Three months before that, she'd been drinking with her colleagues, something she rarely did, and, a bit tipsy, playfully looked into an online dating site. She wasn't sure how it worked, but when she received the updated list of men, she'd chosen Yuichi.

The reason she'd chosen someone from Nagasaki was simple. If it was someone from Saga she might know him; Fukuoka was too big a city for her; and Kagoshima and Oita were too far away.

But three months ago when Yuichi had said, *Let's meet*, she stopped e-mailing him right away.

Three days ago, too, she didn't feel like actually meeting him. Before going to bed she'd simply felt like talking to someone, even via e-mail. And that had led to a three-day exchange of messages. Now she wanted to see him, a desire that had grown more intense over the three days. She wasn't sure what it was about him that made her feel this way, but when she exchanged messages with him she felt like the person she was back then, the one who didn't get on that bus. Nothing was guaranteed, but if she screwed up her courage she felt as if she'd never have to get on that bus again.

Mitsuyo held her cell phone in the sunlight and read last night's final e-mail.

Well, I'll see you tomorrow at eleven in front of Saga station. Good night!

Simple words, but to her they seemed to glow.

Today I'm going for a drive with him, in his car, she thought. To see the lighthouse. The two of them, going to see this lovely lighthouse facing the sea.

When it gets dark you turn on the fluorescent lights. He'd done it every day without thinking, but now, to Yoshio Ishibashi, it seemed like an unusual, special act.

It gets dark and you turn on the light. Simple as that. But even in performing a simple act, a person runs through a series of feelings.

First your eyes sense it's grown dark. Darkness is inconvenient. If you make things lighter, the inconvenience vanishes. To make it light, you have to switch on the fluorescent lights. And to do that you have to stand up from the tatami and pull the cord. Just pull the cord, and this place is no longer dark and inconvenient.

In the gloomy room Yoshio stared at the light cord above him. All he needed to do was stand up, but the cord was miles away.

The room was dark. But he didn't need to do anything about it.

He didn't mind a dark room. And if he didn't mind, he didn't need to turn on the light. If he didn't need to turn on the light, he didn't need to stand up.

So Yoshio stayed lying on the tatami. The room was filled with the smell of incense. Just a few minutes before he'd asked Satoko, "Why don't you open a window a little?"

"Okay," she'd replied. She was seated in front of the Buddhist altar, but over ten minutes passed with no sign that she was going to get up.

Beyond the darkened room was the barbershop, also dark. Trucks roared past occasionally, just outside, rattling the thin front door. If he listened carefully, Yoshio could hear the faint sputter of the incense and candles burning at the altar.

The wake and funeral for his daughter, Yoshino, were over, but how many days had passed since that? It felt as if it was a while ago that he'd brought Satoko back from the funeral home, sobbing. But it also felt as if he'd said goodbye to Yoshino a half a year ago.

The funeral was at the memorial hall next to the Chikugo River. And lots of people came: relatives, neighbors, old friends of Yoshio and Satoko all jostling to help out. Some of Yoshino's classmates and colleagues came as well. When the two colleagues who were with her on that last night came to offer flowers, they touched her cold face and sobbed uncontrollably, unconcerned about those around them: "We're so sorry, so sorry. We're sorry we let you go by yourself." They were all gathered for Yoshino's sake, but no one spoke about her. No one said a word about why this had happened.

A couple of TV crews were gathered outside the memorial hall. The police were there, too, and what the reporters learned about the investigation from them filtered back to the mourners. The college student who was supposedly meeting Yoshino the night of her death was still missing. Can't tell for sure, one policeman declared, but if it turns out the boy is on the run, then that must mean he's the one who did it.

"They can't even find one college student? What the hell do the police think they're doing!" Yoshio yelled in an angry, tearful voice.

"What are you doing here offering incense? Go out and find the guy!" Totally at a loss, he spit out these angry words, his body shaking uncontrollably.

His great-aunt and others hurried from Okayama and arrived on the night of the wake, and they tried to persuade him to get some sleep. "I know it's hard," they said, "but you have to try to rest," and they laid out a futon for him in a waiting room of the memorial hall. He knew he couldn't sleep, but maybe if he did he'd wake up and find out this was all a dream, so he closed his eyes and tried his best.

Beyond the sliding door he could hear the hushed voices of his relatives mixed in with the occasional can of beer popping open, and crunching sounds as someone chewed crackers. From what he could make out of their conversation, his wife refused to leave the altar and Yoshino's side, and whenever anyone spoke to her she broke down in tears.

Yoshio longed to fall asleep. Here he was, unable to do anything but wait for the young Buddhist priest to show up, the one whose hobby was collecting anime dolls, and he found it pitiful and frustrating. But no matter how hard he tried to close his eyes, he couldn't filter out the muffled voices from the next room.

"It would be better for Yoshino if it does turn out that the college student did it. Think about it—what if it turns out she's involved with one of those dating sites, like the police said? On TV they said if that's true, then she took money to sleep with men."

"Be quiet! Yoshio's in the next room!"

Someone shushed the great-aunt and the others. But after a few moments someone hesitantly brought it up again.

"That college student has to be the one. Otherwise he wouldn't run away, right?"

"That makes sense. Maybe he found out about her getting money from other men and they had a fight. And things escalated after that. . . ."

A draft of cold wind blew in from the kitchen, which was next to the barbershop. Still lying down on the tatami, Yoshio stretched out his legs and pushed the sliding door shut. The darkened room now lost every last bit of light.

"Satoko . . ." he called out listlessly to his wife.

"Yes?" she replied, sounding as though she were replying to a question from five minutes ago.

"Shall we have something delivered for dinner?"

"Okay."

"We could call Rairaiten."

"All right."

Satoko answered but made no move to get up. Still, Yoshio felt this was the first time he and his wife had actually had a conversation the whole day, which she'd spent frozen in place in front of the altar.

Yoshio had no choice but to get up himself. He pulled the cord for the fluorescent light and it blinked a few times and came on, revealing the worn tatami and the cushion he'd been sitting on. On the low table was a stack of extra gift boxes for mourners, and on top of that a bill from the funeral home.

"You'll have people visiting you at home," the funeral director had explained.

Yoshio looked away from the table, dialed the number for Rairaiten, and ordered two bowls of vegetable ramen. The owner of the store answered, very awkwardly, "Ah, Mr. Ishibashi. Of course. We'll bring it over right away."

After he hung up he could still hear Satoko sniffling. No matter how much she sobbed she couldn't sob out all her pain.

"Satoko." Yoshio crouched down again on the tatami and called out to his wife's back as she sat there, leaning toward the shelf on the altar. "Did you know that Yoshino was seeing this college student?"

It felt like the first time since the murder that he'd used his daughter's name. Satoko lay prostrate before the altar now and didn't reply. She was no doubt sobbing again; the candle on the shelf was flickering as her body shook.

"Yoshino isn't the kind of girl they say she is. She wouldn't go with guys and . . ."

His voice started to shake and before he knew it, tears were running down his cheeks. His wife began sobbing aloud, crying with clenched teeth, just as Yoshino used to do as a child.

"I won't let him get away with it! I don't care what anyone else says, I won't allow it!" But his voice wouldn't work. The words stuck in his throat and he gulped them back.

Some time ago, he couldn't remember exactly when, Yoshino had made her usual Sunday evening call to them and she and Satoko were on the phone for a long time. The call came in just before Yoshio was about to take a bath, and continued long after he finished, so they must have talked for over an hour.

After his bath Yoshio was enjoying some *shochu* mixed with oolong tea, watching TV and half listening to their conversation. From Satoko's answers Yoshio could surmise that Yoshino had been asking questions like "When you and Dad first met, who was the first to say 'I love you'?" and "Since Dad was in a band and girls were really into him, how did you get him to fall for you?" To each of these Satoko gave an honest answer.

Usually at this point Yoshio would yell at them for talking too long, but considering the topic he wasn't sure what to say, and instead drank at a faster pace than normal.

When Satoko finally hung up he asked, feigning ignorance, what they'd talked about, and Satoko, a happy look on her face, said, "Yoshino has somebody she likes."

For a second he was taken aback. Yoshino likes a man? But then he thought it was touching, cute even, that she'd phoned her parents asking about how they'd first met.

"She's going out with somebody?" Yoshio asked brusquely.

"I don't think they're actually going out yet," Satoko replied. "You know, she always tends to act sort of tough in front of boys. She's kind of stubborn, not so open. . . . But it sounds like she's really fallen for this guy. She was crying a bit. She's still a little girl in a way, isn't she, calling her parents about this instead of talking with her friends."

Yoshio didn't say anything, but instead drained his cup of *shochu*, and Satoko added, "The boy is apparently the son of a family that owns an upscale inn in Yufuin or Beppu or someplace."

About a half a year ago Yoshio had taken a trip with the barber's union to an inn at Yufuin and he was remembering what the town was like. The inn they stayed at was a cheap place, but when he went for a stroll he'd run across a famous old inn with a huge entranceway. The owner's beautiful young wife just happened to be standing at the entrance, and though she recognized from the *yukata* they were wearing that they were staying at a different inn, she casually called out to them. When Yoshio and his group commented on how great the air was in Yufuin, the lovely young woman smiled and said, "Please come back and visit us again!"

That night, as he stared at Satoko's backside as she washed the dishes, he pictured Yoshino in a kimono standing in the threshold of that nice old inn and smiling at him. He grinned wryly at how his mind had leaped ahead a few steps, but actually it didn't feel too bad to imagine a future like this for her.

Staring at Satoko now, collapsed in tears in front of the altar, Yoshio again muttered, "He won't get away with it. . . ." If he could go back in time, he'd go back to that night, grab the phone away from Satoko, and tell Yoshino, "I don't want you to have anything to do with that guy!"

It felt awful not to be able to do that. All he'd done was casually imagine his daughter standing there in a kimono, and he'd ended up feeling sad and impotent.

❋

Koki Tsuruta realized that Keigo Masuo had been on his mind for several days.

There had been no word from the police since they came the day after the murder, so he'd relied on reports in the papers and on TV to follow events.

A classmate he was friends with had murdered a woman and was on the run. Put it like this, and it sounded like he was involved in quite a drama, but actually his days were pretty ordinary, as he stayed holed up in his room overlooking Ohori Park, watching his favorite movies—*Ascenseur pour l'échafaud* and *Citizen Kane*. Before he went to sleep each night, he'd switch to porn and make sure to come.

A classmate murdering someone and running away—it sounded like some lousy script he'd written himself. If it actually did become a film, it would be kind of boring. Still, the facts remained: Masuo really had killed a woman and was running from the police. This was no crummy script, but reality.

Ever since the incident, and actually before the incident, Koki had stopped going to school. He was sure the school must be in an uproar over what Keigo had done. He could picture everyone running around, as if it were the night before the annual university festival.

Keigo had been a well-known figure on campus, and those who liked him and those who didn't were watching, all of them irritated with their selfish desire just to see how this would end up.

Since the murder, Koki had called Keigo's cell phone every day, but he never answered. Koki realized once again that Keigo was his one link with the outside world. He relied on Keigo for everything he heard about school, about other friends, about girls—information that made Koki feel that he was just like everybody else, living an ordinary college student's life.

Where *was* Keigo?

Was he afraid? Was he going to keep on running?

If he's going to get caught, Koki thought, *I don't want any of this turning-himself-in stuff. He should keep on running as much as he can, until the cops have him completely surrounded, a blazing spotlight on him, and he shouts out some memorable line* (which Koki knew he could never come up with), *and then he takes his own life.*

Koki was watching porn as he thought this, and he looked up and saw a fellatio scene on the screen. Morning had come, the sunlight streaming in on the messy room. The chirping of birds from the nearby park mixed with the slurping sounds of the girl in the movie. Before the scene was over Koki came. He tossed the sticky tissue into the garbage can and yanked up his underwear.

But why did he kill her?

Koki couldn't think of a good reason why Keigo would kill the girl. He could picture a girl killing Keigo, who could be pretty cold-hearted. That would be a kind of fitting end to his life.

The girl on the screen was still performing fellatio, and Koki switched off the tape and went around the apartment, squinting in the sunlight, closing the curtains. He'd needled his parents into buying these special blackout curtains that even during the day turned the place as dark as night. Thinking of his parents' money always upset him, but by taming those feelings, he'd been able to persuade them to buy these expensive curtains.

As he sprawled on his bed he pictured the faces of his parents, always calculating how much money they had. How they'd sit there, tapping out figures on their calculators as if the more they stared at their bankbooks, the more money they'd have in their accounts. Koki knew the necessity of money, but he also knew there had to be something more in life. And unless he found it, he couldn't escape this listlessness.

After a while he began to doze, and was jerked awake when his cell phone on the glass table rang.

"Hello?" The man's voice sounded familiar.

"Uh, hello!" He instinctively sat up in bed.

"Sorry, were you asleep?" It was without a doubt Keigo's voice.

"Keigo? Is that you?" Koki said loudly, and the phlegm in his throat made him cough. "Don't—don't hang up!" he managed to say, then coughed loudly and spit up the phlegm. It shot out and splattered on the DVD package of the porn film.

"Keigo? Are you—okay?" Koki asked. There were a million things he wanted to ask, but that was all that came out.

"Yeah, I'm okay," Keigo said, sounding tired.

❦

It was only six a.m. and he figured Koki must be asleep, but Koki picked up.

Keigo hadn't called with the intention of missing Koki—but the moment he heard Koki's voice, he realized he'd been hoping there would be no answer.

He was at a sauna in Nagoya. At the end of the red-carpeted hallway was a darkened room where guests could nap. The public phone was in one corner of the hallway. Next to it was a vending machine selling nutritional supplement drinks, three of the five buttons lit up indicating they were sold out.

"You're really okay?" he heard Koki ask. He sounded as if he'd just woken up, but his voice was tense and strained, and told Keigo in no uncertain terms the situation he was in.

"So where are you?" Koki's voice suddenly grew gentle. Keigo instinctively gripped the receiver more tightly.

He figured they must be tapping the phones in his apartment and his parents' home, but they couldn't be tracing calls from Koki's cell phone. Still, Koki sounded *too* gentle and nice, as if he was putting on an act in front of somebody.

His hand was resting on the phone's cradle and he pushed down hard on it. The call over, a few ten-yen coins plunked down into the coin return, clattering in the silent hallway. Keigo turned. Nobody else was around, just his own reflection in the mirror on a pillar, decked out in the light blue robe of a sauna patron. Keigo replaced the receiver on its cradle. He'd never noticed before how heavy a public phone receiver could be.

He hadn't called Koki because he wanted to tell him something, or to find out what was happening with the investigation. The last few days he hadn't spoken to a soul. At the front desk of the sauna and the hotel, he'd merely nodded or shaken his head in response to their questions. A moment ago when he told Koki he was okay, it felt like the first time in a long time that he'd heard his own voice.

Keigo walked back down the red-carpeted hallway to the nap room. Beyond the curtains he could hear a man snoring, the sound of which had bothered him all night long. The snoring man was sprawled out next to the chaise longue where Keigo had planted himself earlier and it made Keigo want to kick him. But he knew that he couldn't—if he caused a problem here, that would be the end for him. About fifty chaise longues were lined up in the spacious room. These chairs—with their synthetic leather split open and foam rubber sticking out—were the only place where Keigo could now be free.

It might have been his imagination, but as he entered the nap room of the sauna he smelled a feral, animal-like odor. Even after sweating in the sauna and scrubbing themselves clean in the bath, if you put this many men together in one room maybe this smell is unavoidable.

Guided only by the exit light, Keigo made his way back to his chaise longue. The others contained sleeping men in a variety of poses. One man kept his glasses on as he slept. Another had skillfully arranged the tiny blanket provided them to cover himself completely. And then there was his next-door neighbor, gaping mouth emitting thunderous snores.

Keigo cleared his throat loudly and lay down, wrapping the still warm blanket up around him. His throat-clearing only made the man beside him roll over, but did nothing to stop his awful snoring.

When Keigo closed his eyes he could picture Koki's face on the other end of the phone line.

Why did he make the call? And why to Koki? Did he think that Koki would be able to rescue him from this predicament? The more he thought about it, the stupider it felt. In school and out, he had plenty of friends and acquaintances, but he couldn't think of anyone else he could call at a time like this. People tended to flock to him, and Keigo was aware of this. But not one of them was worth a damn. He might hang out with them, but deep down he despised them.

Keigo squeezed his eyes shut, trying to force himself to sleep despite the snores. But closing his eyes tightly only produced more memories, like juice oozing from a piece of fruit, and though he didn't want to think about it, the memories of that night, and running across Yoshino Ishibashi by chance, at Higashi Park, all rushed back at him.

Why do I have to run away, he thought, *just because of a girl like that? And lie here listening to the snores of a stranger?* The more he thought about it, the angrier he became.

Why did he run across her again in a place like that? If only he'd waited until he got back to his apartment to go to the bathroom, none of this would have happened.

He'd been in a crappy mood all that night. He'd gone out drinking in a bar in Tenjin, and then got in his car, which he'd parked on the road, planning to drive back to his apartment. It was just a five-minute drive back to his place, but somehow he was terribly on edge and decided to go for a longer drive instead.

He was drunk. When he looked back on it now, he had no idea where he drove, or how he ended up at Higashi Park. At any rate he was in a bad mood. But he couldn't pinpoint what was irritating him, which bothered him all the more.

He knew any number of girls he could call who'd sleep with him, but the desire he felt tonight was for something more violent, something fierce, like himself and a girl biting each other's skin, drawing blood. What he'd really wanted wasn't to sleep with a girl, but to punch out a guy. But it was too late; he couldn't go back to that night and undo what had happened.

After he'd been driving around the streets of Hakata for two hours, the liquor he'd drunk got to him and he had to urinate. At the end of the street was Higashi Park, and he figured there had to be a public restroom, so he parked his car there. There was a sprinkling of cars in the parking lot alongside the park. After the long drive he was no longer drunk.

He got out of his car and saw, at the end of the road, a young man standing there urinating. His dyed blond hair was visible in the streetlights. Keigo stepped over the low fence and went into the darkened park. He soon found the public restroom. He ran inside, and as he was peeing into the dirty urinal, his urine smelling of alcohol, he heard a strange snorting sound coming from one of the stalls. It gave him the creeps but he couldn't very well stop in the middle of peeing.

The door to the stall opened right then and he flinched, getting urine on his fingers. The guy coming out of the stall was the same age as he. The man cast him an ugly look. In a flash it came to him what kind of guy this was, and Keigo, the liquor helping, him along, called out to the man as he was leaving, "How 'bout sucking me off?" He laughed, and the man came to a halt and laughed, too. "How 'bout *you* suck *me*?"

This enraged Keigo for an instant, but the piss was still coming out hard and he couldn't make a move to hit the guy. He finally finished peeing and ran out in pursuit. The scattered streetlights made the park seem even gloomier. Keigo gazed around, checking the bushes and the walking path, but couldn't spot him.

Being made fun of by someone he'd made fun of—the frustration shot through him. His body should have shrunk back in the wintry wind, but it was filled with a blazing hot irritation. If he could only find the guy and pound him, this bitterness that had filled him all night would be blown away. If he could get hit back as hard as he hit the other guy, maybe even get a bloody nose, he could finally get rid of this pointless frustration.

But he never did locate the guy, so instead he clicked his tongue in anger and stepped over the fence around the park again. The asphalt road was lit up by the orange streetlight. And that's when he spied a woman walking toward him. The woman must have been meeting up with somebody, for she checked each car as she walked by.

Keigo straddled the fence and leaped out from the shrubbery. And at that instant one of the cars parked between him and the woman blew its horn. The horn pierced the air and echoed on the road along the park. Startled by the sound, the woman came to an abrupt halt. She recognized Keigo before he recognized her and he saw a smile spread on her partly shadowed face.

The woman quickly ran over to the car, the clatter of her boots on the road absorbed into the darkened interior of the park. Halfway to the car she shot a quick glance inside, but didn't slow down. Just as Keigo walked past the car he realized that this was that girl he'd met at a bar in Tenjin, the one who wouldn't leave him alone with all her e-mails.

"Keigo!" she called out.

Keigo lifted a desultory hand in greeting. He was concerned about the parked car, and when he glanced over he caught a vague glimpse of a young man's face in the dome light. He didn't get a good look at him, but from the hair color it looked like the guy who'd been peeing outside a few minutes ago.

Yoshino didn't call out to the guy in the car, who was obviously waiting for her, but trotted over to Keigo.

"What are you doing in a place like this?" she asked.

Even in the darkened street Keigo could see how beaming and happy Yoshino looked.

"I had to take a leak."

Yoshino looked about ready to hug him and he took a step back.

"What a coincidence. Our apartment building is just behind here," Yoshino volunteered, pointing to the dark park. "Did you come by car?" she asked, looking around.

"Uh, yeah," Keigo answered, concerned about the blond man in the parked car staring at them.

"Is it okay?" Keigo asked, motioning with his chin toward the car. As if suddenly remembering, Yoshino turned around and shook her head. She frowned and said, unenthusiastically, "Yeah. Don't worry about it."

"But weren't you meeting him?"

"Yeah, but don't worry about it."

"What do you mean, don't worry about it?" Keigo asked.

Yoshino, sounding resigned, said, "Just, ah—just wait a second," and scurried off toward the car.

Keigo certainly hadn't come here to see Yoshino, but he was taken aback by her cheery welcome and realized he couldn't very well just leave.

When Yoshino ran over to the car, the man's face in the overhead light visibly relaxed a bit. But she merely opened the passenger-side door, said a few words to him, then shut the door and came back over to Keigo.

She'd slammed the door so hard the sound reverberated through the street for a time.

"Sorry," Yoshino apologized. "He's a friend of a friend, someone I lent some money to." She looked annoyed.

"Don't you want him to give it back?"

"No, it's okay. I just asked him to transfer it to my account," Yoshino said lightly. Keigo glanced over at the car and saw the man still staring in their direction.

"Going back to the apartment?" Keigo asked.

She'd neglected the man she was supposed to meet up with, and come back to him, but this didn't seem to bother her. She stood there watching Keigo steadily, waiting for him to continue.

"Uh, yeah . . ." Yoshino answered.

Truthfully, Keigo found this type of girl hard to deal with. The kind who was waiting for something, but pretended not to be. Who made of show of not expecting anything but actually was expecting a lot.

If the car the man she had met up with had pulled away right then, Keigo would probably never have given her a ride. He wouldn't have found it hard to just say, "Well, I gotta go. Catch you later," and leave her there. But that other car just stayed put, the man's face—at once angry and sad—still faintly visible in the interior light. It didn't look like the man was going to get out of the car, and Yoshino showed no indication that she was going back to him.

"So your building's nearby?" Keigo said, breaking the silence, and for a second Yoshino was at a loss for an answer. Her smile could have been interpreted either way.

"Want a ride?"

Yoshino nodded happily. He pressed the key to unlock his car. When he opened the passenger door Yoshino crawled inside.

While they'd been outside talking in the cold wind, he hadn't noticed Yoshino's breath, but when she said, shivering, "It's nice and warm inside the car!" he realized she stank of garlic.

His feelings changed as soon as he got in the driver's seat. This girl would be a good outlet for all the irritation he'd been feeling all night.

"You have some time?" Keigo asked as he started the engine.

"Why d'you ask?" Yoshino said.

"You feel like going for a drive?"

"A drive? Where to?" She wasn't going to turn him down, but still she tilted her head as if she had her doubts.

"No place in particular. . . . How 'bout we test our courage and go to Mitsuse Pass?" Keigo teased, and stepped on the gas. In the rearview mirror he caught a glimpse of the blond man's white Skyline.

It's no big deal, she told herself, and her legs, which had been pedaling furiously, came to an abrupt halt. The Saga station, where she was supposed to meet Yuichi, was just across the street.

It's no big deal, Mitsuyo murmured to herself again. Seeing a guy she met online—no big deal. Everybody does it, and meeting him isn't going to change anything.

This morning she'd told Tamayo as she left for work, "I'll be a little late tonight." She realized now that ever since then she'd been telling herself, over and over, that this was nothing to get all worked up over.

She'd e-mailed Yuichi, promising to meet him. He'd asked her where would be a good place, and she'd answered back. He'd asked her what time would work for her, and she'd replied. Simple enough, but as soon as she put down her cell phone, she started to feel uneasy, wondering whether she was really going through with it. Making a date had been easy, but she'd never given any thought to how she really felt about it.

No way am I going through with this, Mitsuyo murmured. *I'm not that brave.*

Perhaps she wasn't, but she did think about what she should wear. And she did imagine the two of them meeting up at the station.

As morning dawned she couldn't see herself actually going on the date. Couldn't see herself going, yet she told Tamayo she'd be late. Couldn't see herself going, yet she changed her clothes and left the house. Wasn't brave enough to actually meet him, but now here she was standing right across from the station.

She must have been standing there for a while, for people rushing to the station passed her. Mitsuyo stepped to one side and sat back on a railing. A middle-aged woman behind her, thinking perhaps that she wasn't feeling well, shot her a sympathetic look. The sun was strong, so she didn't feel the cold. Just the railing digging painfully into her rear end.

It was already past eleven, the time they'd agreed to meet. From her perch on the railing, she could see the traffic circle in front of the station. People were going in and out of the station entrance but none were likely candidates. Just then a white car roared into the traffic circle. The car's tires squealed so loudly as it took the corner that Mitsuyo, some distance away, instinctively stood up. There was no doubt about it—this was the car whose photo Yuichi had shown her in an e-mail the night before. "I can't go through with this," Mitsuyo said softly. But despite her words, her right leg took a small step forward.

What do I do if he isn't happy with what he sees? If he's disappointed by me—what then? These thoughts in mind, she started walking.

"It's no big deal. Seeing a guy I met online is *no big deal*," she repeated, forcing her feet to move forward. She found it incredibly strange that she'd be approaching the car of some man she didn't know. She was surprised that she had this much courage.

The door of the white car opened just as Mitsuyo was about to enter the traffic circle. She stopped, and watched as a tall blond man came out. In the winter sunlight his hair looked several shades lighter than the pictures he'd sent her.

The man glanced in her direction, but soon looked back toward the entrance to the station. He shut the car door and leaped over the railing. Mitsuyo steadily watched this from behind one of the trees that lined the road. The man was younger than she'd thought. Thinner, too, and kinder looking. She was sure she would take it no further. She didn't think she'd find the courage no matter how hard she looked within herself.

The man disappeared inside the station for a moment, then emerged again, cell phone in hand. For an instant her eyes met his. She turned away and sat back down on the railing.

I'll count to thirty and if he hasn't come here by then I'll go home, she thought. He must have seen her face. She wanted him to make the next move. She was afraid that he'd be disappointed once he met her. But she also would hate to run away after coming this far and later regret it.

In the end, she counted to five but then the numbers wouldn't come. She didn't know how long she sat there, but as she stared at her feet a shadow fell over her legs.

"Hey . . ." a timid voice said from above her. She looked up and saw the man standing there in the sunlight filtering down through the leaves of the trees.

"My name is Shimizu. . . ."

Maybe it was the way he stood there, all shy. Maybe it was the way the winter sun shone on his skin. Or maybe it was the fearful look in his eyes. But in that instant something changed for her. She felt as if her life up to that point was now over. Something new was about to begin—she had no idea what—but Mitsuyo was sure of one thing. She was glad she had come.

Mitsuyo tensely smiled at him, and that tension seemed to infect Yuichi as he nervously looked around.

"You're going to get towed if you park there," she said, her first words to Yuichi, and Mitsuyo surprised herself at how calm she sounded.

"You're right." Rattled, Yuichi started to head back to the car but remembered Mitsuyo was there and came to an abrupt halt. His long limbs made his movements look exaggerated and Mitsuyo couldn't help but smile.

After he left the railing, Yuichi constantly glanced behind him, like someone worried that his child might not follow.

"Your hair looks blonder than in the photos," Mitsuyo called out to him.

Yuichi slowed down so he was walking beside her, and scratched his head. " 'Bout a year ago I was looking at myself in the mirror one night, and I suddenly wanted to change something," he mumbled. "Not to look fashionable or anything . . ."

"So you went with blond hair?"

"Couldn't think of anything else," he replied, looking serious.

They came up to the car and Yuichi opened the passenger door.

"I think I know how you feel," Mitsuyo said, and with no hesitation at all got in.

Yuichi walked around to the driver's side. *He must use some kind of air freshener in the car,* Mitsuyo thought, because there was a scent of roses. From the moment she climbed inside she could tell he took very good care of his car.

Yuichi settled into the driver's seat, quickly started the engine, and pulled away. She thought he was going to smash into the taxi in front of them, but he accelerated as if he was sure, down to a fraction of an inch, how much clearance he had. His car barely missed the cab. His fingers gripping the steering wheel looked as if he'd just finished fighting somebody. Not that Mitsuyo had ever seen somebody's hands right after a fight, but the long, knobby, gnarled fingers looked terribly beat up.

As the car moved halfway through the traffic circle, Mitsuyo saw the usual scene of the front of the station. Here she was, riding around in a car with a man she'd just met, yet she didn't feel at all uneasy. It was rather the scenery of the front of the station that looked cold and distant to her. After just a few minutes she trusted Yuichi's driving more than she trusted what she saw outside the window.

"I never imagined I'd be driving around with someone like you," Mitsuyo said as the car drove on, the words escaping her.

Yuichi shot her a glance. "Someone like me?" he asked, inclining his head.

"You know . . . a blond."

Yuichi scratched his head again.

The words had come out inadvertently, but nothing else could express the way she felt.

Cars with local license plates crawled down the road ahead of them, and Yuichi passed them one after another. He changed lanes smoothly, and every time he accelerated Mitsuyo was sucked back into the soft seat. Whenever she was in a taxi and the driver sped up, Mitsuyo tensed up, but strangely enough with Yuichi's driving she didn't feel nervous. His timing cut everything close when he changed lanes, but she was certain that, like opposite poles of magnets never touching, they'd never hit anything.

"You're really a good driver," she said as Yuichi swung around another car. "I have a license but I never really drive much."

"It's 'cause I drive all the time," Yuichi replied.

They were soon approaching the intersection with Highway 34. If they turned left they'd go past the menswear shop where Mitsuyo worked, go straight and they'd connect up with the Saga Yamato interchange on the interstate.

"So what are we doing?" Mitsuyo asked, not looking at Yuichi, as they stopped for a time at a red light. "Should we go straight to the Yobuko lighthouse? Or have lunch first around here?" It was strange how smoothly the words came out. She had no idea what kind of man this was sitting beside her, and was amazed at her own boldness.

Yuichi clutched the steering wheel hard. Mitsuyo looked at his fists and felt as if it were her body he was squeezing.

"How about we go to a hotel?" Yuichi said as he stared at his fists. For a second it didn't hit her what he was asking and she stared vacantly at him. "We can eat and go for a drive . . . after that," Yuichi muttered, his eyes down. He looked just like a child who knew he was going to get scolded but went ahead and begged for a toy anyway.

"What are you talking about?" Mitsuyo gave a quick laugh. Dumbfounded, she turned toward Yuichi and punched him on the shoulder.

Yuichi grabbed her hand. The light had changed and the car behind them blew its horn. He let go of her hand and slowly stepped on the gas.

That's not why I came here! I just wanted to see the lighthouse, she thought. She could think of a number of things to say, but in front of the silent, awkward Yuichi they all felt phony.

"Are you serious?" she replied, so tense her chest hurt, feeling as if the man beside her was already tugging her clothes off. She'd met this guy less than ten minutes ago and yet she was acting this bold. She felt as if she were watching herself from a distance.

Yuichi, eyes fixed forward, nodded. She waited for him to say something, some clever, enticing words, but nothing came.

It had been a long time since she'd seen such open sexual desire. The last time she met a man who'd wanted her this much was back when she worked in the factory and one of the men on the same line who'd been there longer suddenly grabbed her in the parking lot. Mitsuyo had been friendly with him, but still she had struggled and run away. It had all been too sudden; but at the same time, she'd been hoping that something like that would happen, and was afraid he'd find out. She didn't want to admit that that's who she was, a girl waiting for a man to make his sudden, aggressive move.

Almost ten years had passed since then, and she'd mentally replayed that incident over and over. That moment may have decided the kind of life she had now. She felt as if it had changed her into the type of woman who sought out fierce sexual desire from men.

"Going to a hotel is fine with me," Mitsuyo said calmly. Up ahead was a sign for the Saga Yamato interchange.

For some reason she pictured the apartment she shared with Tamayo—their comfortable, snug little place. But today the last thing she wanted was to go back there.

After their car passed the interchange, they headed over a highway overpass that tied all the rice fields below in a large bow and headed in the direction of Fukuoka. They must have been traveling fast, for the billboards and signs they passed sped by in shreds.

"There's a hotel just up ahead." As Yuichi murmured this, it hit Mitsuyo again: *Soon I'm going to have sex.*

Just then she spotted the sign for a love hotel, beyond the fallow fields. Mitsuyo turned to look at Yuichi. His hair wasn't all that thick, and there was a small mole on his chin.

"Do you always take girls to a hotel right away?" she asked, not really caring about the answer. Yuichi had invited her to a hotel as soon as he met her and she'd accepted. That was all that was certain at this moment. Between the two of them right now, that was all that mattered.

"I don't mind . . . if you always take girls to a hotel like this."

A narrow road, almost hidden behind the sign, led to the hotel. Their car slowed down. Potted plants lined the road, not a single one with any flowers. The road led directly to the half-underground parking lot. They hadn't passed any other cars on the way over from the interchange, but still the lot was nearly full.

They parked in the last space they could find. When Yuichi turned off the engine it was so silent they could hear each other swallow.

"It's pretty crowded, isn't it?" Mitsuyo said to break the silence. "Guess 'cause it's Saturday." As she said this she remembered last Saturday, and how a customer had complained because they'd made a mistake with the delivery date on some clothes that were being altered.

Yuichi had sped here without hesitating, but now that the car was stopped he didn't make a move. He just sat there, staring at the key in his hand.

"I hope they have a room open," Mitsuyo said, as casually as she could manage.

Yuichi, still looking down, muttered, "Yeah."

"It's kind of a strange feeling, since we just met and now look where we are."

Mitsuyo's voice sounded muffled in the closed car. The more she tried to convince herself that this was no big deal, the weaker her voice sounded.

"I'm sorry," Yuichi suddenly said in a low voice.

"Why are you apologizing?" Mitsuyo was taken aback. "There's no need to apologize," she said. "It's just that it was kind of sudden, so I was surprised. Women get those feelings, too, sometimes. And when they do, they want to hook up with somebody."

The words came out all of a sudden. She couldn't believe it was she saying this. Women want to have sex, too, she was saying, and when they want sex they go out looking for a guy. And she was telling this to a man she'd just met.

Yuichi stared right at her, his eyes seeming to want to say more. Mitsuyo felt herself blushing. It felt as if all her co-workers were eavesdropping. Not her present co-workers, but all her colleagues back at the factory, even her classmates from high school—all of them listening in and laughing at her.

"Anyway," she said, "let's go in and check it out. Who knows, it may be full."

Mitsuyo quickly opened the door and left the car, as if she were fleeing from the confines of the two of them inside together. As soon as she opened the door, the chilly air from the parking lot flowed in.

Once out of the car her body, warmed by the heater in the car, quickly grew cold. Yuichi got out right away and headed toward the entrance of the hotel.

Sex I can take or leave. I just want somebody to hold me. For years that's what I've been looking for. Somebody to hold me. Mitsuyo said this to herself as she stared at Yuichi's back. This is how I really feel, she wanted to tell him. I don't want just anybody to hold me. It's got to be someone who wants me and I want him to hold me tight.

A panel at the self-service check-in counter showed that two rooms were vacant. Yuichi chose the one named Firenze. He hesitated for a moment, then selected "Short Time" above the panel. Immediately the panel indicated the price, ¥4,800.

Mitsuyo was sick of the kind of life where all she did was look for ways to drown her loneliness.

They rode the elevator to the second floor, to the room right in front of them with the nameplate *Firenze*.

The lock was stuck and it took Yuichi several tries before he could get it open. As soon as the door opened, the bright colors of the room leaped out at them. Yellow walls, an orange bedspread, a domed ceiling with a pseudo fresco painted on it. Despite the bright colors, nothing about it looked fresh.

As Mitsuyo entered, she reached back and shut the door. The heater was on high and the air was stuffy and she felt as if she was going to start sweating.

Yuichi strode over to the bed and tossed the key on top of it. The key didn't bounce at all, but sank into the down comforter.

All they could hear was the heater. The room was less a silent place than one from which all other sounds had been sucked away.

"Kind of a gaudy room," Mitsuyo said to Yuichi, who was still facing away from her. Yuichi turned around and suddenly came over to her.

It all happened in a flash. Mitsuyo had been standing there, arms dangling at her sides, when Yuichi grabbed her and held her tight. His hot breath grazed the back of her neck, his stiff penis pushing against her stomach. Through their clothes, they could feel the other's heart beating. Mitsuyo wrapped her arms around his waist and pulled him closer. The tighter she held him the more she could feel his hard penis against her soft belly.

A room called Firenze, ¥4,800 for a short-time stay. A room in a love hotel that tried to have its own personality, but from which all sense of the personal had vanished.

"Promise you won't laugh," Mitsuyo murmured against Yuichi's chest. He started to draw away, but she clung to him so he wouldn't see her face.

"I'm going to tell you the truth, but you have to promise you won't laugh," Mitsuyo said. "I'm . . . I'm serious when I send out e-mails. Other people might just send them out to kill time . . . but I really wanted to meet somebody. This is sort of lame, huh? And kind of sad? . . . Go ahead and make fun of me. But don't *laugh* at me, okay? If you do, I don't know what I'll . . ."

Yuichi was still holding on to her. She knew it was kind of a rash thing to say, but she felt she had to say it now or she'd never ever say it to anyone.

"Me, too," Yuichi said. "I . . . was serious, too, about the e-mails."

Mitsuyo, cheek pressed against him, heard his voice through his chest.

Water dripped in the bathroom, splashing against the tiles. It must have collected in the faucet and then gushed out. That was the only other sound she heard, besides the beating of his heart as she pressed her face up against him.

Yuichi suddenly moved and crushed his mouth on hers. A rough, hard kiss, his dry lips scraping her. He sucked at her lips, stuck his tongue inside her mouth. Clinging to his shirt, she held his tongue in her mouth. That burning hot tongue felt as if it were wrapped around her whole body.

She felt weak in the knees. Yuichi moved his tongue from her mouth to her ear, his hot breath reaching deep inside and exciting her.

He roughly pulled off her shirt, then her bra, and standing there she let him kiss her breasts. In front of her was the cheap love hotel bed, and she pictured herself sinking down, half naked, onto the down comforter.

He was rough, except for the gentle fingers that stroked her behind. Her body wanted it even rougher. Was she the violent one, or Yuichi? She couldn't tell. It was as if she was simply manipulating Yuichi, using him to roughly, violently caress herself.

She was naked now, in front of this man. Under the too-bright fluorescent lights, she felt him stroke her thighs, grab her butt, and Mitsuyo felt that any minute now she would cry out.

Yuichi lightly lifted her up and carried her over to the bed. He almost tossed her on top of the comforter, then tore off his shirt and T-shirt. Yuichi's hard chest crushed her breasts. Every time he moved, Mitsuyo's nipples slipped across his skin.

Before she knew it she was lying facedown on the bed, sunk deep in the comforter, as if she were floating on air. Yuichi's hot tongue traced a line down her spine. He stuck his knees between her legs and no matter how much she resisted, her legs opened wide.

She buried her face in the pillow, which smelled of detergent. All the strength drained away from her. Yuichi caressed her roughly, almost as if he were trying to break her. At the same time, he held on to her tightly, as if to repair the damage.

He destroyed her, repaired her, and repeated the process. Mitsuyo no longer knew if she'd gotten destroyed, or if she'd been destroyed from the very beginning. If it was Yuichi doing the breaking, she wanted him to break her even more violently. If her body was broken from the beginning, she wanted his gentle hands to restore her.

"I don't need to see him ever again. Just this one time. This is just for today," she murmured as he caressed her. She didn't really feel this way, but she had to tell herself this, or else she couldn't accept this shameless self, the one she'd never really seen before, the one writhing in ecstasy on the bed.

She heard the metallic sound as Yuichi undid his belt. She had no idea how long she'd been like this on the bed, but it seemed as if Yuichi had been caressing her for a long time. Fifteen minutes? Thirty minutes? No, it felt more like he'd been stroking her with his fingers, his hot body crushing her, for a whole night—or was it two?

She felt her body grow lighter. The bed creaked and the vibration made her head fall off the pillow. She opened her eyes and saw Yuichi standing there, naked.

She hadn't been crying, but she saw Yuichi's penis through a kind of haze. All the strength drained out of her; even moving her fingers seemed like too much trouble. He was gazing down at her totally nude body from above, but she felt no embarrassment at all. One of Yuichi's knees came up beside her face. The mattress sank down and her face rolled over toward him. He cupped his large palm behind her head to support it, and Mitsuyo closed her eyes and opened her mouth.

Yuichi's hand supporting her head was gentle, but the penis jabbing deep inside her mouth was brutal and relentless. Again she didn't know if she was being treated gently, or roughly. Was she suffering? Or happy? As she clutched at the sheets over and over, she had no idea. She knew she must look like a total slut. And she detested Yuichi—and loved him—for forcing her to lick him like this.

She reached around and grabbed his butt. Her nails dug into his sweaty behind. Trying his best to stand the pain, Yuichi cried out. And Mitsuyo wanted to hear that voice more.

I really do want Mitsuyo to be happy.

I never call her *onesan*—older sister. But still inside me I feel like I might be calling her that.

We have a younger brother, and he calls her *onesan*. It's weird to say he does it in my stead, but that's what it feels like. Me he just calls Tamayo.

People often say twins know what the other one is thinking. But Mitsuyo and I were never like that. Don't get me wrong, we got along okay, and stood out in school, being twins and all. So when we were in elementary school we were always together, and tried to protect each other from our classmates' curious eyes. Yeah—I think we did sort of stand out in elementary school. But once we entered junior high, another set of twins from a nearby elementary school came to the same school and they were ten times cuter than us. Kids can be really cruel, and it wasn't long before we were being called the ugly twins. That didn't bother me too much—if a boy said that, I'd chase him and hit him with a broom or something. About this time our personalities, you might say, the overall impression you got from us—hairstyle, clothes, interests—slowly started to be different from each other. . . .

We weren't planning to go to the same high school. I wanted to go to a regular co-ed school, while Mitsuyo applied to a private girls' high school, but she failed the entrance exam.

Anyway, soon after we started high school, we found boyfriends.

Mine was typical—the star of the soccer team—but Mitsuyo went out with this guy named Ozawa who was not exactly a negative kind of guy, but he never seemed to be able to do anything well, neither school nor sports. He gave up on the volleyball team after only a month.

If Ozawa paid a bit more attention to his hairstyle and clothes he might have looked okay, but he had zero interest in that kind of thing. Not that he had any particular interest in anything else . . . Anyhow, when Mitsuyo said something about how she liked Ozawa I went like, Whoa! What's with that? It was then, I guess, that I realized that Mitsuyo and I are two different people.

Since my boyfriend was the star of the soccer team, I had a lot of rivals for his attention, and sometimes things didn't go so well. Mitsuyo and Ozawa, who didn't have any competitors to deal with, got along better than me and my guy. They always walked home together, pushing their bikes side by side. Most every evening she'd stop by Ozawa's house, but she'd be sure to be home by six-thirty, in time for dinner.

Even twins who get along well have things they can't ask each other. School ended around four o'clock every day, and it took twenty minutes to walk to Ozawa's house, so even if she rode her bike back home afterward, it means that they were alone, just the two of them, for about two hours and fifteen minutes every day. Rumors started about them at school and people starting asking me, not her, whether she and Ozawa had done it. As her younger sister I felt, intuitively, that she and Ozawa had, you know. I wanted to know for sure, but I couldn't ask her straight out.

I remember it was just after the end of summer vacation. Mitsuyo was at Ozawa's as usual, and my cheerleading squad's practice was canceled that day so I went home early. We were sharing the same room and I'd never done a thing like that before, but something possessed me, I guess, and I opened Mitsuyo's desk drawer and looked at the notebook Mitsuyo and Ozawa used to exchange notes. I was sure it would be totally boring. I was a little worried what I'd do if there was bad stuff written in there about me, but that's about it.

I flipped through it and was surprised to find every page filled with tiny writing.

I read through it, nervous that Mitsuyo might come home. As I read, I felt a shiver up my spine. . . . Basically she said something like this:

"I've always liked you, Ozawa-kun. But recently I've started to like certain parts of you—your right arm, for instance, your ears, or your fingers, your knees, your front teeth, your breath. ☺ Not the whole of you, but parts that make up you. I don't want anybody to take them away from me. At school and other places, I don't want anybody else to see you. ☺."

I had always thought that Mitsuyo wasn't the type to get attached to things. When we were little, she always gave me and our brother all of her candy or cakes. I guess that comes from being the oldest daughter. But in this diary that she and Ozawa exchanged, this was a Mitsuyo I'd never seen before.

Here are some other quotes: "Today Onotera from No. 2 class was talking to you about something, right? I found it funny how annoyed you looked." "I can't wait to graduate and live with you! We can live together, right? You know, that apartment we saw from the outside the other day looked really nice. You could park a car right outside when you buy one, and once we have kids they can play in the garden." It sounded different from the usual Mitsuyo, more aggressive.

As I read more, I was thinking how Ozawa must find it kind of annoying. I got frightened and quickly stashed the notebook back in the drawer.

I'd always thought of Mitsuyo as an unselfish, disinterested person. But here I discovered a side I'd never seen before, her karma or something. Her hidden greed, I guess, and it made me feel sad, or sorry for her.

Anyhow, Mitsuyo and Ozawa broke up before they graduated from high school. Rumor had it that he started to like another girl who attended the after-school college prep course he was in. Mitsuyo never said a thing to me about it. And I never dared ask. . . . I don't remember her getting all upset or crying when they broke up.

Maybe she did cry, but off by herself. . . . Anyway, it was all a long time ago.

After we graduated from high school, there were really only two guys she went out with. Neither relationship lasted very long. Mitsuyo isn't the type, like me, to play around with guys much. Sometimes I've wished she were a bit more outgoing. We're living together now, but deep down I think sometimes I'm doing this all for her sake, not mine. Like if I got married, she'd be alone the rest of her life.

I really like my sister. She's sort of introverted, but I do want her to be happy.

I don't remember when it was, exactly, but I was on a bus and just happened to glance out and see Mitsuyo pedaling her bike with this very happy expression on her face. Now that I think about it, this was just about the time she started exchanging e-mails with Yuichi Shimizu.

Body temperature has a smell to it, Mitsuyo found. Just like smells can mix together, so can body temperatures.

When the phone rang signaling that their time was up, Yuichi was still on top of Mitsuyo. The thermostat was set too high in the love hotel and their bodies were glowing with a sheen of sweat. Yuichi had beautiful skin. His beautiful skin was covered with sweat as it penetrated Mitsuyo's body.

Worried about the phone, Yuichi stopped moving for a moment and Mitsuyo called out, "Don't stop!"

So he ignored the phone. A few minutes later there was a knock on the door, but until then he continued to penetrate her.

"Okay, okay! We're leaving!" Yuichi growled. As soon as he yelled out, he penetrated even deeper inside Mitsuyo and she bit her lip.

Fifteen minutes had passed since Yuichi said they'd be out soon. Holding his sweaty body under the blanket, Mitsuyo laughed, "Aren't you hungry?"

His response, as he lay there panting, was to kick off the blanket.

"There's a really good grilled-eel place nearby," Mitsuyo said.

The blanket fell to the floor and the two of them, naked and cling-ing to each other, were reflected in the mirror next to them. Yuichi was the first to get up, the vertebrae of his back clearly reflected in the mirror.

"It's an authentic eel place, they have grilled eel without sauce and everything."

As Yuichi started to get out of bed, Mitsuyo grabbed his hand and pulled at it. "You want to go there?" she asked. Yuichi twisted around and looked at her for a while, and finally gave a small nod.

Mitsuyo got out of bed and headed for the bathroom. "We don't have time for that," she heard Yuichi caution her.

"We're already over the time limit and will have to pay extra," she said.

It was a cute little bathroom with yellow tiles. *I wish they had a window,* Mitsuyo mused. She could picture a window and outside that a small garden, and Yuichi washing his car.

"After we have eel you better take me to the lighthouse!" Mitsuyo called out. There was no reply, but she went ahead and enjoyed a hot shower. It wasn't even two o'clock yet. When she thought of the long weekend ahead, the hot water splashing on her seemed like it was singing and dancing for joy.

"If we don't have time, why don't we take a shower together?" Mit-suyo shouted out to Yuichi over the sound of the water.

"Is Yuichi Shimizu your real name?"

Staring straight ahead, Yuichi nodded.

They'd left the love hotel and were in the car heading toward the eel restaurant. Mitsuyo was still warm from the shower.

"Well, then I have to apologize. My name is Mitsuyo Magome. I was using Shiori because—"

"It's okay," Yuichi interrupted her. "Everyone uses fake names at first."

"Everyone? You mean you've met that many girls like this?"

The road was empty of other cars and they didn't get stopped by traffic lights. Every time they approached a traffic light it turned green.

"Well, that's okay."

Since Yuichi didn't respond, Mitsuyo withdrew her question.

"This is the same road I used to use to go to high school," Mitsuyo said as she gazed at the passing scenery.

"See that sign for the discount shoe place over there? If you turn there and go straight, there's our high school, in the middle of a bunch of fields. And if you go back on this road toward the station there's my old elementary and junior high schools. . . . And a bit further down this road toward Tosu is where I used to work. . . . I guess I've never really left this road, have I. . . . All I've done is go back and forth along this one road all my life. . . . That place I used to work at was a factory for food products. All the other girls my age said it was monotonous work and they hated it, but I didn't mind that kind of production-line work."

Their car was stopped at a rare red light and Yuichi, stroking the steering wheel, turned toward Mitsuyo.

"It's the same with me," he murmured. Mitsuyo inclined her head, at first not knowing what he was talking about, and he went on. "I've always stayed close to home. All the schools I went to— elementary, junior, and senior high—are all just down the road from my house."

"But you live near the sea, right? I envy you. I mean, look where I live."

The light changed and Yuichi slowly accelerated. Mitsuyo's hometown, a dreary succession of stores along the road, flowed by.

"Oh, there it is! You see the eel-shaped sign? It really is good, and pretty cheap, too."

She was starving. She hadn't felt this hungry in ages.

During the morning Keigo Masuo slipped out of the sauna, trying not to be noticed.

He'd wanted to sleep in the nap room until past noon, but as the number of visitors declined, he was afraid the staff might start to notice him. He couldn't believe that a "Wanted" flyer with his photo on it had made its way all the way to this sauna in Nagoya, but still, when he'd gotten the locker key from the guy at the front desk a while ago, he could swear the man gave him a strange look.

Numb from lack of sleep, Keigo came out onto the street, and the combination of the bright winter sky and the fact that he'd been in a darkened room hit him, and he stood there for a moment, dizzy in the light.

He headed off in the direction of Nagoya Station, checking how much he had in his wallet. He'd withdrawn five hundred thousand yen when he left Fukuoka, so he should still be all right, but he couldn't very well use his ATM card where he'd run to, so the cash he had on hand was his last resort.

It was sunny, but the wind was cold. The cold wind lashing the rows of skyscrapers around the station chilled him. The collar of his down jacket was clammy with sweat and grime. He'd bought new underwear and socks at a convenience store, but didn't want to spend all his money on a new jacket.

As he came to the traffic circle in front of the station, Keigo took shelter from the wind behind a direction billboard. In front of him, crowds of people were streaming up from the underground shopping mall into the station.

Yesterday he'd read through a few of the newspapers at the sauna but didn't find any reports of the murder. The talk shows had spent so much time covering it, but now they'd moved on to covering another murder that had taken place a few days ago: a housewife who'd grown exhausted taking care of her sick father-in-law had killed him. Not a single word about the murder at Mitsuse Pass.

Behind the direction billboard Keigo lit a cigarette. He took a puff and suddenly realized how hungry he was. He stamped out the cigarette and went down to the underground mall. Keigo walked down one step at a time, weaving his way through the hordes of people

ascending the stairs toward the station. With each step, two thoughts
came to him: *At this rate I'll never be able to escape. But I just don't
get it.*

He'd never felt like he wanted to kill that girl. He'd never even
wanted to have anything to do with her. But there was no doubt
about it—he was the one who'd driven her to that freezing pass, and
he was the one who had left her there.

As soon as Yoshino Ishibashi had climbed into his car on the street
along Higashi Park, Keigo had started driving. He'd said they could
go to test their courage at Mitsuse Pass, but soon after he started out
he regretted it. Especially when Yoshino began talking about the
friends she'd had dinner with.

"Those girls I was with when we met in that bar in Tenjin? You
remember them, right?"

It appeared that Yoshino was silently agreeing to go for a drive with
him, because she snapped on her seat belt.

"I don't know." Keigo shrugged, hoping to cut short the conversation, but she went on blabbing away.

"You remember. There were three of us? One was Sari? She's tall
and has a sort of stern-looking face. . . ."

Keigo just drove around, speeding through intersections to beat
the light. Before long they'd left Higashi Park far behind and the
overpass for the city highway loomed above.

"Are you taking off from school tomorrow?" Yoshino asked.

Yoshino had, without asking, adjusted the car heater, and now was
trying to open his CD case at her feet.

"Why are you asking?" He didn't want to keep the conversation
going and didn't want her rummaging around in his CDs without
permission.

"I was just thinking if we go for a drive now, it'll be pretty late
when we get back. . . ." Yoshino placed the CD case on her lap, but
didn't open it.

"How 'bout you?" Keigo said, motioning with his chin.

Things had just happened, and here she was riding with him, but
Keigo was irritated at himself for driving around aimlessly.

"Me? I have to go to work. But if I call in and tell them I'm going directly to see a client, then it doesn't matter if I'm late."

"What kind of job do you do?" Keigo asked without thinking, and Yoshino gave him a playful rap on the shoulder.

"I don't believe it," she said coquettishly. "I told you already— I work at an insurance company."

Something must have made Yoshino happy, for she giggled. Keigo waited patiently for the laughter to subside and then said, coldly, "Something smells like garlic. Do you smell it?"

Yoshino's expression froze and she clammed up.

Without a word, Keigo opened the passenger-side window. The cold wind blew Yoshino's hair around. The garlic smell flowed out of the car, quickly replaced by chilly air swirling up around their legs.

The car had left the main shopping district behind without being stopped at a single red light, a rare feat.

Keigo thought Yoshino might not speak after being ridiculed like that, but she took a stick of peppermint gum out of her handbag and explained, "I had *teppan gyoza* for dinner."

With the Christmas season in full swing, the trees along Tenjin were lit up, the sidewalks filled with couples strolling along arm in arm. Keigo stepped on the gas and blew past them.

"Sari and Mako seem to think that you and I are going out. I told them we aren't, but they wouldn't buy it." Yoshino babbled on and on, chewing the gum with her back teeth. No matter how roughly Keigo swerved to change lanes or how much he slammed on the brakes, she wouldn't stop talking.

"We're not going out . . ." Keigo said coldly. *Who the hell would ever go out with you?* he said to himself.

"Keigo, what kind of girl do you like?"

"None in particular."

"Isn't there a type you like?"

To avoid answering, he sharply swerved and wound up on Route 263, the one that leads to Mitsuse Pass.

"You know, when I was taking a leak back there at the park, a gay guy tried to put the moves on me," Keigo said, changing the subject.

"Are you serious? What'd you do?"

"I shouted, *I'm gonna kill you!* and he ran away. I wish they'd keep them out of places like that," Keigo vented, but Yoshino didn't seem particularly interested.

"Yeah," she said, "but regular places are closed to them, right? So that's the only place they can go. Don't you feel a little sorry for them? I mean, there're all kinds of people in the world." She popped another stick of gum in her mouth.

Keigo had just been trying to change the subject and hadn't expected her to argue with him. He didn't know how to respond.

They'd left the showy shopping district behind and the road grew more deserted, but still the streetlights were strung with banners announcing Christmas sales. A pathetic scene, drained of all color and life.

Yoshino was silent until she spit out the gum and wrapped it in a tissue. She didn't tell him she wanted to go back. He kept missing opportunities to pull off, and so they continued south along Route 263 toward the pass.

Up until they started to climb to the pass, they saw hardly any other cars coming in the opposite direction. In the rearview mirror Keigo occasionally caught a glimpse of the light of a car far behind them, but no cars ahead. Their headlights palely lit up the cold asphalt of the road over the mountain pass. Every time they rounded a curve their lights shone on the woods and the complex patterns of the bark on the trunks.

Yoshino continued to chatter, but Keigo ignored her and focused on his driving. Yoshino had pulled a CD out of the case without asking—"Oh, I love this song!" she'd said—and played a sugary ballad over and over.

As she was hitting the repeat button for the umpteenth time Keigo suddenly was struck by a thought: *This is the kind of girl who's going to get murdered by a guy someday.* *What* kind of girl he meant he couldn't say, exactly. But he was convinced that she was the sort of girl who could enrage a man so much he'd strike her down.

As Keigo maneuvered around the increasingly sharp curves, he thought about this girl beside him, happily humming along to the insipid ballad, and what the future held for her.

She'd work as an insurance saleswoman, save up a tidy sum of money, enjoy her days off, gazing at herself in the mirror of some brand-name stores. *Who I really am . . . Who I really am . . .* would become her pet phrase, but after working for three years, she'd finally realize that the image she'd created of herself wasn't who she really was at all. She'd give up on carving out a life on her own, and somehow find a man and pour all her problems out on him. Which would only put the man in a bind. *What are you going to do with my life, now that you've ruined it?* This would become her new pet phrase, and her hopes for her children would swell in inverse proportion to her frustration with her husband. She'd compete with the other mothers at the park, eventually forming a neat little clique that would gossip and bad-mouth others. She wouldn't realize it, but as her little clique grew tighter, she'd bad-mouth those outside her group exactly the way she did back in junior high, high school, and junior college.

"So how far are we gonna drive?"

"Hm?" Keigo said curtly to this sudden question. The ballad had finally ended, replaced by a strangely cheerful tune.

"Are you really going over the pass? There's nothing beyond here. During the day there's a good curry shop, and a bakery, but not this time of night. . . . Oh, you know that noodle place we passed? It's closed now, but have you ever been there? It's supposed to be really good. One of my friends said so. . . . What's the matter? How come you're so quiet?"

The words spilled out of her, as if in time to the cheerful music. *She really does think we're on a date,* Keigo thought.

"Your family runs a really nice inn in Yufuin, right? And a big hotel in Beppu? So your mother must be the mistress of the places, huh? I bet that's a lot of responsibility."

"Yeah, my mother is the mistress of the place, but that's nothing for you to worry about," Keigo said. He surprised himself at how cold his voice was. Yoshino looked puzzled.

"The two of you are different types."

"Huh?" Yoshino asked, still confused.

"My mother and you are different types of people. You're more the maid type, don't you think? If you were working in our inn, I mean."

Keigo suddenly slammed on the brakes. Yoshino pitched forward.

When he'd spied the entrance to the tunnel, Keigo had instinctively turned off onto the older mountain road. Now they were almost at the summit of the pass.

"I want you to get out. I can't stand having you in my car anymore."

Keigo stared right into her eyes, but Yoshino was still stunned and his words didn't register.

The upbeat song played on. *Your love makes me strong*, the lousy singer belted out, in a voice as appealing as fingernails scraping across glass.

"I want you to get out," Keigo repeated, his voice flat, face expressionless.

"What are you talking about?"

In the dark car Yoshino's eyes went wide. She tried to smile, hoping against hope that this was Keigo's idea of testing her courage.

"You're kind of a slut, you know that?"

"*What?*"

"How can you just jump into a guy's car like this, without even thinking? Somebody you don't even know? Most girls would refuse. The kind of girl who leaps at an invitation to go for a drive in the middle of the night isn't my type. So just get out. Or do I have to kick you out?"

Keigo pushed her. She finally seemed to understand that this was no joke.

"But . . . if I get out here . . ."

"If you stand over there, somebody will stop and give you a ride. You'll ride with anyone, right?"

Unsure what she should do, Yoshino clutched her handbag in her lap.

Ignoring her, Keigo reached over her and opened the passenger-side door. He gave it too hard a shove, and it swung open and banged against the guardrail. He could smell the cold soil outside, and the freezing mountains beyond.

"Get out!" Keigo commanded, giving Yoshino's thin shoulder a shove.

Yoshino twisted aside, and his hand slipped off her shoulder and dug into her neck.

"Stop it!"

"I mean it! Get out!"

Keigo kept on pushing her resisting body, almost as if strangling her. He felt the warmth of her skin, which only made him more irritated. His thumb dug deep into her neck.

"All right! I get it," Yoshino said, and unfastened her seat belt. Perhaps out of fear, her voice sounded strangely defiant. Keigo lifted one leg from under the steering wheel and, muttering, kicked Yoshino hard in the back.

"Ow!" Yoshino fell out and hit her head on the guardrail. The clang rang out, echoing down the guardrail and out into the pass.

To me, the name Mia fits her more than Yoshino Ishibashi. So is it okay if I call her that? Mia-chan?

I teach elementary school kids at an after-hours *juku*, so I'm used to hearing names like that that don't sound exactly Japanese, the kind of names that are trendy now. In the class I teach, there's a boy named Raymond, and girls named Sheru and Tiara. It's enough to make a teacher pull out his hair.

As I've told you a couple of times already, I don't have any interest in little kids. I just happen to be a *juku* teacher. . . .

But anyhow, kids' names these days sound kind of, you know, like the fake names girls use on dating Web sites. It's like there's an imbalance between the person and his name, and I remember when I first took roll call I felt sorry for them. They talk about gender-identity disorder, right? Pretty soon I think we're going to see people with *name-identity* disorder.

So what I was saying was, other than Mia-chan I must have met about ten other girls on online dating sites. Mia-chan would have been the second, or maybe the third one I met. Her face and body weren't exactly my type, but when I think about it, now I can see she was a kind, gentle sort of girl. When she showed up for our date and immediately asked me to reimburse her for the taxi it did upset me a little, I'll admit it, but still there was something, I don't know, sort of kind about her.

I mean, take a look at me. I'm fat and hairy, and look like a bulldog. No way I'm going to be popular with the ladies, and I'm not. But even a guy like me, if a girl says one nice thing it makes me feel like I'm not completely hopeless. Mia-chan was good at making a guy feel like that. But I could be wrong.

We were in the hotel, just after we'd done it, and I was about to pay her. All of a sudden she goes, "I wonder if we hadn't met in the dating site if we would have hooked up."

"You never would have given me the time of day," I said, laughing, but Mia-chan, with this sort of sad look on her face, said, "I wonder. There is the age-difference thing, but when I was in junior high, I really liked my biology teacher and he was kind of chubby, too."

Yeah, I know it was just an empty compliment. I was handing over the money to her, and threw in an extra two thousand yen. But Mia-chan seemed like she really meant it. She had this look on her face like, *Yeah, maybe if we had just run across each other on the street, we might have gotten together.*

Men are idiots and we never forget words like that. Oh, well, guys who are popular would forget it right away, but for someone like me who has worried about how to talk to girls ever since college, even a transparent, empty compliment stays with you. It gives you more confidence. This was a long time ago, but back when I was in college one of the older girls in the tennis club I was in said, "Hayashi-kun, you understand people right away. When I'm with you, I feel like you see right through me." It's weird, but after that I came to rely on what she said. Whenever I wondered what kind of man I was, I always remembered what that girl told me. . . . She told me later she had no memory of ever having said that, but to me these were truly important words. It might be a bit of an exaggeration, but over the past twenty years those words have helped keep me going as a man.

You must think this is pretty stupid, right? That I'm a real loser. But a guy like me needs a woman like that. It doesn't matter if it's just transparent flattery. Without that, I'd be left with nothing.

Mia-chan was the kind of girl who said those things. Maybe not consciously, but she's the sort of girl who might say something that a guy like me would cling to for twenty years.

When I heard that she'd been murdered, it made me sad. She's just a girl I met online and saw only once, but I'll never forget her. "The guys I respect the most," she told me when I took her to an Italian restaurant, "are the ones who know good food."

After he'd finished breakfast on Saturday, Yuichi went out without telling anyone where he was going. Fusae thought he was going out for a drive as usual and would be back for dinner, so she made meatballs, one of his favorites. But Yuichi never came back, so she went ahead and ate the slightly too sweet meatballs herself.

On Sunday morning he still hadn't come home. Yuichi often went out, aimlessly, on weekends and spent the night away, but for Fusae, being alone in the house only brought back unpleasant memories. Memories of Dr. Tsutsumishita—the man who held those health seminars at the community center—and being surrounded by rough young men who'd forced her to buy that expensive herbal medicine. It was such a frightening experience that she remained upset and shaky.

In the afternoon she called Yuichi's cell phone. He picked up right away.

"What d'you want?" he said, like he couldn't be bothered.

"Where are you?" Fusae asked.

"Saga."

"What are you doing in Saga?"

Fusae had expected that he would be driving and would hang up right away, but when he didn't she asked him this.

Yuichi didn't respond. "What d'you want?" he repeated.

Fusae asked him when he would be back. Again Yuichi evaded her question, merely saying, "I won't be needing dinner," and hung up.

After this, Fusae went to the hospital in Nagasaki to see Katsuji. She listened to his usual complaints about the nurses for a good half hour, then she thanked the nurses and left.

In the bus on the way back the voices of those men forcing her to buy the herbal medicine came back to her in a rush.

"What d'you mean you're not going to buy the medicine!"

"Just who the hell do you think you're dealing with, old woman?"

"I don't care if you don't sign, we're still gonna come to your place every single day!"

The men's voices pulled her back to that place and time, and seated on the special Silver Seat reserved for the elderly in the bus, she began to shake uncontrollably.

Yuichi finally came back home after eleven that night. As she heard the front door open, Fusae, in bed, felt relieved and called out, "I'm glad you're back! You want to take a bath?" she went on. She hesitated to get up out of bed, which was just getting warm.

"Nah, I already took one," she heard Yuichi say from beyond the sliding paper door.

Fusae eventually left her bedroom and followed after Yuichi into the kitchen. Her bare feet on the hallway floor were ice cold. Yuichi had taken some sausages out of the refrigerator.

"You must be hungry," Fusae said.

"Not really," Yuichi said, but he ripped open the plastic package with his teeth and crammed a sausage into his mouth.

"You want me to make something?"

"No. I already had dinner."

Fusae called out to Yuichi as he was exiting the kitchen.

"What?" Yuichi said, annoyed, as he continued to gnaw on the sausage.

Fusae felt oppressed by the look on his face and she sank limply to a chair. She hadn't planned to tell him, but the words just spurted out.

"The other day on the way back from the hospital . . . You remember the man who held the seminar at the community center? . . . The one about herbal medicine?"

This was her own house, and this was Yuichi with her, so she was safe, but still she was on edge, as if she would start shaking again at any moment. Just putting that experience into words frightened her. She had to force herself to breathe.

But just as she was going to continue, the cell phone in Yuichi's pocket rang. Without a word to her, Yuichi answered.

"Hello? . . . Ah, yeah. Yeah, I just got back. . . . Tomorrow? . . . I have to get up at five, but it's okay. . . . Yeah, me, too."

As he turned the doorknob, Yuichi looked happy.

"Yeah, okay. I'll call you tomorrow. . . . Huh? . . . Yeah, I know. Okay, then. . . . What? I told you it's okay. . . ."

Fusae sat there eavesdropping. Just when the conversation seemed about over, it started up again. Yuichi took his hand off the doorknob, ran his fingers along the pillar, and turned over a page on the calendar that was pasted to the wall.

It had to be a girl on the other end, probably the person he spent the weekend with. Fusae had never seen Yuichi look so happy. Well, maybe he was happy at other times, but secretly, somewhere Fusae was unaware of. In the twenty years since she'd taken Yuichi in, she'd never seen him with such a look of utter bliss.

CHAPTER 4

WHO DID HE HAPPEN TO MEET?

Toward evening several groups of customers came in all at once. Mitsuyo took care of two men in their midtwenties. As they pawed through the racks of suits, their banter was like a comedy routine; from what Mitsuyo heard, she gathered that the shorter of the two had just had a successful interview for a new job and had dragged his friend along with him.

"I've always worn work clothes, so I'm kind of lost when it comes to choosing a suit."

"Yeah, but usually when guys buy suits they bring their wives along."

"Don't be an idiot. If I bring her with me, she's going to choose the cheapest possible outfit, from the suit to the shirts and ties."

"So what? You're planning to buy the top-of-the-line brand?"

"No, not really. Just something in the middle, you know?"

They went on, grabbing one suit after another from the rack and holding it up to see how it looked.

"They're so young looking," Mitsuyo mused, "but already married." She kept her distance, patiently waiting for them to ask her something.

The floor manager, Kazuko, stood over by the fitting room, tape measure around her neck. She'd just finished a break and Mitsuyo had asked her if she had a little free time tonight. "Maybe we could go out for a drink," she said.

Kazuko tilted her head at the unexpected invitation, then replied, "That shouldn't be a problem. My husband's going to be a little late tonight. But where should we go? How about that new *kaiten sushi* place next to the new bar, the Bikkuri?" Kazuko seemed unusually up for the idea.

Once they decided on a place, Mitsuyo was about to go back to her station, but Kazuko grabbed her hand. "You took last Saturday off," she said with a grin, "so I was kind of wondering what was up. . . . Any good news?"

"No, nothing really," Mitsuyo said. "I just thought we hadn't gone out for dinner in a long time." She managed to get away, but couldn't keep from smiling.

After leaving the love hotel on Saturday, she ended up spending the whole day with Yuichi. They'd eaten eel, and were planning to go to the lighthouse, but as they left the restaurant it started pouring so they gave up and went to another hotel.

On Sunday evening Yuichi drove her back to her apartment and they had one long last kiss in the car. That was two days ago, and Monday evening they'd talked for three hours on the phone. Tamayo had come back from work while they were still on the phone, so the last thirty minutes Mitsuyo sat on the staircase outside in the freezing wind.

Less than a day had passed since then, but she was dying to hear his voice again.

She looked up and noticed that the two-man comedy team was rummaging through the rack along the wall. The suits on this rack were three thousand yen more than the others and no extra trousers were included.

"Oh, I went to see that new movie *Fishing Nut*—the comedy," one of the men said.

"By yourself?"

"No way. I took my son."

"To that kind of movie?"

"Kids like them."

"Are you kidding? The only kind my little one's interested in are the anime specials."

Though in their midtwenties, they acted more like college buddies. But here they were talking about their kids and picking out suits.

Mitsuyo watched them, amused. The men may have sensed her presence, for the shorter one turned to her and said, "Excuse me. Could I try this one on?"

His friend grabbed it away and teased him. "You gonna go with this one? Kind of looks like a host in a bar or something."

The first guy, who seemed more easygoing, said, "You think?" and gave the suit another look.

"Why don't you try it on?" Mitsuyo smiled. "It does have a certain shine to the fabric, but if you wear a white shirt with it it'll look more subdued."

Her advice seemed to give the man confidence again, and he strode over to the fitting room. His friend, like someone not really in the market for a suit, casually flipped through the price tags.

The suit was a perfect fit. Mitsuyo handed him a white shirt to see how it would look, and the combination went well, strangely enough, with his baby face.

"How do you like it?" she asked as the man turned from side to side, checking himself out in the mirror. His friend had sidled over and said, "You're right. It really doesn't look all that gaudy." In the cramped changing room the man nodded in the mirror to Mitsuyo and his friend.

Mitsuyo took her well-worn tape measure from her pocket and measured the cuffs to see how much would need to be taken up.

When it rains it pours: there was one customer after another, not just browsing but actually buying, and she sold a number of suits.

The store finally closed for the day, and at the table next to the register Mitsuyo was going through the day's sales receipts in the half-darkened floor. "This only happens on the one day we plan to go out for a drink," she said.

Kazuko, herself with a fistful of receipts, said, "You got that right."

Mitsuyo nodded a reply and checked the clock. Eight forty-five. By this time she'd normally have changed and be pedaling home on her bike.

"Is it going to take you much longer?" asked Kazuko, who had already finished sorting out her own paperwork.

"Give me another fifteen minutes," Mitsuyo said as she flipped through the receipts.

"I'll wait for you in the break room," Kazuko said, and went downstairs. Mitsuyo was left alone on the half-lit, gloomy floor, her legs chilly now that the heat had been turned off.

Right then she heard the ring tone on her cell phone, which she'd left on the register stand. She reached for it, thinking it was Tamayo, but saw Yuichi's name instead. Her thumb still stuck in the sheaf of receipts, she picked it up with her other hand.

"Hi, it's me," she heard Yuichi say. Looking around to make sure she was alone, Mitsuyo answered happily, "Hi! What's up?"

"You still at work?" he asked.

"Yeah. Why?"

"Do you have plans today?"

"By today, do you mean right now?" Her happy voice echoed in the empty floor. "Aren't you in Nagasaki? Did you finish work already?" she asked.

"I finished at six. I drove my own car to the construction site today, and was thinking about going to see you right after work."

The signal was cutting in and out, as if he were driving already.

"Where are you?" Mitsuyo asked. Before she realized it she was standing, and her thumb had slipped out of the sheaf of receipts.

"I'm almost on the highway."

"Highway? You mean the Saga Yamato?"

Mitsuyo glanced toward the window. From the Saga Yamato interchange it took only ten minutes to get here. She sat back down. "I wish you'd told me sooner you were coming," she pouted happily.

They agreed to meet in the parking lot of the fast-food place next door, and Mitsuyo hung up. An almost painful thrill of joy shot through her as she thought of Yuichi coming to see her so unexpectedly on a weekday night.

As she quickly checked the receipts, she could picture Yuichi's car whizzing down the streets. With each receipt she stamped, she felt his car get that much closer.

She rushed through her receipts in five minutes. She turned off the rest of the lights on the floor, and as she ran into the locker room on the first floor she found Kazuko there, already in street clothes, pouring a cup of strong-smelling *dokudami* herbal tea from the thermos she always carried with her.

"That was fast."

"Uh . . . yeah." For a moment Mitsuyo was at a loss for words. She hadn't forgotten about their plan to go have a drink, but things had changed so quickly she hadn't had time to formulate an excuse.

"What's the matter?" Seeing Mitsuyo so flustered, Kazuko was worried.

"Well, it's just . . ."

"What's wrong? Did something happen?"

"No, nothing. I just, ah, had a phone call. . . ."

"Phone call? From who?"

Mitsuyo still faltered. She wanted to tell Kazuko of her change of plans, of meeting Yuichi, but somehow the words wouldn't come.

Kazuko watched Mitsuyo carefully. "How about we go next time? Any time's fine with me." A meaningful smile crossed her lips.

"Sorry," Mitsuyo said.

"Your boyfriend decided to come see you all of a sudden, is that it?" Kazuko smiled, unfazed by the abrupt change of plans. "I was pretty sure you had a boyfriend. I mean you took a day off on the weekend, and you've been floating around with this happy look on your face the last few days."

"I'm really sorry," Mitsuyo apologized again.

"Don't worry about it. . . . So, is he from Saga?"

"No, from Nagasaki."

"He suddenly decided to come all the way from Nagasaki? I guess this isn't the time to go out for a drink with me! Come on, you'd better change." Mitsuyo was standing there like a statue and Kazuko gave her a friendly pat on the rump to get her moving.

After Kazuko had left and Mitsuyo was alone in the locker room, she hurriedly changed out of her uniform. As she was changing, her cell phone rang with a message from Yuichi. *I'm here*, it said.

Glad I wore the leather jacket today, Mitsuyo thought. The down jacket she usually wore had a dirty collar. That morning she'd pondered whether to wear it one more day before sending it to the cleaners, and had decided against it.

This was the same leather jacket she'd worn when she met Yuichi that past weekend. She'd bought the jacket a year ago, when she and Tamayo had gone shopping in Hakata. She'd hesitated over the price—¥110,000—but in the end had decided to go ahead and splurge.

She locked the locker room, handed the key to the night watchman, and left by the back door. The cold wind whipped at her feet and she pulled her muffler tight. The huge parking lot was a sea of white lines, and beyond the fence was the fallow field and a steel pylon.

She turned and saw the familiar white car parked next to the fast-food place. The place wasn't crowded and Yuichi's car, polished to perfection, was the only thing sparkling under the streetlights. Mitsuyo walked along the highway, hurrying to the parking lot next door.

As she entered the parking lot, the headlights of Yuichi's car came on. He must have been watching her all the way over. Mitsuyo gave a small wave to the dark interior of the car. As she got closer Yuichi snapped open the passenger-side door from inside. As soon as it opened, the interior light flicked on and she could see him, still dressed in his work clothes.

"I'm freezing," Mitsuyo said, shivering as she hurried inside and sat down. She hadn't met his eyes as she did, and the car again was dark inside. "Did you really come straight from work?" she asked, turning toward him.

"If I'd gone home first I'd have been even later," Yuichi said, turning up the heater.

"You should have called me sooner."

"I was thinking of it, but figured you were still at work."

"If I couldn't see you today what were you gonna do?" she teased.

"If I couldn't see you, I guess I'd just go home," he answered solemnly.

Mitsuyo placed her hand on top of his, which was resting on the gearshift. It may have been his work clothes, but this time, the car smelled old and dirty.

The car stayed for a time in the fast-food-restaurant parking lot, and didn't move. Meanwhile, three other groups of customers had exited the restaurant and driven off. No other cars replaced them, and as the number of cars decreased it felt as if only theirs was left, like a small boat in a vast sea.

Minutes passed and Mitsuyo's fingers remained entwined with his. Wordlessly their fingers spoke to each other.

"You have to go to work early tomorrow?" Mitsuyo asked as she gripped his middle finger. On the highway beyond the fence a car sped up.

"I get up at five-thirty," Yuichi said, stroking her wrist with his thumb.

"Doesn't it take about two hours from here to Nagasaki? We don't have much time."

"I just wanted to see you. . . ."

The digital clock on the dashboard showed 9:18.

"You have to go back, right?" Mitsuyo asked.

The thumb stopped stroking her. Yuichi paused. "Yeah. If I don't go back tonight, I'll have to get up at three," he said, forcing a smile.

I wanted to see you so much. I just had to see you, so I drove here right from work. Yuichi didn't put it into words, but his fingers conveyed this message clearly as he stroked her wrist.

They could go to a love hotel now and spend a couple of hours together. But then he'd have to drive back to Nagasaki. That meant he'd get home around one a.m. Even if he went to sleep right away, Yuichi would have to go to his exhausting job with only four hours of sleep.

Two hours is fine, Mitsuyo thought, *as long as I can be with him. But I want him to get as much sleep as he can, too—even an extra hour.*

"If only my sister weren't at home. . . ." Mitsuyo surprised herself. She'd never thought of her sister as a bother before. She'd always worried instead about when Tamayo would be back.

"You want to go to a . . . hotel?" Yuichi asked. He seemed hesitant, as if worried about tomorrow morning.

"But if we go to a hotel it'll be really late when you go home."

"Yeah, you're right." Yuichi's fingers on top of the gearshift tensed.

"Nagasaki and Saga are so far away," Mitsuyo murmured. "No . . . that isn't what I mean," she quickly added, shaking her head. "It's not that. . . . It's just that you came all this way and I wish we could spend more time together."

"It's a weekday. Nothing we can do about it," he muttered resignedly. He sounded cool about it, and Mitsuyo couldn't help but say, "You're so serious, you know that?"

"I can't take a day off. It's my uncle's company."

"But it's hard for me to get Saturday off. It's almost impossible for me to get two days off in a row like last time." She sounded a bit miffed and the instant she said that Yuichi's fingers went limp.

He came to see me, Mitsuyo thought. *He didn't come all this way just to be told that we don't have time to see each other. He drove two hours to see me, after doing his backbreaking job.*

"You want to park next door?" Mitsuyo tugged at his fingers. "The store's closed and there won't be any other cars. We can talk for a while. If you park behind the building, nobody can see you from the road."

Yuichi glanced over the fence toward the darkened menswear store, and quickly released the parking brake.

"Hold on a second," Mitsuyo hastily added. "You probably haven't had any dinner. Let me buy you something."

"No, I had some *udon* at a rest area. I couldn't wait," Yuichi laughed.

He drove out of the fast-food-restaurant parking lot and over to the lot behind Wakaba. Behind the store it was dark, the only light an illuminated billboard for makeup in the field beyond the fence.

"Next Friday's a holiday, so I was thinking of going to Nagasaki. Just a day trip," Mitsuyo said. The car had come to a halt and Yuichi's hands were resting on the steering wheel. He suddenly reached out and placed his hot hand on her, stroking her earlobe and neck. Without a word, he kissed her. For a second, Mitsuyo was taken aback, but before she knew it he was all over her. She closed her eyes and let him have his way.

It was after ten p.m. when they left the parking lot. Mitsuyo wanted to stay in his arms forever, but she knew that that would make it all the harder for him the next morning. After they left the parking lot, Yuichi headed to her apartment without needing directions. He deftly changed lanes, zooming past one car after another.

"Three days from now, I'll take the bus to Nagasaki," Mitsuyo said, letting herself sway back and forth with the motion of the car, a lulling feeling she was already used to.

"I finish work at six," Yuichi said, pulling up close to the car in front.

"I have the day off, so I was thinking of going in the morning and doing a little sightseeing by myself. It's been years since I've been in Nagasaki. . . . Last year my sister and I went to the Huis Ten Bosch theme park, though."

"I wish I could show you around. . . ."

"Don't worry. I'll just eat some *champon*, go see the cathedrals. . . ."

It usually took fifteen minutes by bike to go home but at the speed Yuichi drove, it took only three. As he did the last time, Yuichi steered his car down the unpaved path right up to the apartment building.

"Darn it—my sister's home." Mitsuyo looked up to the second-floor window, where the light was on. "I wish we had more time," she added in a low voice, and as she did Yuichi's dry lips covered hers again.

"Drive carefully," she said. Yuichi nodded, lips still glued to hers. For a second it seemed as if he wanted to say something more, so she pulled away a bit. But he just looked down and was silent.

Mitsuyo watched as the car pulled away down the dirt path. When he came out on the paved road he beeped his horn once and shot away.

I'm so lonely, she thought. *I can't wait to see him again.* Mitsuyo stood there watching until his rear lights disappeared.

She remembered how when Tamayo was going out with a guy who was a hairdresser, she'd said the very same thing. That she was so lonely. That she couldn't wait to see him again. At the time, Mitsuyo couldn't understand her feelings, but now she did. She understood, and wondered how anyone could stand it. She wanted to run after his car—or fall to the ground and cry her eyes out. If she could only be with Yuichi, anything was possible.

Yuichi wasn't sure how much time had passed since Mitsuyo's figure in the rearview mirror, waving goodbye, had disappeared. At an intersection near the on-ramp to the highway, he had to stop for a red light. He pulled his wallet out of his back pocket and saw he had less than five thousand yen. If Mitsuyo had agreed to go to a hotel, he would have had to take the surface streets home, no matter how late that made him. Fortunately she'd been worried about his job, so he still had enough money to take the highway.

He'd been dying to see her. Although they'd only met a few days ago, he was scared to death the relationship would end. At night, no matter how long he talked with her on the phone, he couldn't rid himself of this fear. As soon as he hung up he couldn't stand it, convinced he'd never see her again. When he slept, he dreamed she was gone. As soon as he woke up in the morning he wanted to call her, but hesitated since it was five a.m.; he thought about her all day long at work. By the end of the day today, he couldn't stand it, and before he knew what he was doing, he was heading toward Saga. Maybe he'd already made an unconscious decision to do just that, which is why he took his car to work instead of riding in his uncle's van.

The red light seemed to take forever, and Yuichi pounded the steering wheel. If another car hadn't been right beside him, he would have slammed his forehead against it in frustration.

When I was little, he recalled, before Mom took me to live with my grandparents and we were still living in an apartment in the city, she said she'd take me out to see my father, and I was so happy getting ready, and riding the streetcar together. "When we get to the station we'll transfer to a train," she explained. I asked her, "Is it far?" and she said, "Way far away."

In the crowded streetcar, she clung to the strap. And I held on to her skirt. When the streetcar started to move, some men seated in front of us began to elbow each other and laugh. They were laughing at my mom, who'd forgotten to shave her underarms. Mom turned all red and hid her underarm with a handkerchief. It was a hot day. The packed streetcar lurched to one side and her handkerchief slipped off and the men tried to keep from laughing.

We got to the JR station and transferred to a train. Trying so hard to hide her underarm on the lurching streetcar had left Mom covered in sweat. As we were waiting at the crowded ticket counter to buy our tickets, I said, "I'm sorry" to her. Mom looked at me vacantly, her head tilted. "It's so hot, isn't it?" she said. She smiled, and wiped my sweaty nose with that handkerchief.

A car horn blaring behind him brought Yuichi back to the present. He accelerated abruptly and his body, clinging hard to the steering wheel, was snapped back against the seat. He was so distracted he didn't merge into the highway but went straight over the overpass.

He slowed down to do a U-turn and switched on the radio to get his mind on other things. The local news was on. Yuichi did a huge U-turn, and the on-ramp to the highway loomed closer.

"In another story, in the case of the murder that took place just after midnight on the tenth of this month at Mitsuse Pass, the twenty-two-year-old man police have been searching for as a material witness has been found. Last night a clerk at a sauna in Nagoya contacted police, who immediately took the man into custody. He has been transferred back to Fukuoka, where police are questioning him about the incident. As we get more details, we will update this story on the eleven o'clock news."

The news ended and an insurance commercial came on. Yuichi steered back, away from the highway on-ramp, and stepped on the gas. He cut in front of another car and the driver blared his horn. Yuichi sped up more, overtaking another car. Finally he slowed down and pulled off the road, coming to a stop in front of a vending machine.

A nostalgic Christmas song was playing on the radio now. Yuichi switched stations but couldn't find any more news about the murder at Mitsuse Pass. He held on to the steering wheel, even though his car was stopped. A huge truck roared past, the blast of air rocking his car.

Yuichi shook the steering wheel, but no matter how much he tried, it didn't move an inch. He tried again, but the harder he tried to shake it, the more his own body shook back and forth.

They'd captured the guy. The guy who'd been trying to escape. They'd arrested that guy who'd taken Yoshino Ishibashi to Mitsuse Pass. He found himself muttering these words, and as he did, for some reason he pictured again the scene, years ago, when he and his mother had gone to see his father. The men on the streetcar chuckling at her hairy armpit. Standing at the crowded ticket window and his mother's face as she wiped the sweat from his nose. Why that day would come back to him now, he had no idea. But he couldn't erase the images from his mind.

We took the streetcar to the JR station, Yuichi recalled, where we boarded a train. Mom had me sit down at a window seat, and she sat next me, dozing.

Just after Dad left, Mom used to cry every night. When I got lonely and sat down beside her she'd stroke my head and say, "Let's just forget about anything sad, okay? Let's just *totally* forget about it," crying even more loudly than before.

From the window I could see the ocean. I was sitting on the mountain side of the car and on the other side, the ocean side, were two elementary school brothers wearing caps, traveling with their parents. When I leaned over to catch a glimpse of the sea, my mom woke up and said, "Sit down. It's dangerous," pushing my head down. "Once we get there, you can see the ocean as much as you like."

I don't know how much longer we were riding after that, but all of a sudden I dozed off like her.

"We're getting off now," she said, grabbing my arm, and I stumbled off the train still half asleep. We left the station, walked for a while, and arrived at a ferryboat dock.

"We're going to take the ferry and go over there," my mom said, pointing to the other shore.

In the parking lot of the dock there was a line of cars. "They're all going to go on the ferryboat with us," my mom told me.

Just like she'd told me on the train, there was the ocean, right in front of me. And way off on the far shore was a lighthouse. The first one I'd ever seen.

Yuichi's cell phone rang. He was still sitting in the car by the side of the road, hands tightly clasping the steering wheel. Trucks continued to roar by right next to him, the air blast lifting his car up each time they passed.

He pulled his cell phone out of his pocket. The caller ID said *Home.* When he answered it, it was his grandmother, sounding a bit hesitant and timid.

"Yu—Yuichi? Where are you?"

It sounded like somebody was right beside her, and she was checking with that person as she spoke.

"What d'you want to know for?" Yuichi asked.

"The—the police are here." She tried her best to sound upbeat, but her voice was trembling. "Where are you? Can you come back soon?"

Another truck roared past. Yuichi hung up, and almost reflexively his fingers began to move on the keypad.

Is that right? So Yuichi still remembers that time? . . . He must have been five, or maybe six then. . . . I was sure he'd forgotten all about it. As I told you before, after Yuichi started working for me I treated him even more like a son. He's really gotten good at his job these days, and was even thinking of getting a crane operator's license.

If you think about it, that was how he came to live with his grandfather and grandmother. Really? So Yuichi still thinks he was going to see his father that day? That's pretty sad. What happened was, that was the day his mother abandoned him.

I don't know what Yuichi told you, but back then his mother was at the end of her rope. Everybody told her she shouldn't get involved with that worthless guy, but she ignored them and did it anyway. Things went okay until Yuichi was born, but before three years were up the guy ran off and left them. I'm not trying to take her side or anything, but she did get a job in a nightclub and thought she could make a go of raising Yuichi. But things never work out that easy, do they? Working in a place like that, she took up with another bad guy, who spent all her money, and she got sick. . . . She should have called her home for help, but she couldn't. So she ended up alone, with no one she could rely on. . . .

So anyway, his mother was desperate. She lied to Yuichi, telling him they were going to see his father, even though she had no idea where the guy was.

She abandoned Yuichi there at the ferry dock that day. He sat there, waiting, all alone, until the next morning. She said she was just going to buy their tickets, and ran away, but what she did was hide behind the pillars of the pier until morning.

The next morning, when one of the ferry workers found him, Yuichi refused to budge. "My mom told me to wait here!" he said, and actually bit the guy on the arm.

Apparently as she left his mother told him, "See that lighthouse over there? Just look at that lighthouse. I'll go buy our tickets and be right back."

His mother got in touch a week later. She said she felt like she was going to die, but I don't buy it. So after that, Yuichi was taken over by Child Protective Services and Juvenile Court, but his grandparents took him to live with them, and not long after that his mother took up with another man and disappeared.

The whole parent-child relationship is a strange thing if you think about it.

Just around the time Yuichi started to work for me, the topic came up and I asked him if his mother had ever contacted him. His grandfather was doing poorly around then, and I figured if things turned out bad I should be able to get ahold of her to let her know about the funeral. It was just a thought I had that I blurted out.

I was positive that after she took up with that last guy there'd been no word from her. I asked his grandparents and they told me, "She sends us a New Year's card every couple of years. Each time it's a different address. . . . Probably she's with a different man each time."

I asked Yuichi if she ever got in touch. He shook his head and I thought that was the end of it. But then he added, "If it's about Grandpa's condition, I already told her."

"You told her? You mean . . . you have kept in touch with her?"

"We go out to eat sometimes."

"What do you mean by sometimes?"

"Once a year, maybe."

"Do your grandparents know about this?"

"No, they don't," Yuichi replied, shaking his head. His grandpa took great pride in the fact that he'd raised Yuichi, so it must have been hard for Yuichi to say anything about it.

"Don't you get angry when you meet her?" I said this without thinking. I mean, look, his mother abandoned him there at the ferryboat dock, without anything to eat, and he ended up stuck with his grandparents.

But Yuichi said, "No, I'm not angry. I don't see her enough to get angry."

"Where is she now, and what's she doing?" I asked.

"She works at an inn, in Unzen." This was about three or four years ago.

Apparently he's driven over a few times to see her. "What do the two of you talk about?" I asked.

"Nothing much."

I know I can't forgive his mother for what she did. I can still picture Yuichi at the ferry dock, abandoned. It's not just me. His grandfather and grandmother, and the other relatives, feel the same way. But this parent-child relationship really is strange, isn't it? None of us forgave her, but Yuichi did.

After seeing Yuichi off, Mitsuyo sat for a while on the staircase outside her apartment. The hard concrete chilled her backside, and from an apartment on the first floor, she could hear a young man soothing a baby.

Finally she couldn't stand the cold so she headed back to her apartment on the second floor. She opened the door and called out, "I'm back!"

Tamayo, from the bathroom, called out, "You had to work overtime?"

"Uh, yeah," Mitsuyo answered, and took off her shoes. She went down the hallway to the living room, where she saw a plate on the table. It looked like Tamayo had been eating stew.

"Did you make this yourself?" she asked, turning toward the bathroom, but there was no response.

She slid open the door to her small bedroom. Yuichi must be on the highway already, she thought. She found herself next to the window, pulling aside the lace curtain. A stray cat loped across the spot where she and Yuichi had said goodbye. Just then a car pulled off the main road at a high speed, almost spinning out as it headed in her direction. The cat, about to scurry toward the garbage cans, was illuminated in the bluish headlights.

Mitsuyo instinctively clasped her hands together. "Watch out!" she said to herself. The car came to a halt, just shy of hitting the plastic garbage cans. The cat, shrunk back in the headlights, scampered away.

"Yuichi?"

The car that had skidded to a halt there was definitely his. The headlights illuminated the empty space where the stray cat had been.

Mitsuyo closed the curtains and raced to the front door. She was in such a hurry she couldn't get her heels into her shoes. As she grabbed her bag, Tamayo called out, "Where are you going?" Mitsuyo didn't reply and ran out of the apartment.

From the staircase she could see Yuichi inside the dark car, head down against the steering wheel. The car's headlights shone on the filthy garbage cans. As she ran down the stairs she came to an abrupt stop. *Was this all a hallucination?* she suddenly wondered. *Did I want to see him so much I'm having a hallucination?*

Still, as she slowly approached, the gravel crunched under her feet. She rapped on the window with her fingers and as she did Yuichi bolted upright. *What's the matter?* she wordlessly mouthed. Yuichi's eyes as they followed her lips looked like they were gazing at something else, something far away.

Mitsuyo rapped on the glass again, asking with her eyes again the same question, *What's the matter?* As if in reply, Yuichi looked away. She tapped the window once more, and Yuichi, clutching the steering wheel, eyes down, slowly opened the door. Mitsuyo took a step back.

Without a word he got out of the car and stood in front of her. Looking up at him, Mitsuyo again asked, "What's wrong?"

A car rushed by on the main road; the weeds along the road whipped in the blast of air. Yuichi suddenly grabbed her and held her tight. It was so quick that Mitsuyo let out a short cry.

"I wish I'd met you earlier," he said as he held her against his chest. "If I'd met you earlier, none of this would have happened. . . ."

"What do you mean?"

"Please get in the car, okay?"

"Huh?"

"Get in the car!" Yuichi suddenly said roughly, and grabbed Mitsuyo's arm, pulling her around to the passenger side.

"What is going on?" Mitsuyo tried to pull away, her heels digging into the gravel.

"Just get in!"

Almost holding her under his arm, Yuichi opened the passenger door. With both doors open, the wind rushed through, carrying out the heated air from inside.

"Wait—wait a second!" Mitsuyo said, resisting. She didn't mind so much getting in the car, but she wanted to know why.

"What is up with you? *Tell* me!"

As he pressed her down, Mitsuyo grabbed his wrist. After his harsh words, and the rough treatment, Mitsuyo was surprised to feel his trembling wrist feel so frail.

Yuichi shoved her inside, slammed the door shut, and hurried around to the driver's side. He almost tumbled inside and, breathing raggedly, he released the parking brake. The tires sprayed gravel as he shot down the path. He roared past the vacant lot in front of the apartment building and turned sharply to the left. As he turned, he nearly crashed into a car coming from the opposite direction, and Mitsuyo screamed.

They barely missed the other car and sped down the dark path through the rice fields.

Fusae turned off the light in the bedroom, sat up in her futon, and, without making a sound, crawled over toward the window. With a trembling hand she parted the curtain a bit. Outside the window was a cinder-block wall with a few blocks missing, and through the holes she could see the narrow road in front. The patrol car that had been outside was gone now. Instead, a black car was parked there, and in the light from inside the car she could see a young plainclothes detective talking on a cell phone.

An hour before, Fusae had called Yuichi, the local patrolman and the plainclothes detective standing in front of her as she did. She could barely follow their directions to call him. Before she called, they warned her not to let him know they were there, but she'd blurted it out. When he heard this, Yuichi hung up.

It was all so unexpected. They'd all thought the Fukuoka college student was the murderer, but he wasn't. Even so, she still couldn't understand why the police had come here again.

"Yuichi has nothing to do with this," she insisted, her voice trembling, but the police wouldn't relent. "Just call his cell phone," they told her. The instant she let slip that the police were there, they couldn't hide their anger and disappointment. This is one worthless old lady, they must have thought, and their expressions were exactly like those of the men who had forced her to buy the Chinese herbal medicine. The irritated men who told her just to *Sign it already!*

She took her hand from the curtain. Usually the only sound she heard in this neighborhood was the waves, but now, with several strangers hanging around outside, she could sense their presence, even with the windows closed.

She closed the curtains and crouched down next to the wall. It seemed as though the wall were shaking, but she knew it was her. If she stayed still, the shaking would only get worse; she was about to faint. The Fukuoka college student they'd arrested apparently hadn't murdered that young woman. He'd taken her to the pass—that much was certain—but what he said about events after that didn't make sense. He said that before he gave her a ride she'd been at Higashi Park, in another man's car, a car with Nagasaki plates. Apparently the other man looked like Yuichi.

In the dark kitchen, Fusae lowered the phone from its shelf and cradled it. She lifted the receiver and, still trembling, dialed Norio's house. The phone rang for a long time, and finally Norio came on, sounding sleepy.

"Hello? It's me, Fusae. Were you asleep?" Norio sounded out of sorts and Fusae spoke quickly.

When Norio realized who it was, he grew tense. "Did something happen to Katsuji?"

"No, that's not it," Fusae said. But the next words wouldn't come. She realized she was sobbing.

"What is it? What's the matter?" Norio asked. His wife sleeping next to him must have woken up, for Fusae heard him explain to her, "It's Auntie Fusae. I don't know. . . . No, it isn't Katsuji."

"Yuichi isn't coming back. . . ." That was as much as she could get out between sobs.

"Yuichi? What do you mean he isn't coming back? Where did he go?"

"I don't know. The police are here and I don't know what's going on."

"The police? Was he in an accident?"

"No. But I just don't understand. . . ."

"What don't you understand?"

"I called him and told him the police were here and he hung right up. . . . If he wasn't involved in the murder he wouldn't hang up like that."

As he listened to Fusae's tearful voice, Norio crawled out of his futon, slipped on a cardigan, and looked over at his wife, Michiyo.

"I'll come over," he said. "I can't follow what you're saying over the phone. Just stay put. I'll be right over."

Norio hung up and muttered to Michiyo, who looked extremely

worried, "Yuichi seems to have gotten himself in some sort of trouble."

"Something happened to him?"

"I don't know. Maybe he got in a fight or something. Fusae's crying so much I can't figure out what's going on."

Norio stood up and turned on the fluorescent light. The clock showed eleven-thirty. He took off his pajamas and tossed them on top of the rumpled futon, then reached for the neatly folded work clothes beside his pillow. They'd had the stove on until a short while ago but now, as he stood there in his undershirt, he shivered in the cold.

"I have no idea what happened, but whatever you do, don't hit Yuichi, okay?" Michiyo said as she helped Norio change his clothes. "We're supposed to be looking out for him, so you have to be on his side, you hear?"

"Okay! I get it!" Norio growled. Was it a fight? A car accident? Without buttoning his jacket, Norio leaped out of the house. He climbed into his work van and headed for Yuichi's house. The road was empty of cars at this hour and the lights were green the whole way. Norio felt uneasy. He knew that Katsuji hadn't died, but the dull agitation he'd felt still had hold of him.

Whether Yuichi had been in a fight or an accident, if he was injured he'd have to take time off from work. *I don't know the details yet*, Norio thought, *but I'd better get in touch with Yoshioka or Kurami as soon as I can. Tomorrow they'll have to get to the work site on their own, and I can call them on their cell phones and tell them what they need to do.*

As these worries ran through his mind, Norio arrived at the fishing village where Yuichi lived. The moonlit harbor was calm, the fishing boats still. But there were three or four cars he didn't recognize on the normally deserted pier and a few people milling about, talking. Norio slowed down and drove onto the pier. His headlights shone on the fishing boats and he spotted some uniformed police and residents who had come out to see what was going on.

Norio parked and switched off his lights. He saw a group of locals milling about like the sea bugs that slither over rocks near the ocean. A shiver went through him and he jumped out of his van.

"Hey, Norio!" The residents' association head was the first to recognize Norio. "What's up? Something happen with Yuichi?" he asked as he approached, hunching his neck down against the cold.

Someone else behind him spoke to a policeman, saying, "That's Yuichi's uncle there!" and as soon as he heard this the young policeman hurried over. "Didn't the police just come to your place?" he asked, flustered.

"No," Norio said, shaking his head. "I just got a call from Yuichi's grandmother and came over as soon as I heard."

"I see. Well, I guess you must have just missed them."

"My wife's at home, though."

The policeman turned to a patrol car parked some distance off and shouted, "The suspect's uncle is here!" The door of the patrol car opened and the sound of the static-filled police radio mixed in with the sound of the waves.

"I need to ask you some questions, okay? I understand that Yuichi works for you?'

Before he knew it, Norio was surrounded by police and local residents.

"If it's all right with you, I'd like to see his grandmother first," Norio said firmly, cutting them off.

The next morning Mitsuyo withdrew thirty thousand yen from an ATM at a convenience store next to the road. Since graduating from high school ten years earlier, she'd been steadily saving her money, but most was in a CD and her ordinary account had only what she needed from week to week. So after she withdrew thirty thousand, there wasn't much left.

She put the cash into her purse, went to the checkout stand, and bought two cans of hot tea and three rice balls. As she was paying, she glanced outside and saw Yuichi in his car, parked down the road, staring in her direction.

Mitsuyo left the store and hurried over toward the car, the two cans of hot tea in her hands. Yuichi opened his window and she passed him the tea and then pulled out her cell phone, thinking she had to call her store.

The store's manager, Mr. Oshiro, answered. Mitsuyo had been sure that Kazuko would answer and she was flustered for a moment, but then she said, in an intentionally subdued voice, "Ah, hello, this is Miss Magome. My father suddenly became ill, so I'm sorry but I need to take the day off." She was able to smoothly repeat the lines she'd prepared.

"Is that right? I'm sorry to hear that," she heard her manager say curtly. "Actually, that girl who came for an interview, I'm going to have her start work this afternoon, so I was going to have Miss Kirishima move over from the casual corner to suits."

She'd called him to ask for a day off and here he was telling her all about personnel changes he was planning.

"If his illness lasts a long time, that could be troublesome. And we're getting into the year-end bargain sales, too. . . . Anyhow, as soon as you find out any more, be sure to let me know."

With that, the manager hung up. She'd felt apologetic at first about making the call, but he'd dealt with her so abruptly she felt as if he was making fun of her.

She'd only been standing outside for a few minutes, but the freezing wind had chilled her fingers. As soon as she got in the passenger side of the car, Yuichi handed her a can of hot tea.

"I called work and took the day off," Mitsuyo said, smiling.

"Sorry 'bout that" was all Yuichi had to say in response.

The night before, after he roared off from the apartment, Yuichi drove by the bypass and down the frontage road toward Takeo. The flat road gradually became hilly, and until they entered the hill country, Yuichi didn't say a word.

"Where are we going?" They'd been driving for fifteen minutes and Mitsuyo had finally calmed down enough to talk. Still, Yuichi was silent.

"This car is so spotless. Do you clean it yourself?" She couldn't stand the silence and said this as she stroked the dashboard. The warmth of the dashboard, warmed by the heater, reminded her of Yuichi's body when he'd held her a few minutes ago.

"On days off, I don't have much else to do. . . ." They'd been driving for nearly twenty minutes when Yuichi finally spoke. Mitsuyo couldn't help laughing. He'd been so rough when he forced her to come with him, but now sounded so meek.

"Sometimes I catch a ride to work with the husband of an older woman I work with," Mitsuyo said, "and his car is like a garbage dump. He says, *Come on, get in! Get in!* but it's like, with all the junk where am I supposed to sit?" Mitsuyo laughed at her own words but when she glanced at Yuichi his expression hadn't changed.

Yuichi suddenly brought the car to a halt just past a tiny village, right at the point where they were about to enter a dark mountain road. He slowed and steered toward the shoulder, the tires crunching gravel. At a break in the guardrail just up ahead was an unpaved path, barely wide enough for a compact car, that stretched up into the hills.

Yuichi kept the engine running but doused the lights. In an instant the world in front of them disappeared. With nothing to be seen outside, Mitsuyo looked over at him. And right then he leaned over and tried to get on top of her.

"What . . . what are you . . . ?"

The emergency brake got in the way when he tried to find a place for his hand, and Mitsuyo could feel his frustration. Her seat fell back and she brought her legs, which had unconsciously spread wide, back together again.

Yuichi, on top of her, roughly kissed her lips, her chin, her neck. As her body sank back in the seat, it was strange how perfectly it fit her, almost as if she were tied down. Mitsuyo glanced out the window. From her horizontal position she could see the night sky, beyond the black trees. The sky was full of stars.

As Yuichi continued to cover her with kisses, she slowly pushed back on his chest. He clutched her tighter and she pounded on his chest. For a second his arms went limp.

"What's wrong?" Mitsuyo asked, so close her breath went into his mouth. "I don't know what happened, but you don't have to worry. I'll always be with you."

She hadn't rehearsed these words and was surprised at what she'd said. Her words seemed to seep into Yuichi's skin. On the shoulder of this dark mountain road without a single streetlight, inside their parked car, all that existed were her words, and his skin.

"If you don't feel like talking about it, I'm okay with that. I'll just wait until you feel like it." Mitsuyo slowly pushed him up, away from her, and Yuichi let her have her way.

"I just don't . . . know what to do . . ." he murmured. "I was planning to go home. But I felt like if I said goodbye to you now, I'd never see you again."

"So you came back?"

"I wanted to be with you. But I didn't know what I should do to be with you. . . . I didn't know what to do. . . ."

Mitsuyo pushed her seat up and reached out and touched Yuichi's ear. They'd been in the warm car for quite a while, but his ear was surprisingly cold to the touch.

"I was planning to take the highway home. But all of a sudden I remembered something from the past."

"From the past?"

"When I was a kid and my mom took me to see my father. What happened back then."

He let her finger his ear as he spoke. She could tell something was troubling him, and she wanted more than anything to know what it was. But she felt as though once she did know, Yuichi would disappear from her.

"Let's just be together," she said, gently stroking his ear.

Another car drove past, lighting up the dark world outside. The guardrail stretched out far ahead, glaringly white.

"Why don't we stay somewhere tonight, forget about work tomorrow, and go for a drive instead?" Mitsuyo said. "I mean, we haven't gone to Yobuko lighthouse yet. The other day we spent the whole time in a hotel."

Under her hands, Yuichi's ear grew warm.

✿

Seated on the step that separated the barbershop from their living quarters, bathed in the winter sun, Yoshio Ishibashi stared out at the road. Several days had passed since his daughter's funeral, but he had yet to reopen his shop. He knew he couldn't go on like this forever, grieving, and this was the end of the year, besides, usually a busy time for him. But as soon as he thought of reopening, he felt lethargic. If he did reopen, would anybody come? And if they did, he knew they'd talk with him warily, unsure of what to say.

Yoshio roused himself to stand up. All he had to do was take a few steps, go outside, and plug in his barber's sign—and ordinary, everyday life would return. But reopening the shop wouldn't bring Yoshino back.

He sat back down and was staring at his feet when there came a knock at the glass door. He looked up and saw the detective from the local precinct who had attended the funeral, face pressed against the glass, peering inside.

Yoshio gave a huge sigh, got to his feet, and trudged over to open the door.

"I'm sorry to bother you so early," the detective said, his voice overly loud.

"It's all right," Yoshio said curtly. "I was just sitting here thinking about reopening the shop."

"Well, you might have already heard it on the news yesterday, but they found that college student."

The detective said it so matter-of-factly that at first Yoshio could only respond with a simple, "Oh, is that right?" But then, when it hit him, he raised his voice. "What? What did you say?"

"They located that college student in Nagoya."

"Why didn't you tell me earlier?!"

"The thing is, we had to look into something last night, and we didn't want to get in touch until we'd got everything straightened out."

Yoshio had a bad feeling about this. Arresting that college student should mean they'd caught Yoshino's killer, but the detective didn't seem excited by events.

Yoshio sensed something behind him, and turned and saw his wife, Satoko, on all fours peering out in their direction.

"Ah, hello, Mrs. Ishibashi. Well, from what the college student has told us, and the facts at the scene, it would appear he is not the perpetrator. Though we are certain that he took your daughter to Mitsuse Pass." The detective rattled on quickly so he wouldn't be interrupted.

Before Yoshio realized it, Satoko had come out to the entrance and was seated formally there, legs tucked neatly beneath her. Yoshio clutched the white barber's coat in his hands and said, "What—what do you mean the college student isn't the criminal? You have to tell us everything!" Yoshio looked about ready to grab the detective by the collar, but Satoko reached out and clutched his hand.

"Well, we've established that the college student did drive your daughter to Mitsuse Pass. She ran into him at the park near the building where she lives."

"By run into him, you mean she was planning to meet him there?"

"No. Masuo . . . I mean the college student . . . according to him, your daughter was meeting someone else there and just happened to meet up with him."

"Who is this other person?"

"That's what we're trying to find out. According to what this college student told us, there was definitely another person involved. He told us what this other man looked like and the type of car he was driving."

"So—what happened to Yoshino?" As Yoshio shouted this, Satoko shot the detective a solemn glance and began stroking her husband's back.

"They drove to Mitsuse Pass. There they apparently got into an argument and that man . . ."

"What? What did he do?" This time it was Satoko, not Yoshio, who fired back.

"The man forced your daughter to get out of the car."

"In the pass, where there's nobody around? Why would he . . ." Satoko looked about to cry, and now it was Yoshio who stroked her back.

"They apparently quarreled, and he pushed your daughter, and then her neck . . ."

Unable to bear it any longer, Satoko began to quietly sob.

"Rest assured, we grilled the college student thoroughly. He ended up blubbering and it was pretty pathetic. But he's definitely not the one who killed her. The finger marks left on your daughter's throat were larger than those of the college student's hands. The difference between a child's hands and those of an adult . . ."

The detective stopped speaking and Yoshio sat there, glaring at him.

"So who was my daughter meeting, then? Don't hide anything from me. Was it someone from one of those dating sites or . . ." He couldn't go on.

After the detective had finished his explanation and left, Yoshio slumped down in one of the barber chairs. Satoko, still seated formally at the entrance, was wringing her hands and sobbing.

Our daughter is killed and she cries, he thought. *They can't find the criminal and she cries, and she cries when it turns out the suspect is innocent.*

According to the detective, Yoshino was supposed to meet a blond man with a white car. Yet she lied to her colleagues from work, and when she left them told them she was meeting this college student named Keigo Masuo. And even though she was meeting this other man, she only exchanged a few words with him and went with Masuo, whom she'd run into by accident.

They were talking about his daughter, the daughter he'd raised, but when Yoshio reviewed the events of that night, he just couldn't picture Yoshino being part of it. It felt like someone else, some unknown woman who'd been pretending to be Yoshino.

When the two of them arrived at Mitsuse Pass they got into some kind of argument. Yoshio had no idea what they argued about, but *that guy literally kicked my daughter out of the car,* he thought. *On that dark, deserted mountain road—he kicked my daughter out!*

The detective had said they didn't know yet exactly what happened after that. The chances were good that the man she was waiting for in Higashi Park knew something about it.

Yoshio had been sure all the time that the college student had done it. He'd promised himself that when they caught him he'd kill him himself, with his own hands, right in front of his rich parents with their high-priced inns.

Yoshio realized that he'd been hoping that this college student was indeed the murderer. *Otherwise,* he thought, *my daughter has been snatched away by some unknown man, some man she met in an indecent way. My daughter isn't the type of girl that TV programs and magazines should find amusing. She just happened to meet some stupid college student and got killed by him. She wasn't like those disgusting girls you see on TV and in the magazines all the time. She couldn't be! Satoko and I didn't raise her like that. The daughter we raised so lovingly—there's no way she could be like all those idiots on TV.*

Yoshio took the white barber's coat he'd been clutching and flung it at the mirror he'd been staring at. The coat just spread out and barely grazed it.

Yoshio got to his feet and leaped out of the shop. If he sat there any longer, he knew he was going to scream. As he closed the front door he heard Satoko calling out "Honey!" to him, but Yoshio was already running.

202 · V I L L A I N

Yuichi drove through Tosu and then toward Yobuko. The scenery flowing past changed, but they never seemed to get anywhere. When the interstate ended, it connected up with the prefectural highway, and past that were city and local roads. Mitsuyo had a road atlas spread out on the dashboard. She flipped through the maps and saw that the highways and roads were all color-coded. Interstates were orange, prefectural highways were green, local roads were blue, and smaller roads were white. The countless roads were a net, a web that had caught them and the car they were in. All she was doing was taking off from work and going for a drive with a guy she liked, but the more they tried to run away, the more the web of roads pursued them.

To shake off this bad feeling, Mitsuyo snapped the book shut. Yuichi glanced over at the sound and she lied, saying, "Looking at maps in the car makes me feel kind of queasy."

"I know the way to Yobuko," he said.

That morning, after they'd left the love hotel and eaten the rice balls they'd bought at the convenience store, Mitsuyo had asked him, "Shouldn't you call your work and let them know you won't be in?"

"No, it's okay" was all he said, shaking his head and avoiding her eyes.

She knew it didn't make up for Yuichi not calling, but Mitsuyo phoned her sister, who was already at work.

"Oh, thank goodness!" she said. "I was thinking that if you didn't get in touch today, I might have to call the police." She sounded both relieved and angry.

"I'm really sorry," Mitsuyo said. "A whole bunch of things happened—nothing to worry about, though. Anyway, I'll tell you all about it when I get home."

"You mean you'll be back today?"

"I don't know yet."

"What do you mean you don't know? I thought you might be at work, so I phoned your store. Mrs. Mizutani said, Gee, sorry to hear about your father. I played along, but come on, Mitsuyo . . ."

"Sorry. Thanks for covering for me."

"What's happened? You gotta tell me."

"I don't know. . . . I just wanted to take a day off. You've done that yourself, right? Remember when you were a caddie and played hooky from work?"

Yuichi was listening intently to this conversation as he drove.

"Is that all?" Tamayo asked, still not totally convinced.

"Yeah, that's it," Mitsuyo insisted.

"Well, okay then. . . . But, where are you?"

"I'm on a drive."

"A drive? With who?"

"With who? Well, it's sort of . . ." She hadn't meant to do so, but she realized her voice had softened, making it obvious to her sister that she was with a man.

Picking up on this, Tamayo said, more loudly this time, "No! Are you kidding me? When did this happen?"

"I'll tell you all about it when I get back," Mitsuyo replied.

They had just entered Yobuko Harbor, where there were stands lining the road selling dried squid.

Tamayo still wanted more information, but Mitsuyo cut her off and was about to hang up, when she heard Tamayo say, "Is it somebody I know?"

"See ya," Mitsuyo said, and hung up.

They parked in the parking lot away from the harbor, and when they got out of the car they were hit by a blast of cold wind from the sea. There were several more stands near the parking lot, and the wind blew the strands of dried squid hanging down.

Mitsuyo shivered. "The food there is really good," she said to Yuichi as they got out of the car. She pointed to a bed-and-breakfast-cum-restaurant next to the seaside.

When Yuichi didn't reply she turned to him, and he suddenly murmured, "Thank you."

"Huh?" Mitsuyo said, holding down her hair in the sea wind.

"For being with me the whole day," Yuichi said. He was still clutching the car keys tightly.

"But I told you yesterday. How I'd always be with you."

"Thanks . . . Let's eat some squid over there and then drive out to see the lighthouse. It's kind of a small lighthouse, but they have a little park there with a great view from the end of it. And it's nice just to walk there." Yuichi had hardly said a word in the car, but now the words poured out of him.

"Okay."

The sudden change in him left Mitsuyo at a loss for words. A young couple in another car drove into the parking lot, and Mitsuyo took Yuichi's arm to guide him out of the way so the other car could pass.

"Is squid really all they have?" Yuichi asked cheerfully, as if something had been opened inside of him.

Taken by surprise, Mitsuyo nodded, "Ah, yeah," and went on to explain the menu. "You start off with squid sashimi, then they have deep-fried legs or tempura. . . ."

It wasn't yet noon but the restaurant was filling up. The tables on the first floor, which ringed a tank of live fish, were full, so when Mitsuyo told the middle-aged waitress in her white apron that there were just the two of them, she urged them to try the second floor.

They went up the stairs and removed their shoes. They were led down a creaky hallway to a dining room with a large window overlooking the sea. The room would probably fill up soon, but at this point it was empty, with eight tables lined up on the worn-out tatami. Mitsuyo went straight to a table by the window. Yuichi, seated across from her, couldn't keep his eyes off the scene of the harbor below them. There were rows of squid-fishing boats, and far off, beyond the breakwater, the surface of the sea glittered in the winter sun, whitecaps leaping about. Even with the window closed they could hear the sound of the waves breaking against the wharf.

"The view's much better from here than on the first floor," Mitsuyo said as she wiped her hands with the hot towels. "We kind of lucked out."

"Have you been here before?" Yuichi asked.

"My sister and I came here a couple of times, but we were always on the first floor. The first floor's okay, though, with the live-fish tank and everything."

The waitress brought them hot tea and Mitsuyo ordered two set lunches. As she turned to look at the scenery outside Yuichi murmured, "It reminds me of my neighborhood."

"Oh, that's right. Your house is on a harbor, isn't it?"

"Not a harbor like this, just a fishing village."

"You're lucky. I love this scenery. You know they have those articles in magazines that introduce fancy restaurants in Hakata or Tokyo? Every time I see the seafood in those articles, I think, *I bet it's expensive and doesn't taste half as good as the squid in Yobuko.*"

"But don't girls like that kind of restaurant?"

"My younger sister always wants to go that famous French place in Tenjin, I forget the name. I like places like this. The food's so much better. On TV they'd probably say the food here is second-rate gourmet fare or something. I can't stand that. 'Cause the ingredients here are great."

Mitsuyo got all this out in a burst of enthusiasm. Without realizing it, she was getting increasingly excited at the prospect of skipping work and having the whole day free. She suddenly noticed that Yuichi's shoulders were trembling and his eyes were red.

"What's wrong?" she asked. Yuichi's fists were balled tight on the tabletop and were audibly shaking.

"I—I killed someone."

"*What?!*"

"I'm sorry. . . ."

For a moment she couldn't grasp what he was saying. "*What?*" she repeated, startled. Yuichi just looked down, clenching his fists and didn't say another word. His eyes were tearful, his shoulders trembling. Mitsuyo stared at his tightly clenched fists on the cheap table-top. She could see them, right in front of her.

"Wait a second. What are you telling me?" Mitsuyo reached out her own hand but then, confused, pulled it back. It felt like some-body else's hand.

"You killed somebody?" she said. Outside the window was the calm harbor. The fishing boats bobbed in the water, their lines creaking.

"I know I should have told you before this. But I couldn't. When I was with you, it felt like all of this might disappear. Though I knew it wouldn't. . . . I wanted to be with you today, just one more day together with you. Yesterday I was thinking of telling you in the car, but I didn't know if I could get the whole story out." Yuichi's voice trembled terribly, as if shaking in the waves.

"Before I met you I knew another girl. She lived in Hakata. . . ." He paused after each word. For some reason Mitsuyo recalled the pier they'd just been walking along. It was beautiful off in the dis-tance, but now she saw all the garbage floating there, washed by the waves. A plastic bottle of laundry detergent, a filthy Styrofoam box. A single beach sandal.

"I got to know her through the Internet and met her a few times. She told me if I wanted to see her I had to pay for it. . . ."

Just then the *fusuma* slid open and the middle-aged waitress in her apron came in carrying a large serving plate.

"Sorry it took so long."

She placed the heavy-looking plate on the table.

"You can use the soy sauce on the table there."

The white plate was heaped high with colorful seaweed, on top of which was an entire squid. Its body was translucent, clear through to the seaweed below. Its silvery, metallic-looking eyes were unfocused and stared into space. Its legs alone were still writhing, as if they could escape from the plate.

"The legs and whatever else you leave we'll make into tempura or deep-fry for you," the waitress explained, giving the table a tap for emphasis, and then she stood up. They thought she was about to leave, but she suddenly turned to them. "I see I haven't gotten your drink orders yet," she said with a friendly smile. "Shall I bring beer or something?"

Mitsuyo shook her head quickly. "No, we're fine," she said, her hands, for some reason, held up as if holding a steering wheel.

The waitress left, keeping the *fusuma* open behind her. The two of them were alone again in the dining room. Yuichi sat there, head hung down, in front of the plate of squid. Though she'd just heard an unbelievable confession from him, Mitsuyo still reached out and, almost without thinking, poured soy sauce into two smaller plates.

She stared at the two plates with soy sauce for a moment, unsure what to do, then pushed one in front of Yuichi.

"I don't know where to begin," Yuichi murmured as he stared at the plate. He paused. "That night that girl and I had made a date to meet. In a place called Higashi Park in Hakata."

As he began, Mitsuyo found herself wanting to ask questions, but she held back. What kind of woman was she? How many times had they met before this? Yuichi's story tumbled out in bursts, and in the gaps, Mitsuyo thought of one question after another. Finally she asked, "When did all this happen?"

Yuichi looked up. He tried to reply, but his lips were trembling so much he couldn't form the words.

"Before I met you . . ." he managed to say. "Remember when you sent me e-mails? It was before that. . . ."

"You mean the first message?"

Yuichi shook his head listlessly.

"I didn't know what to do back then. . . . I couldn't sleep, it was terrible, and I wanted to talk with somebody. . . . And then you started e-mailing me. . . ."

They could hear the waitress greeting newly arrived customers down the corridor.

"That night I made a date to meet her, but she made a date to meet another guy at the same place. 'I don't have time to see you tonight,' she said, and got in this other guy's car. And they took off somewhere. . . . I felt like she was laughing at me and I couldn't stand it, so I followed them. . . ."

On the table in front of them, the squid's legs were squirming and writhing.

❀

The night was cold, so cold he could see his breath.

In his rearview mirror he saw Yoshino, walking along the path by the park. Yuichi gave his horn a tap to signal her. Startled by the sound, Yoshino stopped for a moment, stared ahead of her, and then hurried over. It all happened quickly. She didn't run to his car, but ran right past him. Flustered, he turned to see where she was going and saw her run up to a man he'd never seen before.

Yoshino grabbed the man's arm in a friendly way and started to talk with him. The whole time the man was looking over in Yuichi's direction with this spiteful look in his eyes. It must be a coincidence, her meeting him here. Once she said hello, she'd come back to him.

As he expected, Yoshino soon walked over. Yuichi was about to open the passenger door, but anticipating this, Yoshino picked up the pace, opened the door herself, and said, "Sorry. Tonight's not going to work out. Just transfer the money to my account. I'll e-mail you the info later."

Then she slammed the door shut and almost skipped back to where the other man was. It happened so quickly. So quickly he had no time to even open his mouth, let alone figure out how he felt.

The man standing in the road wasn't looking at Yoshino as she approached, but at Yuichi, staring at him. He seemed to be smiling, laughing at Yuichi, but Yuichi couldn't tell if that was just the way the light from the streetlight hit him.

Yoshino got in the man's car without glancing back at Yuichi. The car was a dark blue Audi A6, the kind Yuichi could never afford no matter what kind of loan he put together. The car headed down the

empty, tree-lined road beside the park, its exhaust white in the freezing night air.

I've been abandoned, Yuichi realized. The little scene had been
so abrupt. He felt his blood boil beneath his skin, as if his whole body
were engorged by anger.

Yuichi stepped on the accelerator and sped away. The man's car
was up ahead at an intersection, about to turn left. Yuichi had shot
off so fast it almost appeared that he intended to ram the other car
from behind. Actually what he had in mind was to cut it off from the
front and grab Yoshino to get her back. It was less an articulate
thought, though, than a physical reaction.

After turning at the intersection, the man's car headed straight
toward the next light. Yuichi stepped on the gas, but the light
changed and cars started to move in from both sides. There weren't
so many of them, though, and when there was break in the traffic he
sped through the intersection, ignoring the red light. About a hundred meters later he caught up with the car carrying Yoshino.

Yuichi gunned his engine as if he was going to rear-end the other
car, but right as he got up to it, he changed his mind. He was still
enraged, but knew that hitting the other car would damage his own.

He sped up and pulled alongside the man's car. As he drove, he
glanced over at the car and saw Yoshino in the passenger seat, beaming as she talked to the man. All he needed was a word of apology
from her. It was Yoshino who broke their date and he wanted her to
tell him she was sorry.

The road headed toward the Tenjin shopping district. Yuichi
slowed down and continued to shadow the car. Several other cars
pulled into the space separating them, but by the time they reached
the road heading to Mitsuse Pass, no other cars came between them,
even when Yuichi opened up the gap.

Occasional streetlights lit up the red mailboxes and neighborhood
notice boards along the dark street. The road started to rise, and
Yuichi followed the headlights as they palely illuminated the pavement. It looked as if a clump of light were ascending the narrow
mountain road.

Yuichi followed, maintaining an even distance. With each curve, the car's red taillights looked brighter, and each time they lit up, they dyed the forest ahead a deep red. The man was driving fast, but was a poor driver. Even with curves that weren't so sharp, the guy stepped on his brakes right away. And each time he did, Yuichi's car got closer. Yuichi made sure to slow down, and the man's car pulled farther ahead of him. Still, though, every time it rounded a curve on the dark road, Yuichi could spot the car's lights through the thick trees.

The car came to an abrupt stop just near the top of the pass. Yuichi hurriedly braked and switched off his headlights. In the darkness, the red taillights looked like gigantic, glaring red eyes.

Hands on the wheel, Yuichi stared at those red eyes in the woods. It was as if only the pass itself were breathing. A moment later, the interior light of the other car came on, and the shadows of the man and Yoshino were moving. It all happened quickly. The door opened and Yoshino was getting out. The man kicked her in the back. Yoshino was like an animal struck by a car. She collapsed by the side of the road and struck her head sharply on the guardrail.

The man's car shot away, leaving Yoshino crouching down, facing away from the guardrail. For a second Yuichi wasn't sure what he'd just witnessed, and was about to take off after the man's car. But as soon as he'd released his parking brake he could picture Yoshino, left behind beside the road. Lit up by his red taillights, Yoshino looked as if she were on fire. Yuichi hurriedly set his parking brake again. He yanked it so sharply there was a weird sound from the undercarriage.

Once the man's car rounded the next curve up ahead, all color faded from the scene. Yoshino's red-dyed figure was about to be swallowed up by the darkness of the pass. Yuichi wasn't sure how much time had gone by after the man's car drove off, but he nervously turned on his headlights. The lights didn't quite reach to where she was crouched down, but it helped more than the weak winter moonlight.

He released his parking brake again and lightly stepped on the accelerator. The bluish headlights inched down the road toward Yoshino as slowly as water soaking into a cloth. When the headlights finally reached her, she looked up fearfully, squinting into the brightness. Yuichi set his parking brake again and opened his door. Yoshino clutched her handbag defensively.

"Are you okay?" Yuichi called out, but his voice was swallowed up in the dark pass. The only sound was that of the car engine, like the earth rumbling in the distance.

As Yuichi stepped into the light, Yoshino's expression changed.

"What are you doing here? Did you follow me? Just quit it!" she yelled, clutching her handbag to her and crouching by the roadside.

"Are you—okay?" Despite her yells, Yuichi continued to approach her, reaching out to help her to her feet. But Yoshino brushed away his hand.

"You saw it all?" she said. "You're unbelievable!" She struggled to her feet.

"What happened?" Yuichi asked. As she staggered to her feet in her high-heeled boots, Yuichi took her hand, which felt as if pebbles were embedded in it.

"Nothing happened! I don't have to tell you anything!" She brushed away his hand and started to walk off. Yuichi took her arm again.

"Why don't you get in the car. I'll give you a ride home." When he said this, Yoshino glanced toward his car. The two of them stood there in the headlights, as if this were the entire world.

Yuichi tugged at her arm and she shouted, "Enough already! Leave me alone!" She shook free.

"You can't walk back from here!" Yuichi retorted, pulling her arm hard. His timing was off and the movement made Yoshino, who was starting to walk, slip. She lost her balance, and fell right in front of the car. Yuichi reached out hurriedly to support her but his elbow pushed her right in the back. Yoshino twisted in a strange way and banged right into the grille of the car. As she reached out to break her fall, her little finger got stuck between the front of the car and the bumper.

"Ouch!" her scream echoed, enough to send a flock of birds sleeping in the dark woods shooting into the air.

"Are you okay?" Yuichi hurriedly tried to lift her up. Yoshino's finger was still stuck. He put his arms under her sides and tried to lift her up again, but as he did so she screamed and her little finger bent back at an awful angle.

It all had happened in an instant. The blood drained from her face, lit by the bright headlights as she crouched there, and each single hair on her head stood on end.

"I . . . I'm sorry. . . . I'm really sorry."

Yoshino, her faced twisted in pain, finally pried her finger loose, and clenched her teeth. "You murderer!" she screamed the moment Yuichi rested his hand on her shoulder. He pulled away.

"You murderer!" she screamed. "I'm going to tell the police! Tell them you assaulted me and kidnapped me. How you kidnapped me and almost raped me! We have a lawyer in our family, so don't think you can get away with this! I'm not the kind of woman to go out with a guy like you! You're a murderer!"

Yuichi knew it was all a lie, but he found his knees shaking.

When she'd gotten it all out, Yoshino started to walk away, holding her injured finger. Once away from the car, her figure was sucked up into the blackness of the pass.

"Hey—hold on a second," Yuichi called out, but she walked on.

As the sound of footsteps grew farther away in the darkness, Yuichi ran after her.

"Don't lie like that! I didn't do anything!"

As he shouted this and ran toward her, Yoshino halted, and turned around. "You better believe I'm going to tell them!" she yelled. "I'm going to tell them how you kidnapped me and raped me!" Even though he was in a mountain pass in the middle of winter, Yuichi's ears were filled with the loud buzzing of cicadas echoing from all the hills. A buzzing so loud he wanted to block out the noise.

He didn't know what he was afraid of. She hadn't been kidnapped or raped. He knew it was a lie, but he turned pale as if he had really committed these crimes. *You're lying! That's a lie!* he desperately shouted inside his mind, but instead he heard the pass whisper back:

Who will ever believe you? Who in the world will ever believe you?

The only thing there was the dark mountain pass. There weren't any other witnesses. *There's nobody to testify that I didn't do anything. I didn't do anything!* He could picture himself trying to explain things to his grandmother. Himself, shouting out, *I didn't do anything!* to the people surrounding him. He recalled his voice when he was a child at the ferryboat dock, explaining, *My mom will be coming back!* His voice when nobody believed him.

Yuichi grabbed Yoshino's shoulder.

"Don't touch me!"

As she pushed him away, her arm hit Yuichi's ear. Pain shot through him as if he'd been struck by a metal rod. Instinctively, he grabbed her arm. As she struggled to get away, he pushed her down until he was sitting on top of her on the chilly pavement. Yoshino's face in the moonlight was twisted in anger.

"I didn't do anything."

He held down her shoulders. In a voice at once pained and snarling, she shouted back, "Who's ever going to believe you! You murderer! Help!" Yoshino's screams shook the trees in the pass. Every time she screamed, Yuichi's body trembled in fright. If someone ever heard these lies of hers . . .

"But I didn't do anything. I didn't do anything."

Yuichi shut his eyes. He was desperately pressing down on her throat, so frightened he couldn't help it. No one could ever hear these lies she was spouting. He had to kill these lies quickly or else the truth itself would die. And the thought terrified him.

Several squid-fishing boats were tied up at the wharf. The lines that tied them up were slack, and schools of small fish swam up from the bottom of their hulls. A moment ago, a little girl had pedaled her tricycle over to where Mitsuyo and Yuichi stood on the wharf, then pedaled back to where her mother was at one of the stands.

Mitsuyo and Yuichi had left the restaurant without finishing their meal. By the time Yuichi had finished his story, the squirming legs of the freshly prepared squid on the platter had gone limp. Fortunately, no other guests had come into the second-floor dining hall. The middle-aged waitress, however, had checked in on them a few times.

When he finished speaking, Yuichi had simply said, "I'm sorry," in a small voice. Mitsuyo was silent and he went on. "I'm turning myself in now," he said.

Mitsuyo nodded, her mind blank.

Just then, the waitress came over and asked, "You're not that fond of sashimi, then?"

"It's not that," Mitsuyo lied. "I'm just not feeling very well."

Mitsuyo stood up and Yuichi looked at her, resigned. "Let's get out of here," she said. Yuichi was amazed; he had expected her to leave him there. When they apologized to the waitress for leaving all the food, she said, "It's okay. It's on the house."

They left the restaurant and walked along the wharf where the boats were anchored. Without really realizing it, they were heading toward the parking lot. On one level, Mitsuyo knew she was going to get into his car, the car of a man who'd murdered someone, but as she walked along the cold, windswept wharf, there seemed to be nowhere else to go. She was amazed at herself for having listened to him to the end, without screaming, without getting up and running away. What he told her had been too overwhelming, so overwhelming that her mind wouldn't function.

As they came to the end of the wharf, Mitsuyo stopped and looked down at all the garbage bobbing up against the wharf.

"I'm going to go to the police right now."

Staring down at the flotsam, Mitsuyo nodded.

"I'm really sorry. I never meant to cause any problems for you, Mitsuyo. . . ."

Mitsuyo nodded again before he'd finished. The little girl on her tricycle was pedaling over to them again. A pink ribbon tied to the handlebars looked about to rip off in the cold, stiff wind.

The girl pedaled between them and started back to her mother at the squid stall. Mitsuyo watched her, pedaling furiously away.

"Forgive me," Yuichi said, bowing to her and heading off alone to the parking lot. His back looked as if it had shrunk one whole size. As if he would break down in tears if she touched him.

"Which police station are you going to?" Mitsuyo called out.

Yuichi turned around. "I don't know. I guess if we go into Karatsu there must be a station somewhere," he said.

What do you care? part of her mentally shouted. *Get out of here as quick as you can.* But she also felt terribly frustrated. She had to say something.

"Don't leave me here alone," Mitsuyo said. "If you leave me here by myself, what'll I do? I'll go with you, to the police. We can go together."

A blast of wind from the sea blew her words away. Yuichi stared at her intently. And then, without a word, he started walking away again.

"Wait!" Mitsuyo shouted, and Yuichi halted.

"I can't let you do that. You'll get in trouble," he said without turning around.

"I already am in trouble!" she shouted. A middle-aged woman cleaning squid on the other side of the road shot them a glance.

Without replying Yuichi set off again and Mitsuyo ran after him. She'd wanted to say something, but not that.

When he reached the parking lot Yuichi stopped, and clenched his fists as his shoulders shook.

"Why did things turn out like this?" he moaned.

The sound of Yuichi's crying drowned out the slap of the waves against the breakwaters. Mitsuyo walked around in front of him and took his tightly clenched fists in her hands.

"Let's go to the police," she said. "We'll go together. . . . You're scared, aren't you? To go alone? I'll go with you. If we're together . . . if we're together I know you can make it."

Yuichi's hands trembled in hers. He nodded again and again.

"Yeah . . . yeah . . ." he said, and she could feel him trembling, and feel each nod.

❦

It was past two p.m. when it started to get cloudy. After he heard the detective's explanation, Yoshio Ishibashi had run out of his shop, walked the three minutes to the parking lot where he rented a space, and got in his car. Where he was headed, though, he had no idea.

The Fukuoka college student wasn't the murderer after all. Instead, it was some man she'd met on an online dating site. That's what the police had told him, but he still wasn't convinced. He wasn't even convinced that his daughter had been part of all this. It had to be some kind of mistake. Somebody, for whatever motive, must be out to get them.

Yoshino is still alive somewhere, he told himself. *Waiting for me to come and rescue her . . . but I don't know where she is. Everybody I ask keeps telling me she's dead.*

He drove aimlessly. He knew these streets well, but through his tears Kurume looked like a place he'd never seen before.

His car was one that Yoshino had picked out, back when she'd just entered high school. He'd told her he didn't want any bright colors, but she kept insisting he had to get a red car. "Red is so cute!" she'd said. He finally compromised, buying a light-green compact.

The day the car was delivered, they took a picture of the three of them posed in front of it. Yoshino was overjoyed, and no matter how much Yoshio tried to persuade her, she wouldn't allow him to remove the plastic protective sheets over the seats.

He drove aimlessly for hours around Kurume. He just wanted to see Yoshino. He wanted to know where she was. He could hear her voice, calling out for help, but where his daughter was, he had no idea.

Before he knew it, he was heading toward Mitsuse Pass. He drove out of Kurume onto the highway, crossed the river, and suddenly realized he was driving down a road through the fields in the Saga plains. Before him lay the mountains of the Sefuri range.

The weather started to cloud up right about the time he stopped at a gas station. He went to the restroom as they were filling up his gas tank, and from the small window he saw the dark rain clouds moving in over the mountains. The clouds spread out until they hid the peak of the pass and began to approach the plain where Yoshio was.

It began to sprinkle right as he left the restroom. There was an outdoor sink, but he didn't wash his hands there and instead sprinted for his car, whose gas tank was full now. A girl about the same age as Yoshino trotted over and handed him the receipt. It was wet with the rain. Yoshio paid her and pulled out. In the rearview mirror he could see the girl in the rain, standing there, bowing as he left.

It began to pour just as he started up the road to the pass. The low rain clouds covering the sky turned the road dark and gloomy.

Yoshio switched on his headlights. Beyond the wipers he could see the pale asphalt road rising up. Rain lashed his windshield and his wipers moved so quickly that it looked as if they would blow away.

The headlights of cars descending from the pass lit up the beads of rain on the windshield. The rain drowned out the sound of his engine, and even from inside the car, all Yoshio could hear was the sound of rain whipping against the trees.

On the day of Yoshino's funeral his cousin, who worked in a factory in Kurume, had said, "Someday I'd like to light some incense in memory of Yoshino at the spot where she died." So many things had happened to him so quickly, and Yoshio couldn't reply at the time, but one of his female relatives had added, "If you go, I'd like to go, too. And place some flowers there, and some of the sweets that Yoshino liked . . ."

He knew they were only being kind to him, but it felt to Yoshio as if accepting their kindness would mean saying goodbye to Yoshino forever.

"I'm not going" was all he said to them. His relatives fell silent.

He couldn't recall when it was, but at some point after the funeral, he saw a scene on TV picturing flowers and cans of juice lined up at the site of the murder. Perhaps his relatives had quietly visited the site after all, or maybe complete strangers had gone to offer flowers to Yoshino, who had been the brunt of so much criticism. When Yoshio had seen this, he sobbed. The criticism of Yoshino in the press and on TV had been indirect, but the obscene faxes and letters he'd received were anything but.

Sorry your prostitute daughter was killed? She asked for it.

I slept with your daughter once. ¥500 for the night.

No wonder that girl was murdered. Prostitution's against the law.

You should have sent her more spending money!

Some of them were handwritten, others printed from a computer. It had gotten to the point where Yoshio was afraid when the mailman arrived every morning. He'd disconnected the phone, but still heard it ringing in his dreams. It seemed as if the whole country hated his daughter, as if everyone in Japan despised him and his family.

The rain grew stronger as he climbed the pass. The fog was thick, mist accumulating a few dozen meters in front of his car.

Just before the entrance to the Mitsuse Tunnel, there was a sign indicating the old road. The sign loomed up for an instant, as if someone had momentarily blown away the fog with their breath.

Yoshio hurriedly turned and started down the narrow old road. As the road narrowed even more, it felt as if his small car would be engulfed in the cascade of water rushing down the cliffs. The rain washing down the face of the mountain struck the cracked asphalt and then plunged to the cliffs below.

On the main road he'd passed a few other cars, but on this older road, he saw not a single one. The guardrail protruded, as if there'd been an accident. And that's when his headlights lit up the bouquets and plastic bottles lined up on the ground. The bouquets, wrapped in clear plastic wrap, seemed about to be swept away in the rain. Yoshio slowly braked. In the fog, these items placed in memory of his daughter somehow stood up to the pounding rain.

He reached for the umbrella that had slipped to the floor in the backseat, and stepped out into the downpour. The car engine was still running, but all he could hear was the roar of the rain, as if he'd wandered behind a waterfall.

The umbrella was heavy as the rain beat down on it, and the cold rain stung his cheeks and neck. Yoshio stood in front of the offerings lit by his headlights. The flowers were wilted, and the stuffed porpoise toy that someone had left was drowning in muddy water.

Yoshio picked up the soaked toy. He hadn't meant to grip it so hard but found cold water dripping between his fingers. He knew he was crying, but in the cold driving rain he couldn't feel the tears flow down his cheeks.

"Yoshino . . . ," he said without thinking. The faint voice turned into white breath and left his lips.

"Daddy's here, honey. . . . I'm so sorry it took me so long. Daddy's come to see you. You must be cold. And lonely. But Daddy's here."

He couldn't stop. Once his mouth opened, the words just kept pouring out.

The rain slapped against his vinyl umbrella and flowed to his feet. As it struck near his feet it soaked his dirty sneakers.

"Daddy . . ."

Suddenly he heard Yoshino's voice. It wasn't an illusion, she was clearly calling to him. He spun around. His umbrella slanted to one side but he didn't care that he was getting soaked.

The headlights of his car shone on the fog. And standing there was Yoshino. She didn't have an umbrella, but wasn't wet at all.

"Daddy, you came to see me?" Yoshino was smiling.

"Yeah, I did." Yoshio nodded.

The downpour was striking his hands and cheeks, but Yoshio no longer felt the cold. The freezing wind blowing down the road, too, went around the light.

"What are you . . . doing in a place like this?" Yoshio asked. Tears and his dripping nose combined with the rain to flow into his mouth and he could barely get the words out.

"Daddy, you came to see me. . . ." Yoshino, enveloped in light, smiled.

"What . . . what happened here? What did they do to you? Who did this to you? Who? . . . Who? . . ." Unable to bear it any longer, Yoshio broke down and sobbed.

"Daddy . . ."

"Hmm? . . . What is it?" Yoshio wiped his tears and runny nose with his wet jacket sleeve.

"Forgive me, Daddy." In the light, Yoshino looked apologetic. Ever since she was a child this was the sort of look she gave him when she apologized.

"You don't need to apologize for anything!"

"Daddy . . . I'm so sorry. I'm sorry you had to go through this. . . ."

"You don't need to apologize. No matter what, I'm your father. And no matter what, I'll protect you. . . . I'll always protect you."

The sound of the rain whipping against the trees grew louder. As the sound grew, his daughter looked about to disappear, and he yelled out her name. "Yoshino!" Sobbing, he stretched out a hand toward the light and his daughter, fading from view.

In an instant Yoshino had vanished. All that was left was the headlights illuminating the downpour. Calling out her name, Yoshio frantically looked around him. The wet guardrail stretched out around a curve and disappeared, and beyond that was a dense, dripping forest.

He no longer cared that he was drenched. Yoshio ran to where he'd seen Yoshino standing. But the rain-soaked cliffs stood in his way, and the wet grasses brushed his cheeks. Yoshio touched the cold rock face with his hands and called out Yoshino's name twice. His voice pierced the rocks.

He turned and saw that his umbrella was lying in front of the flower offerings. He hadn't noticed that it had fallen, but now it was upside down and filled with rain.

Just then it started to get a bit lighter out. He looked up and saw a small patch of blue sky, far off, barely peeking through the thick clouds. Rain continued to spatter at his feet, and his trousers were soaked to the knee with muddy water.

"Yoshino . . ."

His soaked body was frozen, his breath white.

"You didn't put Daddy through anything bad. I can put up with anything if it's for you, honey. If it's for your sake, Mom and Dad can put up with anything. . . ."

His voice gave out and he knelt down on the soaked pavement.

"Yoshino!" he cried out one last time to the sky. But no matter how long he waited, she did not appear again on the foggy mountain road.

It kept on raining and his wet clothes were heavy.

Daddy, I'm so sorry.

Trembling now in the cold, Yoshio heard his daughter's voice again in his ear. "Yoshino . . ." he murmured once more. The name fell to the wet pavement and formed a ripple in a puddle.

"I'll never forgive him! Never!" Yoshio pounded the wet pavement a few times with his fist. Blood oozed out from his hand, into the freezing rain.

Finally, he stood up in the rain and with his bloody hand picked up one of the wilted bouquets of flowers someone had left by the roadside.

"I'm telling you there's no way. Me a murderer? Kill that kind of woman? You gotta be kidding!"

Victoriously, Keigo Masuo went to the counter to get his second beer, then happily began to gulp it down. He'd been questioned by the police for just one night, but was acting as if he'd been released from jail after many years.

Seated on the sofa were a dozen or so of Keigo's friends, including Koki Tsuruta. As Keigo stood there downing his beer, they looked up at him almost reverently.

Koki had barely touched his beer, but now he took a sip. As the group discussed what they had thought when they heard that Keigo had disappeared, they were so loud they drowned out the late afternoon music in the café, and even the clatter when a waitress dropped a plate.

It was after two that afternoon when they'd received an e-mail from Keigo. Koki had been in his apartment, asleep as usual, when the e-mail came in saying that anybody who wanted to hear what had happened should drop everything and come to the Monsoon Café in Tenjin. Koki was sure it was a practical joke, but a few minutes later Keigo phoned him. "Did ja see the message?" he said in a carefree voice. "You gotta come. I'll tell you all about life on the run." Koki had a million things he wanted to ask him, but Keigo just laughed. "Too much trouble to repeat the story to everyone individually, so I'd like to just tell it once to everyone." And then he abruptly hung up.

The Monsoon was the kind of upscale café college students liked, where they served alcohol during the day, and the food and prices were reasonable enough. The kind of place where the management spent all its money on the interior design.

When Koki got there, ten or so people were already waiting for Keigo, but the guest of honor had yet to arrive. They all knew Keigo had been arrested in Nagoya, and were loudly speculating about how he had to be innocent, since the police had let him go.

When Keigo showed up outside the glass-enclosed café, a shout rose from among his friends. Some young girls, bent over their uninspired lunches, looked up to see what the commotion was about.

As Keigo came in, he winked at a waitress he apparently knew, and announced, "I, Keigo Masuo, have now been freed!" and spread wide his arms and bowed. Some of his friends clapped, others burst out laughing.

Keigo started off by telling his impatient fans why he was late. Earlier that morning, he'd been completely cleared of all charges by the police and released, and had gone back to his condo to take a shower. Which perhaps explained why he didn't have the pathetic look of a runaway criminal that his friends had pictured.

As soon as Keigo sat down among them, they peppered him with questions: "Okay, so what really happened?" "You really didn't kill her, right?" "If you didn't, then why run away?" Keigo stopped them and turned to the vacant-looking waitress standing there and ordered a Belgian beer.

"One at a time, guys. . . . I guess you could say it was simply a misunderstanding on my part."

"A misunderstanding?" everyone around the table asked.

"Yeah, you could say that. I don't know where to start. Hey, did they redecorate this place?"

Keigo was the one who'd called them all together, but he seemed to find the conversation kind of boring. Koki, sitting beside him, tried to get the story back on track. "Why don't you start by telling us what happened that night," he asked.

"Yeah, right, that night . . ." Keigo glanced up at the ceiling fan, then looked back at them. "Well, it's true I was with that girl that night," he began. "I was feeling kind of irritated. You guys get that way sometimes, right? There's no real reason for it, but you feel kind of disgusted by things, and then you can't sit still."

The young men all nodded.

"It happens, am I right? Well, that night I was feeling like that, so I decided to get in my car and race around. I was driving around and had to piss, so I stopped at the Higashi Park, and that's where I ran into her."

"Did you know her?" the man seated farthest from Keigo asked, leaning out over the table.

"Uh, yeah, I did. Koki, you knew her, too, right? Remember those three girls who worked for an insurance company we met at a bar in Tenjin? The ones who were like fresh off the farm? Some of you must have been there that night?"

Several of his friends finally remembered. "Yeah, that's right," they said.

"It was one of them. After that, she wouldn't let up with the e-mails. Oh, yeah—that's right! The police checked out my phone and there were still a few of her messages on it. You want to see them?"

Want to see some e-mail from that girl who was murdered at Mitsuse Pass? Keigo was proudly asking them, and the group of men leaned forward expectantly. For a second, Koki had a creepy, bad feeling about it, but he was carried along by the enthusiasm of the others, so he felt he couldn't object.

Keigo pulled out his cell phone and scrolled through his e-mails. "So anyway, I happened to run across that girl that night and gave her a ride. That was my first mistake. . . ."

He paused, then continued. "She was looking at me with these dreamy, *please-take-me-somewhere* eyes. Like I said, I was in a bad mood, so I just thought, Why not take this slutty girl somewhere, get it on, and that might make me feel better. So I gave her a ride. But she'd apparently had *gyoza* and her breath stank, and that sort of made me lose interest. So anyway, after we drove up to Mitsuse Pass I couldn't stand being with her anymore and left her there."

Keigo was roughly scrolling through the messages on his phone, apparently having trouble locating the older ones. His friends grew impatient watching his fingers move.

"If you just left her there, then why run away?" somebody asked, and Keigo's fingers stopped. He looked up and grinned.

"The girl didn't want to get out, so finally I got physical. I wasn't really thinking. And she hit her neck and it wound up like I was strangling her."

As one, the men surrounding him gulped.

"No, that isn't why she died. I was just pushing her out the door and accidentally pushed against her neck, that's all. But when I heard that that girl had died there, at the pass, and there wasn't anyone else around at the time, I jumped to the wrong conclusion and thought, Wow, what if that was why she died. . . ."

Keigo laughed, trying to ease the tension, and gradually his laughter spread to the others. Koki, however, felt disgusted. He looked around, but he was the only one with a grimace on his face.

"So that's why you went on the lam for a couple of weeks?" someone asked, and Keigo nodded sheepishly.

"As the girl was getting out of the car, I gave her a huge shove with my foot and she fell out and hit her head on the guardrail. . . . But she didn't really get hurt or anything."

As Keigo nonchalantly continued, Koki felt as if he was going to vomit. Just as Koki was about to stand up, Keigo finally located the old e-mails.

"Oh, I got it! Here they are."

He placed the cell phone on the table and someone stood up behind Koki and bent forward eagerly, leaning against him. Koki lost his balance and nearly hit his forehead against the table.

"Here, check it out!"

Hands went in all directions, in an attempt to grab the cell phone. Finally the guy seated across from Keigo grabbed it, and pushing away everyone else, he started to read the messages aloud in a high-pitched, girlish whine.

Just then they heard some loud girls' voices near the café entrance. The men turned to look at the commotion and found three girls from their college, the core of a flashy group that hung out with Keigo — Keigo's entourage, as others referred to them.

"Keigo!" one of the girls shouted and the three of them ran over to him in a group.

"What're you girls doing here?"

The men scrunched over on the sofa to make room and the girls squeezed in. As soon as they sat down, they peppered Keigo with the same questions the men had earlier, and Keigo, being Keigo, gave them the same answers as before.

While Keigo and the girls were talking, the men passed around Keigo's cell. Koki could tell from their expressions what sort of messages the dead girl had sent him. To him it felt as if the murdered girl's body itself were being passed around from one pair of hands to the next.

A girl who'd sent one e-mail after another to a guy with no interest in her had been murdered at Mitsuse Pass. Keigo, sitting next to him, hadn't murdered her. Still, if Keigo hadn't met her that night — even if was just coincidence — the girl would never have wound up at the pass.

It was Koki's turn to see the phone. Beside him, Keigo was entertaining the girls with the story of how he was interrogated by the police, and it was hard to tell how much was true and how much was being embellished for their benefit. Like, did they really shine a bright light on Keigo as they interrogated him, just like in a TV drama?

"A drama," Koki muttered to himself. He looked down and saw the e-mail from the murdered girl. He didn't want to read it, but he couldn't pull his eyes away.

Universal Studios sounds like so much fun!

The words leaped out at him.

❀

There was a patch of blue sky off in the distance, but raindrops were still striking the windshield. Drops mixed together and silently flowed down the glass, followed by more.

The car was stopped by the road that ran along the coast. The wet asphalt had changed color, making the surrounding scenery look dark. The inside of the car where Mitsuyo and Yuichi sat was as dark as if it were twilight.

Down this road was the police station. Just a few dozen yards more and they would enter its grounds.

They had no idea how long they'd been sitting there. Had they parked just a moment ago, or sat there the whole night? Mitsuyo reached out to touch the rain on the windshield. She was inside the car and of course couldn't really touch it, but her fingertips felt as if they were wet. It was hard to see very far beyond the car.

For the last few minutes she'd noticed Yuichi's ragged breathing beside her. If she turned, she would see him, but she couldn't bring herself to look. She was seized by the fear that if she did look over, it would all be over.

At the Yobuko pier Mitsuyo had told Yuichi she'd go with him to the police. *I can't let you do that. You'll get in trouble,* he'd insisted, but she'd almost forced her way into the car.

She was with a murderer, but Mitsuyo didn't feel afraid. It felt less like she'd met a murderer than like somebody she already knew had committed a crime. It had happened before she'd even met him, but still she felt frustrated and exasperated, as if she could have done something to prevent it.

They'd driven away from the parking lot in Yobuko and headed toward the center of Tosu. Until they hit the city, they didn't say a word to each other. The roads were empty, and they soon neared the city center. As they did, a sign for the Tosu Police Department appeared by the side of the road. Yuichi shook the steering wheel nervously and slowed down.

A few dozen yards ahead was a cream-colored building standing alone in a large lot. A traffic-safety banner hung from the building, billowing in the strong wind from the nearby sea.

There were no other cars on the street.

"I think . . . you'd better get out here, Mitsuyo," Yuichi said, hands on the wheel, eyes avoiding hers.

That's when it started raining. The sky had become cloudy, and now raindrops were drumming against the windshield. A young mother pushing a baby carriage down the street hurriedly pulled on its plastic hood.

"You'd better get out here, Mitsuyo," Yuichi repeated, and fell silent.

She was silent, too. "So that's it?" she finally muttered.

Yuichi kept his eyes down, staring at his feet. She didn't know what she hoped to have him say by asking that, but simply being told to *get out here* was too sad to bear.

They were silent again. The rain on the windshield began running down the glass in rivulets.

"If they see you with me you'll get in trouble," Yuichi murmured, his hands tightly clasping the wheel.

"You mean if I get out here, I won't get in any more trouble?" Mitsuyo said roughly.

"Sorry," he said.

She had no idea at all why she'd said that. The last thing she wanted to do at this stage was to abuse him.

"I'm sorry," she said in a small voice.

In the side mirror she could see the young mother from behind as she pushed the baby carriage. The young woman was walking along at a normal speed, though she must have wanted to sprint to get out of the rain. Mitsuyo let out a huge sigh. She felt as if she'd forgotten to breathe for the past few minutes.

"After you go to the police, then what?" This came out of her mouth before she'd thought it through. Yuichi stared at his hands on the wheel, then looked up and shook his head as if he hadn't a clue.

"If you give yourself up, then they won't punish you as much, right?" Mitsuyo said.

Yuichi shook his head again as if he had no idea.

"Someday we'll see each other again, won't we?"

He looked toward her and she saw the tears welling up in his eyes.

"I'll wait for you," Mitsuyo said. "No matter how many years it takes."

Yuichi's shoulders began to shake, and he kept on violently shaking his head. Mitsuyo reached out and touched his cheek. She could feel his shaking through her fingers.

"I'm . . . scared. I might get the death penalty."

Mitsuyo gently held his ear. It was burning up.

"If I hadn't met you, Mitsuyo, I wouldn't be this scared. I was kind of nervous before, thinking they'd arrest me, but I couldn't give myself up. But I wasn't this scared. I knew my grandparents would cry about it, and I'd feel sorry for all they'd done for me, raising me, but it didn't hurt as bad as it does now. If I hadn't met you . . ."

Mitsuyo listened as the words streamed out of Yuichi. She could feel his ear grow even hotter in her hand.

"But you still have to go," Mitsuyo said. She felt him shaking, and could barely get the words out. "You have to give yourself up, and pay for what you did. . . ."

Yuichi nodded, as if all the energy had drained out of him. "I might get the death penalty. . . . Then I'll never see you again."

The phrase *death penalty* simply didn't register with Mitsuyo. She knew what it meant, of course, but all the meaning had drained out of the term, and she could only comprehend it as *goodbye*.

Mitsuyo took his trembling hands. She wanted to say something but nothing came. The two of them were not simply saying goodbye, since *goodbye* still held the hope of a future. Mitsuyo felt she was making some huge mistake, and she desperately clutched Yuichi's hands. Something was coming to an end, she knew. Right here, right now, something decisive was coming to an end.

That's when the memory of a scene came to her. It came so suddenly she couldn't recall where and when she'd seen it. She closed her eyes and tried to conjure up the details. Desperately she squeezed her eyes shut, and finally a vague, unfocused scene floated before her.

Where am I? she murmured. But what she pictured, like a single photograph, was a frozen scene, and when she tried to see the other parts they wouldn't materialize.

Two young girls were standing before her. Their backs were to her, and they were giggling happily together. Beyond them was an older woman, her back also turned, her face to a wall. She was talking. No, it wasn't a wall. A kind of window. Beyond a transparent board there was man's face, a man selling tickets.

Where am I? she asked herself again. She kept her eyes shut and recalled a map of routes above the ticket window.

"Oh!" Mitsuyo suddenly called out. It was a map of bus routes. She was standing at the ticket window for the long-distance buses from Saga to Hakata.

The instant she realized this, the still scene came alive with sound and movement. From behind her was an announcement for the arriving bus. The girls were giggling. The old woman who'd just bought her ticket was putting away her purse as she left the ticket window, and was heading over to where the bus had just pulled in.

It had to be. There was no doubt about it. This was the bus to Hakata, the one that was hijacked.

Don't get on that bus! In her mind, Mitsuyo yelled out to the old woman. But no one heard her.

Don't buy them! she screamed again, but no sound came out. Her legs began to move forward in the line, and she was trembling all over. If nothing stopped her, she was going to buy a ticket herself. *My cell phone!* she remembered. This was the moment that her friend called. When her friend informed her that her son was sick, could they reschedule?

Mitsuyo rummaged frantically through her handbag, but couldn't come up with her cell phone. The young girls had bought their tickets and were happily traipsing over toward the bus. *I can't find my cell phone. I can't find it.* The man at the window said, "Next!" calling out to Mitsuyo. She didn't want to, but her legs carried her forward. She struggled to run away, but her face approached the counter and her mouth moved on its own.

One adult for Tenjin.

My cell phone's gone. The one that's supposed to ring right now.

Almost ready to scream, Mitsuyo opened her eyes. In front of her was a rainy street, and beyond that a rainy police station. She looked over at Yuichi. And right then it happened. A patrol car was coming toward them from the opposite direction. It slowed down, put on its turn signal, then made a right turn into the grounds of the police station.

"No way!" Mitsuyo shouted. "No way! I don't want to get on that bus!"

Her voice was loud enough to echo inside the car. Startled, Yuichi held his breath.

"Start driving! *Please.* Just for a while, just for a while is okay. Get us out of here!" Yuichi stared at her, wide-eyed. "*Please!*"

For a moment, Yuichi didn't know what to do. Mitsuyo kept on shouting, and her panic finally infected him. He hurriedly released the parking brake and stepped on the gas.

They roared past the police station, and soon turned left. The road ran along a concrete embankment. Ahead was the prefectural yacht harbor, its large sign dripping in the rain. Yuichi stopped the car there. The police station was still visible.

As soon as they had started driving again, Mitsuyo began to sob. Having to say goodbye to Yuichi meant she had to get on that bus. Get on that bus and have that boy come at her with a knife.

Yuichi kept the engine running, but switched off the wipers. In an instant the windshield was wet, the scenery before them a blur.

"No! No way!" Mitsuyo shouted as she stared at the blurry windshield. "No way! If I have to leave you now, I have nothing left. . . . I thought I was going to be happy! After I met you I thought I was finally going to be happy! Please don't take that away from me!"

Yuichi wavered, then reached over to Mitsuyo, touching her shoulder, and swiftly pulled her close. Mitsuyo roughly tried to break free, but Yuichi held her even tighter, and all she could do was stay still and cry in his arms.

"I'm so sorry . . . so very sorry. . . ." His voice sounded as if it were biting her neck. Mitsuyo shook her head as hard as she could. Her cheek struck his with each shake of her head. "I'm so sorry . . . so sorry I couldn't do anything for you. . . ." Mitsuyo couldn't tell if she was crying, or if it was Yuichi.

"*Please!*" she pleaded into his shoulder. "Don't leave me behind! Don't ever leave me alone!" She knew they couldn't run away, but still she shouted for them to do exactly that. "Let's run away!" she cried. "Let's run away together!" She knew she was never going to be happy now, but still she shouted out, "Stay with me! Don't leave me behind—ever!"

Never before had Fusae cursed the passing of time. But it had been six days since she'd heard from Yuichi, and she suddenly noticed that the rest of the world was about to celebrate the end of the year.

Fusae was born the third child of a tatami craftsman from the outskirts of Nagasaki City. When she was ten, her father—about to depart for the war front—died of tuberculosis, and that same year, her mother had given birth to her second son. Now she was left to care for four children: her fifteen-year-old elder daughter, ten-year-old Fusae, her four-year-old older son, and the newborn infant boy.

Through some relatives, Fusae's mother found a job working at a restaurant in the city called Seyokan. Her fifteen-year-old daughter was working in a factory as part of the wartime student work corps, so it fell to ten-year-old Fusae to take care of her two brothers.

Occasionally her mother would steal eggs from the restaurant and bring them home. This was the best food they had. Late one evening, her mother still had not come home, so Fusae and her older sister went to the restaurant to find her. The head clerk had discovered her mother stealing eggs, and had tied her to a pillar in the kitchen. The two girls, in tears, apologized for their mother. When their mother saw them, she quietly sobbed, still tied to the pillar.

The rationing system had started by then, and Fusae had to line up with the adults to get her family's share, her four-year-old brother in hand, the baby on her back. When rations were plentiful, the adults would sometimes let her go to the front of the line, but when commodities were in short supply the frenzied housewives kept pushing her out of the way. The arrogant man in charge treated Fusae and her brothers like stray dogs. He'd shove them aside, tossing their ration of potatoes and corn at them. Fusae and her brother desperately scrambled in the dirt to pick up their potatoes.

How dare you! How dare you make fun of me! Fusae wanted to scream, holding back tears as she grabbed for the potatoes.

Life didn't get any easier after the war. Miraculously, their family didn't lose a single member to the atomic bombing, the one stroke of luck they had, her mother said. Fusae graduated from junior high and began working at a fish market. There she met Katsuji, and they were later married. It took her some time to have a child, and her mother-in-law occasionally abused her, but gradually life got easier, and before she knew it she had two daughters and they were able to take a yearly vacation at a hot-springs resort. Fusae kept on working at the fish market even after she got married.

Until now she'd never wished for more time, but waiting in vain for the past few days for word from Yuichi, she'd felt a bitterness about the way time slowed down, something she'd never experienced.

Usually Fusae was busy on New Year's Eve preparing *osechi ryori*, the special New Year's dishes, putting up festive decorations at their door, and getting the New Year's rice cakes ready, but this year she sat alone in her kitchen.

In the morning, Norio's wife had brought over a small lacquered box of *osechi ryori*. "I thought you probably hadn't done any cooking," she said. "I noticed the detectives aren't outside today," she added.

"The last few days the local patrolman's been coming by to check on me, but that's all," said Fusae. Still, Norio's wife just had a quick cup of tea and then left, perhaps concerned that the house was still under surveillance.

Katsuji was still in the hospital, but initially he'd been given permission by his doctor to go home for the three-day New Year's holiday. That was the plan until he complained of pain and nausea, so they decided he would stay in the hospital after all.

Norio, not Fusae, was the one who updated Katsuji on Yuichi. Fusae didn't know what Norio told him, but when she went to visit her husband there were times she was so uneasy that she started to cry. Katsuji didn't ask her a thing. Instead, he just complained as usual. A few days before, though, after she'd given him his sponge bath and was getting ready to leave, Katsuji muttered, "Why, when I have one foot in the grave already, do I have to go through something like this?"

Fusae left the hospital room without replying. She didn't get right on the elevator, but went to a restroom, where she broke down. Katsuji had had a hard life, she thought. They'd both gone through a lot to get to where they were now as a couple.

Fusae vaguely reached out for the box of *osechi ryori* that Norio's wife had brought and slid it closer. When she opened the lid, the bright colors of the shrimp leaped out at her. She picked up one of them and realized she hadn't eaten a thing since breakfast.

It was already past twelve. Fusae planned to visit Katsuji in the afternoon, so she picked out some of the foods she knew he could eat and got a plastic container down from the shelf.

She was just transferring the *konbu* to the container when the phone rang. For a second, she hoped it was Yuichi, though over the last few days she'd been let down dozens of times. Maybe, she thought, it was Norio, who was worried about her, or perhaps her elder daughter, always concerned about her own children's future.

Chopsticks still in hand, she answered the phone and heard a familiar young man's voice.

"May I speak with Mrs. Fusae Shimizu, please?"

He spoke so politely that Fusae replied, "Yes, this is she."

"Mrs. Shimizu?"

As soon as she said yes, the man turned haughty. Fusae had a bad feeling and clenched the chopsticks tightly.

"Thank you for signing the contract with us the other day. I'm calling about next month's delivery."

As the man rattled on, Fusae tried desperately to interject. "What? What are you talking about?"

"Excuse me? As you recall, Mrs. Shimizu, you signed a contract at our office for health foods."

The man's words remained polite, though she could sense how irritated he was.

"You do remember this, I hope."

Fusae was overwhelmed. "Yes, I suppose," she said. Her knees were shaking. She remembered the young men at the office and how they threatened her. Her hand holding the phone was trembling, too, and the hard receiver banged against her ear several times.

"The contract, as you know, is a yearly contract."

"A year—a yearly contract?" Fusae said in a low voice, trying to hide her trembling.

"A yearly contract is exactly that. We received your first payment, so next month will be the second. The second payment doesn't require a membership fee, so it comes to exactly two hundred and fifty thousand yen. How will you be paying? By bank transfer? Or shall we come to collect it? By the way, if you do a bank transfer, the fee for that is your responsibility."

It wasn't the man's voice that scared her. But as she listened, she had the illusion that she was back in that office, forced to sit there, surrounded by those agitated, intimidating men. They'd told her she had to sign and then they'd let her go home, and with a trembling hand she'd picked up the pen. In her mind now, this scene overlapped with the one from years ago, of scrambling to pick up her ration of potatoes that had been flung to the ground.

In a small voice Fusae said, "I . . . I can't do that."

"What? Old woman, what did you say?"

Shaken, Fusae hung up. Almost as if to crush the receiver under her, she leaned into it as she hung up. Silence returned to the kitchen. Fusae collapsed into her chair. The instant she sat down, the phone rang again, shrilly. She didn't pick up the receiver again, but it was as if she had. She could clearly hear the angry shouts of the man: "Listen, old woman! What the hell do you think you're doing? You can't run away! We're gonna pay you a little visit right now!" Fusae put her hands over her ears, but no matter how much she tried to block out the sound, the phone kept on ringing.

The phone kept on ringing, but at twenty-one rings it finally stopped.

Mitsuyo looked over from the phone by the bedside to the restroom, where Yuichi was.

It was way past checkout time, and if they didn't hurry they'd have to pay a late fee. She knew this, but still couldn't bring herself to get out of bed. Yuichi, shut up alone in the bathroom, no doubt felt the same way. The love hotel charged ¥4,200 per night, and they were supposed to be out by ten a.m. But when they did leave, there was nowhere else for them to go.

She'd lost track of how many days she and Yuichi had been wandering, spending the nights in love hotels. In front of the Karatsu police station, when they'd decided to run away together, they'd planned to leave Kyushu as soon as they could. They never discussed it, but they didn't head for Shimonoseki and the Kanmon Bridge that would take them to Honshu. Instead they spent the days driving back and forth across the border between Saga and Nagasaki, finding a cheap love hotel each night, hurried out every morning by a phone call informing them that their time was up.

She suddenly remembered it was New Year's Eve and felt oppressed, cornered. Did Yuichi remember what day it was? She knew they wouldn't bring it up.

This is impossible. We can't go on running, she'd told herself over and over, but as she repeated the words she'd asked herself: *But what's so impossible? What can't we run away from?* Was this life going from one love hotel to the next really so impossible? Or was it the life she imagined after she lost Yuichi?

She had to do something. But she had no idea what else to do, other than leave this love hotel and search for the next one. As long as she kept on looking for the hotel, another day would pass.

Mitsuyo reluctantly pulled herself out of bed. "Yuichi," she said in the direction of the toilet. "It's about time we leave." No answer, just the sound of running water.

Yuichi was fastening his belt as he emerged from the bathroom and Mitsuyo passed him his socks. Last night she'd rinsed them with water and put them out to dry, but they still felt damp.

"You didn't sleep, did you?" Mitsuyo said as he tugged on the socks.

"No, I did," Yuichi said, shaking his head, but she noticed the dark circles under his eyes.

As she watched him put on his socks he said, apologetically, "I woke up a few times, but I think you're the one who didn't get much sleep, right?"

"No," Mitsuyo said, "I'm okay. We should park somewhere and take a nap," she went on, trying to disperse the heavy feeling that had taken hold of them.

They couldn't sleep well in the beds in hotels, but strangely enough they slept soundly for an hour or so when they parked their car beside the road, or in a parking lot.

As Yuichi got dressed, Mitsuyo casually opened the guest book on the table.

Here I am again with Takashi. This is the third time for us—By the way, this was our two-month anniversary so we went to see a movie in Hakata and stopped here on the way back. I really like it here—it's cheap, and clean. Oh, and I definitely recommend the chicken nuggets! They're probably frozen, but real crunchy!

Without really thinking about it, Mitsuyo continued to read through the girlish writing.

On the next page, in pink fluorescent pen she saw this:

Today Akkun and I did the dirty deed for the first time in a month. Since April we've lived far away from each other, which makes me soooo sad. Boo hoo!

Beneath it there was a mangalike sketch of a guy, probably by the girl, and in the dialogue bubble over it, in a stronger hand—no doubt that of the man—were the words *I'll never cheat on you!*

Mitsuyo closed the guest book and placed it back on the table.

Just as they were leaving, Mitsuyo turned and looked back at the room. The down comforter had been straightened, but the white sheets underneath were wrinkled and tossed about, a sign of last's night's insomnia. Mitsuyo was struck by a sudden thought. Which was bigger—this bed or Yuichi's car? You can stretch out on the bed, but can't go anywhere. The car's more confining, but in it you can go anywhere you like.

Yuichi looked concerned—Mitsuyo was just standing there, spacing out. He tugged her arm.

They walked down the orange-carpeted hallway to the stairs, which were painted white. They put the key in the box at the front desk, and were heading for the half-underground parking lot when they saw a cleaning woman, broom in hand, staring at the license plate of Yuichi's car. Yuichi came to an abrupt halt and his heels squeaked on the floor. The cleaning woman glanced over in their direction. But she turned right back to his car.

Mitsuyo pulled Yuichi by the arm and ran toward the car. As if trying to sound them out about something, the cleaning woman said, "Excuse me—I wanted to—" but they ignored her and quickly got in the car. Yuichi got in first, and while she was waiting for him to unlock the passenger side, Mitsuyo was exposed to the woman's eyes.

She avoided looking at her, though, and was soon in the car and they took off. The plastic curtain at the parking lot's exit licked their windshield as they left, and once outside, the winter sunlight illuminated the car's interior. Until they left the hotel grounds, Mitsuyo could barely breathe. She knew that if she looked in the rearview mirror she'd see the cleaning woman, broom in hand, watching them go, but something, perhaps fear, kept her from glancing back.

"That woman saw it. Didn't she," she said. Yuichi didn't respond.

Once they were out on the main road, Mitsuyo finally worked up the courage to glance in the mirror. All she could see was a van following them. The cleaning woman, and the entrance to the hotel itself, had disappeared.

"She saw it, I know she did," she almost shouted.

"Our license plate . . . She . . . she saw the number," Yuichi said. Frightened, he stepped on the gas. The van behind them faded in the distance.

"What should we do? We can't go on like this. . . . We can't use this car anymore!"

"Yeah, I know . . ." Yuichi said.

She had known this day would come. But as one day followed the next, and nothing happened, she'd begun to feel that they weren't running away so much as pursuing time. But while they made their way from one love hotel to another, reports about Yuichi were making their way down the web of connected highways and roads, down the interstate, crossing prefectural borders, traveling down prefectural and city roads.

"If we keep this car," Mitsuyo said, "they'll find us. We have to ditch it."

When he heard these words, Yuichi gulped.

Mitsuyo knew they couldn't escape. The only destination awaiting them was jail. She could try to convince herself otherwise, but that was the reality of it. Still, she couldn't say goodbye to Yuichi. Not yet.

"Let's ditch this car somewhere! If it's just the two of us, we can hide out." Mitsuyo was desperate to get away.

I've known Yuichi since grade school, about twenty years, and sometimes I can't figure out what's on his mind. Other guys say he's hard to approach, but I think they're reading too much into it. I don't think he's thinking anything. It's like he's a ball that's left lying on the playground for a couple of days. The kids play with it all day and then when it gets dark someone gives it a final kick and it rolls over by the horizontal bars. The next day someone else gives it a final kick and it comes to rest under a cherry tree. . . . This makes Yuichi sound pretty pathetic, but it never bothered him to be treated like that. He actually prefers it that way. When I suggest we go somewhere for a drive, or go do something, he's usually happy to oblige. He wouldn't do it if he didn't want to, right? I've never forced him to do things with me.

Not long after the murder, I actually went over to Yuichi's house. That evening I e-mailed him from a pachinko parlor and he said he'd drop by on the way home from work. We played the slots for a while, and then went to his house, where his grandmother made dinner for us.

Was he acting? I've thought about it a lot, but he seemed the same as always. Maybe he was really trying to act normal, but even though he'd killed somebody not too long before, he looked like the same old Yuichi. After dinner we went up to his room for a while, and he sprawled out on his bed like usual, and was reading car magazines. . . . He said, "If I didn't have a car I never could have gone anywhere." And I went, "Yeah, but what about trains or walking? People can go anywhere they want to." I laughed when I said this, but Yuichi didn't reply. . . . Somehow I can't forget those words now. *If I didn't have a car, I never could have gone anywhere.* Or the look on his face.

Everybody knew how crazy Yuichi was about cars. Cars aren't my thing so I don't know the details, but somebody told me once that Yuichi's was tuned to professional specs, and come to think of it, his car was featured once in a specialty magazine, *Car* something or other. "This is a national magazine!" he said, excited for once, and he must have bought five copies to keep. It was just one of those black-and-white photo spreads at the back of the magazine, but it was a whole page and they showed Yuichi, looking kind of tense, standing next to his precious car.

Yeah, I remember now. This was around the time he fell for that massage-parlor girl. He said he gave her a copy of the magazine.

I really feel sorry for him about that whole thing. I was actually worried Yuichi might commit suicide back then. I'm not trying to justify him or anything. I mean, he was spending every day at a massage parlor, trying to pick up this girl who worked there. But there they were, sharing all their hopes for the future, and Yuichi decided to rent an apartment in the city for the two of them, and right when he did, the girl disappeared.

He didn't tell me anything at first, but one day out of the blue he said, "Hifumi, I'm going to move soon, so could you help me?"

Yuichi isn't the talkative type like me. So this was really unexpected. I asked him why he was moving and he said, "I'm going to live with a girl." I was astonished. I mean, with a girl in that kind of business, besides. I didn't pry any further, but I had a bad feeling about it. The week after that, I think it was, I helped him move. And right after that, the girl quit the massage parlor and vanished.

About a month later, I helped him move again. Yuichi told me all about the reasons for it without any prompting from me, and I couldn't believe it. He'd never discussed any of the details with the girl. When they were at the massage parlor, she'd just mentioned the type of life she'd like to live someday. Yuichi's always been that way. He's always leaped from point A to point D, imagining the intermediate steps, and never telling anyone what he had in mind. When she happened to tell him, "I'd love to quit this job and live in a small apartment with a guy like you," the first thing he did was go out and rent an apartment. Unbelievable.

❁

The first three days of the new year were almost past, with none of the traditional soba, *osechi ryori*, or good-luck first visit to a shrine. Ever since she'd heard that the Hakata college student wasn't the killer, Satoko hadn't done any cooking, so Yoshio bought two *makunouchi bentos* for them at the take-out place in front of the station.

He made hot tea for them, and placed the *bento* in front of Satoko. As she listlessly separated the disposable chopsticks, she murmured, "So *bento* shops are still open during New Year's. . . ."

"Yeah, it was actually pretty crowded."

Satoko looked about to reply, but silently speared a boiled carrot instead.

Yoshio had yet to tell Satoko about seeing Yoshino in the pouring rain at Mitsuse Pass. He knew she'd believe him if he did, and would insist that he drive her there. But when he thought about going and the possibility that they might not see Yoshino again, he couldn't bring himself to explain what had happened.

He'd driven up to the pass three days in a row after that, hoping to catch another glimpse of his daughter. But that first day was the only time Yoshino appeared and called out to him. After that, no matter how much he waited, he neither saw her nor heard her voice. On the third day he visited, he was surprised to find one of Yoshino's co-workers there, a girl named Mako Adachi.

Mako said she'd come a number of times to lay flowers there for Yoshino. She took the local bus up to the pass and then walked along the back road to the site.

Yoshio gave Mako a ride back to Kurume station. In the car they hardly spoke, but she did tell him that she was quitting at the end of the year and moving back to her parents' home in Kumamoto. Yoshio asked her what she planned to do there.

"I don't know yet," she said. "I just don't feel comfortable in the city anymore." She told him how she once spotted Keigo Masuo in Tenjin after he was released. She didn't talk with him, of course, but just seeing him made her feel bitter. "That might be the reason I decided to go back home," she said. Yoshio asked her for Keigo's address and at first she said she didn't know it, but after a moment's hesitation, she told him the name of a well-known building right next to his condo, a place everyone knew.

The call from the police came just as Yoshio and Satoko were finishing their *bentos*. He was expecting to hear that they'd captured the suspect, but all he learned from the detective—the same one who'd visited him the other day—was that although they'd been sure the suspect had already fled Kyushu, his abandoned car had been found near Arita, in Saga.

Yoshio hung up and told his wife what he'd heard. Strangely enough, he felt nothing at the news. Satoko was silent and placed the lid back on her half-eaten *bento*.

Yoshio figured that that was the end of it, but Satoko suddenly murmured, "So the police are working even during the New Year's holidays." For a moment she sounded like the old Satoko, before Yoshino had died. She wasn't exactly smiling, but perhaps trying desperately to do so. "The police never give up, do they? They do their best even during New Year's," she murmured, her lips drawn back tightly, as if they were numb.

"Yeah, even during New Year's, so I'm sure they'll arrest the guy soon," Yoshio said.

"Arresting him won't bring back Yoshino," Satoko said, her expression gloomy again.

"The day after tomorrow I'm going to reopen the shop," Yoshio said, trying to change the subject.

"I'll believe that when I see it." Satoko smiled.

It was the first time she'd smiled since the murder. The smile was halfhearted, but he was proud of her for trying.

"Satoko, there's something I wanted to tell you. . . ."

He was going to tell her about what took place at Mitsuse Pass, how Yoshino had apologized to him. He wanted to tell her about it, but somehow the words wouldn't come.

Satoko put the leftovers in the plastic bag they came in, and tied the ends tight, then tied them again. She did it so many times there finally wasn't enough slack left to tie it anymore. Yoshio took the bag from her and dumped it heavily in the kitchen wastebasket.

Satoko stared at the wastebasket and said, "Honey? . . . I just don't get it. Why did that college student leave Yoshino up there at the pass?" She paused. "That's what I want to know," she went on. "When she called us and said she was going to Universal Studios, she mentioned his name. . . ." Her gaze was still fixed on the wastebasket.

"Did she say she was going with him?" Yoshio asked.

"*I don't know yet* was all she said, but she seemed happy. *I hope we can*, she said."

Yoshio didn't know what to say. Out there was a man who had murdered his daughter. And another who had stepped on her heart. His hatred should be aimed at the one who killed her, but all he could picture was Yoshino being literally kicked out of that car.

The next morning Yoshio drove to Hakata.

❦

Holding her breath, Mitsuyo listened to the voices and footfalls of the young men outside. Yuichi was crouched down beside her, his arm around her shoulder.

The men had just arrived here by car a few minutes before. The moment Yuichi heard the sound of their engine coming up the narrow logging road, he grabbed Mitsuyo's hand and yanked her into the shack next to the lighthouse.

The lot where the men had parked was a little bit away and they heard the footsteps of three or four people getting closer. "This place gives me the creeps," they heard one say. "The last time I was here, the road was blocked off."

The door in the shack where Mitsuyo and Yuichi were hiding was made of frosted glass, and the lines of iron in the reinforced glass were sharply defined in the moonlight.

Before they knew it, the young men's voices and footsteps were right outside the door. The door suddenly banged as they roughly tried to pull it open.

"Is it open?"

"Nah, it's locked."

"Want to use a rock and break the glass?"

Shadows moved beyond the frosted glass. Mitsuyo inched closer to Yuichi and they clasped each other's numb hands.

"Don't do it. There's nothing inside anyway."

As he said this a large rock clunked down on the ground. Apparently one of them had actually picked up a rock.

Yuichi was crouching next to a large plastic bottle of water. It was almost ready to fall over.

"The road back that way's really dark, so you better watch out!"

One of the men—who'd apparently started to walk toward the lighthouse—was shouting, and then the shadows outside the door grew distant, kicking pebbles as they went.

Mitsuyo reached out and grabbed the bottle. Yuichi, thinking she was trying to hug him, pulled her closer to him, the bottle now in her hand.

The men were apparently heading toward the cliffs.

"It'd be cool to come here to see the first sunrise of the year," one of them said.

"But that's west, isn't it?"

"I wonder when was the last time they used this lighthouse."

"It isn't much fun here if it's just four guys."

Mitsuyo and Yuichi held their breath and listened.

Because of the cold, the men stood there only about a minute and then headed back to the shack.

Please, Mitsuyo prayed, *please just go away*.

Beyond the frosted glass they saw one shadow pass by, then a second, and a third. Right when they were waiting for the last one to pass, a fist pounded on the glass. Mitsuyo nearly cried out, burying her face in Yuichi's shoulder just in time.

The men stood there for a while, discussing where they should go next. An engine roared to life in the parking lot.

Mitsuyo tapped Yuichi's shoulder twice and, relieved, she nodded. The sound of the engine faded in the distance.

Yuichi stood up and carefully opened the door and peered out. Mitsuyo stood behind him, and when she looked outside, she saw the car winding its way down the logging road, its high beams lighting up the road ahead.

The winter sky was full of stars, and they could hear the waves crashing against the cliff nearby. The strong wind shook the little shack, bending the plywood boards nailed to the windows. Mitsuyo took a deep breath. She looked and saw the lighthouse, bathed in moonlight.

They'd abandoned their car a few days before in Arita. When

Yuichi couldn't decide what to do, Mitsuyo said, "Let's go to a light-house." She knew they couldn't escape, but she couldn't suppress the desire for one more day, one more hour together.

"There's one lighthouse they don't use anymore," Yuichi murmured, finally bringing himself to get rid of his car.

Without a word, Yuichi took his sleeping bag out of the trunk, a red sleeping bag he apparently used when he went on long drives. They took a train, and then a bus, and finally arrived. Mitsuyo let Yuichi lead her by the hand; she had no idea where they got on the train, or where they were going.

They rode the bus along the seacoast and got off at a small fishing village where the lighthouse was. In front of the bus stop was a small convenience store and a tiny gas station, but other than that there were only twenty or thirty homes, with fishing nets hung out to dry in the gardens.

They walked a little while from the bus stop and passed a shrine, next to which was a steep logging road. At the entrance to the road were signs saying *Not a Through Road!* and *Closed Ahead!* The thick weeds growing along the road made it even narrower. The two of them held hands and walked up the road for nearly half an hour, feeling as though they were walking through a prairie.

"We're almost there," Yuichi said, many times, his hand on her back to help her along the steep road.

When they reached the road's end, the sky opened up and there was the lighthouse.

"See, there it is," Yuichi said, smiling for the first time since they'd abandoned his car.

Beyond the logging road was a parking lot. There wasn't a single car there, of course, and the asphalt was missing in places, with weeds shooting out through the cracks. Beyond the parking lot was the lighthouse, surrounded by a fence. They slipped through a break in the fence, the shabby lighthouse looming above them, looking ready to topple over. Below it was a similarly grubby lighthouse keeper's shack, painted white. Yuichi tried the doorknob and the door opened easily.

Inside, the space was empty and dusty, the light shining in illuminating the dust in the air. In one corner of the shack were plywood boards leaning against the wall and a pipe chair, the foam rubber sticking out of the cushion. The floor was littered with sweet-bun wrappers and empty juice cans.

Yuichi laid one of the plywood boards on the floor and tossed his sleeping bag on it. Then he took Mitsuyo by the hand and led her outside, right below the lighthouse. A single bird, a kite, was circling in the winter sky. The sky seemed close enough to touch.

The lighthouse looked out over the sea that lay beneath the cliff. A chain blocked the way and there was no path past this point. She could hear the waves crashing against the cliff. Gazing at the scenery spread out before her, it felt less like a dead end than a starting point. From here one could go anywhere.

"I bet you're starving," Yuichi said. Mitsuyo, gazing out at the distant horizon, nodded. The sun was out, but the wind was so cold they soon sought shelter again in the shack. They spread the sleeping bag out on top of the sheet of plywood and ate the lunches they'd bought at the convenience store in front of the bus stop.

"Are you sure nobody's going to come here?" Mitsuyo asked, and Yuichi, his mouth full of rice, nodded.

"Do you really think we can stay here?" she asked, and then Yuichi stopped chewing.

"We can buy some candles and food at the convenience store down there. . . ." As he spoke, his voice grew softer.

Ever since they'd run away from the Karatsu police station, they hadn't discussed the most important point of all. They knew they couldn't escape. But they both felt the same way: that they wanted to be together right up until the moment they were arrested. They just couldn't say it aloud.

The threatening phone calls she'd received at the year's end stopped after New Year's. She knew she couldn't just crouch in fear in the kitchen, but she was so afraid of the phone ringing, of those men pushing their way into her home, that she found herself trembling even while she was sitting down.

So when the front doorbell rang she was even more startled. *They're here*, Fusae thought. But it turned out only to be the local patrolman.

"Grandma, you at home?" he called out.

She nearly collapsed from relief and hurried to the front door.

"Have you heard Yuichi mention a friend by the name of Mitsuyo Magome? A girl who works at a clothing shop in Saga?" The policeman asked this as soon as she opened the door, without even saying hello. The cold wind rushed in. The patrolman rubbed his hands as he spoke and Fusae could only weakly shake her head.

"I see. So you haven't heard of her. It looks like Yuichi took this girl with him when he ran away."

"Took the girl with him?"

"Yeah, we don't know if he forced her to go, or whether she went voluntarily."

Fusae sat down heavily on the step up from the entrance. Knowing, perhaps, that asking any more questions was pointless, the patrolman patted her on the shoulder. "They found Yuichi's car in Arita," he added, and then left.

All Fusae could manage to do was stare at his retreating back.

Yuichi abandoned his car. He gave up on his car. . . .

She could see him, walking far away from his car. *Where are you going!* she shouted to him, but he kept on walking, disappearing into a dark forest she'd never seen before.

Just then the phone in the kitchen rang. She was about to call after the patrolman, but she knew that he'd come about her grandson, the murderer, and wouldn't listen to some complaint about threatening phone calls.

If she didn't answer the phone, those men would definitely pay her a visit. If she did answer the phone, maybe they could find some sort of solution. All she could do was cling to this hope. She walked back to the kitchen and, hands shaking, lifted the receiver.

"Hello? Mom? It's me, Yoriko. What is going on? They're saying Yuichi is a murderer! That can't be true, can it? Tell me what's going on!

"Hello? Talk to me, Mom!"

Yoriko was hysterical. She didn't let Fusae get a word in edgewise. "Honey . . ." was all Fusae was able to say.

"The police came to my workplace! Like they thought I was harboring him or something. And they even went through the company dorm. . . ."

"How are you? Okay?"

As her daughter spoke, Fusae remembered how strong-willed she was, even as a child. When Yoriko entered junior high, she started going out at night. On weekends their tiny fishing village was shaken by the roar of motorcycles as a gang pulled up. Katsuji would grab her by the hair to try to stop her, but Yoriko would kick free and run off. More than once, Yoriko was taken into custody in the city and they had to pick her up at the police station. Once she graduated from high school, she started working at a bar, but this didn't turn out so badly. Working full-time helped her to grow up, and Fusae remembered how, on one of her rare visits home, she politely poured sake for her father and said, "Dad, you should drop by our bar sometime for a drink," handing him her business card.

But then she went and married a worthless man who ran out on her. Yuichi had been born by this time, and she gave him up to her parents to raise. Ever since then the only contact they had was a phone call every couple of years, an afterthought on her part. She'd say things like "I'm really sorry about what I did to you, Mom," or "Next time let's go on a trip to a spa together," but in all that time she never once came home.

"Yuichi a murderer? It's got to be a mistake."

Fusae had no idea how to respond.

Yoriko sighed deeply. "You've been with him all this time. . . . How could you have raised him to become someone like that!" she shouted. "Anyway, I told the police he wasn't going to come here. The only time I see him is when he comes to pester me for money.

He knows how poor I am, but he'll come and wheedle a thousand yen, two thousand, out of me and leave."

"You two see each other?" Fusae said, shocked.

Yoriko stopped. "Anyhow, that's what I told the police," she said, and without waiting for a reply, she hung up.

Fusae was dumbfounded. She was surprised that Yuichi had been secretly meeting Yoriko, but even more shocked that he was trying to get money from her. It was easier to believe that he murdered someone than to believe he wanted money from his mother.

With the sunlight streaming in the glass window, the air in the shack grew a little warmer. Inside the sleeping bag, Mitsuyo kissed Yuichi on the neck.

Sleeping on the hard plywood board, despite the padding of the sleeping bag, made her back and sides ache, and she'd woken up often during the night. When she did, she could see her breath, and though her ears and nose ached in the cold, the snug sleeping bag let her feel Yuichi's warmth all the more.

Next to the plywood board were some plastic bags full of the remains of the *bento*, bread, and drinks they'd consumed over the last few days. Lying here, it felt as if they were on a magic carpet flying through the sky.

Feeling Mitsuyo stirring, Yuichi woke up, murmured "Good morning" into the hair at the back of her neck, and pulled her close.

"I'll go to the convenience store later on," Mitsuyo said. The warm air in the sleeping bag spilled out around their shoulders.

"You'll be okay by yourself?" Yuichi asked, yawning.

"I'll be fine. I think it's better if I go alone."

"I'll go with you down to the road, and hide in the bushes and wait for you."

"I told you, I'll be fine." In the tight sleeping bag Mitsuyo gave his chest a couple of playful taps.

The previous day they'd gone together to the convenience store. They'd been there several times, and when they were at the checkout stand the woman at the cash register asked, "You're not from around here, are you?"

Mitsuyo immediately replied, "Uh, yeah. We're spending New Year's with some relatives who live in the area."

"Is that right"? the woman asked. "And where are you from?"

Without thinking, Mitsuyo said, "Saga."

"Where in Saga?" the woman asked.

"From, uh, from Yobuko."

The woman seemed about to say something more, so as soon as she got their change Mitsuyo pulled Yuichi by the hand and hurried out of the store.

If that same woman was working the register today, she might very well ask Mitsuyo where their relatives lived. If it came to that, they couldn't use that store anymore. To find another store, they'd have to walk the road all the way to the next town.

Yuichi got out of the sleeping bag, slipped on his sneakers, and headed to the toilet. The lighthouse hadn't been in operation for years, but luckily the water was still on. The toilet wasn't exactly clean, but Mitsuyo felt like giving a prayer of thanks for the running water, as if it had been left by some secret ally.

"The place looks so much cleaner now," Yuichi murmured admiringly as he stepped into the toilet.

"Well, I spent two hours cleaning up."

Yuichi looked over at Mitsuyo, still in the sleeping bag, and said, "While you're at the convenience store, I'll try to cover over this broken window." He pointed to the window facing the sea. He'd used some plastic tape he'd bought to temporarily cover the broken glass, but the wind still blew between the cracks.

After Yuichi had used the toilet and was heading outside with a plastic bottle of water, Mitsuyo asked, "Besides food, what else would you like me to buy?"

"Besides food? . . . Well, how about a deck of cards?"

"A deck of cards?"

As soon as she said this, she realized he'd been joking. Yuichi's eyes narrowed in the winter morning light. He howled, laughing at her.

Mitsuyo finally got up and folded the sleeping bag, still warm from their bodies, neatly on top of the plywood board. She followed the sound of Yuichi gargling and when she stepped outside, she saw the sea laid out before her, glittering in the sun, seagulls drifting low in the sky.

"It's so beautiful," Mitsuyo said, lost for a moment. Yuichi spit out the water near his feet and said, shyly, "You know what? I had a dream last night."

"What kind of dream?" Mitsuyo took the plastic bottle from him.

"You and I were living together. Remember how we were talking about that before we went to sleep? What kind of house we'd like to live in? In my dream, we were living there."

"Which one was it? The house? Or the condo?"

"The condo . . . But in this dream you kicked me out of bed." Yuichi gave a short laugh. Mitsuyo took a drink of water and said, "But I really did kick you from inside the sleeping bag."

Yuichi faced the sea and stretched lazily. His fingertips seemed to be almost grazing the sky.

"Later on, maybe we can gather some weeds and lay them on top of the plywood."

"I wonder if that would make it softer."

Mitsuyo took another swig of water. It hadn't been in a refrigerator, but the water was freezing cold.

Everybody blames me, saying Yuichi did what he did because I abandoned him, but it was my mother who really raised him. I'm not blaming her or anything. It's just that on TV and in magazines they're treating me like the villain in all this. There was this announcer on TV, who looks like she couldn't care less about other people's lives, and she gave a neat summary of everything that happened in my life. Then some big-shot commentator added his take on it. They discussed the murder from all different angles, but the conclusion was always the same: the mother who abandoned her kid is the real culprit.

After I left Yuichi at the ferryboat pier at Shimabara, I thought about killing myself many times. But in the end I couldn't do it.

When I went to see my parents, they said they'd raise Yuichi, and they even took away my parental rights. It was like they were telling me to get lost.

But I was still his mother. I might have lived apart from Yuichi, but I was always thinking of him. And I never once hid his existence from the men I was seeing.

I didn't stay in touch because I knew my mom would say something like "If you're not going to raise him, then don't call us." And I also thought it would hurt Yuichi to be reminded of his mother, now that he had gotten used to living with my mom. But I never forgot him. I waited until he entered high school, and then I secretly got in touch. I figured when he was in high school, he'd be old enough to understand the dynamics between men and women.

It was kind of awkward seeing him again, at first. But we're mother and child, and there should be something we have in common. I can still remember what the noodles tasted like the first time we met. I was surprised to see how much pepper he put on his noodles, and when I asked him about it he said, "Grandma's food is always kind of bland, so I use tons of pepper, hot mustard, mayonnaise, and ketchup." Somehow when I heard this, I knew my parents were taking good care of him, and I was relieved.

After that, we met about once every six months. When school was in session we met during his summer or winter breaks, and we'd have a meal together. He was always very quiet, but still he came whenever I asked.

One day I was feeling really depressed. After we ate in Shimabara,

Yuichi gave me a ride back to my apartment, and in the car I suddenly burst into tears. I had so many problems. I wasn't getting along well with the man I was living with, at work I'd been transferred to a section I hated, and I was starting to feel emotionally unstable. Plus I was feeling like an awful woman for having left Yuichi. I knew I was pretty young when I left him, but if I had had my life together a bit more, I might have spared him those sad and painful memories.

I bawled my eyes out then, right in his car.

Please forgive me, I sobbed, for being such an awful mother. I've been so awful, yet you still come to see me when I ask you to, and you never act angry. And you call me Mom, despite what I did to you. It's so hard on me to meet you like this. I'm the only one at fault here, so I wouldn't blame you if you hate me. I realize this is the cross I have to bear.

I kept on crying and crying. I didn't even notice we'd pulled up in front of my building. It's just that . . .

I finally stopped crying in the car and was about to get out when Yuichi suddenly said, "Mom, can you lend me some money?" For a moment I couldn't believe my ears. This was a boy who'd always refused to accept any allowance I gave him, even a thousand yen. I was startled, but I opened my wallet right away and handed him five thousand or ten thousand, whatever I had. Through my tears, I asked him what he was going to use it for and he said, "What does it matter?" and shot me this scary look.

After that day, every time I saw him, he asked me to give him some spending money or lend him some cash. At first I gave it to him, to sort of atone for my sins, but I was scraping by on ¥120,000 or ¥130,000 a month. I didn't have any spare cash. All he wanted when we met was money, and more money, so I didn't call him as often anymore. But then he began dropping in on me unannounced, telling me it wasn't payday yet and he was broke. He'd grab whatever I had, one thousand, two thousand yen, and leave.

Of course, part of the blame for why he committed this murder lies with me. But if you ask me, I've been punished enough. Think about it. How a parent feels when their child forces them to give them what little money they have. It's a terrible feeling. You feel totally hopeless. Some days he looked like the devil to me. I almost hate him now.

※

"Ouch! That hurts!" Mitsuyo screamed. She was sitting on the sleeping bag, her legs spread out in front of her, and Yuichi was giving her a foot massage.

"If this spot here hurts, that means your neck's weak, Mitsuyo."

He couldn't tell if it really hurt her or whether she was laughing, but he found it amusing nonetheless, and continued to press down hard with the base of his thumb.

"Ow! Wait! Wait a second!" She tried as hard as she could to wriggle away, but Yuichi's large hands wouldn't let her go.

"I get it. I'll stop. . . . But let me ask you, does it hurt here, too?"

"Ow!"

"And here?"

"Do I look like I'm not in pain?"

"If it hurts here, that means you're not getting enough sleep."

"I know that! How do you expect me to sleep on top of a sheet of plywood?"

"But you were snoring last night."

"I don't snore. But I talk in my sleep sometimes."

As if to persuade her to stay put, Yuichi began gently massaging her calves.

Until a short time before, they'd been enjoying the sun at the base of the lighthouse. Cold wind whipped up from the cliff, but Yuichi had lit a fire in a small metal drum he'd found and they sat beside it, eating some of the bread they'd stocked up on. The dried branches crackling in the flames made them forget the previous night's cold weather.

"If we bought some rice cakes at the convenience store, do you think we could roast them on that drum?" Mitsuyo asked as she was getting her calves massaged.

"If we had something we could use for a grill, we could," Yuichi replied.

"How do you usually spend New Year's?" she asked, as Yuichi put on one of her socks for her.

"New Year's? I go over to my uncle's house on New Year's Eve and drink with the guys from work. Then in the middle of the night we pay our first visit of the year to the shrine. And on the third I go for a drive, I guess."

"By yourself?"

"Sometimes. Sometimes with Hifumi, a friend of mine. How about you?"

"We always have the big New Year's sale on the second. I know it's kind of weird, considering where we are and all, but it's been ages since I've had such a relaxing New Year's."

Mitsuyo tugged on the other sock herself. A relaxing New Year's— she knew it was a silly thing to say, but the words just slipped out.

What was I doing last New Year's? she thought.

Mitsuyo pulled on her shoes and walked outside, leaving Yuichi sprawled on the sleeping bag. This was the western edge of Kyushu, but even here the sun went down early in the winter. It had been high above her, making the surface of the sea glitter, but now it was a faint red, fading into the horizon.

Mitsuyo walked over to the base of the lighthouse, leaned over the chain handrail, and gazed down at the cliff far below. Waves crashed against the base, eroding the rocks.

Last New Year's Eve it was past six-thirty when she'd finished work. It was the last day of their end-of-year sale and they'd closed up early, but being on her feet all day left her exhausted.

She spent every New Year's Eve back at her parents' house, but last year she rode her bike back to her apartment first. Tamayo had left a few days before on a group trip to Hokkaido, leaving behind a forgotten copy of her itinerary on the table. Thinking she'd spend the hours before she went back to her parents' home doing a thorough year-end cleaning, Mitsuyo began by washing the windows. She wet a cloth in cold water and leaned out the window, completely absorbed in the task.

The next morning, New Year's Day, she and her family gathered around to eat the special dishes her mother had prepared. Then they went for a first visit to the local shrine, but when they got back there was nothing else left to do. Her younger brother and his wife and son went home by car, and her mother started watching the New Year's specials on TV, her father snoring away beside her.

With time on her hands, Mitsuyo rode her bike over to a shopping center that was open all year round. The huge parking lot next to the road was full, and many of the customers inside the shopping center were dressed in their New Year's best.

She wasn't shopping for anything in particular, but she stopped first in the bookstore. At the front of the store was a shelf of bestsellers and she picked up one, a love story that had been made into a movie, but just thinking about work the next day made her put it down again. She left the bookstore and went to the CD store. She picked up a copy of Yuji Fukuyama's song "Sakurazaka," which she heard a lot on the background music at work, but after toying with the idea of buying it, she put it back.

From the window of the CD store, she could see outside. Her bike was parked there, and somebody had thrown an empty juice can into her basket. For a moment everything looked blurry, and that's when she realized she was crying. Mitsuyo ran out of the store, looked for a restroom, and dashed inside. She had no idea why she was crying. It wasn't because somebody had thrown an empty can in the basket of her bike. . . .

There were no books or CDs she wanted. A new year had just begun, but there was no place she wanted to go, no one she wanted to meet.

She went into a stall and couldn't stand it anymore. Tears gushed out and she realized she was bawling.

Now Mitsuyo gazed at the sea, unconcerned about the freezing wind blowing up from the cliff. The sky, clear during the day, was suddenly covered with thick clouds. If the temperature dropped any more, she thought, tonight might be the first snowfall of the year.

She sensed something behind her. Turning around, she saw Yuichi, hunched up against the cold.

"You'd better go to the convenience store before it gets dark."

Yuichi came over and stood beside her, leaning out and looking down at the cliff. She saw his prominent Adam's apple in the faint evening sun shining through the clouds.

"Yuichi, if I hadn't asked you to run away with me, would you have gone to the police?"

The question came out all of a sudden, but she'd been thinking about it for several days now. Staring at the cliff, Yuichi was quiet. "I don't know," he said, but no matter how long she waited, he didn't elaborate.

"There's one thing I'd like to make sure of."

Yuichi tensed up a bit at her words.

"You didn't make me run away with you. I wanted you to take me with you. If anybody ever asks you, I want you to tell them that."

Yuichi frowned, uncertain. Mitsuyo felt as if she'd just said good-bye and buried her face in his chest.

"Until I met you," she said, "I never realized how precious each day could be. When I was working, each day was over before I knew it, and then a week just flew by, and then a whole year. . . . What have I been doing all this time? Why didn't I meet you before? If I had to choose a whole year in the past, or a day with you—I'd choose a day with you. . . ."

As he stroked her hair, she began to cry. Yuichi's hand, just out of his pocket, was warm as a blanket.

"I'd choose a day with you, too, Mitsuyo. That's all I ever need. . . . But I can't do anything for you. I wanted to take you to all kinds of places, but I can't take you anywhere."

Mitsuyo pressed her cheek against his chest.

"I wonder how many more days we can be together," Yuichi

mumbled sadly. And right after that, a single flake of snow landed on the handrail and melted away.

※

Powdery snow suddenly began to fall onto the pavement and melted. Keigo Masuo was walking down the sidewalk, and when it started snowing, he halted and looked up at the sky.

Before he knew it, the world was covered with powdery snow. The overcast Hakata streets seemed to fade out of focus. A mailbox nearby looked far away, while the high-rise building across the street loomed closer.

Yoshio Ishibashi, following him, kept about ten yards back. Between them, countless powdery snowflakes fluttered down from the sky.

With each step, Yoshio had to suppress the desire to rush forward. Keigo had no idea he was being followed, and continued walking, one hand thrust in his jeans pockets, his shoulders hunched against the cold.

Two days earlier, Yoshio had surprised himself and run out of his home in Kurume.

This college student who had kicked Yoshino out of his car on top of Mitsuse Pass lived on the top floor of a luxurious building. Yoshio had ridden the elevator to the eighth floor. As he rode up, he felt the weight of the wrench concealed in his pocket. The door to Keigo's condo had a bell but Yoshio knocked. He knocked at the thick front door over and over. "Come out, you! Come out!" he yelled.

But no matter how much he knocked, the door remained shut, and he suddenly realized his nose was pressed again it and he was sobbing.

"Come out. . . . Nobody's going to make fun of my Yoshino and get away with it. . . ."

There was no sound from the other side of the door.

Fighting back his tears, Yoshio stepped away. He got in the elevator, and as he did, the whole scene rushed back at him: Yoshino being kicked out of the car at Mitsuse Pass. He slammed his fist against the elevator door.

He hadn't come here to grill the boy about why he'd abandoned Yoshino. Asking that wouldn't bring her back. No, he'd come as a father, a man who couldn't let anyone break his daughter's heart. All he wanted was to protect her feelings.

Yoshio went out to his car, parked in front of the condo, and called his wife on his cell phone.

"I won't be back tonight, but don't worry," he said in a rush of words. "I'll be back as soon as I finish up what I need to do here."

After a pause, Satoko asked, "Where are you?"

"Hakata," Yoshio answered.

After more silence she said, "Okay. Be sure to come home as soon as you're done."

It was snowing harder than before. Keigo almost skipped along and, ignoring the red light, crossed at the intersection.

Yoshio tightened his grip on the wrench in his pocket. As he stepped into the crosswalk, he nearly collided with a taxi making a left turn, and the driver blasted his horn. Yoshio came close to falling, but pushed hard against the bumper of the cab and managed to keep his balance.

The taxi driver rolled down his window. "What the hell do you think you're doing?" he shouted angrily. Two high school girls, wrapped in mufflers and waiting for the light to change, stared. Keigo, already on the other side of the street, glanced back for a moment at the commotion.

Yoshio ignored the driver and took off after Keigo. The driver went on blaring his horn.

When he got to the other side of the street, Keigo was far away. Yoshio sped along in the snow. The wrench banged against his ribs as he ran, the snowflakes melting on his face forming lines of water down from his eyes, like tears.

Just then, Keigo noticed the approaching footsteps and turned around. Yoshio rushed toward him and Keigo edged backward. "What the . . . ?" he said.

Yoshio stood right in front of Keigo, his ragged breath white in the air. Yoshio was struck by how tall the young man was, or rather, how short he himself was. But he stood his ground, glaring up at Keigo, who was glaring down at him.

"Are you Keigo Masuo?" Yoshio asked, more loudly than he needed to.

"Who are you, old man?"

Keigo took a step back. Yoshio stuck his hand in his pocket and felt the heavy wrench.

"Yoshino died because of you."

"*What?*"

"My precious daughter died because of you."

Yoshio glared up at him, unblinking. A flash of fear crossed Keigo's eyes.

"Why the hell did you do that?"

"Do what?"

"Why did you—abandon Yoshino at the pass!"

At Yoshio's angry shout, a cat appeared from behind a light pole, bristled, and scampered off.

"What are you talking about?"

Keigo tried to run off but Yoshio grabbed his arm. Keigo attempted to twist away.

"I didn't kill her! I didn't do anything!" Keigo broke free from his grasp, but as he did, his elbow struck Yoshio hard in the face. Everything turned blank and Yoshio fell to his knees. Still, he managed to grab Keigo by the legs to keep him from escaping.

"Let me go! What the hell do you think you're doing?"

Keigo roughly tried to shake free. His knees scraped the ground and a dry pain shot through him. Keigo tried to walk, dragging Yoshio behind him.

"Let me go!" he yelled.

At that instant all the strength drained out of Yoshio's arms. Keigo slipped free and almost instinctively kicked him in the shoulder.

Yoshio flew out horizontally and hit his head on the guardrail of the street with a dull thud.

"I didn't do anything!" Keigo said again. He looked furious and he bolted down the street. In the increasingly white world that surrounded him, Yoshio lay there watching his retreating figure.

"Wait. . . . You have to apologize to Yoshino. . . ." He'd meant to shout this, but all that came out was white breath. Keigo had disappeared into the swirling snow. A single cold flake of snow landed on Yoshio's eyelashes and melted.

"Yoshino . . . Daddy's not going to give up."

As his consciousness grew dim, he could see Yoshino as a young child, toddling along. . . . Where is this place? Some ferryboat dock? There's the sea over there. And Yoshino's running across a huge parking lot. She's holding a snack, some *chikuwa* from one of the stands, and she's running toward the sea.

"Are you all right?"

Just as he was starting to lose consciousness, he heard a voice. A young man put his arms around Yoshio and helped him to his feet.

"Can you stand?"

"That guy . . . you have to . . . chase him. . . ."

As he made this desperate plea, the young man looked in the direction that Keigo had vanished in.

"Why . . . why do you need to chase Keigo?" the young man asked uneasily.

Nearby a black crow was pecking at a bag of garbage. As it tried to tug the bag along the ground, the garbage became covered in snow.

The pitch-black crow shook its head as it tore open the convenience-store bag. A crumpled wrapping for a *bento* flew out of the hole in the bag. A light layer of snow covered the asphalt, dotted with the crow's footprints. As it spread its wings, they brushed against the glass of the phone booth.

With the freezing receiver held to her ear, Mitsuyo lightly tapped the glass with her foot, hoping to drive the crow away. Startled, the bird leaped back a step, the plastic bag in its beak.

"Hello? Hello? Who's calling?" Tamayo asked cautiously.

"Sorry I haven't gotten in touch."

"Mi—Mitsuyo? Where are you? Why haven't you called me? Are you by yourself? Are you okay?"

Mitsuyo couldn't get in an answer to this flurry of questions. "Calm down, okay?" she managed to say.

"What do you mean, *calm down*? Do you have any idea how panicked I've been? They said you've been taken away by a murderer. Please—tell me you're all right! Is that guy with you?"

"No, I'm alone right now."

"Good. But you have to run away. Right this instant! Where are you? I'll call the police!"

"Take it easy, all right?"

Tamayo sounded as if she really was going to call the police at any minute. That made sense, Mitsuyo thought. Ever since the night that Yuichi half dragged her away in his car, after she'd told Tamayo not to worry, they had exchanged a few e-mails, but she never answered Tamayo's questions about what was going on. They'd kept this up until her cell-phone battery died.

"Are you really alone?" Tamayo asked again. "If you really are, then I want you to say *Call the police right away*."

"What're you talking about?"

"If that murderer isn't with you, say it."

Tamayo was serious, so Mitsuyo gave in and repeated the line. "The guy I'm with," she added. "He really isn't an evil person, you know."

From the other end of the line, she heard a disgusted sigh.

According to Tamayo, detectives had been staking out their parents' house. The police were convinced that Yuichi had forced Mitsuyo to go with him, and after the New Year's TV programs ended and regular programming started up again, the talk shows began showing scenes of Mitsuyo and Tamayo's apartment building, though they blurred out the name, and they didn't give the sisters' names or show their photos. The investigation was progressing better than they'd expected.

As she listened to Tamayo, Mitsuyo thought of Yuichi, back on the logging road. I'm fine going to the convenience store myself, she'd told him, asking him to stay back in the shack, but Yuichi was worried about her going alone and he had accompanied her down the hill, where he was hiding now in the bushes. The snow must be piling up in those bushes, too, she thought.

"But he really didn't force you to go with him, did he?" Tamayo asked.

"No, he didn't," Mitsuyo answered firmly.

"So what are you planning to do? How can you stay with a person like that?"

Mitsuyo had no idea how to respond. Tamayo broke the silence and said, tearfully, "My God, of all people in the world, why did you have to choose a murderer?"

"Tamayo?"

The crow outside had flown off somewhere, its footprints filling with newly fallen snow.

"I did something terrible, didn't I. . . ." Mitsuyo said.

On the other end of the line Mitsuyo could hear her sister gulp. "If you know that," Tamayo said, "then you'd better—"

"But this is the first time in my life I've felt this way. I want to be with him, even if it's just one more day."

"You want to be with him? That's a little self-centered, don't you think?"

"Huh?" Mitsuyo clutched the receiver tighter.

"I hope you're not telling me you want to run away with this guy. No matter how much you love him, you can't tie him down with the way you feel. It'll be painful, but if you really love him you have to take him in to the police. The more you two run away, the more guilty he'll be."

Before she realized it, Mitsuyo pressed the hook with her numb finger. All she heard now was an inorganic whoosh of the dial tone.

Tamayo hadn't told her anything she didn't already know. She hadn't expected her sister to understand, but the conversation had only reinforced what she expected—that no one else was on their side.

It had stopped snowing when she left the phone booth.

Leaving footprints behind in the light dusting of snow, she headed for the convenience store across the street. She'd already bought their food, but she'd seen a ¥480 pair of gloves and she wanted to go back and buy them for Yuichi.

You can't tie him down with the way you feel.

Tamayo's words, and her own footprints, followed her.

The parking lot of the convenience store was empty except for one lone car, its engine running. The exhaust from the tailpipes was as white as cotton. Normally she would have noticed it right away, but perhaps because she'd been unsettled by Tamayo's words, or perhaps because the car blended into the snow, she didn't see right away that it was a patrol car. The moment she did, her legs went weak, and she couldn't move.

The heat inside the store clouded the windows, and she couldn't see inside. Still, she could barely make out a figure at the register that looked like a policeman.

He's coming out. The policeman's coming out.

She tried as hard as she could to walk away, but her legs wouldn't move. As the automatic doors slid open, she finally was able to walk. There was still some distance between her and the policeman. She was just about to glance back when someone tapped her on the shoulder.

"Excuse me," a man's voice said, close by.

She turned and found herself face to face with a young patrolman. His hat was lightly covered with snow. His nose was red in the cold, his breath forming a cloud that almost hid his face.

"Is something wrong?" the patrolman asked.

He smiled at her. He seemed to have been watching Mitsuyo from behind and saw how she had stood there, stock-still, on the road.

"No . . ."

She turned her face away and strode off. At that instant the patrolman's eyebrows, stiff in the cold, twitched.

"Hold on a minute. You're Miss Magome, aren't you?"

Mitsuyo, about to break into a run, felt these words behind her. A truck drove past. The ruts in the snowy road led straight to where Yuichi was waiting for her on the logging road.

Yuichi . . . Mitsuyo called out silently.

The ruts in the snowy road led to a narrow alley. The sunlight and shade cut the road neatly in two, with only the snow on the sunny half dazzling in the light.

Fusae bent over and walked straight ahead, so as to stay within the space between the ruts. Once out of the alley there was the pier, and past that the bus stop. She'd checked the bus schedule. Now if the bus would only come on time.

"Do you have a comment for us?"

"How do you feel now? Any feelings for the victim's family?"

"Yuichi really hasn't gotten in touch with you?"

"Do you know the girl he ran away with?"

Fusae stared at her feet, avoiding the cameras and reporters surrounding her. The spot in the snow where she was about to step next had been trampled down, leaving behind a dark footprint.

There'd been only a scattering of reporters up till now, but this morning they suddenly multiplied. Last night she'd talked to Norio on the phone, and he'd said they'd finally released Yuichi's photo. Right after talking with him, the phone rang again. She was sure it was Norio, but it was yet another threatening call from the health-food people. "Listen, old woman, you haven't transferred the money to us yet!" the voice on the other end growled.

Fusae hung up immediately, but the phone rang every fifteen minutes until after midnight. Fusae put the futon over her head to block out the sound. More than anything, she felt frustrated at her own fear spilling over into tears.

That morning when she turned on the TV, the first thing she saw was a talk show reporting on the murder. They didn't show Yuichi's photo, but rather a graphic of Mitsuse Pass straddling the Saga and Fukuoka prefecture border, and the highway in both directions. Symbols indicated the murdered girl's apartment in Hakata, the apartment on the outskirts of Saga City where Yuichi's girl lived, and Yuichi's home here in Nagasaki. One more symbol showed where Yuichi's car had been abandoned, in Arita, and where a witness had seen them in a hotel.

The report said it wasn't clear yet whether Yuichi had forced the girl to go with him, or whether she'd gone along voluntarily. According to the employee of the hotel who had spotted them, "the girl seemed to be pulling him by the hand," to which an ill-tempered commentator added disgustedly: "If they're running away together, the guy's an idiot, and so is she. What I mean is this is the kind of girl who latches on to guys like that. It's disgusting."

Surrounded by reporters and cameras, Fusae finally made it to the bus stop. The microphones thrust at her occasionally brushed against her ears.

Even at the bus stop, the barrage of questions didn't let up. Fusae didn't say a word, which led one irritated reporter to shout, "Does your silence mean that you admit it's true?" trying to force her into making a comment.

Luckily, there was no one else at the bus stop, but along the way, there were local housewives watching Fusae and the reporters, looks of pity on their faces. The bus finally arrived and Fusae, mumbling an apology, stepped forward. The reporters made room for her, though some clucked their tongues in disapproval. She grabbed the handrail and was climbing in when several reporters tried to get on as well. Five or six passengers were already aboard, all of them staring in amazement at the crowd at what was normally a deserted bus stop in a little fishing village.

Fusae hunched over and sat down in the seat behind the driver. The reporters were all scrambling, vying to get aboard. Fusae sat there, staring at her shoes, their tips covered in mud and snow.

"Just a second here. Who do you think you are?" the bus driver growled, his voice booming over his microphone. "You can't do interviews in the bus. You have to get permission!" The reporters all froze.

"It's dangerous. You'd better all get out!" the driver shouted. He looked around to shove the reporters back.

"Yelling at an old lady isn't going to help anything," the driver added, to everyone. Fusae recognized his face in the rearview mirror. This was usually an unfriendly driver, a bit erratic in his driving, the one driver along this route she always hoped to avoid.

"Watch out now, I'm shutting the door!" The driver forced the door closed and the bus slowly pulled away.

Fusae looked back down at her shoes. It wasn't until they reached the next bus stop that she realized she'd been crying, thankful to the driver for his kindness.

The bus left the road along the sea and headed into the city. Fusae felt as if everyone was staring at her and couldn't bring herself to look up, but as new passengers boarded at each stop, the atmosphere inside the bus gradually changed. As they reached Katsuji's hospital, Fusae pressed the button next to the window. "We'll be stopping at the next stop," said the driver curtly.

The bus slowed down. Fusae waited until it came to a complete stop before she grabbed hold of the railing and stood up. She wanted to thank the driver but didn't have the courage, and headed toward the exit at the back.

The door hissed open. No one else was getting off. She glanced toward the driver and was stepping down when he suddenly said, "It's not your fault. You hang in there now, y'hear?"

A stir ran through the bus for a moment after the driver's words echoed through the sound system. Fusae didn't know how to react. The passengers turned to look at her, standing on the steps, and she fled. She turned around, but the door closed and the bus just drove away.

It had all happened so quickly. Left behind, alone at the stop, Fusae could only stare blankly at the receding bus.

You hang in there now, y'hear?

The words echoed again in her mind, and she hastily bowed in the direction of the bus.

It's not your fault.

She repeated the driver's words to herself. Behind her was the hospital and going inside meant taking care of her ill-tempered husband, then back home to the crowd of reporters outside, and a night spent trembling in fear at more threatening phone calls.

"You hang in there now, y'hear?" she murmured again.

Running away won't help anything, she thought. *And no help's on the way, no matter how much I wait. It's no different from when they threw those rationed potatoes and I had to scramble around to pick them up. I need to be strong. I'm not going to let them make fun of me anymore. Be strong. Nobody's going to make fun of me anymore. No way. No way am I going to let that happen.*

When Yoshio awoke, he was on a makeshift bed in a hospital. He must have lost consciousness, but his mind was clear now. All he felt was pain.

Yoshio looked around him. His bed was in a hallway, not a room. He tried to sit up, but a man's arm shot out from the bench beside him and rested on his chest. "You better lie down for a while," the man said, but Yoshio pushed back and sat up. A nurse was scurrying away down the long hallway.

"You have a mild concussion. . . . They're going to put you in a ward soon," the young man beside him said uneasily, glancing back and forth between Yoshio and the retreating nurse. This was the young man who'd helped him up after he'd hit his head, Yoshio recalled, and he was about to thank him, when another memory came and he was silent for a moment.

"You're a friend of Keigo Masuo, aren't you?" he said as he lowered himself from the makeshift bed. The young man's face stiffened and he asked, more hesitantly, "What sort of . . . relationship do you have with Keigo?"

Yoshio looked straight at him. The young man was tall and lanky, his eyes somehow lifeless. Trying to avoid Yoshio's wordless stare, the young man said, bowing his head, "My name's Koki Tsuruta. I know Keigo from school."

"If you're his classmate, you must know where he is now, right?" Yoshio asked. He knew the boy wouldn't answer him. He got up and set off toward the elevators.

"Wait up!" Koki's voice followed him from behind. "Are you . . . that girl's . . ."

Yoshio halted and turned to face Koki. He realized his jacket was lighter than before and he reached in his pocket. The wrench was gone.

"Is this what you're looking for?" Koki pulled the wrench out of his yellow backpack.

"You saw what happened, didn't you? The guy kicked me, too, and made me lose consciousness. I can't just go back to Kurume like this. I couldn't stand it. But I don't expect you understand how I feel."

Yoshio reached out and grabbed for the wrench from Koki. Koki hesitated for a moment. "All right," he said. "But don't try anything stupid, okay?" And he meekly handed over the wrench.

As I was taking Yoshino Ishibashi's father over to the café where Keigo always hung out, I called Keigo on his cell phone. When he answered, he sounded really worked up. "Koki, is that you?" he said. "Where are you? Get over here, okay?" He went on: "Something crazy just happened to me. Guess who I ran into? The father of that girl who died on Mitsuse Pass! *Y'all killed mah daughter!* the guy said and tried to grab me. God, it was wild! I gave him a good kick." Keigo's voice was loud, and I could picture his entourage around him, egging him on.

After we left the hospital, Yoshino's father walked beside me. I hung up the phone and said, "He's in the usual place," and he said "Is that right?" and nodded.

At the time, I didn't understand why I was taking him to meet Keigo. I can't express it well, but when I saw Mr. Ishibashi in the snow, clinging to Keigo's legs, it was like I was smelling the scent of a human being for the first time in my life. I'd never noticed the scent of humans before, but for some reason Mr. Ishibashi's scent came through clearly. Compared to Keigo, he looked so small, so small it made me sad.

I spend most of my time holed up in my room, watching movies, so I've seen tons of people crying, being sad, angry, and full of hatred. But this was the first time I realized that people's emotions have a distinct odor. I wish I could explain it better, but when I saw Mr. Ishibashi clinging to Keigo's legs, it was like, I don't know, like I could really feel this whole crime for the first time. . . .

The feeling of Keigo's foot as it kicked Yoshino out of his car, the cold of the ground as she touched it. The sky Yoshino saw as the criminal strangled her, the feeling of her throat under his hands as he wrung her neck. I could suddenly feel it all, as clear as day.

A person disappearing from this world isn't like the top stone of a pyramid disappearing. It's more like one of the foundation stones at the base. You know what I mean?

Truthfully, I don't think Mr. Ishibashi could ever hurt Keigo. Not then, when they confronted each other, or later on in their lives. Keigo will always come out on top. Still, I wanted Mr. Ishibashi to stand up to him and say something. I didn't want him to silently lose out.

✱

As she walked from the bus stop in front of the hospital, Fusae took her worn purse from the bag hanging heavily on her wrist. Inside was a sheaf of supermarket receipts, four-thousand-yen bills, a large five-hundred-yen coin all by itself, and a handful of other coins.

The only snow left along the seaside road was underneath the trees lining it. On the road itself the snow had melted and the cars splashed muddy water.

Fusae put her purse back in her bag. The bus driver's words were helping her along, but something else had burst within her. She had finally shaken free of the fear that had controlled her these past few weeks. She left the seaside road and headed toward the back road that led to Dutch Slope.

She was trying to recall the time when Katsuji's second cousin Goro visited with his family, from Okayama, on a vacation to Nagasaki. They weren't all that close to them, but Katsuji was enthusiastic about it and showed them all over town, then took them to a Chinese place for dinner. Yuichi must have been in elementary school back then, so it would have to be twenty years ago.

Goro's wife was a frumpy, strong-willed woman who was constantly complaining about how high the entrance fees were to places they visited, how expensive the coffee was. They had a daughter, Kyoko, who'd just gone into junior high, and she and Yuichi played together during the trip.

Fusae recalled showing them Dutch Slope. She was tired of the complaints and so she walked ahead and caught up with Yuichi and Kyoko. As she did, she overheard Kyoko say, "Yuichi, you're lucky your grandmother's so pretty." Yuichi didn't seem interested and went on kicking pebbles as he walked, but Kyoko continued. "I wish my mom was like your grandmother and wore a pretty scarf when she went on a trip."

Fusae was embarrassed, and kept her distance. The scarf she was wearing was cheap, and these words of praise were coming from a girl in junior high, but Fusae couldn't hide the pride she felt.

Afterward, on visits to open-house days at Yuichi's classroom and parent-teacher-conference days, Fusae was never without a scarf around her neck. Nobody ever told her how nice she looked again, but without the scarf she might not have had the courage to be among the young mothers.

As she walked down the cobblestoned backstreet toward the shopping district, Fusae wondered how long it had been since she'd bought a new scarf. Not just a scarf—she hadn't bought any new clothes in ages. What was the last thing she had bought? Was it that imitation-leather coat she got at Daiei? Or the light blue sweater from the local clothing shop?

She'd walked down this street for years, but now she noticed a clothing store she'd never seen before. The place was small, the entrance nearly blocked by a wagon piled high with sweaters that were obviously catering to a middle-aged female clientele.

Fusae stopped and gazed inside the shop. Perhaps because it was still light out, the inside of the store looked dark, with a couple of old mannequins set up as though they'd like nothing better than to flee. Large price tags were attached to the clothes on the mannequins, the printed price crossed out in red, the reduced price written over it. But that, too, was crossed out, without a new price written on the tag.

Fusae walked over to the wagon outside and picked up the nearest sweater, a purple one. She held it up and saw that it was too small for her. The woman at the register stood up, and after a moment's hesitation, Fusae returned the sweater to the wagon and went inside the dark store.

Fusae merely nodded to the clerk when she greeted her, and as she fingered the white jacket one of the mannequins was wearing, the woman came over and said, "That material feels very nice. It's so soft."

The original price on the tag said twelve thousand yen, but that was crossed out, and the reduced price of nine thousand was crossed out as well. She turned her eyes and saw colored scarves hanging next to the register. Noticing where Fusae was looking, the clerk said, "Those are on sale, too."

Fusae walked further back into the store and picked up a bright orange scarf. There was a mirror to one side reflecting her in her dark gray coat. Fusae slowly wrapped the scarf around her neck. Perhaps a bit too bright for her, she thought, but the color went surprisingly well with the coat.

"How much is this?" she asked.

"The color looks really good as an accent," the clerk said while she straightened the scarves. "Let me see," she added, checking the price tag. "This one would be three thousand eight hundred."

Fusae had no makeup on, and the scarf was all it took to make her face look much brighter. She had only four thousand yen with her, but she unwound the scarf from her neck and handed it to the clerk. "Here you go. I'll take it," she said.

"Here you go."

The policeman in the driver's seat held out his hand, which held a handkerchief. The handkerchief, pure white cotton, looked strange in his rough fingers. He must be married. The handkerchief was nicely ironed and had a faint scent.

Mitsuyo was seated in the backseat of the patrol car. Beside her was the plastic bag full of food she'd bought at the convenience store. The heaters clouded the windows and she couldn't see outside. She took the handkerchief and wiped away her tears.

When the patrolman had her sit in the backseat, Mitsuyo cried. He wasn't sure what to do, so he asked about her health, about where Yuichi was, and then contacted his precinct via radio. But Mitsuyo was so shaken she could barely hear her own voice, let alone his.

She held the handkerchief against her face, and the patrolman hung up the radio and said, "Miss Magome, we're going to go to the station first. A policewoman will be there and we'll talk more." He started the engine.

The patrol car pulled out of the convenience-store parking lot. Mitsuyo could just make out the clerk and the customers in the store watching them. She realized that she was trembling and pulled the bag of groceries onto her lap and hugged it tightly.

Would Yuichi realize what was going on? Would he run away?

The car was heading toward the intersection where the logging road went up to the lighthouse. Turn left here and they could see the thicket where Yuichi was hiding. Mitsuyo couldn't bring herself to look in that direction, and held on more tightly to the shopping bag. She squeezed it too hard, and a sweet bun popped out and fell to the wet floor near her feet.

Yuichi . . . Yuichi . . .

Until the car completely passed the intersection, Mitsuyo repeated his name to herself over and over.

She wanted to force the door open and leap out, but the car was racing along too quickly. It had happened too suddenly, with no time to say goodbye. She held the handkerchief to her face all the way to the police station. The policeman helped her out of the car, and they went into the small, deserted local station. The inside smelled of kerosene from the heater, and curried rice.

"Just—just sit here for a while."

The patrolman guided her to a bench next to the window. Cold wind blew in the open front door, scattering papers on the desk. The phone on the desk was ringing. The policeman hesitated, but decided to close the front door first. As soon as he shut it, the phone stopped ringing.

Mitsuyo sat down on the cold, hard bench and grasped the plastic shopping bag to her again. The handkerchief in her hand was damp with sweat and tears.

The patrolman was about to say something to her, but he seemed flustered and stopped. He took off his cap, laid it on the desk, and lifted the receiver of the phone.

"Yes. We just arrived. . . . No, she isn't hurt. She is a little upset, yes. . . . No, I haven't asked her yet."

Mitsuyo listened to the patrolman's replies, and thought again of Yuichi, hiding in the thicket. With the light covering of snow, he must be freezing. The frozen leaves and branches must be stabbing his numb hands and cheeks.

On the wall opposite the bench was a local map taped to the wall.

The station was marked in red. She saw the village where the convenience store was, and the lighthouse where they'd hid.

"Excuse me. I need to use the restroom," Mitsuyo said, standing up. The patrolman put his hand over the receiver and after a moment's hesitation, opened the door to the back room. Mitsuyo nodded her thanks to him, then gestured to ask whether it was all right to close the door. The patrolman, phone to his ear, nodded, and she shut the door.

The back room was six mats in size and a futon was spread out on the tatami for the policemen to use for naps.

"I'm sure the man is still around here. . . . No, there's no place where they could hide out for long. . . ."

Mitsuyo heard the patrolman's voice through the door. Next to a door that said *Restroom* was a window. On impulse, she opened the window. She stood on top of a metal folding chair and scrambled out.

She didn't look back. She climbed over the low wall behind the station, ran through the garden of a nearby house, and emerged onto an alley. Beyond the narrow alley was a hill, and on top of the hill was the lighthouse. Mitsuyo felt Yuichi was calling to her, and she knew that even if she had to crawl up the steep slope on her hands and knees, she would make it back to the lighthouse.

As he walked next to Koki, Yoshio wondered whether he could be trusted. He'd been nice enough to take him to the hospital, but after that he'd announced that he was a friend of Keigo's. The whole thing made Yoshio uneasy.

"Do you know Yoshino, too?" he asked.

Koki's pale cheeks, which looked as if they seldom saw the sun, reddened. "Ah, no I don't. I never actually . . ." he said evasively.

Koki silently headed toward the shopping district. He wasn't taking a taxi, Yoshio noticed, and he walked right past the subway, so the shop that jerk is in must be right around here.

"You go to the same college as that guy?" he asked.

"Uh . . . yeah."

"You don't like him much?"

"No, we're good friends."

Yoshio barked a short laugh at this. *If you're such good friends, then why are you taking a man you don't know to see him, a man who's carrying a wrench?*

"I left home planning to kill him. Do you have any idea how I feel?"

It felt weird, talking about this with a good friend of the man who'd kicked his daughter in the back and abandoned her.

"You have parents?" he asked.

"Yes," Koki replied briefly.

"You get along okay?"

"Not really." The reply left no doubt how he felt.

"You have somebody you really care about?"

At this, Koki halted and looked puzzled.

"Somebody who, when you think about their happiness, you feel happy, too?"

Koki shook his head. "I don't think he has anyone like that either," he muttered.

"There're too many people in the world like you," Yoshio said. "Too many people who don't have anyone they care about. Who think if they don't love anyone else then they're free to do whatever they want. They think they have nothing to lose, and that makes them stronger. If you have nothing to lose, there's nothing you really want, either. You're full of confidence, and look down on people who lose things, who want things, who are happy, or sad sometimes. But that's not the way things are. And it's just not right."

Koki stood there, stock-still, the whole time. Yoshio nudged him and said, "Come on, which way is it? Are you taking me, or what?"

Koki came to a halt outside a glass-enclosed restaurant fronting the main street. White words in a foreign language danced across the glass. Inside, young girls were poking around in large bowls of salad.

Yoshio left Koki standing outside and walked in. He was met by a rush of sound—music playing, the clatter of dishes in the kitchen, customers laughing.

He didn't spot Keigo at any of the tables, or at the counter that wrapped around the kitchen area. Yoshio ignored the waitress who came over to seat him, and strode into the restaurant. Two young men were seated on cushioned seats, facing toward Yoshio. They were gazing up at Keigo, seated with his back to the entrance, who was doing all the talking. The two friends were laughing uproariously.

Yoshio walked straight toward them. Keigo didn't notice him coming and went on talking, gesturing all the while as he spoke. "So get this. The old fart grabs me and says, 'It's y'all's fault, hear me? That mah daughter's dead!' The guy was so serious you couldn't believe it. So desperate. God! I'd laugh my ass off if I ever saw that old fart's face again. You know the type—like the old men that Macchan imitates sometimes?"

The two friends were laughing, right in front of Keigo. But Yoshio couldn't figure out what was so amusing. A father trying that hard for the sake of his murdered daughter—what's so funny about that?

The two friends finally noticed Yoshio and glanced at him. Following their gaze, Keigo turned around, and gulped.

I just don't get it, Yoshio thought. *This guy who can laugh at other people's sorrow. I don't get it. And I don't understand how these friends of his can laugh along. And I don't get these people who send letters abusing and slandering Yoshino. And these talk-show commentators who've labeled Yoshino a slut. I just don't understand them.*

Yoshino. He silently called her name. *Daddy doesn't get it at all.*

Keigo was standing up in front of him. He was speechless, his face pale. The wrench Yoshio was gripping in his pocket seemed suddenly light.

"Is it so funny?" he asked. He really wanted to know. Keigo took a step backward.

"Go ahead, try living that way," Yoshio said, the words pouring out. "If you can live like that, laughing at everybody else, go ahead." Yoshio was so sad he couldn't stand it.

Keigo and his friends stood staring blankly. Yoshio took the wrench out of his pocket and tossed it at Keigo's feet. And without another word, he left.

Yoshio arrived back in Kurume after four p.m. that day. He'd been gone two days, and when he thought about Satoko, who had probably spent the whole time crying, he considered how worried she must have been. It pained him deeply.

He parked in the lot a little way from their house, and trudged heavily toward home. After Yoshino was gone, he felt drained of energy. He'd stood in front of Keigo, who'd ridiculed him, but had left without doing a thing. Was this the right choice, or had he made a mistake? He had no idea.

He emerged from the alley where the parking lot was and could see in the distance the sign *Ishibashi Barbershop*. For a moment he couldn't believe it. After Yoshino had been killed, he hadn't once switched on the light on the barber pole outside the shop, but now he could swear it was on and revolving.

Dubious, Yoshio stepped up his pace, and as he approached his shop he could see that indeed the barber pole was revolving. He started running. Out of breath by the time he reached the shop, he yanked open the front door. There weren't any customers inside, just Satoko, dressed in her white barber's coat, folding freshly laundered towels.

"You . . . you opened the shop?" Yoshio asked.

Surprised by his sudden appearance, Satoko, eyes wide, said, "Oh! You startled me." She went on, smiling, "If I don't open it, who will? Mr. Sonobe came in a while ago for a cut."

"And you cut it?"

These past few years, Satoko had grown to hate touching customers' hair, and had avoided working in the shop. But here she was now, decked out in her barber's coat, right in front of him.

"You must have been worried," Yoshio said.

Satoko went back to folding the towels and silently shook her head.

"Well, I'm back," Yoshio said.

The setting sun shone through the glass door, and the name *Ishibashi Barbershop* formed a shadow at their feet.

❈

Fusae declined to have the scarf wrapped and tied it around her neck. The clerk had shown her a special way to tie it. Fusae paid and left the shop. Just a scarf, but buying it made her feel light and happy.

She cut across a park and came out behind the bus terminal. At night the area was lined with small stands selling food and drinks, but it was still early and there were only a few stands there, all locked up with tin sheets and chains. Down the road was a large pay-by-the-hour parking lot, and beyond that the bustling shopping district.

She'd seen this parking lot before, back then, from the window of that room where she was surrounded by those men. She'd been so frightened she couldn't lift her head, but the leader of the group, who occasionally spoke to her kindly, brought her a cup of hot tea, and she managed a quick glance out the window.

Fusae continued down the street, and was at the fence around the parking lot when, taking a deep breath, she slowly turned around and glanced up at the building behind her. It was the kind of old multiuse building you find anywhere, with a narrow staircase up to the second floor. She could make out the bottom half of the blue door of the elevator.

A young family, the father holding his little daughter on his shoulders, was walking nearby, perhaps on their way to have a meal in Chinatown. The little girl had on a kind of Santa Claus hat that she evidently found uncomfortable and was trying to yank off, while her mother walking beside her adjusted it.

Fusae clutched the bag in her hand more tightly, took another deep breath, and set off again. She thought she was walking along pretty steadily, but she began to feel something trembling beneath her, as if she were walking on a board floating in the water.

She went into the gloomy building. As she stepped onto the first step of the stairs, its tiles starting to come off, she suddenly felt like fleeing and grabbed on to the handrail.

Yuichi, honey—where are you?

She walked up another step.

Remember that no matter what happens, Grandma's always on your side.

You need to do what's right, too. You're scared, aren't you? But you can't run away. You have to do the right thing. Grandma's not going to let them beat me, either.

Fusae touched the elevator button. The heavy bag made her arm tremble. The door opened. It was a tiny elevator that couldn't hold more than three at a time. She went inside and pushed the button for the third floor. She kept on pushing it until the door closed.

The elevator door opened again and she stepped out into a dim hallway. A single door was at the end.

Yuichi, you can't run away. I know you're scared, but you can't run. Running away's not going to change anything. That's not going to help anybody.

Fusae found herself muttering this aloud as she walked down the corridor. She stood in front of the door and could hear men laughing inside. Her body felt tense. The sound of a TV mixed in with the laughter. She heard a girl on a roller coaster: a thundering sound, the girl's shrieks, and every time she shrieked, a roar of laughter from the men watching, right behind this door.

Fusae gritted her back teeth and turned the cold doorknob. The door was unlocked and opened easily, cigarette smoke wafting out.

She saw the backs of three men, sprawled out on a sofa in front of the TV. The one who looked the youngest noticed Fusae standing there. "Yeah?" he said, as if he couldn't be bothered. Fusae took a step forward. The man who'd spoken to her stood up, and the other two stared at her.

"Whaddaya want, old woman?"

The man who'd stood up approached her. The other two had gone back to watching TV.

"I never intended to . . . sign a year's contract," Fusae managed.

"Huh? What's that?" the young man said as if he hadn't heard her.

"I never intended to make a year's contract!" she shouted. "And I want you to cancel it." Things started to swim before her eyes, and she felt about to faint. At the shout, the two on the sofa turned around again.

"I want you to cancel it!" she shouted, the spit flying. "I don't have that kind of money, so you have to cancel it!"

The bag in her hands swung around as she spoke and struck a shelf. The three men burst out laughing, but Fusae didn't hear them.

"I've struggled all my life. And I'm not about to let people like you make a fool out of me!"

Her breathing ragged now, Fusae strode out of the office. She bumped against the walls on both sides as she walked down the corridor. *If they want to come, let 'em*, she thought. *They want to laugh at me, let 'em*. But beyond the door to the office there was no laughter, no footsteps about to chase after her. The gloomy hallway was so silent it was creepy.

The setting sun was just grazing the horizon. Yuichi was standing on the far edge of the cliff following a pair of seabirds with his eyes as they flew off into the sun.

Without waiting for sunset, he walked back to the caretaker's shack at the lighthouse. It wasn't warm inside, but he could feel how chilled he'd become standing on the cliff.

On the plywood board was the sleeping bag that Mitsuyo had folded up, the orange-juice pack she'd drunk, the box of chocolates she'd eaten, the pebbles she'd lined up. Yuichi sat down on the folded sleeping bag. He could feel the cold concrete below the plywood board.

While he was hiding in the thicket, snow that had accumulated on the leaves had fallen onto his neck. He'd shrugged his shoulders at the cold and the melted snow ran down his back. Mitsuyo was just buying a few things at the convenience store and should have been back a long time ago. Worried, he'd emerged from the bushes. Just before Yuichi came out on the main road, he spotted a policeman walking from the bus stop in his direction. Yuichi quickly hid behind a light pole. The policeman posted a notice of some kind on a bulletin board across the street, and started walking back toward the bus stop.

Yuichi waited, checking out the situation. He was just about to step out onto the main road when a patrol car, siren blasting, roared by. He hurriedly hid again behind the light pole.

He waited another five, then ten minutes, but no Mitsuyo. Maybe she'd noticed the patrol cars, too, and had taken the path, the one past the shrine, back to the lighthouse. Thrusting aside weeds as he went, Yuichi made his way up the hill. But no matter how long he waited at the lighthouse, Mitsuyo didn't return.

Yuichi flicked at the pebbles of different sizes and colors she'd lined up in a neat row on the plywood board. Did they mean anything? Yuichi scooped them up. As he squeezed them, they clicked against each other in his palm.

Mitsuyo . . . He called her name as he fingered the pebbles. No other words came. A sudden commotion was coming from the base of the hill. Usually he and Mitsuyo couldn't hear anything from down there, but now something ominous was filtering up the slope.

Pebbles still in his hand, he ran outside. The sun had set now, and the border between the sea and the mountain had vanished. Red lights of a patrol car were visible among the faint lights of the town below. Not just one, but many, coming from all directions, red lights converging on the town. Sirens, like waves, rang out from down below.

In all the commotion, the mountain seemed all the more silent. Yuichi turned away and gazed at the towering lighthouse. It soared upward, as if propping up the night sky.

He remembered when he was a child, when his mother abandoned him and he'd stared across to the lighthouse on the other shore.

"I'll be right back," his mother had told him, and disappeared. Yuichi had believed her. He waited and waited but she never returned. *It must be because I did something bad,* he'd thought. And he'd tried his hardest to think what that could be. But no matter how hard he thought about it, he couldn't figure out why she'd be so mad at him.

The last ferryboat was just leaving then. Yuichi, tired from waiting, was walking along the pier when a little girl ran up to him from the parking lot. She must have just learned to walk, for she didn't seem to know how to put the brakes on her running feet. Yuichi reached out and held her to stop her from running. The little girl's look of relief was something he could clearly picture, even now. As the girl's father ran over and lifted her up, the girl reached out to Yuichi and offered him the stick of *chikuwa* in her hand. Yuichi declined, but the girl's father said, "We just bought it, so please go ahead," and he handed it to Yuichi. Yuichi thanked him and took it.

When he thought about it later, he realized that from the time his mother left him, until the next morning when one of the ferry workers discovered him there, all he ate was that stick of *chikuwa*.

Yuichi tossed the pebbles in his hand at the lighthouse above him. *Mitsuyo . . .* he thought again. The pebbles flew in all directions, only the largest one actually striking the base of the lighthouse.

Mitsuyo might be in one of those patrol cars. She might have been arrested. *If they grabbed her, I have to go rescue her. Go right away and tell them, "I wanted her to come with me. I threatened her and made her come with me."* No. *Mitsuyo will be back. No way the cops got her. She bought a lot of things at the convenience store and will come back, a smile on her face, saying, "Sorry I'm late!" She said she'd be right back. She smiled when she said that, when she left.*

Yuichi picked up a stone from the ground and flung it hard against the lighthouse.

Without Mitsuyo, all he felt was pain. *Mitsuyo is off somewhere right now, alone,* he thought. *The last thing I want is for her to feel this kind of pain. It's enough that I feel it.*

❇

The bark of the tree broke off under her grip and stabbed beneath her fingernails. Mitsuyo gritted her teeth, not giving in to the pain, grabbed a thin branch, and stepped up on top of a boulder.

The woods were pitch-black and wherever she stepped were fallen dead trees. Dead trees she could handle, but not the moss-covered rocks. She slipped on them over and over, tumbling to the damp ground.

After she climbed out the window of the police station, her only thought was to get to the top of the hill, to the lighthouse. On the way, as she was running through the garden of someone's house, an old woman sitting on the porch had called out to her, but she clambered over the wall without looking back and ran into the dark woods.

The snow piled up on tree branches and leaves and she could barely make out her surroundings. She'd lost all feeling in her fingers. She looked up and saw the sky beyond the branches ahead of her. If she could make it that far, she would be at the lighthouse, where Yuichi was waiting. The bushes she grabbed on to had thorns; the thin branches bent back and snapped into her face.

Still she climbed on, clambering over the rocks. The sorrow that had swept over her in the back of the patrol car was pursuing her, and would catch her if she stopped for even a moment. She no longer had the willpower to consider what she was doing, or what she had done. All she wanted was to see Yuichi one more time. It hurt not to have him by her side, right this instant. He was there at the lighthouse, waiting for her, and she couldn't stand to make him feel any lonelier.

She had no idea where this strength was coming from. Or where she found the power to love someone so much.

"Yuichi!"

With each freezing branch whipping across her face, she bit her lip and called out to him.

Yuichi's at the lighthouse, waiting for me. I know he's waiting for me. Have I ever had a place like this before, ever? And I can make it there. . . . If I can only make it, I'll be with the one who loves me. In all my thirty years, have I ever had a place like this? But I've found it now. And that's where I'm heading.

Mitsuyo grabbed at the cold branches with her numb hands and climbed up the wet rocks.

❊

On this day the temperature in the northern part of Kyushu fell below zero degrees centigrade. At five p.m. the decision was made to temporarily lower the speed limit on the entire Kyushu Expressway. Chains were required for cars driving through the mountains and fog started to envelop the cities. The evening news announced that a snowstorm was coming that night and reporters feared that traffic would grind to a halt. It was after five-thirty when Mitsuse Pass was closed to traffic. This announcement scrolled across the TV screen during the entertainment-news report and soon disappeared.

Just around that time, an old woman showed up at a police station in a small harbor town. She explained that twenty minutes before, a young woman had crossed through her garden and gone up into the hills behind. The patrolman, terribly pale looking, took down her report and hurriedly spread a map before him. Today, for some reason, this sleepy harbor town was crawling with police.

Up the hill behind the old woman's house was a lighthouse that was no longer being used. The assembled policemen's fingers rested on top of the map.

"I asked where she was going but she went into the hills without even looking around once."

The policemen didn't hear this last explanation from the old woman, for they were already out the door.

Around the same time, Yuichi had decided to come down off the mountain and was packing up the sleeping bag inside the caretaker's shack. He knew he'd be arrested if he came down to the town, and wouldn't have a chance to ever use the sleeping bag, but still he shouldered it. With the candles out, the shack was dark, though he could see his cold white breath.

Once he came out of the shack, the disturbance in the town below was louder. The police cars that had been scattered about the town had now formed a line of red lights headed up from the foot of the hills to the lighthouse.

Yuichi went limp. He could barely stand.

And then it happened. Branches in the dark thicket shook, and he heard Mitsuyo, feebly calling out his name. "Mitsuyo!" he yelled out.

"Yuichi!" she called back. Branches shook and snow slipped from the leaves. Yuichi leaped over the fence and raced into the dark thicket. Mitsuyo's hair was full of dead leaves and twigs, her fingertips were bloody, her eyes wet with tears.

"I couldn't leave you, Yuichi."

Yuichi blew on her frozen, numb hands.

"I . . . I escaped. I couldn't stand to say goodbye. . . ."

Yuichi stroked her chilled body. Mitsuyo's cheeks were so frozen even his own cold hands felt warm.

He put his arms around her and was leading her back into the shack when Mitsuyo saw the line of patrol cars heading up the logging road and stopped short. The red lights were getting closer to the lighthouse. Sirens echoed through the hills. Yuichi gave Mitsuyo a little shove.

Inside the shack, Yuichi took the sleeping bag from his bag and spread it out. He tried to get Mitsuyo to sit down, for she was clearly exhausted, but she clung to his neck. The sirens were nearer.

"I'm so sorry. I couldn't help you. I'm so sorry," Mitsuyo sobbed aloud as she clung to him. "I knew you were going to get arrested, and yet I begged you . . . to run away with me. . . . If only I hadn't been so selfish. . . ."

Yuichi held her close as she sobbed.

"I couldn't help you at all," she cried, "but you stayed with me. . . . I'm such a terrible woman, yet you're still holding me. . . . Don't say anything, just hold me. . . . It's so hard—so hard when you're kind to me like this. I hate myself—I never did anything for you. I'm terrible . . . terrible. I told you to go to the police then. . . . And then I stopped you. God, I'm so awful."

Yuichi listened. As her cries became louder, so did the sirens. The line of patrol cars was drawing nearer the lighthouse.

Yuichi finally had to peel Mitsuyo away from him. For a moment she stood there, trying to bury her face in his chest, but Yuichi refused to let her. He refused and stood staring right into her wet eyes.

A red light shone through the window of the caretaker's shack, dyeing Mitsuyo's wet face red. When she noticed the light, Mitsuyo tried again to cling to Yuichi. Footsteps drew nearer.

"I'm not . . . the kind of guy you think I am," Yuichi said, and roughly pushed Mitsuyo away, and she fell to the plywood board.

Mitsuyo's short cry echoed in the room. The policemen's flashlights shone in from the far window, the beams crisscrossing each other. And right then, Yuichi straddled Mitsuyo and laid his cold hands on her neck.

Mitsuyo, wide-eyed, tried to shout. Yuichi closed his eyes and squeezed her neck hard. Behind him, the door slammed open and flashlights shone on the two of them.

❁

Let me see, now, when was that? It was when I still looked forward to the homemade lunches he made for me, so it must have been not long after we met. . . . We were eating the lunches in one of the private rooms and talking about something, I don't remember what. Oh—yes I do. It was about our mothers.

I'd totally forgotten about that, but after he was arrested they had all those talk shows about him on TV. And that jogged my memory. His mother was on one of those shows and she nearly tore the head off the interviewer, she was so angry. "I've been punished enough!" she shouted. And when I saw that, I suddenly remembered what we talked about back then.

I was raised by my mom, just her and me, and it might sound strange considering what I do for a living, but the last thing I wanted to do was worry my mother. And when I told him that, he got all serious and said, "Don't tell anybody else, but every time I see my mom I'm always pestering her for money."

A pretty ordinary story, I thought, and gave some noncommittal response. But he looked so serious and probably felt bad, like he wanted to apologize or something. Really, though, it sounded like it was going to be a boring story.

Then he said something unexpected. "It hurts to pester her for money I don't really need."

So I went, "Then you shouldn't do it." I laughed but he thought for a while and then he said, "Yeah, but both of us have to be victims."

At first I didn't get it and was going to ask him what he meant, but right then our time was up and the phone rang.

That was it. He brought me lunches many times after that but never mentioned his mother again.

In the news they've been running stories about him and the confessions, I guess you'd call them, of that girl who was with him to the end, the one he nearly killed. Playing these stories up big, right? Every time I see these, it still gets me. His face when he said that. *Yeah, but both of us have to be victims.*

It makes me kind of want to meet that woman, the one from Saga he took with him. Something about the way he looked back then, I just can't shake it.

I know meeting her isn't going to change anything. Maybe if I send him a letter or something. . . . On second thought, I shouldn't get involved. . . .

Maybe it's like he said in his confession, that at the pass, and at the lighthouse, he was carried away by this sudden urge to kill. Maybe he really *is* that kind of person. . . .

I finally opened my little diner, but had to close it last month. I guess luck wasn't on my side. I got sick soon after we opened. . . . So now I'm back at my old job. I used all my savings to open that shop, and after I closed it, I needed money to live on. . . . It makes me kind of scared when I consider my age, but I couldn't think of anything else to do.

❀

It's like I told you. I don't have anything more to add, or anything I want to correct.

I get a kick from driving women into a corner. When I see women like that, scared and suffering, it turns me on. I never noticed it before, but I think I always had those feelings inside me. My first confession was what the reporters picked up on and ran with. But I did say those things. And I am that kind of man.

I didn't chase after Yoshino Ishibashi because I was planning to kill her. We'd made a date, but then she told me she didn't have time for me. And then she got into another guy's car right in front of me. One word of apology from her, that's all I wanted. . . . So I followed her, and when I got to the pass she'd been kicked out of the other car. . . . I tried to help her, but she refused, said she was going to the police, and before I knew what was happening I'd strangled her.

Maybe it was like that detective told me, that maybe when I was strangling her I realized for the first time I get sexually aroused by women who are suffering. And that's why I didn't turn myself in, but went looking for another girl. Mitsuyo Magome just happened to get in touch with me right then, so I made a date to meet up with her.

When they arrested her, Miss Magome apparently said she went with me of her own free will, but I think it's because I intimidated her and psychologically backed her into a corner. I told her how I murdered Miss Ishibashi, and I think she understood what an evil person I am, that she couldn't escape, and that made her submit to me.

In fact, Miss Magome did exactly what I told her, and since I didn't have any money it worked out well to have her along.

She stood by me, apparently testifying that "I was never intimidated or treated roughly," but I think that's also like the detective said, that even after she was freed she couldn't shake off her terror. You could turn that around and say it confirms what I said: that I used fear to control her.

The whole time we were together, she was jumpy. Everywhere we went—when I told her about how I killed Yoshino, when I forced her to go to a love hotel with me, when she sat in the passenger seat of my car, when we arrived at the lighthouse. She was nervous and scared, and that got me excited.

The detective told me how my grandfather died the morning after I was arrested. He did his best to raise me, and I feel awful about putting him through all this in his final hours.

I feel sorry for my grandma, too, for what I did. I heard how she went to visit both families—the Ishibashis and the Magomes—to apologize. And how they refused to see her . . .

My grandma's a timid person who can't do anything on her own, and it hurts to think about that. . . . My grandparents are totally innocent in all this. Totally . . .

I wrote a letter to Yoshino's parents, but didn't get a reply. Not that I should expect one. Or I guess I should say I know I don't have the right to send them a letter. I can apologize all I want, but it'll never be enough, I know that. Doesn't matter the reasons behind what I did, the fact remains that I did something that can never be undone. I think I should die in order to apologize to them. That's the only thing a person like me can do. But until that day, all I can do is put my hands together in prayer to beg their forgiveness, and keep on apologizing.

I did bad things to Miss Magome, too, I know that, and if the police had shown up a few minutes later, she might have ended up like Yoshino. I'm absolutely sure of this. From the first moment I met her, I may have been imagining that scene, and those feelings.

I've said this over and over, but I never liked Miss Magome. She was a source of funds for me when I was on the run, so I pretended to like her. And as I did, I think I started to deceive myself into thinking I really did feel that way about her.

Now when I rethink it, I realize it didn't have to be Miss Magome. It didn't necessarily have to be her. . . .

If I hadn't met her, though . . .

If I never had met her, I don't know . . .

That night, when Yoshino shouted, "I'm going to report this to the police!" I could have insisted that she was lying, but I didn't think anybody would believe me. Like no one in the entire world would trust what I say. That terrified me, and I ended up doing what I did. But somehow I couldn't admit deep down to myself what I'd done. . . . Which is how I wound up taking the coward's way out and running away . . .

But it's different now. There are people now who believe what I say. I understand that. So I can admit it now, that I'm a murderer. I'm the man who killed Yoshino and dragged Miss Magome along with me. . . . I can just come right out and say it.

Can I say one more thing?

I heard that Miss Magome was able to go back to her job. Is that true?

I guess I won't be able to see her again, right?

I know it sounds stupid coming from me, but I want to tell her to forget all about this, as quickly as she can. . . . And tell her to find her own kind of happiness . . . Could you tell her that for me? I won't see her ever again, but it would be enough for me if you told her that.

I know she must hate me and doesn't want to hear anything I say, but if you'd just—just tell her that, that would be enough. . . .

I'm living in our apartment with my younger sister again. Everybody at work has been very helpful, and I've been able to go back to work this month.

Things are back to normal. My life's the same as it was before I met that man.

Right after the news broke, reporters were trying to force their way into my parents' house, and I didn't know what to do. But now I get up every morning at eight, pedal my bike to work, come back to the apartment in the evening, and make dinner with my sister. . . .

On the last holiday I did something I haven't done in a long while—I bought a CD of a singer I like at the shopping center in the neighborhood. I think I'm getting calmer these days.

I've heard all kinds of things from the detectives about what that guy said, ever since he was arrested. Of course I didn't believe it at first. About him saying he liked to make women suffer and that he took me along just to get money out of me.

I couldn't believe any of it, no matter how much I heard. But finally I understood that I was the one who was really flipping out here. That like an idiot, I'd been so taken in by him, and maybe he really *was* using me.

After that guy's testimony was in all the TV stations and magazines, people stopped throwing rocks at the windows of my parents' house, and though people still come to my workplace sometimes out of curiosity, wanting to take a look at me, I don't get any dirty looks anymore from people on the street.

Because I'm not the woman who ran off with him, but a victim who was forced to. . . .

My sister and other people have asked if I want to move, but I'm the woman who couldn't go anywhere, even when I was running away with that guy. There's no other place I can go.

I've been reading articles about the incident in magazines. But I never can believe it's me they're talking about.

I'm not trying to escape reality. But even when I try hard to remember what happened, it always feels like some other woman who did all those things. Not me.

I think while all that was going on, I forgot what kind of woman I am. I'm a woman who can't do a thing, but I was convinced I could. . . . I ignored the fact that up till then I couldn't do a single thing in my life. . . .

Not too long ago, I went up to Mitsuse Pass for the first time, to lay flowers at the spot where Yoshino Ishibashi passed away. For a long time I didn't have the courage to go, but I thought it's my duty to go there. . . .

My sister said, "You're a victim here, so you don't need to force yourself to go," but that time when we were in the squid restaurant in Yobuko, when he told what had happened, I forgave him. I was just thinking of myself, and I forgave him for violently taking Yoshino's life, no matter why he did it.

I think that for the rest of my life it's my duty to apologize to Yoshino.

The place where she died is a lonely curve in the road, a gloomy place even in the middle of the day. The flowers there were all dried up, but there was a bright orange scarf someone had wrapped around the guardrail like a landmark. I plan to go every month, on the day of the month when she died, to apologize. Not that that will make her forgive me or anything. . . .

I've never met that man's grandmother. I heard she visited my parents' house a number of times, but I was never sure how I should receive her. All I really want to tell her is that none of this is her fault. . . .

No, I'm trying not to follow the trial. At first I thought he was lying to protect me. I wasn't threatened by him, or the victim of mind control or anything. . . . I tried to argue that we were really in love with each other, but people kept on saying no man could be in love with a woman he just met on an online dating site. And if he really loved me, would he try to strangle me?

But those days when we were on the run . . . when we were in that shack at the lighthouse, scared, when it was snowing and we were freezing—I still miss those times. I know it's stupid, but it hurts when I think of those days together.

I guess I was the one who was off in my own little world, convinced I was in love.

I mean, he's the guy who murdered Yoshino. The one who tried to kill *me*.

Isn't it like everybody says? That he's the villain in all this? And I just decided on my own to fall for someone like that.

Right?

www.vintage-books.co.uk